FAMILY SECRET

"Wouldn't you be upset, Papa, if you suddenly discovered something like that about yourself?"

"Something like what?" Lottie said carefully.

But Alison could not put her feelings into words.

"Does Mama know?" she asked him.

Horace nodded.

"Then both of you have lied to me."

"Not exactly, Alison."

"Yes you have!" she flashed. "What other word is there for not telling the truth? And how am I to feel but that my whole life, until now, has been a lie? If my aunt hadn't saved me from it, I should have gone on till the end of my days in ignorance of what I truly am!" She took a wisp of cambric and lace from her apron pocket with a dramatic flourish and delicately dabbed her eyes. "I may never forgive you for it."

Between Two Worlds

MAISIE MOSCO

HarperPaperbacks
A Division of HarperCollinsPublishers

The author acknowledges invaluable research contributed by
Tanya Ossack and is indebted to Carola Edmond and Linda S.
Price for encouragement and guidance.

HarperPaperbacks   *A Division of* HarperCollins*Publishers*
10 East 53rd Street, New York, N.Y. 10022

Previous editions of this book were published in 1983 in
Great Britain by New English Library and in 1984 in the
U.S. by Bantam Books, Inc.

Cover illustration by Donna Diamond

First HarperPaperbacks printing: October 1993

Printed in the United States of America

HarperPaperbacks and colophon are trademarks of
HarperCollins*Publishers*

10 9 8 7 6 5 4 3 2 1

For my sister

Thelma Ballan

PROLOGUE (1895)

The boy lay on his bed, listening to the rumble of cart-wheels on the cobblestones outside. The gray light that precedes nightfall bathed the room in which he had slept all his life. Where soon he would sleep no more.

His eye roved to the marble-topped washstand, which in his schooldays he had used as an improvised desk. On it were his few personal possessions; a hairbrush and comb; the plated gold cuff-links he had received as a *Bar Mitzvah* gift; a copy of Shakespeare's plays, which he had scrimped and saved to buy; and the scrapbook in which he pasted newspaper cuttings about the theater.

In the washstand drawer was the black velvet bag containing his prayerbook and prayershawl. A pang of conscience assailed him. Why did he feel that what he had made up his mind to do meant leaving his religion behind? Because Jewish boys don't leave home to go on the stage. Most were thankful to have a roof over their heads and a job in a sweatshop, would give their eyeteeth to be the son of a businessman, as he was.

"Where are you already? It's nearly suppertime!" came a call from the foot of the stairs.

The boy went to the mirror to tidy his hair and put on the skullcap he wore at table. "What makes you think you've got what it takes to be an actor?" he asked his reflection. He was neither tall nor short, dark nor fair, handsome nor ugly. A nondescript-looking lad. But someone had once told him he had nice eyes.

The savory aroma of chicken soup, drifting from below, conjured up for him the cozy living room behind the shop. It was Friday night and his mother would be fixing the candles into her brass candlesticks, while his sister covered the loaf with a small white cloth on which was embroidered a blue Star of David. His father would be filling the Kiddush cup, making ready to bless the wine.

Week in, week out, the Sabbath Eve ritual was observed; part of the familiar pattern of the boy's existence, like getting up in the morning, munching a bagel and joining his father in the shop. A shiver of apprehension rippled through him as he contemplated stepping forth into the unknown. Supposing he failed in what he was setting out to do? He brushed that possibility aside and went downstairs to tell his family he had taken the first step.

They were halfway through their meal before he found the courage to do so. Three pairs of startled eyes turned to look at him.

His sister's fork clattered on to her plate. "What do you mean you've got yourself a job as a stagehand? You already have a job."

"That, he doesn't need telling," his mother said.

His father sat crumbling some bread.

The boy licked his lips, which suddenly felt parched. His parents' expressions accounted for it. "It's my life," he said defensively.

"Since when?" his father inquired.

"Since I decided it's going to be. Which wasn't easy,

Father. As you had my future all mapped out for me. I've always known what I wanted to be and today, I did something about it. When you sent me to the bank, I called at the Gaiety and asked to see the manager of the company that's playing there this week. He happens to be a great actor and I couldn't believe my luck when he offered me a job backstage. So when the company leaves here, I'll be going with them."

The boy saw his sister's dark eyes brim with tears. She still thought of him as her kid brother, though he would soon be sixteen.

"How will your father manage without you?" his mother asked quietly.

"There's no shortage of shop assistants."

His father smiled bitterly. "But for me, only one son."

Two days later, the boy left home with the sound of his mother's weeping and a final ultimatum from his father ringing in his ears.

They'll get over it, he told himself while making his way to the theater. There, in the bustle of activity of a company about to move on, he was allocated the most menial tasks.

He was wielding a broom when a dainty vision in white addressed him.

"Would you mind removing this pile of dirt?" she requested, fingering her golden curls. "Or I shall soil my Sunday slippers, walking through it."

She was tapping one of them impatiently and he hastened to do as he was bid.

"We haven't met before, have we?" she said conversationally, while he fumbled amid the dust.

The boy was too affected by her presence to reply. She was his employer's daughter. He had seen her arrive at the stagedoor, with her parents and little brother, but would not have expected her to notice him.

"Papa mentioned that he had engaged you. And that you wish to enter our profession," she added with a smile.

He watched her walk gracefully away. She was the loveliest girl he had ever seen. And everything about her had made him painfully aware of his own deficiencies. Briefly, his faith in himself was dashed. Then he squared his shoulders. He had burned his boats and there was no going back.

Life's but a walking shadow, a poor player, That struts and frets his hour upon the stage . . .

MACBETH

ONE

One of Alison's earliest memories was of seeing her father transformed into an ass. Though a decade had passed since she wandered into his dressing room and saw, reflected in the mirror, a hairy creature who spoke with Papa's voice, she could still recall the frightening confusion that had overwhelmed her.

Remembrance was evoked by the sight of her father once again playing Bottom in *A Midsummer Night's Dream.* But to twelve-year-old Alison, perched on a stool in the wings of the Theatre Royal, Bolton, on a winter morning in 1912, it was inconceivable that there had been a time when Shakespeare's characters had not seemed to her like old friends.

A command from her grandfather halted the dress rehearsal. For once, Gregory Plantaine was not acting in one of his own productions.

"Kindly stop fidgeting with your mask, Horace," he rebuked Alison's father.

"I was adjusting it around my eyes."

"You appeared to be scratching its nose."

Poor Papa, Alison thought. Grandpa was always finding fault with him. But appeared not to notice when Uncle Oliver fluffed his lines, after having had what the stagehands called "one over the eight." Or when Mama deliberately upstaged one of her fellow-actors. Was it because Oliver and Mama were Grandpa's children and Papa only his son-in-law?

The rehearsal was resumed and Alison watched her mother flit, light as thistledown, to where the Faeries were gathered beneath a tree. How fragile and lovely Mama looked, clad in drifts of gossamer, a crown of petals upon her flowing hair. It was as if Shakespeare had had before him a painting of her, when he created Titania, the Faerie Queen.

Alison had not inherited the patrician features and fair coloring of the Plantaines. Hers was a different kind of beauty, though she did not yet see it as such; dark and striking. Nevertheless, I am a Plantaine, she thought with a proud lift of her chin. Though her father had once been Horace Shrager, before marrying her mother he had taken her name.

Alison rested her pensive gaze on the glimmering footlights which separated her world from that of ordinary mortals. Oh how fortunate she was to have been born into a theatrical family! To share in the preparations and excitement that heralded an opening night; travel the country with the company; watch from the wings while they performed their nightly offering; eat supper with her elders and hear all the backstage gossip.

The rehearsal was drawing to a close. This afternoon, a final run-through would smooth the remaining creases and tonight the curtain would rise on a new Plantaine Players production. Alison's knees felt weak at the thought of it. How would she feel if she were one of the cast? Not "if." When. Because, one day, she would be. In the family tradition begun when Great-great-grandmother Plantaine founded the company almost a century ago. Part of the tradition was for the Plantaine women to make their debuts at the age of sixteen. Alison must wait four more years for that big moment in her life and impatience now mingled with her trepidation.

During the dinner break, Alison joined her father in the Green Room, where his fellow actors were strengthening themselves with pork pies and strong tea. Horace was seated in a quiet corner, sipping milk.

"Shall I fetch your bottle of physic from the dressing room, Papa?" Alison asked him sympathetically. First-night nerves invariably affected his digestion.

Horace shook his head. A dose of medicine would not ease his troubled mind. He had hardly slept a wink since his father-in-law decided to mount this extravagant production, which had plunged the company heavily into debt. If the outlay was not recouped from box-office receipts—Horace could not bear to think of the consequences.

Gregory Plantaine had not deigned to do so and had waved away Horace's cautionary words with an airy hand. Deigned was the right word, Horace thought, glancing at Gregory's well-known profile, about which there was a touch of arrogance.

Gregory had just entered the room and was talking with some of the cast. The distinguished thespian dispensing *bonhomie* to his lessers! Horace reflected with a bitter smile. As though being a Plantaine placed Gregory on a superior plane.

But all the Plantaines had that demeanor, and lived for their art above all else, Horace had learned. Thirteen years as a member of the family had not produced in him the feeling that he was accepted as one of them. Probably, he conjectured, because he was of a very different breed.

"There's no necessity to look worried, Papa," Alison said in her solemn, grown-up way. "Your portrayal of Bottom could not be bettered."

Horace flicked a stray lock of her blue-black hair away from her face and regarded her affectionately. "Thank you, Alison," he replied, managing to smile. He could not tell her that his anxieties were of a more material nature, and on her behalf.

When had it begun to worry him that his daughter had no place to call home? That all Alison would have to look back upon was an endless succession of theatrical lodgings? The realization had come when Horace finally faced up to another truth: Gregory Plantaine's hope of one day establishing the company in its own theater would never be more than that.

Horace, too, had nurtured a hope: of a little house, in which Alison would grow up. With a school nearby, which she would attend as other children did, instead of being tutored haphazardly by her grandmother.

Horace had even allowed himself to imagine engaging a resident housekeeper, whose presence would end the necessity of Alison spending her evenings at the theater. As a small child, she had slept in the dressing room while her parents were onstage. But you couldn't wrap a girl of her age in a blanket and tell her to go bye-byes, he thought, noting the shadows beneath her eyes caused by lack of sleep. Nor was it suitable to leave her in a lodging-house bedroom alone.

So much for hopes, Horace said to himself resignedly. His own were dependent upon his father-in-law, who saw the future through a rosy mist. As Horace once had—why not admit it? He had not always had his feet on the ground.

He swallowed down the last of his milk and gazed through the window at the gray, Northern sky visible between the chimney pots across the street. It was the kind of street from which he had fled in his youth, from the dreary prospect of a life penned behind his father's shop counter.

For a moment, Horace was assailed by a sense of unreality. How had the raw, stage-struck lad who had joined the Plantaine Players as a menial become the polished man he now was?

A vision of his first encounter with his wife rose before him. Himself tongue-tied and clutching a broom. And Hermione in a frilly white frock, tapping her foot impatiently, while he swept up a pile of backstage litter that was blocking her path.

She had captured his heart the minute he set eyes on her, but he could not have envisaged that three years later they would be married. There had been about her then, as there still was, an air of the unattainable, he thought, watching her enter the Green Room with her brother.

Horace rarely allowed his mind to stray backward. Why was he doing so now? Were his anxieties for his daughter's future linked to his own past? He had never regretted uprooting himself and would not wish upon Alison the claustrophobic ambience of his early years, nor the stringencies that had caused him to rebel. But there had been compensations, unappreciated by Horace at the time. One in particular. The stability in which he had been raised would succor him all his life.

"Mama is sticking to Uncle Oliver like glue," Alison whispered.

It was tacitly understood that on days like today, the Plantaines tried not to let Oliver out of their sight. Opening-night tension was affecting all the cast. If Oliver's nerves got the better of him, he would seek and find oblivion in the only way he knew how.

Hermione blew a kiss to her husband and daughter. She would have liked to go and sit with them, but remained at Oliver's side. She noted the twitch in his cheek, which only a drink would soothe away. The trouble was, with Oliver, one drink always led to another. And the trouble with my husband, she thought, noticing Horace's frown, is he doesn't understand that Oliver is still my little brother who needs me.

A distant memory of herself and Oliver sharing a bed

when they were children returned to her. Oliver had been afraid of the dark and of the nocturnal creaks and rustles in the seedy houses that were their transitory homes. Hermione, who was seven years older than him, had not let him know that she was afraid, and had soothed him to sleep in her arms.

Though Oliver had wept bitterly on her wedding day, he had learned to accept Horace's place in her life. But Horace had never accepted his. Or, she suspected, her loyalty to her parents. Family feeling, Hermione reflected, was something her husband had no respect for. Possibly his background, the people he came from, about whom she could only conjecture because she had not met them, accounted for it.

"Uncle Oliver should get married, then he'd have his own wife to watch over him," Alison remarked precociously to Horace.

But it will never happen, Horace thought. Oliver would go on clinging to Hermione for the only kind of comfort he required from a woman.

Horace sometimes wondered if his wife knew of her brother's preference for his own sex. That the interest Oliver took in some of the young actors who came and went, according to the casting requirements of this production or that, was more than professional patronage.

If Hermione suspected, she would not allow herself to believe it, Horace decided. Despite her thirty-two years, she had retained a childlike innocence. In some ways, Hermione had never grown up.

Horace shifted his gaze from his wife to his brother-in-law. The telltale lines that marred Oliver's handsome face were presently hidden by stage make-up and the artificial smoothness this lent to his complexion accentuated the lack of masculinity discernible in him as a boy.

And Gregory Plantaine had sized up his son then, Horace thought with the benefit of hindsight. Why else would Gregory have stipulated that Horace change his name to Plantaine before marrying Hermione? Gregory had given no reason and Horace had not chanced his arm by demanding one. Horace had not thought about it from that day to this—or he would surely have realized that his father-in-law, who beneath his charming exterior was a crafty old fox, had been ensuring a future generation of Plantaines. Gregory had known in his bones that the continuance of his line could only be achieved through his daughter.

Oliver caught Horace's eye and doffed the crown he was wearing for his role of Oberon, in the debonair manner which was his public image.

He has to play a part offstage, as well as on, Horace reflected with grudging compassion. Society would never allow Oliver to be himself. And Horace did not doubt that the private torment to which Nature had consigned him had driven him to drink.

"The dinner break is almost over and you haven't eaten a thing, Papa," Alison said.

"Nor have you, love."

Alison glanced at the cheese sandwiches on the table. Their landlady was a kindly soul and had packed a picnic meal to sustain the Plantaines during this long day at the theater. "The mood you are in has affected my appetite, Papa."

Horace was warmed by her concern for him, which his wife appeared not to share. Hermione had just left the room with her parents and brother. Not for the first time, Horace was made to feel that the Plantaines were an elite little coterie of which he was only a nominal member.

A surge of loneliness welled up in him. Then he felt Alison's hand on his and the ache was replaced by gratitude for his daughter. She was too young to share his troubles, or to be a companion to him, but she was his own flesh and blood and there had always been a special rapport between them. He surveyed the satiny sheen of her olive skin, her sensuous lower lip and high cheekbones. She reminded him of—

But enough of raking up the past! He picked up the

ass's-head mask lying on the velvet banquette beside him, and went to join the company onstage.

Alison remained in the Green Room. Gregory Plantaine's departure had been the signal for all the cast to leave, and the aftermath of their presence, the smell of grease paint mingling with tobacco fumes, and the sudden silence, hung heavily on the air.

The excitement that had stirred in Alison before the dinner break had fizzled out. It was as though a damp cloth had extinguished the glow inside her. But she could find no tangible reason for it.

In later years, she would pinpoint today as the time when she stopped being a carefree little girl and became prey to the unspoken emotional conflicts of the adults around her. For the moment, unable to comprehend why, she was beset by a feeling that all was not well with her world.

TWO

ermione strode into her dressing room and flung herself down on the shabby chaise-longue which was its sole pretension to grandeur. A tiff with the wardrobe mistress was responsible for her mood. How dare the woman neglect to press Hermione's costume, and to rub salt into her wounds, by pointing out that it was no longer possible to do so every day!

When the tour of *A Midsummer Night's Dream* began, the wardrobe room had been staffed by three. The tour was now in its sixth week and Gregory had been called upon to lessen his overheads, by reducing the number of backstage employees.

Christmas had come and gone, and with it Gregory's hopes of recovering production costs. His confident expectation of long queues at the box office during the festive season had not materialized. Instead, the company had played to sparse houses and was still doing so.

Hermione tried to relax. It had always been her habit

to rest in her dressing room before making up for the evening performance. She wriggled her toes and let her limbs go limp, but was unable to rid her mind of its unhappy thoughts, or to stem the tears that had begun coursing down her cheeks. Oh, how her heart bled for her poor father.

She looked up and saw Alison standing in the doorway.

"What is it, Mama?"

Hermione stretched out a hand to her, but did not answer the question. "Come and sit by me, darling."

"Not until you tell me what's wrong."

The child looks a bit peaked this evening, Hermione registered absently. Or was it the gaslight?

"Tell me, Mama," Alison persisted, "or I shan't come and comfort you."

The irritation Alison was capable of arousing in Hermione flickered to life. Alison was not the daughter Hermione would have chosen. Giving birth to a child who looked foreign had come as a shock to Hermione and she had never quite recovered from it. And as that child grew older, she had revealed characteristics which compounded the injury.

As for Alison's behavior. There were times when one would think she was the mother and Hermione the child. Laying down conditions before she would come and sit by her mama! "I am not required to tell you anything. You are only a little girl," Hermione reminded her.

"If you say so, Mama," Alison replied.

Hermione wanted to slap the sphinxlike expression, that was part of the foreignness, from her face. "And what is that supposed to mean?"

"I shall be thirteen in August and I don't feel like a little girl."

Physically, Alison was a big girl, and the childish clothing she wore did not look right on her. The blue smocked frock under her frilly white pinafore had had to be spe-

cially made for her, as all her garments were; stores did
not stock children's garments in adult sizes.

Alison was destined to be a stately lady, Hermione reflected with a sigh. The very opposite of the Plantaine
women. Hermione bore a strong resemblance to her
dainty mother, who was not just a Plantaine by marriage.
Hermione's parents were cousins.

She eyed her daughter, who was still standing in the
doorway. Alison looked nothing like Horace, whose in-
determinate features and mousey coloring belied his
strong character. But her looks emanated from his family. It was as if their blood alone flowed in Alison's veins.
Not a drop of Hermione's own.

Alison was aware of her mother appraising her. "If
you won't tell me why you are upset, how can I comfort
you, Mama?"

"A kiss would comfort me."

Alison went to her and gave her one, but it was not
accompanied by the warm hug Horace would have received.

Hermione noted this with a pang that stemmed from
the maternal love she had for her daughter, which their
inability to communicate did not diminish.

Horace was at that moment engaged in a confrontation
with his father-in-law. Though neither man had raised
his voice in anger, it could not be termed otherwise.

"With respect, Gregory, you seem to be incapable of
using your head," Horace said.

"Indeed?" Gregory parried.

"If you would only come down to earth, accept that
our solely Shakespearean repertoire is simply not com-
mercial, it might be possible to save the company from
total disaster," Horace declared.

Gregory gave him a condescending smile. "You and I
do not have the same interpretation of total disaster, my
dear fellow."

"And what is yours?" Horace inquired.

"Artistic failure, what else? But then, I am an artist, not a businessman."

"That," Horace told him, "is the root of your trouble. You would rather see the company disband, than lower your personal standards."

"The Plantaine Players will never disband."

"I wish I shared your optimism."

"Some would call it spirit," Gregory rejoined, "and respect my high ideals. Regrettably, you are not among them."

"No," Horace said brusquely. "I am proof that it's possible for an actor to be equipped with common sense. And to a practical chap like me, it seems like lunacy to continue touring our current production."

"The play will close this weekend," Gregory informed him loftily, "as I was unable to raise any more money to pay the cast their wages."

Most men would be sitting biting their nails, if they were as deeply in debt as Gregory Plantaine now was. But he displayed not a trace of anxiety. Nor had he ever, Horace reflected wryly. Despite their differences, and the subtle humiliations he suffered from him, Horace had a reluctant affection for him. Without Gregory's encouragement and teaching, Horace would not have been an actor.

And there was about Gregory an indefinable aura which disarmed all comers, Horace thought, studying his face which was as unlined as that of a man half his fifty-seven years. His mane of tawny hair, devoid of even a hint of silver, completed the youthful picture.

How had Gregory stayed so young? Horace pondered. By clinging to his naive hope that tomorrow would be brighter than today—a philosophy possible only because he lived from day to day. Those whose lives were linked with his were required to follow suit, but Horace was prepared to do so no longer.

"Why won't you listen to reason, Gregory?" he appealed. "It's time you gave some serious thought to the company's future."

"There is nothing for me to think about," Gregory answered affably.

"I am beginning to wonder if you have anything to think with!"

Gregory chuckled, as though Horace had said something amusing.

Horace controlled the urge to give him a good shaking. He doubted that even that would provoke him. Gregory was a man with whom one could not have a row; his dignity prohibited it. And his ego was such that insults of the kind Horace had just delivered made no mark upon him.

"The company's immediate future is not in jeopardy, my dear fellow," Gregory said. "We shall do what we have always done when a small difficulty presents itself."

Horace tried to simmer down, but it was not easy. Gregory's equanimity was exacerbating his own frustration. A small difficulty? The Players had experienced financial problems many times, but never so dire as now. Wasn't Gregory aware that he was facing bankruptcy?

"I shall sell my shares," Gregory said placidly, and as if he had read Horace's mind.

Horace was taken aback. He had not known his father-in-law had any shares.

"They were willed to me by a great-aunt, when I was a lad," Gregory supplied. He laughed like an errant schoolboy. "And, would you believe it, I had forgotten about them."

Horace did believe it.

"A solicitor in London knows all about them," Gregory went on vaguely. "He wrote to me once. A pageful of scrawl about investments and brokers," he added with a shudder. "I remember replying that I would prefer to leave the matter in his capable hands, that I did not wish to be personally involved. I must find his address and get in touch with him."

"I'm amazed that you've remembered about the shares now," Horace told him scathingly.

"I didn't, I'm afraid. Your mother-in-law did."

Horace watched Gregory sit down before the mirror and drape a towel around his shoulders. They were in Oliver's dressing room. Before leaving their lodgings for the theater, they had found Oliver drunk in his room. Gregory would have to take over the role of Oberon tonight.

What were his feelings about his son's tragic plight? Horace wondered. Outwardly, Gregory displayed none. Were sorrow and disappointment tugging at his heartstrings, beneath his urbane facade?

Gregory cut into Horace's conjectures. "We shall keep our heads above water with readings from the sonnets and choice excerpts from the comedies," he cheerfully announced.

This was the Plantaines' habitual way of remaining afloat when they could not afford to engage other actors, for a full production.

Horace could not bear the thought of it. He revered Shakespeare no less than Gregory did, but was not prepared to continue living a hand-to-mouth existence in order to perpetuate the Bard's work. A vision of the Plantaines, himself and Alison included, endlessly trekking from town to town, a drunken Oliver in their midst and sparse audiences awaiting them, added to his depression.

Sooner or later, his father-in-law would somehow manage to raise enough cash to stage another play. As with *A Midsummer Night's Dream,* he would not recoup his outlay, let alone make a profit. And the whole ghastly fiasco would be repeated. Over and over again.

It's like being on a merry-go-round, from which one can never get off, Horace thought. No. A bizarre dance, one step forward, then two backward, was a better description.

"I can't go on this way," he told Gregory. "Nor can I allow my wife and child to do so."

Gregory had begun making up and paused with a stick of grease paint halfway to his chin.

"Unless you agree to put on plays like *The Second Mrs. Tanqueray,* which are good box office, I—"

Gregory allowed Horace to say no more. "In the thirteen years you have been my son-in-law, I have not staged *The Merchant of Venice,*" he cut in pleasantly.

"And I'm not suggesting you should do so now," Horace countered. "On the contrary!"

"Kindly allow me to finish, Horace. I was about to add: lest it embarrass you."

"What are you implying?"

"That money has never been my god." Gregory removed a speck of fluff from the sleeve of his mulberry velvet dressing gown. "But I am not of your background."

The color drained from Horace's face.

"I'm afraid you asked for it, old fellow," Gregory said in the same pleasant tone.

Horace left the room.

He walked numbly along the dank, gaslit passage on which the men's dressing rooms were situated and mounted a flight of stone stairs to where he would find his wife. As was the case in most theaters, the male and female dressing rooms were segregated, in the name of propriety.

His coat sleeve brushed against the whitewashed brick wall as he climbed the stairs, and a musty smell, strongly laced with Lysol, rose to his nostrils. An icy blast froze him when he reached the next floor, which was no less comfortless than the one he had just left, and his teeth began chattering.

How great was the contrast between the backstage ambience of a theater and its public face, he reflected briefly. Audiences would find it hard to equate this warren of dingy passages and peeling doors with the glamorous myth of theatrical life.

But Gregory Plantaine had not found it difficult to equate Horace with Shylock, he thought, as the full significance of his father-in-law's words flooded his mind and senses.

Long-forgotten emotions began churning within him. The defensiveness and aggressiveness which had once lived in him, side by side. The insecurity and uncertainty that he had believed gone forever. And the wariness of those who were not of his faith and held him in contempt.

Memories, too, assailed him; of the fear of being ridiculed and the yearning for acceptance he had known in his childhood and youth; of the ever-present necessity not to offend, and the feeling of being different. That was the strongest memory of all.

When had he stopped feeling different? No matter. His father-in-law had reminded him that he was. A man may forget he is a Jew, but the Gentiles acquainted with him never would.

Horace paused outside his wife's dressing room, unable to bring himself to enter. Did Hermione, too, though he did not doubt that she loved him, measure everything he said and did with the yardstick he had just learned her father applied to him? Probably all the Plantaines did. And what was that yardstick, but the classic preconceptions that adhered to the word Jew. Which Shakespeare had immortalized when he created Shylock.

Horace had not practiced his religion since he was a lad and was surprised at the partisan anger now gripping him. I'm not exactly eligible to champion my race, he thought with grim irony. Though he had not made a conscious decision to reject Judaism, he had turned his back upon it.

Under his parents' roof, he had followed their example. When he left home, it was a relief no longer to be obliged to attend synagogue, or to have to conform to the everyday restrictions imposed by Judaic Law. But the manner of his leaving had been painful as an amputation. His father had told him never to return.

Time had helped to heal the wound and there had been no contact with his family to reopen it. And it was as though Horace's Jewishness had, over the years, slipped away from him. Like a cloak one had habitually worn slipping from one's shoulders, he thought metaphorically.

But it had not slipped away entirely. He had shed the outer trappings of his religion without a pang of conscience or regret, but the feeling imbibed with his mother's milk was still there.

He cast it aside and returned his mind to the matter he must discuss with his wife.

"You look as if you've seen a ghost, my darling," Hermione remarked when he entered her dressing room.

Of my former self, Horace thought with a tight-lipped smile: "I've been talking to your father," he said.

Hermione moved from the chaise-longue to the dressing table and began brushing her hair. "About his plans, I suppose?" She had not expected Horace to approve of them.

"What plans?" he inquired derisively. "A return to his usual haphazard way of trying to make ends meet, is what I would call it!"

Hermione managed a light laugh.

"I won't be a party to it any longer," Horace declared.

"You have no choice, my dear," Hermione answered, carefully avoiding his eye.

Horace addressed her back, which was now as stiff as the brush in her hand. "I have a very distinct choice, love. And I have already made it."

Hermione glanced at Alison, who was listening intently. "I don't care to talk about this in Alison's presence."

"Why not?" Alison asked and received the reply she had anticipated.

"You are only a little girl."

"She will have to know, nevertheless," her father said to her mother. And added, "I'm afraid the time has come for a parting of the ways."

Alison gripped the edge of the chaise-longue, to steady herself. Her inexplicable feeling that all was not well with her world had just frighteningly crystallized. The bottom was dropping out of it.

Horace took in his daughter's apprehensive expression. Hermione was right; it wasn't suitable to conduct this conversation in the child's presence. The air was already bristling with his own and his wife's unspoken animosity and Alison was a sensitive girl.

He fished in his pocket and brought out a bag of sugar candy. "I got these for you," he said to her gently. "Go and sit in the Green Room and read one of your storybooks."

"I prefer to stay here," Alison answered.

"Kindly do as you are told," her mother snapped.

"Must I, Papa?"

Horace gave her a reassuring smile. "If you wouldn't mind, love."

"That child will do anything to please you!" Hermione exclaimed when Alison had left the room. The incident had emphasized her own lack of rapport with her daughter. "And perhaps we should postpone this ridiculous discussion, Horace. I must get ready for tonight's performance and so must you."

Horace consulted his pocket watch and recalled that his parents had given it to him when he was *Bar Mitzvah*. Would the past, once resurrected, give him no peace? He snapped the silver timepiece shut and returned his thoughts to the present—which was traumatic enough.

The actress playing Hippolyta called a friendly greeting as she passed along the corridor to her dressing room, swathed in a long, red feather boa.

"There's still almost an hour left before curtain call," Horace told his wife. "And there is nothing ridiculous about what I have to say to you. I ought to have said it long ago," he added with a weary smile.

Hermione rose from her stool and went to shut the door, which Alison had left ajar. "You've already inferred that you want us to leave the company. Nothing could be more ridiculous than that."

"There's no future for us with the company, Hermione. Our life will never be any different from what we're experiencing now. It isn't a suitable life for a child."

"Really?" Hermione flashed. "My parents considered it suitable for Oliver and me."

Horace doubted that Gregory and Jessica Plantaine had given a thought to their children's welfare. They had smothered them with love, and implanted in them their own impractical attitudes but, in essence, Hermione and Oliver's childhood had been the very opposite of Horace's own. A come and go game of chance.

"I want something better for Alison," Horace declared.

"Do you indeed? Materially better, I suppose?"

"And what's wrong with that?"

Hermione's dainty nose wrinkled with distaste. "That's dependent upon one's personal values, Horace. Those you are expressing make me think it would have been best if you'd stayed where you once were."

For the second time that evening, Horace felt as if he had been slapped.

"My family and I have never shared your concerns," Hermione informed him unnecessarily.

She had not failed to note the whipped look on his face and her instinct was to move to his side and comfort him. But it was he, not she, who had sought this confrontation, she thought with a surge of anger.

She tugged her pink satin robe closer about her diminutive figure and retied the sash with trembling fingers, trying to calm herself. How could she make her husband understand that what he wanted her to do was out of the question?

"If papa had cared to, he could by now have reached the very top of his profession," she declaimed. "His talent has been compared with that of Henry Irving."

Horace was well aware of this and considered Gregory's eschewal of the heights of fame a useless sacrifice. But it would add fuel to the fire to say so. The flame Horace had already kindled within his wife was dangerous enough.

How beautiful she is when her anger is aroused, he thought with an ache in his throat. Hermione's blue eyes had darkened with intensity to violet, and there was a proud grace in the tilt of her head.

"Why do you suppose my father chose not to follow a selfish path?" she went on. "Because nothing would persuade him to desert the family company. I, too, am imbued with that spirit. The Plantaines remain together, come what may. Maintain our artistic standards as best we can. Offer our audiences the most we are able to—"

"You'll have me in tears in a minute!" Horace cut in. "That was a lovely performance, my sweet. But you're not onstage and I'm not here to applaud. I'm your husband, attempting to make you face up to the truth."

"As you see it," Hermione replied.

"And allow me to give it to you unembellished. The Plantaine Players will end up with no audiences," Horace said brutally.

They regarded each other silently.

It's like looking at a stranger, Hermione thought. No, worse than that. An enemy in the camp. Her fists clenched into tight little balls as another gust of anger swept through her. Horace's failure to share her unquestioning dedication to the company had long been a source of distress to her. But she had not expected it to come to this; that he would seek to take her away from everything she held dear.

Horace met her gaze and recoiled from what he saw in

it. But there was, he knew, no lack of hostility in his own. How could two people who loved each other arrive at moments like this? All their shared tenderness forgotten in a blaze of mutual resentment.

"I ought not to have married you," Hermione said.

A cold hand clutched at Horace's heart. "But you did."

"Under the misapprehension that you had in you some loyalty."

Horace allowed the jibe to pass.

Hermione inserted her verbal scalpel deeper. "Not to the Plantaine tradition. Possibly that would be too much to expect, as you are not one of us. But it didn't enter my head that you would prove to be disloyal to the man who took you under his wing and gave you a chance."

Horace stood staring at a damp patch on the distempered wall and noticed that rivulets of condensation were trickling down the grimy windows. The hissing of the gaslights, and the muted rumble of cart wheels outside the theater, heightened the gathering tension in the room and he was aware of a pulse throbbing in his temple.

"I am very grateful to your father," he said in an even tone that belied his feeling. "But my gratitude has not impaired my faculties. Nor can I allow it to prevent me from doing what I know is right. I must provide us with a more secure way of life."

Hermione laughed and the sound was not pleasant. It reminded Horace of her portrayal of the Shrew.

"And how do you propose to do that?" she inquired with barbed sweetness. "I have no doubt whatsoever that I, if I wished, would do very well for myself in London," she added with typical Plantaine arrogance. "I could probably become another Mrs. Patrick Campbell. Or the Sarah Bernhardt of the English theater. I am an actress born and bred. But you, Horace—"

"Yes?" he prodded her.

Dare she say it? Hermione briefly wondered. If she did, it could never be unsaid.

"At least have the courage to speak your mind," Horace goaded her on.

"It wasn't lack of courage, but the wish not to hurt you that caused me to hesitate," she flung at him. "But I shall hesitate no longer. You're unworthy of my consideration. And as you are thinking of taking your chance elsewhere, you had better know your own limitations. You're a competent actor, Horace, but with only a small talent."

Another silence followed.

"So that's your opinion of me, is it?" Horace said, breaking it.

"And I'm sure it is shared by others, though they wouldn't be likely to say it to me. If you weren't Papa's son-in-law, you wouldn't have been cast in the important roles you've played."

Horace sat down as though he were suffering from shock and his legs would not support him.

Hermione was moved to pity him. Then what he was trying to do to her made her, instead, sorry for herself. "If you had let well alone, I wouldn't have had to tell you, Horace. And you'd better forget your wish to separate me from my family. Go if you must. But Alison and I will remain where we belong."

Horace stared down at the floor, his hands clasped upon his knees. He was aware of his frock coat flapping in a draft around his shins, and of his stiff, winged collar encasing his neck. And would remember this whenever he thought of the things his wife had just said to him.

Why was it that the most painful moments of his life were engraved upon his memory together with such irrelevancies? He would not forget the deep scar in the dingy lino, which he was carefully studying now. Nor the musty, backstage atmosphere upon which he had briefly ruminated after his shattering encounter with Gregory. He could recall, too, observing a small crack in the living-room ceiling, when his father told him never to come back.

It must be a kind of defense mechanism, he mused with the remote part of his mind he was allowing to function, the way his attention swooped like an injured bird upon whatever mundanity was nearest at hand. A stunned flailing of the wings of consciousness in the interval between receiving a blow and succumbing to its effects.

He transferred his gaze to his wife's face and was able to maintain his detachment no longer. His whole being felt battered and bruised. How could Hermione look so composed? Probably because she had nothing left to say. She had said it all, and, in so doing, had purged herself of resentment.

Hermione observed Horace's stricken expression and knew there was nothing she could do for him. "You told me the truth as you see it and left me no option but to do likewise," she said quietly. "The truth can be exceedingly hurtful, as you now know."

Horace, who had that evening received a double dose of it, made no reply.

He could not have envisaged Hermione being prepared to be parted from him. She was a passionate woman, the kind who needed a man's love. But the woman who shared his bed was another Hermione. Not the cool creature who had told him to go if he must. Or the cruel one who had cut him down to size.

"I'll die if you leave me," the Hermione with whom he had fallen in love said tremulously.

The trouble with being married to an actress is it's hard to know when she's acting, Horace thought wryly. Whether what you're seeing is an aspect of the real her, or a character she's pulled out of the hat. Hermione was capable of being several different people, one after the other. Horace was too. It was the actor's stock-in-trade. But Horace had never made use of it in his personal life.

Hermione was looking at him with her heart in her eyes. Was this another performance? Calculated to sway

him? If so, it was possible that she didn't know it. It had
occurred to Horace long ago that the line between reality
and make-believe had begun to blur for his wife.

A moment later, she had flung herself into his arms
and was sobbing on his shoulder.

This, at least, is real, Horace thought, stroking her hair.
The warm human contact they had shared for thirteen
years. As the child born of their love was real.

"There is no question of my leaving without you and
Alison," he said.

Hermione covered his face with rapturous kisses, then
she gave him the special smile of a woman saying thank
you to a man from whom she has got what she wanted.
Horace had seen her employ it onstage, countless times.
But there was no mistaking the genuine relief in her eyes.

"All's well that ends well," Hermione blissfully
quoted.

She went to being making up, unaware that for her
husband the mischief begun today had not ended, but
would continue its work inside him.

"And nothing has changed," she added with satisfaction.

Horace watched her wrap a broad band of linen
around her hair, before applying grease paint to her face.
How could she think that nothing had changed? Because, for her, nothing had and she would not give the
matter another thought. But with a few choice words she
had diminished him. Destroyed his belief in himself; as
her father lightly put to flight the comfortable illusion
that had made Horace's life with the Plantaines possible.

Hermione was humming a happy tune while she
worked on her face. And her papa is probably booming
out a merry sea shanty, while he puts the finishing
touches to his! Horace thought. A tide of laughter rose in
him, but he stemmed it. Who wanted to laugh at their
own expense?

Briefly, he allowed himself the luxury of hating both
his wife and his father-in-law, then stemmed the hate as

he had the laughter. He adored Hermione and, possible or not, must remain in the bosom of her family; keep his thoughts and feelings to himself.

Neither Hermione nor Gregory would ever be aware of the damage they had, between them, wrought. They saw only with their own short-sighted vision, their horizons stretching no further than the perimeter of their narrow world.

"If you don't hurry, darling, you won't be dressed in time for your entrance," Hermione prodded him. Bottom made his first appearance in Scene Two.

If the Plantaines had a family motto, it would be: "The curtain must rise," Horace thought, and had a vision of himself lying dead in the wings and Hermione stepping over him, to make her entrance on cue. An empty sensation assailed him, and with it the feeling that he wouldn't give a damn if he never saw a theater again.

"Do get a move on, Horace!" Hermione exclaimed.

But for his wife, the theater was all. The real-life drama in which she had just played a major role had left no impression upon her.

"You look as if you've lost a sovereign and found sixpence," she told him.

Horace was not surprised to hear it. The man he had thought himself did not exist, and the lad he had once been was only a memory. What he had lost was his sense of identity, he thought with grim amusement.

He left Hermione to finish transforming herself into Titania and made the gloomy trek to his own dressing room, oblivious to the familiar last-minute bustle he encountered *en route*.

His reflection in the mirror, when he sat down before it, displayed no outward ravages. But Horace could still feel the terrible emptiness gnawing inside him, and knew he would never be the same again. It was as if his wife and her father had shaken him like a tree and the fruits of his adult years had come tumbling down, revealed for the hollow illusions they were. Only his roots remained sure and solid.

But they were in a place whither he could not return and he fought back a sudden longing to be with his own people. A man must foot the bill for his folly and Horace must pay the price of his. He could take comfort from the love of his wife and daughter, but the rest of his life would be a sham. How foolish he had been to think he could transplant himself in alien ground.

THREE

Oliver awoke with a ringing reverberation in his head. Someone was clanging a bell outside. Where was he? Momentarily, he could not remember. Then the sickly green curtains, through which wintry sunlight was filtering, jolted him to recollection. The company was playing in Leeds this week, and Mrs. Drury was inordinately fond of that unappetising color.

Last week, the Plantaines had stayed with Mrs. Pickles in Liverpool, and Oliver had slept in one of her chastely white bedrooms. And the week before that, he recalled, his room had been a somber brown, which meant they were in Nottingham, at Mrs. Fathingale's house.

Oliver had always attached colors to people, places and events, and they remained pigeonholed in his mind that way. In retrospect, his life seemed a kaleidoscope of briefly experienced sights, sounds and sensations. An ever-changing pattern, yet with a deadly sameness, he reflected bleakly. His own color was a leaden gray. He had never been able to approach each new day with the zest with which his parents and sister were blessed.

Smells were part of the kaleidoscope, too, he thought, wrinkling his nose. Mrs. Drury was scrupulously clean and her bedlinen pristine fresh, but the odor of liniment used by the room's last occupant still hung in the air. As liquor fumes would, when Oliver was gone.

He must get up and go to the theater. The clanging sounded louder and he dragged himself to the window to peer outside. Was there a fire in the street? No. It was the baker, stomping along with his handbell, a laden basket on his arm. Doing his morning round—Oliver had slept through last night's performance.

Missing a performance was a serious misdemeanor for any actor. For a Plantaine, it was a cardinal sin. The Plantaines were nominally Christians, but it was Shakespeare, not Christ, whom they worshipped, Oliver thought. And the theater was their hallowed ground.

He moved to the washstand, thought that its marble surface would make a nice tombstone, and wished he were lying beneath one, as he swigged down the dregs from a handy whisky bottle. He had once said as much to Hermione and she had taken him in her arms to comfort him.

Hermione was dearer to him than anyone in the world. Between them, there was no need of words. But there were times when Oliver could draw no consolation from her devotion to him. When even in a crowded room, seated beside a cheerful fire, a chill wind of despair tore at his heart and soul.

He poured some water into the rose-patterned bowl and noted with distaste that the jug was chipped around its gilded lip. Imperfection offended Oliver. A hollow laugh escaped him, for there could be no more flawed specimen than himself.

After dousing his face with the water, he went downstairs and was met by the sight of his disreputable appearance, reflected in the hallstand mirror. He had not combed his hair, nor fastened his collar, which was hanging outside his crumpled lapels secured only by a back-stud. His cravat looked like a red rag, dangling on his waistcoat. But he had slept in his clothes; what else could he expect?

He ought to return to his room and make himself look respectable. But he wasn't respectable and the hell with pretending to be. An irresistible urge to shock his parents propelled him into the dining room, where the Plataines were eating breakfast.

The landlady almost dropped the tray she was carrying from the room, and stopped in her tracks. "Really, Mr. Oliver!" she exclaimed when she found her tongue. Mrs. Drury had seen him look this way when he was drunk, but there was no excuse for it when he was sober. Only her esteem for his family prevented her from telling him to leave her house.

She marched out with a disapproving swish of her black bombazine skirt. It would never cease to mystify her, how the nice little boy Oliver had been had turned into a man like that.

The Plantaines had always lodged with Mrs. Drury when they played in Leeds, but she had never really got to know them. Her kitchen was lovely and cozy, she thought, while slicing bread for the extra toast Jessica Plantaine had requested. Her other lodgers ate their meals in here, but Mrs. Drury had never suggested that the Plantaines eat in the kitchen—and doubted that they did so in their lodgings in other towns.

There was something about them that stopped you from being familiar. She pronged the bread onto her two long toasting forks. The Plantaines were pleasant and friendly, but not the kind you sat eating fish and chips with, when they got back from the theater at night. They kept themselves to themselves, as if they were aristocracy. And gave a person the feeling that they were.

Mrs. Drury sat before the hot coals in her homely, blackleaded grate, visualizing the Plantaine family seated around the breakfast table. Gregory and Horace, immaculately garbed in gray, each with a pearl pin in his cravat. Jessica in a rust alpaca gown, with a cameo brooch at her throat, and Hermione in an elegant lavender frock. Young Alison, clean and fresh in sprigged muslin.

Mrs. Drury had never seen them look any different. How sad it must be for Gregory and Jessica, having a son like Oliver, she was thinking when the bread caught fire. And, thanks to Oliver, she had burned the toast!

Oliver had joined the family at the table. "Is nobody speaking to me this morning?" he inquired with bravado.

Silence had followed Mrs. Drury's exit.

"You look as if you've been put through a wringing machine," Horace remarked.

And wrung dry, Hermione thought with distress. "Anyone can have an off days, Horace," she said, managing a smile.

Jessica and Gregory continued eating their egg and bacon, avoiding Oliver's eyes. Also, each other's, Oliver noted.

"Are you feeling better, dear?" his mother inquired solicitiously.

"Better than what, Mother?"

Jessica poured a cup of tea for him and did not reply.

"I enjoyed standing in for you, last night," his father chuckled. "So your indisposition did me a favor, Oliver."

"Would you like me to do you another one, Father? Indispose myself again, tonight?"

Alison was sipping her milk, aware of something heavy in the air, as if a thunderstorm was brewing. Her mother and grandparents were smiling. But their smiles looked stiff, as if fixed onto their faces with glue. Her father was carefully cutting a sausage into tiny pieces. And Uncle Oliver was crumbling some toast to bits.

Why had Granny pretended Uncle Oliver was ill, when everyone knew he only missed a performance when he was drunk? And Grandpa had most certainly not enjoyed playing Oberon last night. Alison had heard him remark that he felt highly uncomfortable, because Uncle Oliver's costume was much too tight for him.

It struck Alison, now, that her uncle's drinking was never spoken of by her grandparents. Would they have behaved any differently had she not been present? No. The pretending wasn't for her benefit. She had the feeling that the adults seated around the table with her had forgotten she was there.

Oliver swallowed down his tea, but it did not remove the sourness from his mouth. And nothing could purge it from his soul. Except, perhaps, the unconditional love his parents denied him; of which honesty was an integral part.

He would prefer them to chastise him, call him names, say he wasn't worthy of being a Plantaine, rather than maintain this charade. Who were they fooling except themselves? Even his young niece knew he was a drunk.

But his parents wouldn't let themselves know it. Like Oliver, they desired perfection. They could never reconcile themselves to having bred an imperfect son. Instead, they had brushed Oliver's trespasses, like unwanted dust, under the self-protective carpet of their Plantaine pride.

FOUR

horace was mistaken in his belief that Hermione would not give another thought to their hurtful confrontation.

After Gregory had paid his debts, for which the proceeds of his shares were fortuitously sufficient, the company continued to have its ups and downs. When they were down, which was more often than not, Horace showed no sign of concern. But Hermione was haunted by a secret fear that he would, one day, leave her. There was about him an almost imperceptible change; a quiet self-containment he had never before displayed. As if the discontentment he had not tried to hide from her in recent years was now lying dormant within him.

When they played in towns where a rival company had people queuing to see the popular entertainment the Plantaines would not deign to offer, Horace no longer made caustic comments to Hermione about her father's stupidity. And he sat carefully withdrawn from the conversation, when actors engaged for a Plantaine produc-

tion talked of the success of a company led by a showy
actress called Ruby May.

"That woman is a monster!" Hermione exclaimed one
Sunday morning, when the Plantaines were waiting at
Crewe railway station. They had played last week in Not-
tingham and were traveling to their next engagement in
Oldham.

Alison was seated on one of the company's property
skips, her teeth chattering with cold. "Which woman,
Mama?"

Hermione turned up Alison's rabbit-fur collar against
the cruel March wind and did not reply.

"I think your mama was referring to Miss Ruby May,"
Horace said, surveying a magenta-clad lady with an
hourglass figure, who was standing with a group farther
along the platform.

Alison giggled. "Miss May's hair is almost the same
shade as her coat!"

"It was doubtless dyed to match it," Hermione said
cattily.

"That hardly makes her a monster," Horace countered.

"I was referring to her reputation," Hermione replied.
"I understand she has an elderly husband, but prefers
young men."

Ruby May's private life was well publicized. Pictures
of her with her twin children appeared in the newspapers. Crowds wanting a glimpse of her waited outside the
stage doors of theaters where she appeared. She was
known as the melodrama queen. Though melodramas
were now considered to have had their day, Miss May
continued touring them and played to packed houses.

"It is she and her like who give our profession a bad
name," Hermione opined prissily. "As for the kind of
theater she purveys! Art doesn't enter into it. All she is
concerned with is financial gain."

"I don't understand what you mean, Mama," Alison
said.

"You will when you're older, Alison. You're a Plantaine."

She's also a Shrager, Horace thought. Was it too much to hope that her Plantaine conditioning would, when she grew up, be offset by a latent streak of common sense?

Their train appeared in the distance and Alison went to tell the rest of their party, who were in the waiting rooms.

Horace watched her stride away, a tall and shapely figure, her hair cascading down her back from beneath her crimson pillbox hat. Soon, she would be fourteen and only her face was still childish.

Hermione observed his poignant expression. "A penny for your thoughts?"

"I was thinking that Alison will be grown up before we know it. And how sad it is that she doesn't know my family," Horace added as that feeling overtook him.

Hermione stiffened. "Sad for them, certainly. But they have only themselves to blame."

The mere mention of her husband's family was anathema to Hermione. How could it not be? she thought. Horace had written to tell them of his marriage and, a year later, of Alison's birth. They had not acknowledged the letters, as if Hermione and Alison did not exist for them. But nor did their son, it seemed, once he had left home.

Hermione had, from the outset, considered their attitude to Horace extraordinary. Her parents would not have behaved as though she were dead, if she had not fulfilled their expectations. They would have hidden their disappointment and would, somehow, have come to terms with it. As they had about Oliver.

Horace had not mentioned his family for years and Hermione could not understand why he was suddenly thinking about them. "When Alison was born, you made me a promise," she reminded him.

"I haven't forgotten it. Nor have I broken it," Horace replied.

As Alison was unlikely to have any contact with the Shragers, Hermione had seen no reason to burden her with the unhappy details. Alison had been told that her father had no family. In effect, this was so.

Knowing she had Jewish blood in her veins could be for Alison the heaviest burden of all, Horace reflected, watching her help Jessica Plantaine on to the train, and thinking of the pleasure his own mother was missing.

But, he mused, Minna Shrager would have other grandchildren to brighten her old age. When Horace left home, his sister Lottie had just become engaged to Lionel Stein. They had planned to marry that year, and probably had a houseful of kids by now. Lionel was then a traveling salesman, but was the kind who had an eye to the main chance and, Horace surmised, would now be firmly entrenched in the Shrager family business.

Hermione saw that her husband's expression had shadowed with emotion. She had thought he had stamped out the love he once had for his family, as their treatment of him deserved. But he had only set it aside. If a reconciliation with them were possible, would she want it? Oh no!

An imaginary family portrait of her in-laws rose before her eyes, darkened by their anonymity into a menacing huddle and framed by her own acrimony. They were not her kind and it had been a relief that she would not have to know them. Nor would she have them complicating her life and Alison's now.

Horace had taken her arm and was escorting her to the train. "I don't want you ever to break that promise," she said intensely. "Alison is a precocious and difficult girl and—"

"If you mean she has an inquiring mind, I agree," Horace cut in, defending his daughter.

"Too inquiring by far," Hermione declared. "But I want the matter of your family to remain a closed book."

For once, Hermione was not to have her way. The book was opened for Alison by her Aunt Lottie a few days later and, as Hermione had feared, would never again be closed. But even Hermione could not have foretold how deeply it would enmesh her daughter.

While Lottie Stein was making her way to Oldham's Hippodrome Theatre, Alison, unaware that she had a paternal aunt, was in Horace's dressing room, watching him morosely remove his makeup after the evening performance.

Horace had changed into his dressing gown and Alison took down the tartan kilt he had slung over the screen, and folded it, her brow wrinkled into a thoughtful frown. The Players were currently staging *Macbeth,* which was supposed to be unlucky. Was the thing that had made Uncle Oliver go to pieces affecting Papa?

Because luck seems to be a major influence, for good or ill, in the shaping of their careers, or possibly because theater people inhabit a world of the imagination, most are superstitious to a high degree. Alison could remember seeing her mother carefully tear up the envelopes in which good-luck telegrams were delivered before a première. Not to do so was said to tempt Fate.

Her father was the kind who thumbed his nose at superstition. But even he, Alison had noted while the play was in rehearsal, had adhered to the unwritten rule that prevailed in the profession. *Macbeth* must never be referred to by its title, or disaster would surely descend.

Last night, a stagehand had thoughtlessly broken the rule in Oliver's presence, just before the curtain rose. Oliver had gone onstage unable to remember his opening lines. He had pulled himself together, but had given a terrible performance and had since been consoling himself in his usual way.

Gregory had asked a young hopeful, engaged to play one of the soldiers, to take over Horace's part of Macduff. Nowadays, though Oliver did not know it, either Horace or Gregory undertook to understudy him—just in case. And tonight Horace had found himself playing the role he had once coveted. Most actors yearn to play Hamlet, but Horace's high peak of challenge had been Macbeth.

But his performance had been uninspired and drab, he reflected while creaming the grease paint from his face. He had spent the afternoon making sure he knew the lines and cues, but with the disinterest with which he now approached all his parts. Without so much as a flicker of excitement. Because acting had become for him only a job and all he was able to bring to it was the technique he had acquired with the years. The spark once within him had been snuffed out when he learned from Hermione that he was second-rate.

"May I say something personal, Papa?" Alison asked tentatively.

"No, you may not!" Hermione had just entered the room.

Hermione would have liked to make a few personal comments to Horace, herself, but curbed the urge. His lifeless performance had, by contrast, made her portrayal of Lady Macbeth seem melodramatic. Why else had the audience tittered from time to time? As if they were watching Miss Ruby May!

Alison had been going to ask her father if the superstition had put a blight on him; that something had, she could read in his expression. And she agreed with what was written in her mother's. Papa had been a failure as Macbeth.

Then something else occurred to Alison. Her father was never at his best when the company was playing in Oldham. When they were here, he didn't take Alison for walks around the town, as he did in their other venues, and rarely left their lodgings except to go to the theater. Once, Alison had celebrated a birthday here, but Papa had made her wait for the coral necklace he'd promised her, until they moved on to their next engagement.

Alison was wearing the necklace now and toyed with it

thoughtfully. "What is it about Oldham, Papa, that always sets you on edge?"

Her parents exchanged a quick glance and the mystery deepened for her.

Horace was startled by Alison's perceptiveness.

"Whenever we come here, you're gloomy," she persisted when he did not reply.

Hermione made light of it. "Perhaps it's because Papa met me here," she joked.

"Really?" Alison exclaimed. "Why didn't I know that?"

Horace managed to smile. "Probably because you've never asked us where we met."

It struck Alison then that there was a good deal she did not know about her parents. Her mother did not like being questioned. And something, she knew not what, had stopped Alison from quizzing her father about himself.

She would not have known he had first joined the company as stagehand, if Nellie Lamb, who had been the Players' wardrobe mistress for twenty years, had not told her. And he never spoke of his childhood, the way Mama sometimes did. But a person had to have a childhood. Was Papa brought up in an orphanage, with nobody of his own to love him until he met Mama? Alison conjectured.

She was about to learn that quite the opposite had been the case.

"There's a lady askin' fer yer, Mr. Plantaine," the stagedoor keeper called from the corridor. "Are yer decent? If yer are, Ah'll cum in, wi't note she asked me ter fetch yer."

Hermione opened the door. "Thank you, Ned. Would you mind waiting until my husband has read it?" She handed the note to Horace and watched him scan it, and his face turn as white as the paper upon which it was written.

Horace wet his lips, which suddenly felt parched. "You had better show her in, Ned."

"Show who in?" Hermione demanded when Ned had gone.

"My sister," Horace said swallowing hard.

"And what brings her here? After years of wanting nothing to do with you?"

"It seems that my father is seriously ill."

"I am sorry to hear that," Hermione said stiffly. "You may do as you please, Horace. But I would prefer not to meet her." She swept to the door, but had to step back to allow Lottie Stein to enter.

The two women surveyed each other.

"You must be Horace's wife," Lottie said with a wan smile.

"I am indeed. But isn't it a little late in the day for you to recognize me?" Hermione left without another word.

Not until she had shut the door behind her did she remember Alison's presence in the room, but could not bring herself to go back inside and get her. And it no longer mattered, Hermione thought resignedly. Alison had just learned that the Plantaines were not her sole relatives. The damage was done.

Alison was watching her father and his sister embrace each other. Tears were streaming down both their faces. She herself was too stunned to speak.

"How long has it been, Lottie?" Horace said after they had released each other.

"Too long," Lottie replied. "And such a terrible waste."

They exchanged a long glance across the awkward chasm of their estrangement, briefly bridged when they had held each other close.

What was Lottie thinking? Horace wondered. Had cold recrimination superseded the warmth she had just displayed?

Was that shame in Horace's eyes? Lottie could not be sure. But he had plenty to be ashamed of.

Alison wished she had left with her mother. It was as though she was watching a scene in a play, so tense was the atmosphere. Her father's expression was anguished and she couldn't bear to see him this way. Ought she to leave now? She wanted to, but could not make herself move.

"You haven't introduced me to my niece, Horace," Lottie said breaking the silence. "Alison is a lovely name," she said when Horace had done so.

"I'm the only female Plantaine not to be called after a Shakespearean heroine," Alison informed her. "They always have been."

"My wife wanted to continue the tradition and call her Viola," Horace told Lottie. "But I've always liked the name Alison." It was the only matter in which he had stood fast, he reflected wryly. His sole scccessful attempt to assert himself over the Plantaines.

"Why don't you sit down, Lottie?" he said.

Lottie seated herself on a straight-backed chair which stood against the wall. "I was waiting for you to invite me to."

"Since when does a sister need to stand on ceremony with her brother?" Horace answered.

They eyed each other awkwardly again and Alison felt the tension return to the room.

"Since the brother made himself a stranger," Lottie replied.

Her gloved hands were gripping her bag, which she had placed upon her lap. She was wearing a coat of some soft material in a muted shade of gray, with a matching hat tilted on her blue-black hair. In the shadows cast by the gaslight, she seemed almost to merge with them, and Horace was assailed by the feeling that she was not really there, but a specter sent to haunt him.

"Why did you come?" he suddenly flung at her. "You could have written to tell me about Father."

"But it wouldn't have had the same effect."

No, Horace thought bitterly. Her coming had opened

up a can of worms which would never stop wriggling so far as his daughter was concerned. Alison's gaze was riveted to Lottie. He ought to send her from the room, but there was no way to undo what had already been done. He would have to tell her the whole story when Lottie had gone, and hope she would understand.

Lottie rose from the chair, as if she could not remain still. Her face was now flushed with feeling, which shone, too, from her eyes.

"I've always wondered who I look like and now I know," Alison said to her.

Lottie went to kiss Alison's cheek. "You wouldn't have had to wonder, Alison, if pride and principle were never put before love."

"Whose pride and principle, Aunt Lottie?"

Horace felt like a bystander at a family reunion. His sister was gently stroking his daughter's hair.

"Your Grandfather Shrager's," Lottie replied to Alison. "Which, until now, I felt it my duty to uphold, as your grandmother did."

"I don't understand," Alison said confusedly.

"Of course not. How could you? What happened between your father and his family was long before you were born. But me, I have a new motto," Lottie said, looking at Horace. " 'Let the past be the past.' "

Only a supreme optimist would believe that possible, Horace thought, and recalled that his sister had always been one. "It isn't that simple," he declared.

"Why not? If everyone wants it? Father may not have long to live," Lottie said tremulously. "Would a man deny his only son's right to stand beside his deathbed? And you, Horace. Will you let him go without making peace with you? How could he rest in his grave?"

Another silence descended and Alison could not bear it.

"You must go and visit my grandfather, Papa!" she cried.

How quickly and easily she had claimed the Shragers

as her own, Horace thought, noting the gleam of diamonds in Lottie's scarf pin. The family business must be doing well, he registered in one of his moments of protective detachment.

"If Father dies, it will be your duty to say the *Kaddish* for him," Lottie reminded her brother.

"What does that mean?" Alison inquired.

"The *Kaddish* is the mourners' prayer, Alison," Lottie explained. "When a Jew dies, it is recited by their male next-of-kin."

Alison's confusion was plain to see.

Lottie looked at Horace incredulously. "Doesn't your daughter know you're a Jew?"

"There seemed no point in telling her."

"I see."

"But only from your point of view. Not from mine." Not for anything would Horace reveal that it had been his wife's wish.

"There is only one right point of view," Lottie declared. "And that is that Alison was entitled to know."

"I agree," Alison said. Why was her voice trembling? "And it means I'm half-Jewish, doesn't it?"

"Does that make you so unhappy?" Lottie asked, observing her distressed expression.

"I'm not sure how I feel. I mean—well it's a shock, isn't it?" Alison turned her gaze upon her father.

Was she eyeing him accusingly? Yes, and he deserved it. All Horace was able to say was, "I suppose it is."

"Wouldn't you be upset, Papa, if you suddenly discovered something like that about yourself?"

"Something like what?" Lottie said carefully.

But Alison could not put her feelings into words.

She had been raised as a Gentile—which, technically, she was; Judaic Law deems a child to be of the religion of its mother—and had absorbed the age-old misconceptions about Jews. Horace reflected. He could see her troubled thoughts flickering in her expression. This wasn't easy for her.

"Does Mama know?" she asked him.

Horace nodded.

"Then both of you have lied to me."

"Not exactly, Alison."

"Yes you have!" she flashed. "What other word is there for not telling the truth? And how am I to feel but that my whole life, until now, has been a lie? If my aunt hadn't saved me from it, I should have gone on till the end of my days in ignorance of what I truly am!" She took a wisp of cambric and lace from her apron pocket, with a dramatic flourish and delicately dabbed her eyes. "I may never forgive you for it."

"I agree with everything she's said," Lottie told Horace.

Alison inclined her head, graciously, "Thank you, Aunt Lottie."

"Only I felt like clapping," Lottie added.

"I wasn't acting. I meant it," Alison declared vehemently.

"I'm sure you did, love. But the way you said it took my breath away."

Horace too, despite being the subject of his daughter's castigation, had felt he was witnessing a performance. Alison's tone, posture and gestures had ranged within the space of a minute from passionate anger and righteous indignation to the pathos of a tragedian, and had been carefully controlled throughout.

"Who does she take after, Horace? You or her mother?" Lottie asked with a smile.

Horace returned the smile, but did not reply. Alison, he had just learned, was blessed with that indefinable quality known as stage presence. One day she would hold an audience spellbound, as she had him and his sister a moment ago. She had inherited the gift God had bestowed upon the Plantaines. And, like her mother, would use it offstage, as well as on, he thought wryly.

"Bring Alison with you, when you visit Father," Lottie said. "Her cousins will be charmed by her."

"Fancy me having cousins!" Alison exclaimed. "How absolutely marvelous!"

"My Conrad is nearly eighteen," Lottie told her brother, "and already in the business. It's quite a big store, these days. My husband helped to make it one, but don't tell Father I said so. Father thinks he did it all by himself and Lionel lets him think so. You remember Lionel, don't you?"

"He isn't the kind one forgets." Horace's impression of him had proved correct.

"You never really took to him, did you?" Lottie said astutely. "But if you hadn't left home, you'd have found out what a wonderful man he is. There's nothing he wouldn't do for Mother and Father."

Horace retained the feeling that anything Lionel Stein did was calculated to help himself.

"Lionel didn't want me to come here to see you," Lottie revealed. "He was afraid it would upset me."

Or his own apple cart! Horace thought unkindly. Namely, the dying patriarch's will, which Horace's timely return to the fold might conceivably cause to be changed in his favor.

Alison put an end to her aunt's wifely eulogy. "Have I any girl cousins, Aunt Lottie?"

"Two." Lottie smiled. "But neither of them looks like me, the way you do." Looking at Alison was like seeing herself, as a child.

"How old are they?" Alison inquired. "Is either of them my age? I'll be fourteen in August."

"I know you will, love. Your daddy wrote to tell us when you were born." Lottie glanced at Horace apologetically. "Father forbade me to reply. It was the same when you let us know you were married."

"You were telling me about my cousins," Alison reminded her impatiently.

"Your cousin Emma was born on the same day as you, Alison."

Alison cried out with delight. "We're not just ordinary cousins, then. We're twins!"

"But Emma is as quiet as a mouse and you are the very opposite," Lottie said with a chuckle. "A person could forget Emma is in the room. But her sister Clara is a young madam and already has boys flocking around her, though she's not yet sixteen."

"I can't wait to meet them," Alison declared. "Especially Emma."

A tug-of-war had begun raging inside Horace. His interpretation of letting the past be the past was not Lottie's. He had put it firmly behind him, together with those who had caused him to do so. And would be wise to leave it that way. He could not shut out his memories and had given up trying to, but the intrusion into his life that his sister was proposing, and herself represented, was preventable. He could stop it from happening. Did he want to? His reason said yes. But his heart was saying no.

"When will you come, Horace?" Lottie asked.

She was taking a lot for granted! "We leave Oldham on Sunday," he said abruptly.

Today was Friday.

"Then you must come tomorrow."

"I haven't said I'm coming at all."

Lottie had never been one to shilly-shally. "Are you?"

"Yes," Horace heard himself say. The black sheep would do his duty, then go on his way. And the father who had cast him out could rest in peace.

"I knew you would do the right thing, Papa," Alison said solemnly.

But it was not duty alone that had swayed Horace. The blood tie he had sought to sever still held fast. Family feeling, too, which seeing his sister had, against his will, resurrected. And oh, the sweetness of surrender. With his decision, a blessed tranquility had enveloped him. Was it because his heart had won?

FIVE

After Lottie had gone, Horace was told by the stagedoor keeper that his wife had left the theater with her parents.

"You mustn't blame Mama for leaving without us," Alison said, on the tram to the outlying district of Hollinwood, where their lodgings were. "There was no point in her waiting," she added sensibly.

"I shan't say a word to her about it," Horace replied. He had not expected his wife to hang around while he remained closeted with his sister. On the contrary. And was steeling himself for the words Hermione would, no doubt, fling at him.

Alison looked along the slatted-wood seating that stretched from one end of the vehicle to the other, empty of passengers at this hour. "How eerie it is, having the tram to ourselves," she remarked, linking her arm through her father's. "As if there's nobody but you and me in the world."

They were trundling past the darkened buildings on

Manchester Road, and pools of light spilling from the streetlamps onto the rainswept pavements lent a ghostly look to the deserted sidestreets.

"Everyone's tucked up in bed," Horace answered.

"It isn't as late as that, Papa. You and I haven't had our supper yet."

"It is for the folk who live around here, Alison. They have to be up at the crack of dawn, to work in the cotton mills."

"How awful for them," Alison said, and it struck Horace that his daughter knew little or nothing about ordinary people's lives.

Only on Saturday nights was Oldham's town center thronged. And littered with discarded pieces of greasy newspaper, in which fish and chips had been wrapped. Horace could still remember vividly the festive weekend excitement that had pervaded the air, and the tangy smell of the vinegar with which the piping-hot food was liberally splashed.

On week nights, people had stayed by their firesides, and still did. A man might drop in for a pint at his local, but he would go home early, munch the cheese and pickles that was a ritual Lancashire supper, bank up the fire with small coal, and get to bed.

Men who had a drop too much and did not return on time would be fetched by their wives. Or a child might be sent to get them, Horace recalled with a reminiscent smile. How many times had he, in his youth, seen a scraggy little lad or lass loitering outside a pub, beseeching anyone within earshot, "Please will yer fetch me dad?"

There was something about the northern industrial towns, his native one included, that Horace found chilling. When he had lived here, there had been days when he was unable to smile. The drabness of his surroundings had permeated his soul. Yet his fellow citizens had gone around with happy faces. He could hear the tram conduc-

tor whistling a tune now, and jingling the coppers in his
leather money satchel, in brisk accompaniment.

But Lancashire working folk had always been known
for their good humor. A line of shawled and clogged mill
girls, arms linked and singing lustily, on their way home
from work, was a common sight. And women placidly
gossiping beside spick-and-span doorsteps, while their
husbands applied a coat of bright paint to woodwork neglected by the landlord, was, on summer evenings, a familiar scene.

They were the kind who bought their boots and shoes
from the Shragers' store. Horace could remember serv-
ing them and the dreariness of his days. His father had
thought there was something wrong with him, because
he hadn't wanted to dedicate his life to fitting footwear
on sweaty feet. Walter Shrager had not understood that
his son had wanted nectar, not bread and butter.

In those days, my eyes were pinned to the stars, Horace reflected. Only in retrospect did he see what had
been there in front of him. That down on earth, those
who had settled for their lot were engaged in a struggle to
survive. Not had he felt for them then the compassion he
had now.

"You're looking very thoughtful, Papa," Alison said.
She had sensed his pensive mood and had left him to
himself, but they had almost reached their destination.

"I was thinking about the people I used to rub shoulders with, when I was a lad, Alison. How on earth can
your Grandfather Plantaine hope to sell Shakespeare to
them and their kind!" Horace exclaimed.

Alison smiled. "I don't think Grandpa would approve
of the way you put it."

How well she knew Gregory! "But that is, nevertheless, what the company is doing. Audiences pay to see a
play, don't they? So they're buying something. Would
you fork out your money, Alison, for something you
didn't want?"

"Certainly not. I don't have that much to spend."

"Nor do most of the folk your grandpa is trying to interest in seeing us perform. He reminds me of a missionary trying to convert heathens. But most people don't want to be educated in their leisure time. They want to be entertained. When they have a bit of cash to spare, they spend it on the sort of entertainment the Plantaines— excluding me—despise."

"You mean Miss Ruby May's sort, don't you, Papa?"

"I mean whatever will make people laugh and cry, without exercising the brain. Miss May's sort of theater may not be art—as your Mama said—but it is certainly entertainment. And those who perform it are eating better meals than we are!" Horace said ruefully as he helped his daughter off the tram.

Alison waited for him to put up his umbrella and took his arm.

"Now it's you who is looking thoughtful," Horace said, eyeing her profile while they crossed the main road.

"Well you've just given me something to think about, haven't you?"

"And I'd like you to consider what I've said very carefully."

"I shall, Papa."

Horace twined his fingers through hers. The rest of the Plantaines would have said there was nothing to think about. More and more, his daughter was revealing that in her was a strong streak of the Shragers' astuteness, and that, despite her conditioning, she had retained an open mind.

"For some reason, I feel a very special bond with you tonight, Papa," she said.

"Oh?" Horace answered carefully.

"Perhaps it's because I've found out that you and I have something special in common, something that the other Plantaines don't have."

"You're referring to our Jewish blood, I presume?" Being able to use the word "our" in that sense had a profound effect upon Horace. He would never feel alone on alien ground again.

Alison nodded. "Now I've got over the surprise, I don't mind being half-Jewish."

Horace steered her around a puddle as they neared their lodgings. "You could, if you preferred, think of yourself as half-Gentile," he said with a smile.

"Oh no, Papa, it sounds much more interesting the other way round. Besides, Jesus was a Jew, wasn't He? And nobody thinks badly of Him."

She had found a way of coming to terms with her new status. And the rapport between them had strengthened; Horace, too, was aware of it. He had a lot to be thankful for.

They found their landlady, as usual, clutching a duster in her hand. Mrs. Baines was a dedicated cleaner and pursued her crusade against grime at all hours of the day and night. She was polishing the hallstand mirror. "Good evenin' and mind yer both wipes yer feet on't mat," she said briskly.

"That mirror looks perfectly clean to me, Mrs. Baines," Alison made the mistake of saying.

"Aye. But yer not me, are yer, luv? Most folk wouldn't notice a pile of muck if they fell over it." Mrs. Baines paused only to breathe upon the mirror ferociously, before giving it another rub. "Can yer 'ear me, Len?" she shouted.

"Ah'd 'ave a job not ter!"

The kitchen door was open at the far end of the long narrow lobby, and Alison and Horace could see Mr. Baines reading by the grate, resplendent in a woollen undervest, workman's trousers, and red suspenders.

"Put that dratted newspaper down!" Mrs. Baines ordered, "an' fetch me some coal. An' tell our Ivy ter dish up two more 'elpins o' tripe'n onion pie!" She gave Horace and Alison a rebuking glance. "Our two late customers is 'ere!"

Ivy Baines appeared in the kitchen doorway, her

mousey hair in a half-frizzed state and a pair of curling tongs in her hand. "Why does me dad need ter tell me?" she shouted to her mother, "when Ah can 'ear yer meself?"

Horace and Alison, who had been shedding their outdoor garments, reluctantly left the domestic pantomime to continue without an audience. The antics of the Baines family never ceased to fascinate them—Mrs. Baines had just removed Horace's hat from the hallstand, in order to polish the peg upon which he had hung it.

In the dining room, the rest of the Plantaines were eating their pudding.

"Forgive us for being late," Horace said.

Nobody replied.

"We seem to be in everyone's bad books, Papa," Alison said with a naughty wink at him.

Fortunately her mother did not see it. Hermione's gaze was glued to her plate.

Oliver had risen from his bed, washed and changed and got himself downstairs, but there was a glazed look in his eyes. "The only person in my bad books is me," he said sullenly. Then he stood up abruptly, and left the room.

"How did the reunion go?" Hermione asked Horace, after Ivy Baines had plunked his and Alison's supper before them, Hermione had not intended to inquire, but was unable to prevent herself from doing so, or keep the sarcasm from her tone.

"Swimmingly, Mama!" Alison answered before Horace had decided how best to do so. "Especially for me."

Three pairs of blue Plantaine eyes gazed at her thoughtfully. Then Gregory and Jessica resumed carefully spooning up their dessert.

Hermione continued to survey her daughter. "I should like to know how a person can be reunited with someone they've never met before, Alison."

Alison evaded the question. Inexplicably, she had not felt that her aunt was a stranger. And how exciting it was to have suddenly discovered that she had cousins! She spent the next few minutes talking about them.

"Isn't it lovely for me, Mama?" she concluded happily.

Hermione glanced at Horace, who was giving his undivided attention to his food. "Get on with your meal," she instructed Alison, who had not yet touched hers.

"Papa is going to take me to meet our family, before we leave Oldham," Alison said, forking some tripe into her mouth.

"Is he indeed?" Hermione put a bright smile on her face and sprinkled some sugar over her semolina. "Mrs. Baines's milk puddings are never sweet enough," she remarked to her parents.

"And her vegetables are a little on the soggy side, for my taste," Jessica declared.

"But she makes an exceedingly good cup of tea," Gregory said with a chuckle. "When all else fails, one can comfort oneself with that."

"The dreadful dishwater brew that Mrs. Livesey serves is no comfort," Jessica said. "If her house were not so cozy, I shouldn't want to continue staying with her when we play Bradford."

"For me, Mrs. Livesey's saving grace is her Yorkshire pudding," Hermione declaimed.

"But when it comes to cakes and pastry, there is no beating dear Mrs. Palmer," Gregory put in. "Her delicious confections make me wish we played Salisbury more often," he said, helping himself to one of Mrs. Baine's rock buns, which were aptly named.

"But Mrs. Palmer's mattresses are lumpy," Hermione sighed.

Horace sat toying with his food, for which he had no appetite, listening to his wife and her parents continue their banal discussion. If necessary, they could, and would, spin it out indefinitely, he thought against the murmur of their voices. The Plantaines' experience of landladies, each of whom had her pros and cons and idiosyncrasies, was limitless, and any subject would, for them, be preferable to the one Hermione had abruptly brought to an end.

But Horace was not surprised when she reopened it with him in private, later that night.

"What is this nonsense about you taking Alison to visit your family?" she said, after Horace had extinguished the gaslight and climbed into bed beside her.

"I don't see what harm it could do," he replied evenly.

"Then you don't know your daughter as well as I do. She is unsettled enough after having met your sister. If she meets your whole family, she will want to remain in touch with them—with the children especially. There'll be no end to it."

"Why should there have to be an end to it?"

"Have you forgotten, Horace, how badly your family has treated you?"

"No. And I shall always carry the scars. That doesn't mean I don't understand why they behaved as they did."

But there was no way Horace could explain to his wife the primeval Jewish attitude toward filial obligation and parental entitlement, passed down from generation to generation. For a son and heir to up and leave, as Horace had done, was equivalent to thumbing his nose at his parents and all they stood for. His subsequent marriage outside the faith had compounded the blow he had dealt them, sealing his fate as an outcast.

Hermione knew the facts, but the emotional complexities surrounding them were beyond a Gentile's comprehension, he thought resignedly. Horace had not expected his parents to acknowledge his marriage and fatherhood, and recalled that it had been Hermione who had insisted upon letting them know.

Why had she done so? he pondered, lying beside her in the intimate darkness. His hand wandered absently to her thigh, but she pulled away, reminding him that the barrier his sister's visit had raised between them would not magically disappear, but must somehow be surmounted.

"I love you, Hermione," he said quietly and it occurred to him that he had not told her so for a long time.

"But not enough," she answered.

Was she asking him to choose between herself and his family? The few words she had exchanged with Lottie returned to Horace's mind:

You must be Horace's wife, Lottie had said.

I am indeed. But isn't it a little late in the day for you to recognize me? Hermione had replied.

Horace was aware of her lying aloofly on her half of the bed, according him the same coolness she had displayed to his sister. As if she now saw him as a defector to the other side. Why had he not realized until now that she, too, had been injured? That she had wanted her in-laws' recognition of herself and her child.

"I gave your family two chances," Hermione said as though she had divined Horace's thoughts. "The first when we were married. The second when our daughter was born. I would have gone with you to see them, whenever we played Oldham," she added with an abrupt laugh.

They lay listening to the rain beating on the slate roof. Together in the nighttime silence, but isolated from each other by their private thoughts.

For Hermione, her sister-in-law's sudden appearance had, in retrospect, the quality of a bad dream. Lottie was part of the sinister picture that Hermione had, over the years, painted in her imagination. And Alison's striking resemblance to the woman had been frightening, emphasizing Hermione's feeling that her child did not really belong to her, but to the alien tribe whence her husband came.

Tonight, a spider's web had superimposed itself upon the imaginary family portrait. Horace, she now knew, had not escaped from it. But Hermione would not allow it to enmesh her daughter.

Horace was visualizing himself with his wife and child at his parents' fireside. If things had worked out differently, his mother would have insisted upon them staying in her house, when the Players were in Oldham. Alison would, from time to time, have experienced the home life she had never known.

But "if," as so often in life, was the operative word. As life itself sometimes seemed the empty exercise that Shakespeare summed it up to be, in *Macbeth*. A person did what they had to do, laughed and cried, ate and slept, but in the end, what did it all mean?

"If your father were not ill, your sister wouldn't have come!" Hermione said vehemently.

"And if we had some sausages, we could have sausage and eggs—if we had the eggs."

"What exactly is that supposed to mean?"

"That many things are conditional, as I have just been painfully thinking. But there are times when one cannot allow that to influence one's actions."

"I see."

"My sister did come. And I intend to visit my family."

"That doesn't surprise me, Horace. I've always known that you don't have a proud bone in your body," Hermione said cuttingly. "But you're not taking Alison with you. I don't want her head filling with the kind of ideas your people live by. Their code of conduct is a very strange one. And I am qualified to judge it, having been on the receiving end."

There was nothing Horace could say in reply.

SIX

Minna Shrager stood by her parlor window, waiting for her son to arrive. "What time is it?" she asked Lottie.

"Five minutes later than the last time you inquired. Why don't you look at your watch, Mother?"

Minna glanced down absently at the silver fob watch pinned to her cardigan. "I forgot to wind it up."

Lottie was not surprised. Her mother had been distracted all day. And how today had dragged, Lottie thought. She had come to her parents' home immediately after breakfast, with her daughters, and they had stayed for lunch.

Usually they only came for Saturday tea, and were joined here by her husband and son when the store closed. But this was not an ordinary Saturday. Lottie had thought it best not to leave her mother alone. And Lionel had arrived with Conrad, an hour ago, to lend his father-in-law moral support.

Lionel's arrival had, for Lottie, deepened the sense of family crisis pervading the house. It was not just their grandfather's illness that had, today, caused her children to tiptoe about and converse in hushed voices. They too were aware that something momentous was about to happen, and that the skeleton in the family cupboard would soon appear before their eyes.

A fine way to think of your brother! Lottie chided herself. But wasn't that what Horace had become? Her children knew of his departure from the fold, and that he had married-out. It was inevitable that they viewed their uncle as the very opposite of what a good man should be.

Minna plucked nervously at some fluff that had attached itself to her sleeve. How would the reunion with their son affect her husband? Outwardly, he had displayed no reaction when she told him Horace was coming. But that was Walter Shrager to a tee. Minna reflected with the bitterness she sometimes felt toward the marriage partner her parents had chosen for her, when she was a girl of sixteen.

She had borne him four children, two of whom had died in infancy. Minna had wept when her baby daughters were taken from her arms to be laid to rest. Walter had not shed a tear. Nor had he jumped for joy when Lottie was born and the doctor pronounced her a healthy child. Not until Horace's birth, five years later, when her husband had presented her with a dozen carnations, had Minna realized that Walter had been waiting for a son.

The only other occasion on which he had given her flowers was Horace's *Bar Mitzvah*. As though providing him with an heir who would continue his line was the one thing she had done for him, Minna thought now.

"What are you brooding about, Mother? As if I didn't know!" Lottie said edgily.

"I was thinking that I shouldn't have been surprised that your father took what your brother did so hard."

"Has he never talked about our Horace, even to you?"

Minna shook her head. For eighteen years she had not

been allowed to mention her son's name in her husband's presence. If Walter had voiced his feelings, ranted and raged even, it would have afforded her some relief. Instead, he had banned the subject and there were times when this enforced silence had felt to Minna like a wall between them.

She had begun to think Walter had forgotten he had a son. Then she had found an old newspaper cutting in the tobacco jar he had used when he smoked a pipe. In recent years, Walter had smoked only cigars, but the jar had remained on his bureau in the bedroom. Minna had needed some change for tram fare and had seen her husband drop a few coppers in the jar when he emptied his pockets at bedtime.

The cutting had come tumbling out with the halfpennies and pennies, crumpled, but still readable. "Young actor to marry into theatrical family," the headline had announced—and Minna had found herself reading about her son's engagement.

The Shragers never went to the theater, but even Minna had heard of the Plantaines. The company had been well-known when she was a girl. But she could not have envisaged that she would one day have a son who would leave home and join it, and who would pile insult upon the injury he had inflicted upon his family, by changing his name to Plantaine.

Minna would not have known Horace had done that, had she not found the cutting. Had Walter kept it to help him harden his heart? Minna wondered now, as she had when she read it. She was not even sure that Walter still loved his son. Minna could not turn off her maternal feelings like a tap. How Walter felt, she would never know, he was a good husband, a family man, and she would grieve for him when he was gone, but his children and grandchildren had always feared him a little. He exuded no warmth and kept his feelings locked within himself.

Lottie heard her mother sigh, and thought how careworn she looked, frail, too. Minna had never had weight to spare and the pounds she had shed since her husband was taken ill had rendered her hollow-cheeked and thin as a reed.

"You look as if a good meal wouldn't do you any harm, Mother."

At lunchtime, Minna had fed Lottie and the girls with large portions of roast chicken and had herself sat picking at a wing.

Minna surveyed her comely daughter. "If I stuffed myself with food from morning till night, I wouldn't be your shape," she said, while admiring Lottie's new white silk-blouse and black marocain skirt. "Your figure is inherited from your Grandma Shrager, who was a buxom lady. She was also, like you, a fashionable one."

"Which nobody could call you!" Lottie answered with a smile.

Minna glanced down at her nondescript brown frock. "My tastes have always been simple, Lottie. If I'd had the figure for it, maybe I'd have wanted to dress up. I sometimes wonder why your father agreed to marry such a flat-chested girl."

"Maybe he thought marriage and motherhood would fill you out," Lottie joked.

"He should've known better. It didn't have that affect on my mother. Or hers. I come from a thin family."

"And our Horace takes after you," Lottie remarked, reminding them both that the wanderer had not yet put in his promised appearance.

"Is Horace still as boney as when he was young?" Minna asked after a moment of silence. It was best to keep on talking, she thought. The waiting was a terrible strain.

"I didn't notice a paunch bulging under his dressing gown," Lottie answered dryly.

"Is he ill?" In Minna's world, a person did not sit around in a dressing gown if they were well.

"For goodness' sake, Mother!" Lottie was becoming

edgier by the minute. Horace had said he would be here soon after lunch and it was now three-thirty.

"Is Horace ill?" Minna repeated anxiously.

"Of course not. I saw him in his dressing room, after he'd come off stage and had taken off his costume. His wife wasn't dressed, either. She was wearing a wrapper."

"You didn't tell me you'd met her."

Lottie's reference to her sister-in-law had slipped out. She had decided not to mention her and had no intention of being drawn into a conversation about her now.

"What was your impression of her?" Minna persisted.

Lottie managed to shrug vaguely. There was no need for Minna to know that her daughter-in-law was a haughty bitch! "She was only in the room for a minute, Mother. And I was more interested in looking at Horace."

"Who wouldn't be, after all these years?"

Lottie had been distressed by her brother's appearance. The sparkle he had had as a lad was no longer evident. There had been a beaten look about him—but with that wife, who could be surprised? Lottie's encounter with Hermione was like being doused with cold water.

All that remained of the Horace she remembered was his appealing way of looking at you. He had inherited those expressive hazel eyes from Minna, Lottie thought when her mother turned from the window. They were Minna Shrager's sole claim to beauty and made you forget how plain she was.

Lottie's younger daughter had inherited them, too; Emma was a small replica of her grandmother.

Lottie glanced at her watch. It would soon be teatime. Minna had prepared a special spread for her son's homecoming. A huge platter of dainty sandwiches had been added to the usual Sabbath afternoon repast of *strudel* and *kuchen.* And a dish of thinly sliced lemon. Horace had always preferred lemon tea. There was lump sugar, too, which he had loved to eat like candy. And Minna had

got out her best lace-edged cloth and napkins, as though
Horace were an honored guest.

She had asked Lionel and Conrad to bring a rarely
used gateleg table from the attic, so she could lay it for tea
in the invalid's room. Lionel had done as he was bid, but
Lottie had sensed his disapproval of his mother-in-law
going to so much trouble for her errant son.

Walter Shrager had lain back on his pillows, with the
shadow of a smile on his face, watching Minna—who had
not allowed Lottie to help her—painstakingly complete
her task. Was her father's smile one of pleasure, or bitterness? Lottie wondered now. It had been impossible to
tell what he was thinking—but then it always was.

Walter would probably make no comment if Horace
didn't come, but Lottie could imagine what her husband
would have to say. Lionel had taken the unprecedented
step of leaving the senior shop assistant in charge of the
store, in order to be here.

Minna was again looking hopefully through the window. "It's still raining," she said, watching a man in a
drenched overcoat hurry by. "I hope our Horace has remembered to put on his galoshes."

Mother hasn't lost her everyday concern for him, Lottie thought. She still worries, like I do about my children,
in a hundred-and-one small ways. It wouldn't surprise
me if she lies awake in bed on winter nights, wondering if
our Horace is warm enough! Lottie said to herself with
compassion for her mother, and a surge of anger because
Horace did not deserve such devotion.

"Supposing Horace doesn't turn up? He may have
changed his mind about coming," she said.

Her mother shrugged, without moving her gaze from
the garden gate. "It will upset me. But what can I do?"

Minna's reply reminded Lottie of her younger daughter. If something to which Emma had looked forward did
not materialize, she would shrug off her disappointment,
as if she ought not to expect things to go right for her.

Emma not only looked like Minna, she had the same

uncomplaining nature, Lottie reflected. It was as though there was, in both of them, a built-in acceptance of whatever might be their lot. And sometimes Lottie feared for Emma's future. Happiness was not always handed to a person on a plate. Often you had to connive or fight for it. But Emma, like her grandmother, took everything lying down.

There was no way Lottie would have remained cut off from one of her children for years and years, on her husband's say so. But Lottie's marriage was a partnership; her mother's was not. Lottie had stuck up for herself with Lionel, right from the start, and he knew just how far he could push her. Her father had had her mother under his thumb all their married life, she was thinking when the garden gate creaked.

She watched Horace walk slowly up the gravel path. "Shall I let him in, or will you, Mother?"

"I think it should be me," Minna replied calmly. Then a great wave of emotion engulfed her. She pulled herself together and went to open the front door.

Horace had just reached the porch.

"We got a new doormat since you left home," Minna said with a smile as he stepped on to it.

Horace wiped his feet. "All right, Mother. I can take a hint! A new house, too," he added glancing around the spacious hall. "Very posh, I must say."

"Like the way you speak, nowadays," she countered. "What happened to your Lancashire accent?"

Horace took off his wet coat and hung it, with his hat, on the gleaming mahogany hallstand. "I lost it, along the way."

Lottie had allowed them a minute or two alone and now joined them.

"Look who the wind blew in, Lottie!" Minna said with the astringent humor she sometimes employed to camouflage her soft center.

Unlike her husband, Minna had been born in England,

and was an incongruous mixture of Lancashire prosaism and the Jewish sentimentality she tried to hide.

Lottie helped her along. "I expect he was passing by and knew he'd get a good tea here."

"There'll be trouble if I don't," Horace joked.

Then they fell silent and he and his mother stood looking at each other. The jocularity had helped them over their initial awkwardness, but nothing could bridge the years.

Horace was shocked by what time had done to Minna. Or was he responsible for her hair being white? There had not been so much as a frosting upon it when he left home. How old was she now? Only fifty-nine. The same age as Jessica Plantaine. Jessica looked like a girl, by comparison, but she had the Plantaine facility for remaining unscarred by life.

He looks as if all the worries of the world are on his head, Minna thought with an ache in her throat. "How tall you've grown since I last saw you," she said.

Lottie watched them and thought her heart would break. "Give Mother a kiss already, Horace!"

"Unless he thinks he's too big to kiss his mother, now he's grown up," Minna laughed.

Horace hugged her. "I was grown up when I kissed you goodbye, Mother!"

"If you say so." To Minna, he had still seemed a child.

Horace cleared his throat. "This is a lovely house."

"I'm glad you like it."

He smiled. "I bet you never thought you'd end up living in Werneth Park."

"It took me a long time to get used to it, and to having rich mill owners for neighbors," Minna confessed. "How long have we been here?" she asked Lottie. "I can never remember."

"You moved into this house ten years after Horace left home, Mother."

"That's right. And five years after he left, we moved to

our first house. When your father said he'd had enough of living on the shop premises."

My going has become a family milestone, Horace thought. A focal point in time.

They were still standing in the hall and he could see into the parlor—a bigger one than the living room behind the shop—but in it were the family treasures familiar to him from his childhood. The rosewood china cabinet, full of Crown Derby cups and saucers which were never used. A pair of vases with printed roses on their fat bellies and gold-leaf frills adorning their slender necks. The silver candelabrum, in which his mother lit candles on *Yom Tavim,* stood on her mantelpiece, as it always had.

How strange it felt to Horace to have words like *Yom Tavim,* the Hebrew term for Jewish festivals, re-emerge into his mental vocabulary. Pangs of nostalgia were stirring within him. "Do you still keep your brassware in the kitchen?" he asked Minna gruffly.

"Would it be my kitchen without it?"

Horace could remember every detail of his mother's kitchen. The blackleaded range and the soot-furred kettle, kept ever on the boil. The mouth-watering aromas drifting tantalizingly from the oven. The gleaming brass candlesticks in which Minna kindled the Sabbath-eve lights, and the matching mortar and pestle. The clutter of homely bric-à-brac, which included a bunch of wax grapes and a black china cat. The cat had a chipped ear, sustained when it traveled from Austria with Minna's parents, in 1850.

"Is Blacktie still in one piece?" he inquired.

"His tail got broken, but I glued it together again. Your father wanted me to throw the poor creature away."

But Minna never would, Horace thought poignantly. He had not been in this house before, but he felt at home here. It made no difference that he had departed from the cramped living accommodation behind a shop and had returned to a spacious redbrick villa, with a laburnum in the front garden. The ambience his mother created was uniquely hers and would go with her wherever she went. Nothing had changed.

Lottie had slipped upstairs to tell her father that Horace was here.

"When I'm not long for this world, he comes to see me," Walter Shrager said. "But late is better than never."

This was the first comment he had made since he was told his son was coming.

Father is impossible, Lottie thought angrily and would have said so, had he not been so ill. He appeared to have forgotten a very important detail—that he had told Horace he never wanted to see him again.

Lottie had not believed her father had meant it, but time had proved that he had. Or was it possible that a man as intelligent as Walter Shrager had been foolish enough to maintain the long estrangement from his only son, in order not to lose face?

Horace entered the bedroom with Minna and took in the cozy, family scene.

A coal fire burned merrily in the grate. Lottie's daughters were sitting on the hearth rug, Clara's blonde prettiness enhanced by the dancing firelight, Emma a pale shadow beside her. Their brother Conrad, a tall youth who reminded Horace of himself as a lad, was standing with his elbow on the mantelpiece.

Lionel was stationed beside the big, brass bedstead— or so it seemed to Horace. There was something about his brother-in-law's stance, and the guarded expression on his chubby face, that made the word "stationed" apposite.

It was as though Lionel had put himself there to fend off the interloper. And, suddenly, Horace felt like one. With his entrance, the family group had momentarily frozen. A silence had fallen and nobody had yet broken

it. He could hear his watch ticking in his waistcoat
pocket.

He cleared his throat and the scene sprang to life. His
mother and sister busied themselves at the tea table. His
nieces went to help them and his nephew was sent downstairs to fetch the milk, which Minna had forgotten.

The teatime bustle was exactly as Horace remembered
it from his youth. Except that he was no longer part of it.
And his father was lying in a sickbed. Dying.

Horace went to the bedside, but was unable to take
Walter's hand, which he had felt moved to do. One hand,
paralyzed by the stroke that had rendered Walter helpless, was hidden beneath the blankets. Lionel was holding the other.

"So what took you so long, Horace?" Walter said
blandly.

Horace could think of no suitable reply and gave him
a hollow smile.

"Let me have Pa's cup, sweetheart," Lionel said to
Lottie. "You know he likes me to feed him. And make
sure the tea is nice and milky."

Horace could not imagine his father enjoying being
fed by anyone. Their eyes briefly met, but Horace could
read nothing in Walter's expression.

Emma, who seemed even more mouselike than Lottie
had described her, brought Horace his tea, and the slice
of lemon floating in it stirred in him again nostalgia for
his homely past. He had not seen lemon tea since those
days, let alone drunk it.

He took a sandwich from the platter offered by Clara
and bit into it.

"I think that one's chopped herring. You might not
like it," she said.

Horace could remember his mother saying that to the
Gentile neighbors who had sometimes dropped in at teatime and were invited to stay.

"I was brought up on Jewish food, love," he said with
a dry smile.

Clara flushed with embarrassment. "Oh yes. I forgot."

"I expect your uncle did, too, Clara," her father said. "Along with a lot of other things. But all of a sudden, he's decided it's in his interests to remember."

The reunion was not proceeding as Horace had hoped. His brother-in-law was making sure it didn't. If anyone was guarding their interests, it was Lionel Stein!

Horace had divined in advance that Lionel would view his reappearance this way, but had not reckoned on him coming out with it. Lottie was crimson checked. Horace noticed. And so she should be, on her husband's behalf. It was all Horace could do to stop himself from grabbing the crafty little man by his well-tailored lapels and hurling him from the room.

Horace's last-minute, futile pleading with Hermione to allow him to bring Alison was responsible for his late arrival. To his mother's disappointment that she was not to meet her granddaughter, Horace had made the excuse that Alison had a cold, rather than reveal his wife's animosity toward his family. Minna had accepted the lie, but he was sure that Lottie had guessed the true reason.

Alison's presence would have saved the day, Horace thought with affection. His daughter charmed everyone she met and would, by now, have been chattering happily with her cousins. Instead, there was this tense atmosphere.

Horace sipped his tea and made himself swallow down the food with which he was plied. He was aware of his mother and sister hovering apprehensively by the bed, and of the three young people eyeing him as an audience eyes the villain in a play.

But the other central figure in the drama seemed oblivious to it, Horace noted, observing his father's serene expression. It was as though, with the approach of death, Walter Shrager had decided to let what time he had left carry him quietly away on its relentless tide, and the final vicissitudes of his life to wash over him, like the ebbing waves upon a pebbly shore.

"Well," Horace said to break yet another pregnant pause.

"Well what?" Lionel challenged him. "Except that the sight of you is enough to give your poor father another seizure." He wiped a dribble of tea from the invalid's chin and addressed him soothingly. "It isn't good for you to get worked up, Pa."

Worked up? Horace thought. His father was the only calm person in the room.

Alison lay curled up on her bed in one of Mrs. Baines's two attic rooms. The other was occupied by Ivy Baines. Alison could hear her walking around, on the other side of the dividing wall.

When Ivy came home from work on week nights, she had to help in the house and had told Alison she hardly had time to brush the bits of cotton flax from her hair. But on Saturday nights she went dancing with some other mill girls, and began preparing for the outing on Friday evening, when she got busy with her curling tongs.

What was Ivy doing now? Alison wondered. Polishing her dancing slippers? Or tightening the laces in her stays? It was only four-thirty, but Ivy had said it took her hours to get ready for the dance.

Alison would not be expected to wear stays until she was sixteen. Or to put up her hair. Yet Ivy, who was just fourteen, only a afew months older than Alison, had already been laced by her mama in her first corset.

To Alison, those two events in a girl's life were of great moment. When they happened to her, she would be officially grown up. It seemed unfair that Ivy Baines was considered by her mother to be grown up.

Alison did not look forward to being restricted by laces and whalebones, but envied Ivy the freedom they implied. That working-class girls had no option but to grow up too soon, and were predestined for a drudgery she would never know, was beyond her sheltered understanding.

At present, she barely knew the meaning of the term "working-class," and on that wet Saturday afternoon in the spring of 1914 resentment smoldered within her. Alison would willingly have swapped places with Ivy Baines, who had a mama who let her please herself instead of one who told you what to do and not to do, like Hermione Plantaine! And, as though you were a baby, never told you why.

It was then that the first seeds of animosity toward her mother were sown in Alison. Though Hermione did not know it, she had, today, carried her maternal high-handedness too far. Had she explained her true reasons for forbidding Alison to accompany Horace on his peace mission, she might have gained her sympathy. Until now, Alison had harbored a daughter's natural love for her mother and Hermione's personal distress would have caused her to see the matter from her mother's standpoint, too.

But Hermione had not sought her child's understanding and would have considered it beneath her to do so. Such was her lack of wisdom and her Plantaine pride. Even if she had been able to see into the future, known that she was, by this one action, driving a wedge between herself and her daughter that would be there for always, Hermione could not have brought herself to behave differently. It was not in her nature to do so.

Alison lay staring at the new, flower-sprigged paper that Mrs. Baines had bullied her husband into hanging on the attic walls, which she did each spring. Two more lots of wallpaper, and then Alison would be sixteen.

But she didn't intend to wait until then before meeting her cousins. She would like to meet the rest of her new family, too, but having Emma and Clara and Conrad to look forward to was the most exciting thing. Emma especially—Alison had never had a friend.

Somehow, she would find a way of seeing Emma. Meanwhile she would write and say how much she looked forward to them being friends. Papa could post the letter for her and Mama need not know about it.

Such are the circumstances that breed deceit in those who, otherwise, would not have a deceitful thought in their heads. Alison had never in her life told a lie, but had no hesitation in getting paper and a pen from the small case in which she kept her schoolbooks, to write to Emma Stein.

It did not occur to her that by seeking her father's complicity she was forming an alliance with him against her mother. Nor could she have known that once formed, that alliance would affect their intimate family relationship; that once the scales were tipped—and they had always been uneasily balanced—nothing would be quite the same again.

Alison was about to learn that one deceit leads to another.

"I'm happy to see you're writing your weekly composition for me," Jessica Plantaine said, entering the room with a laden tray.

Alison covered the half-written letter with her blotter and hoped her face did not look as red as it felt. "Don't I always, Grandma?" she said.

Jessica put down the tray on the bed and wagged her finger at Alison with mock severity. "Not with the enthusiasm I should like to see." She gave Alison a kindly smile. "I thought we could have our tea together, in your room, as you didn't put in an appearance downstairs."

"That was very kind of you, Grandma."

"Which subject did you choose for your composition, Alison dear?"

Alison popped the letter into her case, lest Jessica decide to find out for herself. "A Rainy Day By The Sea," she said. That was the subject she intended choosing from the list her grandmother had given her, so it wasn't really a lie, she told herself.

"And have you done your sums, dear?"

"No." That was the awful truth. Alison had no head

for figures. Wrangling with even the simple problems in the arithmetic book her grandmother had provided was agony for her.

She carried the tray to the washstand, which had served as an improvised desk, brought the room's sole chair for Jessica and seated herself on the large trunk in which everything she possessed was transported from town to town.

Jessica poured their tea. "Regrettable though it is, Alison dear, multiplication and long division are part of your education."

Alison took a slice of bread and butter and spread it thickly with jam. "But I shall never need to do any sums, shall I, Grandma? I'm going to be an actress, like you."

"Your mama used to say that to me, when I taught her. She didn't mind writing compositions, but sums were purgatory to her. Yet she knew all Shakespeare's texts by heart, before she was twelve, as you did." Jessica sipped her tea and studied her granddaughter. "In some ways, Alison dear, you are exactly like your mama."

But Alison no longer wanted to be like Hermione. "It was nice of you to bring tea upstairs, Grandma," she said to change the subject.

Jessica selected an Eccles cake, to which she always looked forward when the Players were in Lancashire. But today she had little appetite. The turn her daughter's marital affairs had taken did not bode well.

She had left Hermione chatting downstairs with Gregory and Oliver, but had detected the unhappiness behind her smile. Also that Oliver was having one of his bad days, though he was trying to hide it.

Why can we not talk to each other? Jessica thought. Open our hearts and let out the pain, as others do? Because we are Plantaines, came the answer. Too proud to reveal our true selves even to each other. Indeed, the last person to whom a Plantaine would show an unstiffened upper lip was another Plantaine, lest it be construed as letting down the side.

Had Alison inherited that trait? Jessica wondered. She had been brought up to behave as the family did and Jessica could not remember her shedding a tear since her toddling days. Nor did she run to anyone with her childish troubles—or she would not have stayed in her room all afternoon, nursing her disappointment alone.

Licking one's wounds in private was the Plantaine way, Jessica reflected with a sigh. It was not an easy way. Once, she had steeled herself to talk to her husband about Oliver. Between themselves, she and Gregory did not try to maintain the pretence that nothing was wrong. But Gregory had refused to discuss it. Possibly, putting his fears into words was more than he could bear.

Jessica still clung to the hope that her son would, one day, meet a woman who would help him put his life right. That Oliver would give Gregory the grandson for whom she knew her husband yearned. A male Plantaine, to continue his life's work when he was gone.

Gregory had tried to hide his disappointment when Hermione gave birth to a girl, but Jessica had sensed it. There were times when the Plantaines did not have to voice their thoughts, were able to read each other's minds. But it was as though a clamp held down their tongues, prohibiting them from expressing their feelings.

To outsiders, the family had a reputation for taking everything in their stride. You had to be a Plantaine to know how it really was, Jessica thought, refilling her teacup. We are no more invulnerable than anyone else. The only difference is we keep our vulnerability hidden.

Alison was thinking about the lovely time her father was probably having. He would tell her all about it, when he got back. "You're very quiet this afternoon," she said to Jessica.

"Does that mean you regard me as a chatterbox, Alison dear?"

They shared a laugh.

"I was thinking, among other things, what a pity it is you have no brother," Jessica said, though she had not been thinking it from Alison's point of view. "If your mama had been able to have another child, it would have been so nice for you."

"I didn't know she couldn't," Alison said blushing. The facts of life, which she had learned from Ivy Baines, were a source of embarrassment to her.

"What I meant, dear, was it's a shame that no more children have come along." Jessica corrected herself. But perhaps it was a blessing in disguise, she reflected. When Alison was born, Hermione had suffered a massive hemorrhage and had almost died.

"I don't think Mama agrees with you," Alison said. "I once told her I'd like a sister or brother and she said she had quite enough with me."

Jessica smiled. "Well, you are a bit of a handful, aren't you, Alison dear?"

"In what way, exactly?" Alison answered stiffly.

Oh dear, Jessica thought. Why did I say it? "You take everything so much to heart, dear. But you must learn not to show it."

"Why must I?"

"Because it isn't done to parade one's disappointments. Our family doesn't behave that way," Jessica said, aware that she was teaching her granddaughter to be a true Plantaine.

"Is that what you came to tell me, Grandma?"

"Well, I didn't climb two flights of stairs to the attic because I need the exercise, Alison dear. It was quite an effort to do so carrying the tray. But that is beside the point."

"Then please get to the point."

Jessica was shocked by Alison's peremptory tone, which from a child was downright rudeness.

Alison read her expression. "I wasn't being disrespectful, Grandma."

"No. I don't believe you were." The girl could not be blamed for displaying characteristics she had inherited from her papa.

Jessica smoothed a fold in her plum moiré frock and mustered a grandmotherly smile. "All this fuss over such a trifling matter, Alison dear."

"It isn't a trifling matter to me."

There it was again, that dreadful directness. Jessica brushed aside the uncomfortable feeling it produced in her; and the import of Alison's words. When the company left Oldham tomorrow, the child would forget about her father having a family.

"Do cheer up, Alison! I thought if you had some company, and a nice cup of tea, it would help you not to feel sorry for yourself," she declared lightly.

She had said the wrong thing.

"Plantaines aren't allowed to feel sorry for themselves, are they? But I'm a Shrager, too," Alison flashed. Whether anyone likes it or not, she thought.

Jessica needed no reminding. Minna Shrager lit the gaslights in her husband's sickroom and drew the curtains across the big bay window, shutting out the last vestiges of daylight hovering in the back garden.

"I shall have to leave in a few minutes," Horace said.

"So soon?" his mother asked.

"I'm afraid so, or I'll be late for the theater."

"Stay in touch with us, Horace," his sister requested. "You must let us know where you are, from week to week, so we can keep you informed about Father."

"I will."

"And let today be a new beginning," Minna pleaded.

Horace managed to smile and kissed her pale cheek. A new beginning could not turn back the clock. His mother and sister were regarding him with love in their eyes and there was love in his heart for them. For his father, too. But love could not undo what had been done. It wasn't, as Horace had believed it would be, enough.

He was seated beside the fire with the two women. His nieces had cleared the tea table and were now downstairs in the kitchen, washing the dishes for their grandmother.

His brother-in-law and nephew were at the bedside, talking quietly with his father.

"They're probably talking business," Lottie said, seeing Horace glance at them. "Or about whatever the men of a family find to talk about," she added with a long-suffering smile.

She could not have pinpointed Horace's feelings more succinctly. Apart from Lionel, nobody had reproached him. Not even his father, with whom he had exchanged only a few words; but Walter had always been a laconic man. Minna and Lottie had done what they could to make Horace feel at ease and he could not complain about the hospitality. But hospitality was accorded to guests. Outsiders. Horace wasn't one of the men of the family.

After tea, the initial tension had relaxed and he had found himself listening, like a stranger, to the everyday chitchat. References were made to this or that; in-jokes laughed at; petty grievances aired; names mentioned respectfully and also scathingly. All of it was double-Dutch to Horace.

There had also been a "do you remember when . . . ?" interlude, sparked off by Lottie. But the spate of family reminiscences her recollection had evoked did not date back to Horace's time.

He glanced again at the bed, where Lionel was raising Walter in his arms, while Conrad rearranged the sick man's pillows.

"Afterwards, Lionel will move Father from the bed, so we can remake it," Lottie told Horace.

When I've gone, Horace thought.

"My husband comes here every night, to help make Father comfortable," Lottie added.

Horace noted the gentleness with which his brother-in-law laid Walter back against the pillows and knew he had misjudged him. Lionel Stein wasn't just watching out for his own interests. He had been orphaned as a lad, Horace recalled, and was living in digs when Lottie met him. Walter was like a father to him, as Lionel had become Walter's surrogate son.

Horace made his farewells and left, promising to visit them again when he could.

Visit is the right word, he thought, returning by tram to the life he had chosen. He was of them, but no longer one of them.

The conductor came to collect his fare. " 'Aven't Ah seed yer photo, on t'billboards outside t'theater, sir?" he said with awe.

Horace nodded and maneuvered his features into the toothy smile he employed for such encounters.

"Ee, fancy that!" the man exclaimed. He pushed his cap, which was too big for him, to the back of his head and grinned broadly. "Me missis won't believe it when Ah tell 'er Ah've met yer!"

The conductor moved along the tram, telling the other passengers who was in their midst, but Horace was too depressed to enjoy his moment of glory. The aftermath of his excursion to the past was making itself felt.

What had he expected? That the blessed sense of peace his decision to reunite himself with his family had brought would remain with him in their presence? Instead, the iron had entered his soul. Slowly and seepingly, while the clock ticked away the afternoon.

When the front door had finally closed behind him, he had had the feeling that his visit had been like a pebble dropping into a pond, and that the ripples he had felt all around him would not last too long.

He could imagine the air of relief pervading the house after his departure. The black sheep had been and gone and that was that. They would resume their family life, which he had briefly interrupted.

From time to time, they would think of him; thoughts colored by whichever emotion he aroused in them personally. His mother's would be sorrowful and his sister's regretful. His father's he could not divine and they would soon be buried with him. To his nephew and nieces, Horace would remain the symbol of inquity he had doubtless always been for them. And his brother-in-law, he decided with grim amusement, would try never to think of him.

Why was he being so cynical: he pondered while alighting from the tram in the town center. Because cynicism was a form of self-protection, to which he habitually resorted. A padding between himself and the painful truth; which, on this occasion, was that he no longer had a place in the family from which he sprang.

Horace made his way to the theater, oblivious to the Saturday sights and sounds around him. He had to push through the throng coming with laden baskets from the market and was only remotely aware of the pungent aroma of the baked potatoes being sold on a street corner, by an old man crouched over a glowing brazier. A flower seller, in sodden shawl and a man's flat cap, offered him a bunch of her wilting wares, but Horace brushed past her.

The March wind had not allowed him to put up his umbrella and rainwater was dripping from the brim of his hat, running down his face in icy rivulets. On any other evening, he would have been filled with compassion for humble folk like the flower seller, who had to stand on the street in all weathers to earn a crust of bread. But, this evening, Horace was sorry only for himself.

This self-pity would not last; he was not that kind of man. But it would not be easy for him to recover from the effects of his pilgrimage. He had not expected to find his old slippers still warming in the Shrager hearth, but hadn't been prepared for what he had found. The gap his going had left in the family fabric had been woven over by time and events, and it was as if the lad who was Horace Shrager had never been.

"T' rest o' t' family's been 'ere fer 'alf-an-hour, sir," the stagedoor keeper informed Horace. "Mr. Oliver Plantaine arrived wi' em," he added significantly.

There wasn't a stagedoor keeper in the provinces who

didn't know Oliver Plantaine was a drunk, Horace reflected and was relieved that he would not have to take over Oliver's part tonight.

When he reached his dressing room, he found Alison waiting for him.

"You're drenched, Papa!" she said with concern.

"And I wouldn't mind a hot drink, Alison. If you could arrange it."

"I'll ask Nellie to boil up some milk for you, on her gas ring, when you've told me how my Grandfather Shrager is. Is he really going to die, Papa?"

"Probably, Alison." Horace took off his outdoor garments and dried his neck with the towel Alison handed him. "Unless prayers save him," he added with a nonbeliever's sardonic smile. "I was told that your cousin Conrad had been to Manchester this morning, to pray on behalf of the family for my father's recovery."

"Why was it necessary to go to Manchester, Papa?"

"Because there isn't a synagogue in Oldham, love. There aren't enough Jews living here."

Horace went behind the screen to change into his dressing gown. He had been about to tell Alison that there were no kosher-food stores in Oldham, but she would not know what he meant, or realize the inconvenience that lack caused to Jews living outside their own community.

He could remember being sent, as a lad, to the Strangeways ghetto in Manchester to buy the family's meat and poultry from a kosher butcher, and the smell of singeing feathers while he waited in the shop to be served. But Horace had not, in the end, allowed religious scruples to inconvenience him. Filial ones, either. Briefly, he allowed himself to wonder if there was a God, meting out punishment to him, by bringing him full circle, face to face with his past.

"I've written to my cousin Emma," Alison informed him when he emerged from behind the screen.

Horace eyed the envelope in her hand. "Your mama would be most upset, if she knew."

"But there's no need to tell her, Papa. Not if you mail the letter for me."

"Wouldn't that be underhand, Alison?"

"Whose fault is it that we have to be?" she flashed. "Mama's! And what she doesn't know can't hurt her, can it?"

Horace was affected by his daughter's pleading expression and brushed aside his misgivings. "I suppose not. But Mama will find out, if Emma replies to you—"

"Not if she does as I've suggested," Alison cut in. "I was sure Aunt Lottie would be writing to you and I've asked Emma to put her reply in her mother's envelope."

Horace was taken aback by Alison's craftiness. She had everything worked out!

"You and I must stick together from now on, Papa," she said conspiritorially. "I am your daughter too, not just Mama's."

Her words went straight to Horace's bruised heart. This afternoon had enhanced his sense of having no real identity. But whoever he wasn't, he was still Alison's father. And between them were none of the invisible barriers and undercurrents he felt with others; his wife included.

"I'll go and see about your hot milk," Alison said.

Horace watched her leave the dressing room, with a rustle of her green taffeta frock, her mane of black hair swinging about her face as she turned toward the door.

He picked up her letter to Emma, which she had left on the dressing table, and slipped it into his pocket, aware that he was doing so in case Hermione entered, and of the complicity this implied. But, as Alison had said, it was Hermione who had made it necessary. And his daughter was dearer to him than anyone in the world. There was nothing he would refuse her.

SEVEN

By July of that year, the Plantaine Players were far away from Oldham. They had gone on to Bath and were now in Salisbury. Their spring and summer schedule had kept them in the south, providing Horace with a valid reason for not visiting his family.

The company was still touring *Macbeth* and playing to better houses than they had in the industrial north. Salisbury, whose four theatrical venues bespoke its citizens' interest in the arts, could usually be relied upon to provide good box-office takings. But advance bookings were poor on this occasion.

"People are too worried about the prospect of war to go out and enjoy themselves," Horace opined to his father-in-law, at the breakfast table.

Rumors that war with Germany was imminent had reached fever pitch, but Gregory was still turning a deaf ear.

"I do not believe in crossing bridges before one comes to them," he replied to Horace.

Or you would be putting your mind to how the company will fare when war breaks out, Horace thought. If it happened, he intended to join up and Oliver was young enough to be drafted. There would be a shortage of actors, not to mention stagehands. But Gregory was blithely planning another large-scale production!

"Would someone kindly pass me another of Mrs. Palmer's delicious hot rolls?" Gregory requested. "The dear lady's breakfasts are almost as splendid as her teas."

Mrs. Palmer bustled into the room from her adjoining kitchen. "Was somebody taking my name in vain?" she smiled.

She put down the teapot she had brought in and surveyed the handsome family seated around her oval dining table. Theatricals of all kinds had, over the years, graced her home with their presence. But for Mrs. Palmer there were none so thrillingly awesome as the Plantaines. It made a person feel special, just to be with them.

"My husband is forever praising your culinary accomplishments," Jessica told her.

"Really?" Mrs. Palmer said with a modest blush.

"Papa insists that nobody makes cakes and pastries like yours," Hermione said. "And we all agree."

Mrs. Palmer straightened the starched apron she wore over her black alpaca housedress, and patted her snowy hair, which she wore piled so high, Alison thought she must have yards, and yards of it.

"Really?" she said again.

"Truly," Gregory endorsed solemnly.

"Thank you ever so much, sir. Those few words have made my day."

"Did you know Mrs. P. wanted to be an actress, when she was a girl?" Horace said to the others when the landlady had left the dining room. "But she married the late Mr. Palmer instead. He was quite a wealthy man, though much older than her, and promised to get her father out of debt if she agreed to be his wife. That's how she comes to be the owner of this house."

"I don't remember ever meeting Mr. Palmer," Jessica said vaguely. "Do you, Gregory?"

Her husband looked equally vague.

"It was when she was widowed that Mrs. P. began taking theatricals to stay," Horace explained. "She had no children to tie her down, but, by then, it was too late for her to try for an acting career."

"I suppose she thought having theater people to stay was the next best thing," Alison surmised.

Horace exchanged a smile with her. "That's always been my theory, Alison."

"How did you get to know so much about the woman?" Hermione asked.

"And why did we not know it?" Jessica said to her husband. "We've stayed here, on and off, for years and years."

"Since long before Horace's time," Oliver put in through a mouthful of egg and bacon. "I can remember climbing the apple tree in the back garden, when I was quite small."

"And falling out of it!" Hermione recalled with a reminiscent smile.

"But I don't expect any of you but Papa ever asked Mrs. Palmer about herself," Alison said. "I mean, the only ones who ever chat to our landladies are Papa and me."

"I have always considered the occasional pleasantry to be sufficient, Alison dear," Jessica declared.

And this didn't apply only to landladies, Horace reflected. For his wife and her family, those with whom they from time to time rubbed shoulders were allowed to get no closer than that. It was not in the least incredible that the Plantaines knew nothing about Mrs. Palmer and her kind, given their lack of interest in anyone other than themselves.

"What did you do, darling? Accost Mrs. P. in her

kitchen and demand to hear her life story?" Hermione asked him with the barbed sweetness with which she largely addressed him nowadays.

Horace buttered a roll and remained silent, though he had done no such thing. He had pieced together Mrs. Palmer's story from snippets of conversation with her, over the years.

"Papa is the kind of person people like talking to," Alison said, implying that her mother was not.

Hermione put down her knife and fork. "Is he indeed?" She resumed eating. "And you, my dear, are getting altogether too big for your little-girl's boots; forgetting that it isn't your place to speak until you are spoken to."

"If I followed that rule, Mama, I should rarely speak at all."

"And your elders would be most thankful," Hermione retorted.

The child hasn't been herself since that unfortunate episode over her papa's family, Jessica thought. She did not allow herself to dwell on the possibility that this was Alison's true self.

Oliver was shocked by his niece's impertinence, but had to admire her nerve. Alison was an individual, not the carbon copy of her mother that little girls were expected to be. Nor would she ever try to be, as Oliver was still trying to emulate his father. And failing more and more miserably. But he mustn't think about that, lest it cause him to have a bad day in his favorite city.

"I do so enjoy being here," Jessica echoed her son's final thought.

"Me, too," Hermione agreed.

"Quite apart from dear Mrs. Palmer's confections, I consider Salisbury our most pleasant venue," Gregory declaimed. For some reason, his son never got drunk here. "When we settle down in a theater of our own, I would like it to be here."

"That would be lovely, Grandpa," Alison said.

Horace allowed himself a private smile. Astute though Alison was, she had not yet realized that Gregory's oft-mentioned intention was no more than a mirage.

I must describe Salisbury to Emma, when I next write to her, Alison added to herself with the warm feeling that thinking of her cousin always evoked. And, too, with an accompanying pang of guilt, because their correspondence remained a secret from Hermione.

By now, the two girls had exchanged many letters and a bond of friendship was firmly established between them. Indeed, it was difficult for Alison to believe that they had not met. She could visualize Emma now, eating breakfast with her parents and brother and sister in Aunt Lottie's homely kitchen. Alison knew it was homely from Emma's description of the Steins sitting around the fire in the evenings, and of each member of the family having their own regular place at the table. Unlike the Plantaines, who did not even own a table! Alison reflected quizzically.

"It would feel very strange to settle down in one place," she remarked to her elders. "Much as I like Salisbury."

"This is an ideal town for you to grow up in Alison dear," Jessica said as though the Plantaines would be ensconced in their own theater here, next week.

"And if we lived with Mrs. P. permanently, my husband, who is on such friendly terms with her, might be able to persuade her to replace her uncomfortable mattresses," Hermione added.

Horace let the jibe pass. Nor did he bother to say that if the company stopped touring, he would want his own home. The entire discussion was absurdly hypothetical, though no more so than many others in which the family indulged.

But Horace could understand his in-laws' wish to live in this elegant cathedral city, and in Mrs. Palmer's house, which was old, but not seedy. The graystone villa was situated on a tree-lined avenue, near to the Cathedral. In summertime, the scent of lavender and roses drifted into the spacious rooms through diamond-paned windows opening on to an old-English garden.

And there was about Salisbury itself, with the graceful spire dominating the skyline, and the ancient inns in the main square and narrow side-streets, an air of historic splendor. Of which, Horace thought, the family into which he had married was a part.

That afternoon, when Hermione and Jessica were resting and Gregory blithely planning his next production, Horace left the house with Alison, for their habitual stroll. To his surprise, Oliver caught up with them before they had walked a few yards.

"Would you two mind if I accompany you?"

"Why on earth should we mind?" Horace said.

"I wouldn't presume to take it for granted that you welcomed my company, Horace," Oliver answered lightly.

"Don't be ridiculous!" Horace said with an uncomfortable laugh. But Oliver wasn't an insensitive clod and must be aware that Horace was jealous of his closeness to Hermione.

Alison had taken her father's arm and now took Oliver's too. "We're delighted to have you with us, Uncle."

Horace would not have put it quite so enthusiastically. His afternoon outings with his daughter were pleasant interludes away from the Plantaines. But his resentment of Oliver had lately lost its edge. Possibly because Horace's feeling for his wife had changed, he thought, as they strolled past the neat houses in the Cathedral Close.

When had the all-embracing love he'd had for Hermione begun to diminish? Horace mused. When she had diminished him; told him in plain language that he wasn't the man he had thought himself. Since then, he had lost the incentive to rise higher in his profession, and the inspiration that had once enabled him to lend color to a performance.

The feeling that he was only doing a job, as a bricklayer

carries his hod on a building site, now dogged Horace whenever he set foot onstage, and his load felt equally heavy. How different it had been when every performance he gave was a challenge, when he had believed that acting was his vocation.

He would have been better off never knowing that it wasn't. Ignorance was indeed bliss. But his wife had put an end to his illusions, cruelly and for her own ends. Horace sometimes thought it remarkable that he did not hate Hermione, that he still wanted her, despite what she had done to him.

In their intimate moments, when she lay in his arms, gazing up at him with her limpid, blue eyes, he could not believe that so fragile a creature, who excited him to indescribable passion, was capable of wreaking such damage. But when his passion was spent, the damage remained with him.

Horace emerged from his thoughts as they reached the town square. His final one had been that it wasn't a good omen that he was able to assess his marriage so detachedly.

"Grandpa told me there can't be a war, because Kaiser Bill is our king's cousin," Alison said, her attention caught by an army recruiting poster.

Horace smiled. Gregory Plantaine wasn't just an ostrich, he was also an innocent. The very opposite of Horace's shrewd father.

To his doctor's surprise, Walter Shrager was still in the land of the living, which made Horace think his father had changed his mind about going quietly. Or had young Conrad Stein's prayers for the patriarch's recovery been answered? If there was a God, on what did He base His decisions? Compassion could not enter into it, or He would not countenance the horrors of war. Or the inequalities that abounded in His universe. Horace thought, as they passed a beggar, seated on the pavement beside his upturned cap.

Horace tossed a coin into it. Charity was part of the

Jewish way of life and Horace had not shed that aspect of his conditioning. He could remember his mother giving her everyday coat to a charlady who had only a tattered shawl. "Why should I have two coats, when she hasn't got even one?" Minna had said.

On that occasion, Horace recalled with some amusement, charity's proverbial "own reward" had not been a pleasant one. The woman had not turned up to scrub the Shragers' shop floor again. And Minna had, later, seen her coat displayed in the local pawnbroker's window.

"Why are you smiling, Papa," Alison inquired, "if there may be a war?"

Horace returned his mind to the present and his gaze to the recruiting poster, which his daughter was still eyeing. "There'll be plenty of time for not smiling, when it comes."

"Shall you join up, Uncle?" Alison asked. "You'd look rather splendid in army uniform."

"But I doubt if I should make a good soldier, Alison."

"Why not?"

"I can't bear the sight of blood."

The poster was of a smiling rifleman, with an invincible look about him. But Oliver's words brought home to Alison that mangled bodies was what war was about.

"Especially my own blood," Oliver added dryly.

Alison paled and clutched her father's hand.

Was Oliver implying his own cowardice? Horace wondered. "I suppose there's a chance it won't happen," he said to comfort Alison.

She managed to smile, but was gripped by a sense of impending doom. Her father was the kind of man who would consider it his duty to fight for his country.

Horace glanced around the square. Young mothers in summer frocks were pushing baby-carriages, well-dressed matrons window-shopping, and soberly clad gentlemen going about their daily business. Overhead, the sun smiled benignly from a cloudless sky. It was difficult to believe that the storm brewing in Europe would soon be unleashed upon a peaceful England.

"I don't want there to be a war," Alison said childishly.

Horace and Oliver exchanged a smile over her head.

They were passing the Red Lion and Oliver eyed the Inn longingly. But the bar was not open at this hour. In Mrs. Palmer's gracious house he hadn't wanted a drink, but had sat by the window, admiring the garden, wishing all his days were as serene as this. Then he had seen his brother-in-law and niece leave the house together and had been assailed by his own loneliness. The afternoons, when the company was not rehearsing and empty hours stretched ahead of him before it was time to go to the theater, were, for Oliver, unbearable.

"You're extremely quiet, Uncle," Alison remarked.

Oliver laughed. "Who can get a word in, when they're with you?"

"I haven't been very talkative today," Alison answered. "Nor has Papa. The thought of war has affected us."

Oliver agreed. Suddenly, he felt he was approaching a crossroad in his life. No it was stronger than that; as if he were being swept toward one, on a high wind.

The Plantaines were a patriotic family and Oliver no less so than his parents and sister. He would give his life for England if called upon to do so. "How would you like to play Macbeth for the rest of the tour?" he heard himself say tentatively to Horace.

Horace stopped in his tracks. "I beg your pardon?"

"I intend to enlist. Here and now." Oliver's tone had firmed as his thoughts crystallized into the decision.

"Oughtn't you to tell your father, before taking such a step, Oliver? Let's assume, for the moment, that war isn't declared, and there you'll be, stuck in the army," Horace pointed out.

"I'll take that chance."

Alison stood rolling her handkerchief into a tight little ball. She was very fond of Oliver and there was something about him that had always aroused pity in her. "I don't want you to lose a leg, or die on the battlefield," she said to him with a catch in her voice.

"At present, there is no battlefield," Horace said to calm her. The conversation was as hypothetical as the one about the Plantaine Players settling down in Salisbury. But without the absurdity of discussing in detail something that could never happen.

"Take my advice, Oliver. Wait," Horace urged.

But Oliver had waited all his life for the chance now presented to him. He could grasp it or not; the decision was up to him. That was what the crossroads was. And the opportunity to redeem himself in his father's eyes might never come again.

EIGHT

horace was not called upon to take over Oliver's role for the rest of the tour. Only for the week following his brother-in-law's rejection by the army.

Oliver had enlisted on a Monday and was medically examined the following morning. He was found to have a heart defect. Though not serious, it was sufficient for the army to turn him down.

Since then, he had been continuously drunk.

"Where did Oliver get the money to buy all that whisky?" Horace asked Hermione.

It was their final night in Salisbury. The set was now being struck by the stagehands, who sometimes had to work until the early hours to clear the theater of the company's scenery and properties, in readiness for the move to their next venue.

The family had returned to their lodgings for supper and Horace and Hermione were now in their bedroom packing, in order to make an early start the following day.

Hermione was folding one of her gowns and wished she could afford some new ones. Her lack of interest in material things did not extend to her own wardrobe.

"Oliver must have sold his watch and chain," she said resignedly. That afternoon, she had gone to his room to pack his things, while he snored on the bed. The watch had not been there. "Papa will be most upset when he finds out."

The gold timepiece had been left to Oliver by his grandfather.

"This isn't the first time your brother's hocked it," Horace reminded her. "It's enabled him to go on some of his most memorable binges," he recalled. It would not have surprised him if the army doctors examining Oliver had diagnosed cirrhosis of the liver.

"But this time he won't be able to redeem it," Hermione said. "He bought so much whiskey, he must have spent every penny he received for the watch."

"You mean that this time, he hasn't a penny left to put with what you've always managed to give him, so the watch can be redeemed," Horace said.

Hermione finished wrapping a shoe in tissue paper and avoided his eye.

"Did you think I didn't know, Hermione?"

"Why shouldn't I help my own brother?" she flared. "But on this occasion I can't. He'll just have to face the music with Papa."

Horace tossed a handful of collars into his suitcase. "Come, come, my dear. Your papa won't say a word to Oliver."

"But Oliver will know what he is thinking."

Horace opened his wallet. He had been saving to buy Alison a bracelet for her birthday, next month. She would have to make do with something less costly; Oliver's need was greater. "I'll leave some money with Mrs. Palmer and ask her to redeem the family heirloom on Monday," he said stiffly. "She can send it on to Oliver."

"I don't expect you to do such a thing for my sake. Nor was I hinting that you should," Hermione said.

"I'm doing it for your brother's sake," Horace disillusioned her.

"Then I thank you, on his behalf."

Hermione went to Oliver's room to search for the pawn ticket.

The poor devil has been cheated by life again, Horace thought. He had not found it difficult to divine his brother-in-law's true reason for joining up.

When Oliver returned from the recruiting station with his news, the family had been at tea. A moment of surprised silence had followed his announcement, as though it were the last thing anyone would have expected him to do.

Then Gregory had risen from his chair to grip Oliver's hand. "A man must do what he has to do," he had said to the women, who were unable to hide their distress.

The group was imprinted upon Horace's memory like a remembered scene from a play. His wife and mother-in-law seated at the table, with tears in their eyes. His father-in-law surveying Oliver with pride, and as if he had never seen him before. And the expression of pure happiness on Oliver's face.

But Oliver's happiness was to last no longer than the bowl of full-blown roses already spilling their petals in the center of the tea table, Horace reflected as his wife returned to the bedroom with the pawn ticket in one hand and a blue envelope in the other.

Hermione put the pawn ticket on the washstand, with the money Horace had left there to give to Mrs. Palmer. "What is the meaning of this?" she demanded, brandishing the envelope.

Horace tried to still his quaking stomach. "It seems you already know, so why bother to ask?"

Hermione gave him a withering glance. "I know it is a letter received secretly, by my daughter. With your complicity. How else could she have received it, except inside another envelope? One of those which arrive regularly, addressed to you. What I am asking, Horace, is how dare you aid and abet Alison to conduct a correspondence I wouldn't approve of? Behind my back!"

Horace said nothing. There was nothing he could say. He stood guilty of the crime of which he was accused, and any explanation he volunteered would be neither accepted, nor understood.

"I wouldn't know about it now, if I hadn't looked into Alison's room to make sure she had done her packing. She wasn't there. She must have gone downstairs to fetch her bedtime milk." Hermione eyed the envelope with distaste. "This odious epistle was lying on her bed."

Horace managed a feeble laugh. "One could hardly call a letter from a little girl odious."

"Then it's time you realized that everything concerning your family is odious to me."

Hermione's face was paper white, and her eyes had darkened to violet, signifying the depth of her anger. She closed her trunk and fastened it down with tremblinf fingers, oblivious to the wisp of silk stocking hanging over the side, trapped by the lid.

Horace moved it to beside the door, aware of her watching him in stony silence.

"This niece of yours," she said.

"Her name is Emma," Horace answered curtly.

"So I saw, when I read her letter. She must be an exceedingly underhand child, to lend herself to the conspiracy hatched by you and her mother. I am deeply shocked that Alison, who is my daughter, as well as yours, allowed herself to be involved in it. But I blame you. Is this how you people bring up your children, Horace?"

"We bring them up to be normal human beings!" Horace was stung into retorting. "Regrettably, that wasn't how you were reared, Hermione, or you would not be grinding your own axe at your child's expense."

"That's your interpretation!"

"It's the truth. But I wouldn't expect you to see it. You Plantaines never could see beyond your noses."

"May we return to the subject?" Hermione said coldly. "I want you to tell Alison, and your niece, that their correspondence must end."

"Then you're in for a disappointment," Horace answered. "For once, you're not going to get what you want. I ought not have let you have your way about Alison meeting my family. If I'd been firm with you then, there would have been no reason for deceit. I made the wrong decision, but I'm now setting right my mistake. If my daughter wishes to maintain contact with her relatives, you will allow her to do so."

Hermione was momentarily shocked into silence.

And well she might be, Horace thought. In fifteen years of marriage, he had never before put his foot down with her. The anger that had impelled him to do so now, fizzled out and was replaced by an aching regret that he no longer cared enough for her to spare her feelings. But she had brought it upon herself.

"Alison isn't the exclusive property of the Plantaines and you had better accept it," he said finally.

Hermione took off her robe and got into bed. "Is that all?"

"Unless you make it necessary for me to say more."

Hermione lay with her golden hair spread upon the pillow and a pensive expression on her face.

Who is she going to pull out of the hat? Juliet or Ophelia? Horace wondered.

"As you have seen fit to assert your husbandly authority, I have no option but to accept it. That is woman's unfortunate place in society," she declared. And added dramatically: "One can only hope that chaining themselves to the Downing Street railings, as Mrs. Pankhurst and her friends are doing, will succeed in changing our lowly status."

Horace had to smile. His wife had temporarily de-

serted Shakespeare's heroines, in favor of the suf-
fragettes.

"Though I personally doubt that anything ever will,"
she added on a tragic note.

"Kindly spare me the performance," Horace said, getting into bed beside her. If the world were to come to a
sudden end, Hermione would enter the hereafter acting!

"And you can spare me your nocturnal attentions,
from now on," she replied. "If it were possible for us to
occupy separate bedrooms, it would suit me admirably."

"There's no need to draw me a picture. You've made
your point." She had now cast herself in the role of Lysis-
trata, heroine of a Greek drama in which the women
used that ploy.

Horace reached up and extinguished the gaslight,
which in Mrs. Palmer's house was conveniently situated
over the bed. Was there nothing to which Hermione
would not resort? he thought before weariness overwhelmed him.

Hermione lay sleepless. She had not meant to say
those final, terrible words to the man whom, despite everything, she still loved.

She got up and drew back the curtains, to let in the
moonlight so she could see his face. In repose, it was the
face of the boy she had married; who would have put his
hand into the fire for her, if she had asked him to. When
had he begun to change?

Long before his sister poked her nose into our life,
Hermione reflected, casting aside the distress she had
suffered on that account. One day she had become aware
that her husband had no respect for the work the Plantaines were doing. He had been talking with some other
actors in a theater Green Room, and had made it clear
that he didn't believe in art for art's sake.

From then on, Hermione had noticed that viewpoint
coloring all he said and did, and had, more than once,
apologized to her father for her husband's attitude.

It could not be very agreeable to a man like Gregory to

have a son-in-law with such materialistic ideas. But Gregory had never uttered a word against Horace. If he did, Hermione knew it would be just one cryptic question: "What else can you expect?"

Her father had liked Horace from the day he met him and had told the family that he admired his pluck. Not many lads would have found the courage to walk into a theater and ask to see Gregory Plantaine, as Horace had.

Gregory had not required an extra stagehand, but had taken Horace on because the boy had said he wanted to be an actor, and was prepared to do anything in order to make his way.

But the dedication this implied was false, Hermione thought now. No more than a tactic Horace had employed, to get where he wanted to be. Once ensconced in the company and as Gregory's son-in-law, he had tried to turn the Plantaine Players into a money-making enterprise.

As though Hermione and her mother were actresses of the same caliber as Miss Ruby May! Who had just buried her husband, Hermione had read in this week's issue of *The Stage.*

Why do I loathe that woman? Hermione paused to ask herself, gazing through the window at the willow tree standing in solitary splendor in the center of Mrs. Palmer's lawn, its foliage a silvery cascade in the moonlight.

Hermione had never met Ruby May, and was not given to violent likes and dislikes, but the mere mention of the melodrama queen set her teeth on edge. As the sight of her had, that day on the station platform at Crewe.

Was it because Hermione sensed that Horace admired Ruby? The woman's flamboyant appearance would cause any male to turn his head, but a discerning man would recognize her for what she was. Horace, however, seemed to respect her, and had not hidden his respect for Ruby's kind of theater.

Hermione turned from the window to look at her sleeping husband. Her parents had not wanted her to marry him. It was the only time in her life that she had not heeded their advice. She had begged and pleaded with them, until they gave their permission, if not their blessing.

She got into bed and lay gazing at Horace, whom she had tried to transform into a Plantaine. She had had to live with him, and bear his child, to learn the folly of painting over a leopard's spots. It remained a leopard and even if you kept it in a cage it would not lose its feeling for its natural habitat.

Why was she thinking about leopards and cages? It must be the hour? She stifled a hysterical laugh. Then tears stung her eyelids. It wasn't her fault, or Horace's, that their marriage had gone wrong. She had tried to make it work, and had failed—that was what those seemingly ridiculous thoughts meant. And Horace was the product of his background, which his family had now decided not to allow him to forget.

It wasn't surprising they had come to grief. Nothing can succeed against impossible odds, Hermione thought. She and Horace could blend no more than oil and water could. They differed in every way that mattered, but had had the misfortune to fall in love.

Horace stirred in his sleep. If she snuggled close to him, he would take her in his arms and they would kiss and make up. Until the next time.

Hermione lay in an agony of indecision, watching the dawn of another day filter into the room. Her husband slept on. The sleep of the just, no doubt, in his opinion! It must have given him great pleasure to put her in her place. But Hermione had had the last word.

Her rumination had come full circle. She hadn't meant to say what she had finally said. And soon, he might be gone from her. She knew he would enlist immediately, if war was declared. And oh, how long and lonely her nights would be, without him in her bed.

Suddenly, her whole body ached for him. She wanted to lay herself against him, but instead rose from the bed and went to the washstand to sluice herself with cold water.

She had taken off her nightgown and picked up her sponge, when Horace opened his eyes.

Hermione went on with what she was doing, aware of him watching her.

"Shall I do that for you?" he said thickly when she was sponging her breasts.

"No, thank you."

"Well, I've done it before, haven't I?"

"But you never will again."

Horace removed his gaze from her hips and looked at his watch, which was on the bedtable. "It's only five-thirty. Why are you up at this time?"

"I haven't been asleep. I've been thinking."

"What about?"

"You and me."

"And what conclusion did you come to?"

Hermione dried her thighs. "That we weren't made for each other."

"Except in one way. Come back to bed."

She was still fighting her desire, but Horace could not have known it. Hermione was too good an actress. "You seem to have forgotten what I said to you last night."

"Did you mean it?"

She wanted to say no, but her Plantaine pride took charge of her tongue. "Yes."

"Then there's nothing more to be said."

"Only that I shall never come to bed with you in that sense again."

NINE

Alison's fourteenth birthday was not the memorable occasion to which she had looked forward. Most boys and girls stopped being schoolchildren when they reached that age, as Ivy Baines had, and began their adult lives. Alison had expected to waken this morning feeling different, even though her family would not consider she had now grown up. But the only difference between this and her previous birthdays was her father's absence. War had been declared and Horace had enlisted.

Usually, on Alison's birthday, her papa took her out to buy her a present and they had a special tea together in a teashop afterwards. This year she had received his gift in advance. She fingered the blue silk scarf he had given to her before he went away.

"Why are you wearing that thing indoors?" her mother asked. "And on a warm summer night?"

The family had just finished eating supper in their lodgings in Brighton.

"Don't you dare call Papa's gift 'that thing'!" Alison flashed.

"I beg your pardon, Alison. And may I remind you that it was my gift to you, too?"

"But Papa chose it. And it's very dear to me, because he did."

"Of course it is, Alison dear." Jessica interposed to ease the sudden tension. Why was her granddaughter always creating moments like this? "And we all know that you miss your papa very much. But so does your mama. You must apologize to her for your rudeness."

"I'm sorry," Alison said.

But she was not in the least sorry and Hermione knew it. A short silence followed, then Hermione changed the subject. "Have you made any plans for the company?" she asked her father. "About how we shall manage, during the war?"

Gregory was peeling an apple and continued doing so. "It is to be hoped that hostilities will not last too long."

He gave his daughter a reassuring smile, which belied his feelings. Like it or not, Gregory Plantaine had had to lift his head from the sand. His young stagehands had been led by patriotism to desert him, instead of waiting until drafting became necessary. Several of the actors in *Macbeth* had gone with Horace to enlist, and some of the actresses had left to join the Red Cross.

Gregory had had no option but to dismiss the rest of the company and resort to his habitual emergency procedure.

"If the war goes on for a long time, audiences will get fed up with our excerpts and readings," Alison declared.

Her elders exchanged a glance. It was as though, in Horace's absence, she was speaking for her father.

"There was hardly any audience tonight," she added. "I peeped into the auditorium, before the curtain went up."

"You have altogether too much to say for yourself, Alison!" Hermione snapped. Adults didn't need a child to tell them what they already knew! Nor had Hermione yet recovered from the ignominy of the catcalls the Players' makeshift performance had evoked from the gallery.

She was glad that Horace had not been there to hear it, to have his opinion of her father's ideas so graphically confirmed. But she yearned for him every minute and wished she had relented and told him how much she loved him, before he went away to the war.

"People were queuing to see Miss Ruby May in *Murder in the Red Barn*," Alison added, making things worse. "I saw them lining up to book tickets, when we passed by on our way to the theater."

So had Hermione. But she had turned her head the other way.

"Nevertheless, Alison, melodrama has had its day," Gregory declaimed correctly.

"But Miss May can still get an audience for it, can't she, Grandpa? I'd quite like to see her play Maria Marten, myself."

Hermione got up and left the room.

"What have I said to upset Mama now?" Alison asked the others.

As her grandparents and uncle did not know, they were unable to answer. Nor were they accustomed to seeing one of their family behave as Hermione had just done. Except onstage.

"Well, Oliver," Gregory broke the moment of silence. "How are you feeling, my dear chap?"

Oliver had been uncommonly subdued since Horace's departure. "No different from how I felt before being told I'm not hale and hearty," he replied. But his father would continue to inquire about his health, as though he were an invalid and Gregory now had a valid reason for his son not coming up to scratch.

"You must take good care of yourself, old fellow," Gregory urged him.

"If you mean keep off the whisky, Father, why don't you just say so?"

With this, Oliver too left the room.

Jessica and Gregory avoided looking at each other. What was the matter with their children tonight? When Oliver was sober, his behavior was usually impeccable.

"Would you mind if I went to my room, now, too?" Alison asked. There was something in the atmosphere that made her feel uncomfortable.

"Not at all, Alison dear. And we do hope you've had a lovely birthday," her grandmother said.

Alison kissed them both goodnight and wondered why they were always saying that sort of thing. Grandma knew Alison had not had a lovely birthday.

Her grandparents often said things she knew they did not mean. And it occurred to her, as she went upstairs, that they refrained from saying the things they did mean. She had known as well as Uncle Oliver had what Grandpa's telling him to take good care of himself really meant.

To Alison, these observations were puzzling. It would be some time before she understood that Gregory and Jessica were incapable of her own inherent directness, that they were the kind who shy away from confrontation, lest it disturb the pattern of their lives.

But Jessica was presently gripped by an ominous feeling about her son. She wanted to go to his room; cradle him in her arms and tell him that he was deeply loved by his parents. But one couldn't do that with a grown man.

Her husband had not allowed her to cuddle Oliver when he was a child, as he himself had cuddled Hermione. Gregory had not considered it right to be demonstrative with a boy and, when Oliver was still a toddler, had always addressed him as "young man."

She watched Gregory quarter an orange. He was fond of fresh fruit and made sure his landladies, all of whom revered him, knew it. He was wearing his customary pleasant expression, but his eyes were sad.

"You're concerned about Oliver, aren't you, dear?" she said quietly.

Gregory glanced at her, but said nothing.

"I think perhaps you ought to talk to him about himself, dear. It has occurred to me that possibly he believes we don't care enough about him."

It struck Gregory, then, that he had never really talked to Oliver. When the boy was born, he had been ecstatic with joy and had envisaged the close friendship he would have with his son. He had imagined them walking side by side on the seashore, or through a market, enjoying together whatever the company's ever-changing surroundings had to offer. Sharing jokes and experiences away from the theater and their women. None of it had happened.

Oliver had always shown a marked preference for his mother and sister's company. As if he were in some way afraid of his father and was clinging to them for protection.

"He is probably worried about what the doctors told him, despite them saying it wasn't serious," Jessica prodded her husband, who was contemplating the peel on his plate. "And perhaps it would help if you let him know you think no less of him, because he can't do his bit for England."

Think no less of him? Gregory was deeply distressed about Oliver's rejection, but on his son's account, not his own. "I can't talk to Oliver," he replied to his wife. "I never could."

Jessica made light of this. "Well, none of us are very good at opening our hearts to each other, are we, dear? But I do think, on this occasion, you might try."

"You must let me be the judge of what is best, my love."

Gregory could not tell his wife that what she wanted him to do was impossible. There was a door between himself and Oliver which must always remain closed, and behind it was the root of Oliver's unhappiness. A father could not tell his son that he knew he was homosexual, but loved him all the same. Oliver was probably aware that Gregory knew. But the subject remained unmentionable.

For a long time, Gregory had not allowed himself to believe it, though he had sensed, when Oliver was still a boy, a certain inexplicable something about him. And had feared what it might be, when Oliver was in his teens and showed no interest in the opposite sex.

Oliver had been an exceptionally handsome youth and the young actresses, engaged for this production or that, had flocked around him. He had charmingly fended them off. It was then that Gregory had noticed a subtle difference in his son's manner toward the visiting actors, and that there was invariably one with whom Oliver made friends.

"It's as though Oliver had something eating away at him," Jessica sighed.

"Stuff and nonsense, my dear!"

Gregory's heart was heavy and it would be a blessed relief to unburden himself, but he had never indulged in sharing his anxieties with his family, not even with Jessica. Talking about one's problems tended to magnify them.

In Gregory's experience, if you clung tight to your beliefs and your hopes, things usually came right in the end, as if his present problem of how the company would cope in wartime would, somehow or other, resolve itself.

"There must be something troubling Oliver deeply, or he wouldn't drink like he does," Jessica persisted, wishing she had found the courage to say this to her husband years ago.

Gregory kept the smile on his face and patted her hand. The problem of Oliver could not be resolved.

"If we don't know what it is, how can we help him?" Jessica said.

"Don't let your imagination run away with you, my love." She would die of shock if she knew what ailed her son.

TEN

By the winter of 1914, Gregory had managed to get together a cast to stage *Twelfth Night*.

"Your papa would be so pleased that we're getting good audiences," Hermione said to Alison.

"We usually do, at this time of year, Mama."

The company was booked for a four-week run in Bournemouth and tomorrow would be Christmas Eve. Alison was in her mother's dressing room, watching her prepare for the evening performance.

Hermione draped a towel around her shoulders and glanced at the rich brocade gown hanging on the screen. "I had to ask Nellie to take some tucks in my costumes. The pounds seem to be dropping off me."

"I remember your losing several pounds when you last played Rosalind, Mama, so maybe playing Viola is having the same effect upon you—though it's a much less strenuous role."

Hermione smiled and kept her thoughts to herself.

Alison was too young to be aware that a woman could shed weight from pining for her husband. Hermione had had no stomach for food since Horace went away—which was ironical, considering the terms on which they had parted, she thought with a pang.

Alison, too, was thinking of Horace, but he was rarely out of her thoughts. When the company last presented *Twelfth Night,* her father had played Malvolio. And if he had been here now, Alison would have been watching him prepare for the performance, not her mother.

"It won't be like Christmas, without Papa," she said forlornly.

Hermione agreed. But Christmas was not for moping and she made herself sound cheerful. "But we shall have a splendid time, Alison, as we always do."

There was no performance on Christmas night, and wherever they might be the Plantaines spent the day in traditional good cheer.

"This year it will be especially nice," Hermione went on, when Alison remained silent. "Mrs. Harvey is such a jolly landlady. And she let you help her decorate the tree, didn't she dear?"

"But Papa won't see it. Do you think he'll get any plum pudding in the army, Mama?"

"You must write and ask him if they gave him any, Alison. But he'll certainly enjoy the lovely box of goodies we sent him from Fortnums, won't he, dear? It was very observant of you to notice their advertisement in your grandpa's newspaper."

"I told Nellie about it, in case she wanted to send one to her grandson," Alison answered. "But she said she couldn't afford fifteen shillings. She sent him the Hope Brothers' five-shilling parcel of clothing, instead. And one of those boxes with Oxo and Horlicks in it, that another shop advertised, that only cost five shillings. I think it's very thoughtful of the stores to arrange special Christmas parcels for soldiers, don't you, Mama?"

"And of the King and Queen to have sent a Christmas

card to every soldier. So you see, Alison dear, your papa will not think he is forgotten," Hermione declared. "Even the Royal Family has thought of him at Christmastime."

"But I do miss him so much," Alison answered blinking away a tear.

Hermione stemmed her own emotion, or in a minute they would both be sobbing their hearts out! "You are not the only girl in England who is feeling that way," she said, sounding more severe than she had intended.

Sometimes, Alison was led to wonder if her mother missed her father at all. She said that she did, but displayed no sign of it. Even when they saw Papa off at the railway station, after his embarkation leave, Mama had not wept. Nor had she clung to her soldier husband, as other ladies were doing all around them.

Hermione wished her daughter would go away and leave her to prepare for the performance. Hermione was not the kind of actress who could chat while making up and dressing. She had always found it necessary to have a period in which to compose herself and, by the time she made her entrance onstage, would have assumed the character of her role as well as the costume.

But not if Alison didn't allow her to do so, she thought, eyeing the girl's forlorn expression. When Horace was here, it was with him their daughter had kept company before curtain call. But Horace had not minded.

"You must try to be brave about your papa being a soldier," Hermione said to her.

"I'd find it easier to be brave, at the moment, if we had heard from him this week," Alison answered.

"The mail, like many other things, is at sixes and sevens because of the war," Hermione reassured her.

"But you received a letter today, didn't you, Mama? I saw the stagedoor keeper hand it to you." Alison paused and noted that her mother was avoiding her eye. "You didn't tell me who it was from."

Hermione went on applying her greasepaint. Alison

watched her. "It wasn't bad news about Papa, was it?" An icy hand had just clutched at her heart.

"No, Alison. I'm sure he is perfectly well," Hermione declared though she was far from sure. The news from France was not good. "Your papa is not in the trenches, remember."

"But he must have to go there, to carry away the wounded."

Horace was a stretcher-bearer and Alison had a vision of him lying bloodied on the battlefield. She had not been born and brought up a Plantaine without absorbing that most sacred of all theatrical traditions: Come what may, the performance goes on. And it would do so tonight, even if her mother had, this morning, learned she was a widow. But Hermione would delay telling Alison the terrible news, lest Alison make it difficult for her to do what she must.

"You're keeping something from me, Mama!" Alison cried. "I can tell."

I'm not as good an actress as I thought, Hermione reflected with irony. Her guilt must be written on her face. The letter from Oldham had been burning a hole in her housecoat pocket, since she hid it there so that Alison would not find it. Since her daughter's initial deceit, Hermione felt she could not trust her, and would not have put it past her to open and search her mama's handbag.

Hermione took the letter from her pocket and gave it to Alison; she could not spare the nervous energy to maintain her pretence.

"It's addressed to me, Mama. Why didn't you give it to me immediately?"

Hermione made no reply.

"And you've read it, haven't you?" The envelope had been opened. Alison scanned the letter. "You weren't going to give it to me at all, were you, Mama? Because Aunt Lottie has invited me to stay, while Emma is on holiday from school. And you don't want me to go, do you?"

Hermione felt as if she were on trial. How dare Alison make her feel this way! She managed to keep her tone even. "You know how I feel about those people, Alison. But it is your father's wish that you be allowed to keep in touch with them, and I shall say no more than that. About the invitation for you to stay—I simply could not bear for you to be away from me at Christmas. Possibly you can visit them some other time."

Alison eyed her coldly. "If you have your way, Mama, I shall never visit them. Christmas is just an excuse."

Hermione rose from the dressing table with sufficient force to send the stool toppling. "Are you calling me a liar, Alison?"

Alison remained silent, and something in her expression revealed her contempt for her mother. There was the merest hint of a smile curling her lips and an enigmatic glint in her dark eyes.

Hermione stepped forward and smacked her face.

A moment of silence followed. Then Alison turned and left the room.

Oh God, Hermione thought. What have I done? She had never before raised a finger to her child, but had been unable to stop herself from doing it.

She sank down on the chaise-longue. It was not possible to continue making up; her hands were trembling and her palm stinging from the blow she had delivered. Her complexion, she saw in the mirror, had grayed and looked the more so by contrast with the greasepaint streaked upon her brow.

She was still sitting there when the assistant stage manager pounded on the door.

"Thirty-minutes, Mrs. Plantaine!"

"Thank you, Tim!" she managed to reply and forced herself to return to the dressing table and resume transforming herself to Viola.

She was putting on her costume when the final, urgent

request, "Places please!" resounded along the dressing-room corridor.

The actors who opened the play must now hasten to the wings. Viola did not appear until the beginning of Scene Two, but *Twelfth Night* had only a short Scene One, which allowed Hermione little time to dawdle.

Nevertheless, she did not leave her dressing room until the last possible moment, hoping that Alison would return—though what would transpire when they again came face to face was a matter for conjecture.

The child must have hidden herself away somewhere, Hermione thought when she reached the wings without having encountered Alison. There was no such luxury for Hermione. Instead, she must face the glare of the lights, in the guise of another, and keep her feelings secreted inside her.

She gave a passable performance, but missed her cue three times. Hermione's mind had, that evening, deserted the Bard, to concentrate upon her personal drama. She could not stop thinking about Alison. How could what had taken place between them, with its dreadful climax, be undone?

By the time the curtain fell, Hermione had decided that, like it or not, she would have to apologize to her daughter. But when she came offstage, Alison was nowhere to be found.

"Miss Alison left the theater during the performance, Mrs. Plantaine," the stagedoor keeper supplied. "I told her it weren't right for her to go off on her own, when it's dark outside," he added. "But she took no notice."

"No. I don't expect she did, Len."

Hermione blanched at the thought of Alison returning alone, at night, to their lodgings. To reach Mrs. Harvey's house from the tram stop, it was necessary to walk along an ill-lit footpath adjoining Branksome Chine.

Nevertheless, Hermione did not pause to think of her own safety and set off without waiting for her parents and brother to accompany her. She could not face the prospect of explaining the incident to them and hoped to make her peace with Alison before they got back.

The stagedoor keeper stood on the steps, watching her small figure recede along the alley. If he didn't have his job to do, he'd have put on his coat and scarf and seen the little lady to her house, he thought as he returned to his cozy cubicle. Len had known Hermione since she was a child, watching from the wings with her brother while their parents performed. And Hermione had always been lovely to him, not like some of the actresses he had to contend with. Even though she was worried about her daughter, she had given Len a warm smile. She had asked him not to mention to her parents and brother that Alison had left by herself. "Let's keep it a secret, Len," she had said in her beautiful voice. And, of course, Len wouldn't say a word.

Like every stagedoor keeper with whom she had come in contact, Len would do anything for Hermione Plantaine.

When Hermione arrived at the lodgings, she found herself in a situation beyond anyone's help.

The landlady, who was hanging mistletoe in the hall when Hermione entered, said she had not seen Alison.

Hermione paled. "Have you been at home all evening, Mrs. Harvey?"

"Except when I popped next door, to borrow some lard. Fancy me running out of it, dear. I must've made more mince pies than I meant to. I was only out a few minutes, but I did leave the door open—"

Hermione was no longer listening. She raced upstairs, her heart thudding in her breast. Alison's room was empty, and a note was propped up against the dressing-table mirror. Mrs. Havey's "few minutes" absence had been long enough for Alison to come and go.

Hermione read the note and had to sit down on the bed. Her legs felt weak. Was she dreaming this? No, she could feel the notepaper in her hand. And the message on it was all too clear: "Merry Christmas, Mama. I shall be spending mine up north."

ELEVEN

Alison rolled her woolen glove into a ball and rubbed the condensation off the train window, but it was too dark outside to see the countryside slipping by.

She had reached London in time to catch the night train to Manchester. From there, she would take another train to Oldham. The routes between this city and that had been engraved upon her mind over the years, as she traversed them.

Alison was a seasoned traveler, as much at home in a train as other youngsters would be on a tram. Wrapped around her knees was the red tartan rug that served not just for winter journeys, but to keep her cozy when she sat doing her schoolwork backstage, or in a chilly lodging-house bedroom.

She had put on her warmest clothing, and in the capacious leather bag that went with her everywhere, were a couple of russet apples and some bread and cheese. She hoped Mrs. Harvey would not mind her having helped herself from the supper table laid in readiness for the Plantaines' return from the theater.

This thought opened her mind to the matter she had resolutely shut out. Alison's cheek had not stung from the slap for too long, but the hurt inside her was still there. And, by now, Mama would know she had gone.

There were two soldiers in the compartment, both fast asleep. One seemed no older than a schoolboy. Were they going home on embarkation leave? The sight of their uniform heightened Alison's longing for her father. But she was going to his family, who would not treat her as Mama had. Or as though she were not there, as the Plantaines did for much of the time.

Alison brushed this last, disloyal thought aside. She loved her Plantaine grandparents and wouldn't stop loving them just because she now had a second family. And if Uncle Oliver hadn't made it possible, she wouldn't be traveling north now.

She had left her mother's dressing room in a daze, heading nowhere. Then anger had stirred within her and settled into cold determination. By the time she reached the end of the corridor, she had made up her mind what she would do.

But she could not do it without a penny in her pocket. Her piggy bank was in her trunk at Mrs. Harvey's, but there was not enough in it to buy a railway ticket to Oldham. She would have to pawn something, like Uncle Oliver did when he was short of cash.

The only thing Alison had to sell was her coral necklace. Since Papa went away, she wore it all the time, because he had given it to her, and she was loath to part with it.

Oliver had arrived at the theater and had found her standing fingering the necklace. She must have looked upset, because he had put his arm around her and asked what was wrong.

Alison had felt like telling him everything, but had

checked the impulse. If he knew her intention, he would consider it his duty to tell Mama.

"I'm desperately in need of some money," she had said.

Her uncle had smiled wryly. "I know the feeling, my pet."

Alison sat in the train carrying her north and was, in retrospect, ashamed of her own cunning. But she hadn't asked Oliver for money. On the other hand, her conscience butted in, she had let him think she required it for a reason very different from the true one.

She toyed with her necklace which, thanks to Oliver, she had not had to sell. He had swept her along to his dressing room and a few minutes later she had left with some pound notes in her hand.

"I suppose that, with your papa away, you miss the extra pennies he used to give you?" Oliver had said. "But in his absence, allow me to insure that you aren't short of cash to buy Christmas gifts."

Alison was taken aback. "But why should you give me money, Uncle?"

"Because I want to. And there's no need to thank me, Alison."

Alison had kissed his cheek and hastened away. Only now, listening to the rhythm of the train wheels, and the snores of the sleeping soldiers, did it register with her that her uncle had had tears in his eyes.

Uncle Oliver is a very strange man, she thought before slumber claimed her, too. It seemed but a moment later that the plump lady seated opposite gently shook her.

"Wake up, luv. T'train'll soon be at Manchester."

"Is someone meetin' yer, lass?" the lady's husband inquired.

Alison folded her lap rug. "No, as a matter of fact."

The couple exchanged a glance, in which was written their disapproval of a young girl traveling alone.

Alison gave them a smile. "But I know Manchester quite well. I can find my way around."

"I can tell tha's not a Mancunian, lass," the man said, "by thi voice."

"Where does thi come from?" his wife inquired.

Alison paused to think about it. "Well, not from anywhere, exactly," she was constrained to reply. "My family are theatricals, you see, and we're always on the move."

The lady exchanged another glance with her husband, then returned her gaze to Alison. "Fancy not coming from anyplace. You poor lass."

"Theatricals, yer said." The man smiled. "Owt to do wi' that Miss Fanny Horniman, what brought the Manchester Gaiety Theatre a few years back, an' puts on them newfangled plays there?"

"I'm afraid not," Alison replied. "But Miss Horniman is very well known in the theater. I have certainly heard of her. She did a great deal to help the playwright W. B. Yeats, of whom you must have heard."

The man and his wife looked blank.

"My family are the Plantaine Players," Alison told them.

"Well, fancy that!" the lady exclaimed.

"All t'same, lass, yer can't be a day above sixteen, an' if Ah were thi dad, tha wouldn't be traveling on t'night train by thiself, wi' nobody meeting yer at t'other end."

Alison did not tell him she was only fourteen. Her height and build led strangers to believe she was older. "My father is in the army," she said, removing the doubt cast upon his sense of responsibility. "And I am well able to take care of myself."

She had not felt quite so confident when walking from the tram to Mrs. Harvey's, with the winter wind stirring the tall pines that bordered Branksome Chine, and only a sliver of moon to light up the night. But determination to do what she must had strengthened her. And the landlady's absence from the house had seemed destined: Alison had not been called upon to offer false explanations. Together with Oliver giving her the money, it was as though Fate had decreed that nothing would stand between Alison and what she had decided to do.

She put on her hat, and the little fur-tipped cape her parents had given her last Christmas, aware of the solicitous couple watching her.

The man's arms were folded upon his sizable paunch and he was toying with the Albert medallion attached to his gold pocket-watch. He wore a black tie and his wife had about her an air of mourning. She was not funerally garbed and had managed to smile while talking to Alison, but her expression now was the one Alison had seen actresses assume for moments of dramatic tragedy.

"Our son was killed in t'war. Afore he had time ter know he was on t'battlefield," the woman said as though she had divined Alison's private conjecture.

Her husband sighed and patted her hand.

"Folk said t'change'd do me good, so Ah let me husband take me down south, ter visit his sister," she went on. She sat for a moment silently clutching her lizard-skin handbag, which was balanced on her broad lap. "But Ah couldn't rest. All Ah wanted was ter run home."

"Tha's home, now, missis," her husband declared as the train pulled into London Road Station.

"Ah shan't feel better till Ah'm sat by me own fireside," the woman answered.

The portly man lifted Alison's suitcase from the luggage rack. "When summat's wrong, lass, their own place is where a person wants t' run to," he said with a sigh.

Alison thanked him.

"Ah'd carry it down t'platform for yer, if me an' t'missis hadn't got two of our own."

"It isn't heavy," Alison assured him. "But you are very kind."

Northerners were, she thought, heading for the station exit, which didn't mean that Southerners were unkind, but there was a special warmth about the way people up here didn't hesitate to do what they could for you, as though being helpful was second nature to them and

something they enjoyed. Alison was never happier than
when the company was playing up north.

She had to cross town to reach Victoria Station, from
where the Oldham train left, and decided to walk, instead of riding a tram down Market Street. It was a
bright, crisp morning and the fresh air felt good. Her
mother did not enjoy walking and with her father gone,
Alison's afternoons were spent lounging in their lodgings, or at the theater, if the company was rehearsing.

Mama would not allow her to go wandering around
alone—and had probably swooned, Alison thought,
when she found her precious child gone. But Alison was
not in the least sorry for her, and was admiring the splendid entrance to the Corn Exchange, as she neared the
station, when a terrible thought entered her head. If
Papa didn't return from the war, Alison would be at the
mercy of her mother.

Not for a moment did Alison think that being smacked
by Hermione would become a regular thing. But there
could be no going back from the point to which their
confrontation had taken them.

The respect Alison had once had for Hermione had
dwindled as she came, little by little, to resent her. Last
night had put an end to the small amount that was left.
But Papa will come back, Alison reassured herself, and
brushed aside her trepidation about how she would fare
with her mother until he did.

She bought a ticket to Oldham, and ate one of her apples when she was seated on the train. There were not too
many people traveling so early in the morning and Alison had a compartment to herself.

The small suitcase into which she had hastily thrown a
few garments, was on the seat beside her. What was it
that the kind gentleman had said, when he lifted it down
from the luggage rack for her? Alison could not remember his exact words, but something about them had
lodged in her mind. He'd told her that when things went

wrong, a person wanted to run home. And his face had lit up when the train pulled in to his home town.

But Alison had no hometown. She was born in Plymouth, where the company happened to be playing at the time, but when people asked you where you came from, they meant, "Where do you live?" And she had had to tell the couple on the train that she came from nowhere. They were probably, by now, in their own little house—they weren't the kind whose home would be grand. But no house, little or big, was, or had ever been, Alison's home.

The train had reached a stretch of countryside and a piece of straw danced briefly alongside the window, before being borne away. That's what I am, Alison thought. A straw on the wind, swept hither and thither.

She told herself not to be ridiculous. She enjoyed traveling around with the company, didn't she? But the thought she had just had about herself had evoked a strange feeling. A dog had its kennel and a bird its nest, but Alison had no place that was special to her. No comforting haven to run to when things went wrong.

A loneliness of spirit had taken Alison in its grip, though she was too young to recognize it. Until now, despite her theatrical background, she had lived a life as sequestered in its own way as that of a nun. The world outside the theater had been for her a place apart. Those who populated it were not her people and she had viewed them through the telescope imposed by her own insularity.

This was Alison's first venture abroad alone and the telescope had turned upon herself. Suddenly, she was aware of her own isolation. And of a hungering inside her that she did not yet know was a need to belong.

She was destined always to live with those twin emotions, and to tread the tightrope strung between them. But on that winter morning in 1914, Alison was not thinking of what the future might hold in store for her. Nor could she have known that she was on her way to the place that, henceforth, would fill the newly-discovered void in her life. Jessica was trying to persuade Hermione to eat some breakfast.

"I can't, Mama."

"Just a slice of toast, dear. It will help to strengthen you."

"It would be more likely to choke me. Could you have sat down and eaten if I had, when I was a child, given you the anxiety Alison has given me?"

"I don't know what's got into the girl," Gregory muttered from his end of the table.

Apart from expressing concern for his granddaughter's safety on the long journey north, he had made no comment last night. It was out of character for him to have remarked upon her behavior, now—the Plantaines were not given to airing their views about each other.

"Nothing got into her that wasn't already there," Hermione declared with feeling. "We may as well face it, Papa. My daughter is not what we would wish her to be."

Oliver entered in time to hear this. "Have you just discovered that?" he asked his sister, joining them at the table. "I've known it for a long time."

Hermione played with her knife. "Possibly I preferred not to know it."

"Because you are a true Plantaine."

Hermione watched Oliver stir the tea Jessica had poured for him. "Are you implying that you are not?"

"We weren't discussing me. We were talking about you."

"Actually, we were discussing Alison."

"And she's your daughter, not mine." Oliver sipped his tea and glanced at his father. "Like it or not, parents hold some responsibility for the way their children turn out." He gave his full attention to his sister. "And that includes something you just said, Hermione. Why should Alison be what you wish her to be?"

"Because it's the parents who set the standards and the children who follow them, Oliver. As you and I did."

Oliver smiled sardonically. "Don't you mean 'try to follow them'?"

"Alison has not tried."

"No."

"She has gone her own way, though she's only fourteen."

"She has gone her father's way, Hermione. And, in my opinion, you'd have been wiser to let her do so with your permission," Oliver said.

Hermione eyed him angrily.

"Shall we talk about something else, my dears?" Jessica intervened hastily. She had the feeling that her son and daughter were about to embark upon a quarrel, which she had never known them do before.

"No, Mama!" Hermione flared. Then she said something unprecedented. "I am sick and tired of the way this family beats about the bush."

Her parents put down their teacups and stared at her.

"I thought it was normal behavior, until I married Horace," Hermione told them. "It was he who showed me that it wasn't. And allowed me the luxury of getting things off my chest to him, as he did to me. But he always knew he couldn't do it with you."

"Bravo, Hermione!" Oliver applauded.

She returned her attention to him. "I haven't yet finished saying what I have to, to you. You seem to have arranged yourself on my daughter's side, Oliver," she declared with a glint in her eyes.

Oliver surveyed her weary appearance and was filled with compassion for her. "I love you dearly, Hermione."

"But?"

"You are a foolish woman."

"Thank you! The way I feel this morning, that's all I needed to hear."

"Had you not been foolish, Alison would have had no reason to upset you."

Hermione let her brother have the full force of her fury. "For you to defend her, Oliver, is quite indefensible! And I shan't forget that you did. I can think of no reason in the world that would persuade me to desert my family at Christmas, and that is what Alison has done. What else can I think but that she did it deliberately? To hurt me." Hermione had, for the moment, conveniently put from her mind that she had slapped her daughter's face.

Gregory folded *The Times* behind which he had been sheltering. "If everyone will excuse me, I have some letters to write," he said, rising from the table.

"We've never had a family crisis before, have we, Papa?" Hermione said to him cuttingly. "But it's rather different from the professional ones we've had to face from time to time. One can't just sit tight and hope that this domestic anxiety will go away."

Gregory gave her a charming smile. "I have never seen the point of working myself into a lather, Hermione. Nor do I enjoy seeing others do so. But you are wrong if you assume that I don't care. I am deeply concerned for my granddaughter's welfare and suggest that instead of wringing your hands, you send a prepaid telegram to your sister-in-law in Oldham. It would relieve all of us to know that Alison has arrived there safely."

"I'll do it as soon as the post office opens, Papa."

"But I'm not surprised you didn't think of doing so, yourself. Unlike me, you are not of a practical turn of mind."

Gregory left the room while his family were still recovering their breath. He had never been known to make a practical move in his life.

Jessica pulled herself together, then gave Hermione's shoulder a comforting pat and followed him.

"If there's one thing our parents know how to do, it's how to make a graceful exit," Oliver said dryly. His mother always followed her husband's lead, and his father had been walking away from situations since Oliver was a child.

Hermione went to warm her hands by the fire. Mrs.

Harvey had wreathed the mantelpiece with holly. Gaily-hued paper chains were festooned from the ceiling. The Christmas tree stood in the window bay, its tinselled adornments gently swaying in the draught from an ill-fitting lattice. The silver pasteboard star that was its crowning glory had been made by Alison, who would not be here to hang up her stocking tonight.

Suddenly, the festive setting was more than Hermione could bear. Her husband had deserted her for the army and her child for an alien family.

"I must go and send the telegram," she said tremulously.

"Let me do it for you."

Hermione's voice hardened. "No thank you."

They fell silent, but it was not the easy silence they had always shared. Oliver's defense of his niece had driven a wedge between him and his sister. Hermione could do no wrong, in her own eyes. And Oliver had dared to tell her the truth about herself. He would probably live to regret it, but had no regrets now.

"I wonder where Alison got the train fare from?" Hermione muttered. That aspect of her daughter's flight had just occurred to her.

In for a penny, Oliver thought. "I'm afraid I gave it to her," he said.

Hermione was momentarily speechless. "Am I to understand that you conspired with her in this whole matter?" she said when she found her tongue.

Oliver was not given time to reply.

"That you let her persuade you to finance her disgraceful escapade?" Hermione went on before he could utter. "I've always known you were a weakling and a sinner, Oliver—but the depths you have sunk to are quite unforgivable!"

Oliver allowed himself a bitter smile. Hermione could forgive only the trespasses that didn't affect her. He knew her as well as she knew him and ought not to have

expected her to react differently. But a cold disillusion
had settled upon him, nevertheless.

Why bother explaining that he hadn't known what Alison would do with the money? Or that he'd been paying
his debt to Horace, for redeeming the heirloom watch
now restored to its place in Oliver's pocket. That even
had there not been that debt, Oliver would have done
what Horace was not there to do. A few pounds was a
small sacrifice compared to the one being made by those
risking their lives on the battlefield.

His sister was eyeing him with contempt and would not
believe any of it. To do so would not suit her purpose,
which was to play the injured party.

Hermione was now telling him what a magnificent performance he had given last night, as the anxious uncle
worried to death about his niece.

Oliver let her get on with it. Suddenly, what she
thought of him had ceased to matter.

"How could you do this to me?" she asked finally.
Then her face crumpled and she stood forlornly fingering
a button on her blue-velvet frock. "I shall never trust you
again, Oliver. Or care for you the way I did," she said,
severing the special, sibling bond that had always existed
between them.

Oliver shuddered as though the words had cut into his
flesh. Without Hermione, for him there was nobody left.

Since his binge in Salisbury, he had vowed to abstain
and had managed, so far, to do so. Horace's kindness in
redeeming the watch had shamed and strengthened Oliver. The devil with it! he decided now. Booze was his only
comfort; why try not to be the weakling and sinner his
sister and everyone else thought him?

Hermione was gazing through the window, as if she
could not bear to look at him.

"I think I shall retire to my room," he told her.

She did not turn her head, which was as good as saying
Oliver could go to hell, so far as she was concerned—the

family knew he always kept a handy bottle of whisky in his trunk.

His Christmas gift to them would be the satisfaction of knowing he would never see the error of his ways, he thought as he went upstairs.

Come to think of it, why should he spend Christmas with them? he asked himself when he reached the landing. They would enjoy it much more without him. And he without them.

He entered and left his room without having a drink. But he'd make up for it when he got to London!—in the company of some fellow sinners of his acquaintance. The actor who was understudying him could have the pleasure of playing Malvolio to a packed Christmas Eve house. Oliver would not be there to play it.

Where's your professional conscience? he quizzed himself. Missing a performance when you were drunk and incapable was one thing. Planning to do so, while you were still stone-cold sober, was something else. But Oliver felt not a pang.

What did he feel? The urge to hit back at those who gave him credit for nothing but letting them down. What he was about to do would hurt them deeply. Christmas was a family time, but Oliver was thumbing his nose at his family, as his niece had, but his reason was different from Alison's. He was doing it maliciously. For revenge.

He was donning his coat in the lobby, when it occurred to him that the money he had given Alison had left him short. But he would not hock the watch again; to do so would be an act of ingratitude to Horace.

He went to the parlor, where his father was seated writing and his mother knitting. "Could you let me have some cash?" he asked Gregory pleasantly. And added, enigmatically, "I've run short and you know how it is, at this time of year."

Business being currently good, Gregory was able to oblige and hesitated only briefly. His son's period of abstinence was a hopeful sign and to refuse Oliver's request would imply that Gregory did not expect it to last.

"Certainly, my dear boy," he said, taking out his wallet and obliging.

Oliver had read his mind. "I assure you I shall put it to good use, Father," he said dryly.

Hermione was still gazing through the front window when Oliver left the house. This was one Christmas his family would not forget! And Oliver's, too, would be memorable.

He was treading the lonely path beside the ridge when he began to smile. How he wished he could be there to witness his father's discomfort when Gregory realized what he had unwittingly made possible. Would Hermione then see her papa in the same treacherous light as she now saw her brother?

Of course not, though Gregory's action was identical to Oliver's vis-à-vis Alison. But Oliver was a dog with a bad name and the worst was automatically assumed about him. Hermione had tried him and found him guilty without giving him the chance to explain.

But who's had the last laugh? Oliver gloated as he boarded the tram to the railway station. He was still smiling with satisfaction when he seated himself on the London train. Byron was right when he wrote that revenge was sweet.

Alison was asleep when Hermione's telegram was delivered to the Steins' house.

Mrs. Ramsden, who lived opposite, opened her front door and watched Lottie receive the terrifying salmon-red envelope. She had seen the telegraph boy cycle along the avenue and, in wartime, the sight of him was even more ominous than it had always been. A telegram spelt bad news.

"It's all right, Mrs. Ramsden! Nobody's dead," Lottie called to her after she had read it.

"What a relief, Mrs. Stein! Me 'eart was in me mouth.

Ah knew it couldn't be yer dad, o'course. Yer'd 'ardly be gettin' a wire from round t'corner. 'E's out o' danger, now, isn't 'e?"

"Yes, thank God."

Lottie's face felt stiff from trying to maintain her neighborly smile. The telegraph boy was leaning on the doorpost, listening to the conversation. Lottie checked her irritation with Mrs. Ramsden, who was nosey, but goodhearted.

"If yer want a threepenny bit, ter tip t'lad with, Ah've got plenty o' small change," Mrs. Ramsden offered.

"I'm all right, thank you. But if you'll excuse me, I must scribble a reply."

"Nothin' serious, I 'ope?"

Lottie shook her head. Though serious this matter certainly was. She took the stub of pencil the boy handed to her. What could she write to the sister-in-law who was so hostile toward her? And would be even more so, in view of what Alison had done.

Hermione had not economized on words or money and the message had caused Lottie's cheeks to burn. It was a ticking-off, if ever she saw one!

She read it again, while the boy shifted impatiently from one foot to the other. "Your unfortunate invitation for my daughter to spend Christmas with you not me was accepted with neither my permission nor knowledge. Kindly relieve my anxiety by informing me of her safe arrival. Signed H. Plantaine."

Lottie wrote the bare minimum of words necessary to set Hermione's mind at rest. They would not remove her hostility, but there was nothing Lottie could do about that. She had almost added "Merry Christmas" but had decided that the circumstances made it inappropriate.

She gave the reply to the lad and tipped him sixpence, instead of the customary threepence, to compensate for his lengthy wait.

Emma appeared at the head of the stairs, as Lottie was

closing the front door. "What's the matter, Mam? You look upset."

"I am. You'd better come down, love. I want to talk to you."

"Who was at the door? Grandma didn't send someone to fetch you, did she?" Emma inquired anxiously. "Has Grandpa had a setback?"

Lottie shook her head. "And we must stop expecting him to have one, Emma, or we shall all be bags of nerves."

"Aren't the doctors expecting him to have one?"

"I didn't ask. Nor did your grandmother. God has given Grandpa a reprieve. He answered your brother's prayer and that's enough to be going on with."

They went into the kitchen and Lottie sat down beside the big, square table. In the afternoons, its scrubbed surface was covered with a rust chenille cloth and Emma stood toying with the bobbled-fringe trimming.

Why did her mother want to talk to her? And she had said it so gravely. "Have I done something wrong, Mam?"

Lottie managed to laugh. "That will be the day! From you, love, I've never had a minute's trouble. Though your sister makes sure I don't go short of it."

"What's our Clara done now?"

Last Sunday, Clara had said she was going to visit a girlfriend, but had been seen in Manchester, with a boy. The informant was Lottie's kosher butcher, who had considered it his duty to hand over the information along with the chicken and meat.

"Nothing, so far as I know," Lottie replied. "But one day, Clara will realize that a person who does what they shouldn't, secretly, will sooner or later be found out."

Lottie got up to stir the fire. "It's Alison. I want to talk to you about, Emma. Did she tell you her mother didn't want her to come here? That she came without telling her mam? And left her to worry all night about how she would fare, traveling alone?"

"No. But she hasn't had time to tell me, has she? Or you," Emma defended her cousin. "She was falling on her feet, when she got here. She went straight to bed."

Lottie's lips tightened. "She will have some explaining to do, when she gets up." A daughter like Clara was enough to cope with and Lottie intended to make it clear to Alison that she wouldn't countenance underhanded or inconsiderate behavior in her niece.

"If you give Alison a lecture, Mam, on her first visit here, she might not want to come again," Emma said, noting her mother's expression.

"That will be up to her, won't it, love? As you know, it's my way to speak my mind."

Emma looked distressed. "Don't you want Alison to like you?"

"Certainly, Emma. But she must like me the way I am. If she can't, then she and I will never be friends. Now make us a cup of tea, there's a good girl."

Alison came into the kitchen while they were drinking it.

"You look much better," Lottie told her.

"How did I look when I arrived?"

"Like a waif or stray."

Alison smiled. "I'm afraid I felt like one, Aunt Lottie."

Emma brought another cup and saucer from the dresser and poured Alison some tea.

"Two lumps of sugar, please, Emma."

"In this house, we usually put in our own sugar," Lottie said.

For some reason, she did not like to see Emma waiting on Alison. Or the way her plain daughter was looking at her attractive niece—as though Alison were royalty, Lottie thought.

"Stop treating Alison like a queen, Emma!" Lottie said when Emma picked up the spoon to stir Alison's tea. "She's one of the family and I'm sure she doesn't expect special treatment."

"I certainly don't," Alison declared.

But she would receive it from Emma, Lottie sensed, and was inexplicably filled with foreboding. Emma was overly kind and helpful to everyone and never demanded anything for herself, but Lottie had never seen her behave quite this way before. Reverence was the word for it.

But it was time Lottie got down to brass tacks. "I received a telegram from your mother, Alison."

"Oh yes?" Alison said guardedly.

"Would you like to know what it said?"

"There's no need to tell me. I can imagine what it said."

Lottie sipped her tea. "Probably, Alison. But it came as a shock to me."

"I'm sorry," Alison said with contrition.

"For what? Giving me a shock? Or upsetting your mother?"

Alison put down her cup and her expression hardened. "I wouldn't, willingly, do anything to upset or shock anyone. But Mama gave me no option but to do what I did. She didn't hesitate to upset me."

Lottie made a quick decision. "I'd prefer not to hear about it, Alison. What goes on between you and your mother is not this family's business. As we're not in contact with her, we can never hear her side of the story and that isn't fair to her, is it?"

"As you wish, Aunt Lottie. But am I forgiven for unwittingly upsetting you?"

Lottie nodded, dispelling the moment of tension. "And, like I just had to remind Emma, you're one of us, Alison. You must come here whenever you wish. You don't need an invitation." Lottie kissed Alison's cheek. "Always remember, love, that we're here if you need us."

"Why should Alison need us?" Emma asked.

"In a lifetime, who knows?" Lottie said. And with that mother, and living among theatricals, doubly who

knows? she thought. "But I want everything straight between us from the start," she told Alison. "So answer me
this question and we'll say no more about it. If your
mother hadn't sent me the telegram, would you have told
us what you'd done? You see I don't like to have the wool
pulled over my eyes."

"Nor do I," Alison answered. "And the answer to
your question is yes."

"Good, Alison. That's all I wanted to know."

Alison watched her aunt move to the hob to stir something that was simmering there in a big copper saucepan.
Aunt Lottie was a woman you could trust, who would put
her trust in you in return. Alison knew then that she need
never be afraid to tell her anything and that Lottie's
opinions could not be lightly dismissed.

Lottie ladled some of the bubbling liquid from the pan.
"Now come and have your first taste of my chicken soup,
Alison. I'm making it for tomorrow evening, which is
when our Sabbath begins. Usually, I cook the special
meal on Friday, the same day, but this year it is also your
Christmas Day and the family store will be shut. Your
Uncle Lionel, whom you'll soon have the pleasure of
meeting, will be home all day, getting under my feet!"

"Can Alison hang up her stocking here, tonight,
Mam?" Emma asked.

"Why not?" Lottie said while Alison tasted the soup
and pronounced it delicious. "But how will Santa Claus
know Alison is here?" she added with a smile. "We don't
have a Christmas tree in our window, like everyone else
has on our avenue. He must know by now that this is a
Jewish house. He wouldn't expect to find a customer
here."

"I had decided not to hang up my stocking," Alison
informed them, "as I'm not a little girl anymore."

Lottie surveyed Alison's mature figure, and Emma's
dainty, childlike appearance. They were wearing similar
garments; each had on a simple velveteen frock, with
smocking on the bodice. Alison's was bottle-green and

Emma's brown, and both girls wore matching hair ribbons. According to the calendar, they were the same age, but Alison looked years older than Emma. It was difficult for Lottie to believe they had been born on the same day.

"I usually go to church on Christmas morning," Alison said. "It's the only time I do go," she confessed. "On Sunday, our company is always on the move. It's unusual for an engagement to keep us in one place for longer than a week, though we have a lengthier booking just now, in Bournemouth."

"You do have an exciting time, don't you, Alison?" Emma said. "All that traveling around. The only place I've ever been to, apart from Manchester where our synagogue is, is Blackpool. We go there for our holidays."

"I've never had a holiday," Alison told her. "But Papa takes me on the beach sometimes, in the afternoons, when we're playing a seaside town."

Lottie went to the sink to wash the cups and saucers, while the two girls chatted. But it was Alison who did most of the talking.

Words like "backstage" and "greasepaint" were part of Alison's everyday vocabulary. To Emma, listening wide-eyed, they spelt the glamor that went with another world. And Alison herself had about her that aura, Lottie thought, glancing at her. The girl had only to tilt her chin, or gesture with her graceful hands, to command and hold attention.

In appearance, Alison was a Shrager, but with something extra. Lottie had felt it that evening in Horace's dressing room and was aware of it now. Horace, though he was an actor, was not endowed with it. Alison must have inherited that certain indefinable something from the Plantaines. It wasn't surprising that Emma was captivated by her, Lottie thought. Who wouldn't be?

Later, at the supper table, Lottie saw Alison's charm work its magic upon her husband and son. Lionel, who had expressed misgivings about inviting her to stay, was by the end of the meal literally eating out her hand.

He had brought home a box of sugared almonds for the family but, as Christmas Eve was Alison's festival, decided to give them to her. His staff at the store received Christmas gifts from him, so why not his new niece?

"It's only right," he had said to Lottie.

"I agree," Lottie had replied. Her husband was a man of principle and sometimes demonstrated it in unexpected ways.

"If I'd known you'd be here when I got home today, I would've bought you a real Christmas present," he said when he handed Alison the heart-shaped box.

Alison gave him a hug and his family awaited his reaction with interest. Lionel Stein was not the sort of man whom people impulsively hugged.

Lionel's embarrassment was compounded by Alison telling him he was an absolute darling. It was the extravagent language of theatricals, but he could not have known it.

Clara, who was not allowing herself to be captivated by Alison, nudged her brother and giggled.

"What's so funny?" Lionel asked her. "Maybe you don't agree that your dad is an absolute darling?" He got up from his chair and kissed Alison. "Everyone here wishes you a Merry Christmas, love," he told her. "It won't be like a Christian one," he added illogically, "but we'll do our best."

Alison blinked away a tear. Why did she feel like crying, when she was so happy? She opened her Christmas present and offered the sweets to her relatives.

"Pop one into my mouth," Lionel requested with a smile. "Then I won't need any sugar in my tea."

Alison did as she was bid, with a graciousness Lionel's wife and daughters did not fail to notice.

"Shall I pop a sugared almond in your mouth, too, Conrad?" Alison asked mischievously. He had hardly spoken a word, throughout the meal. Nor had Emma—

who seemed unable to take her gaze from Alison's face.

She's so beautiful, Emma was thinking without a shred of envy. It was not Emma's way to aspire to the unattainable. Alison Plantaine was something special and Emma Stein, who would pass unnoticed beside her, was lucky to have her for a cousin. It was enough just to be with Alison and Emma asked for nothing more.

Clara's feelings were rather different. Alison's charisma was for her—though she felt it no less than the others—a threat. Clara Stein was not accustomed to being overshadowed by another girl. Her own appearance was as eye-catching as Alison's.

She watched Alison playfully feed the sugared almond to Conrad. Who do you think you are? The Queen of Sheba? she felt like snapping to Alison. "How long will you be staying with us?" she asked pleasantly, instead. Clara had her father's fair coloring, her mother's tall, shapely figure, and her own brand of calculated guile.

Alison had assessed her in the first few minutes of their acquaintance and had taken an immediate dislike to her. She was aware, too, that Clara did not like her. But between Alison and Emma there was a lovely feeling. It was as though they had always known each other.

"I'd like to stay long enough to get to know my Grandma and Grandpa Shrager," Alison replied to Clara. This, she felt, might not be too easy. They were elderly people and she had gained the impression that her grandfather was a difficult man.

Lottie reaffirmed her hospitality. "You're welcome for as long as you like, Alison," she said, bringing the teapot to the table. "Isn't that right, Lionel?"

"Of course. She's family." Alison had done nothing to deserve the treatment Lionel felt her father's behavior merited. And Lionel found her obvious desire to be one of them touching. But the girl had Jewish blood, albeit diluted, and the warmth that went with it, he had observed.

Though the house had a splendid dining room, the

Steins ate their meals in the kitchen. Emma was getting some tall glasses from the dresser and fixing them into silver holders.

"I'd prefer my tea with milk, if you don't mind," Alison said when her aunt began slicing a lemon.

"Why should I mind? Fetch a cup and saucer for yourself. Tea with milk you don't drink from a glass," Lottie answered.

Her husband raised his eyebrows and her children looked taken aback.

Conrad was the first to speak. "But we had meat for supper, didn't we, Mam?"

"To have milk after meat isn't allowed," Clara declaimed to Alison.

"It's a Jewish dietary law," Emma explained.

Lionel frowned at his wife. "That's right."

Lottie had picked up the teapot to pour, and put it down again.

"It doesn't matter. I'll have lemon," Alison said, wishing she had not created this awkward moment.

"If you want milk in your tea, you can have it." Lottie addressed her husband and children, "Our laws don't apply to Alison, just because she's in our house."

"But in your house, I'd like to do what you do," Alison said with sincerity.

"It isn't necessary to go to such lengths, love. You can please yourself, so long as it doesn't cause us to break any laws. You won't get bacon or ham here. Or butter on your bread, when we're eating the kind of meal we had tonight—"

"I thought you'd forgotten to put the butter on the table," Alison cut in with a smile.

"Dairy foods aren't allowed on the same table as meat," Lottie told her. "But dinner is over now. Fetch the milk jug, Clara."

Clara waited upon nobody, and if she did it wouldn't be Alison! "Emma can fetch it, Mam. I'm tired."

"From walking around town admiring shop windows!" her mother declared scathingly. "While your sister stayed at home to help me."

"Emma doesn't mind doing housework."

"That doesn't mean you have to let her do your share, as well as her own."

"When I'm married I shall have a maid to do my housework," Clara said as if there was no doubt about it.

Lionel brought her down to earth. "First, you have to find a husband."

Sometimes, his elder daughter's ways and ideas scared him. How had he and Lottie produced a girl like Clara, who had such a tip about herself and didn't want to put her hands in water? Lionel pitied the man she would one day marry. The poor chap would find himself donning an apron when he came home from work at night, if he couldn't provide her with a maid.

Lionel's gaze moved to his younger daughter. Now there was a girl who would make someone a good wife. But a man would have to look beneath her plain surface to know it covered a seam of pure gold.

The family had fallen briefly silent, sipping their tea.

Clara bit into a sugared almond. "I don't think I'll have any trouble finding a husband," she said to her father.

Nor did Lionel. But for Emma it would be more difficult. Most young men didn't bother to look below the surface. They fell for the girls who looked like Clara, and if all there was to them was what the eye could see, were married with a child by the time they found out.

Alison glanced at the clock. "The curtain will just be rising on the evening performance," she told her relatives.

"And it will soon be time for you and Emma to go to bed," Lottie informed her.

"But I've slept all day, Aunt Lottie. And I rarely go to bed before midnight," Alison added.

Her cousins could not believe their ears. Though Conrad was eighteen and Clara sixteen, midnight was an unheardof hour for them to retire.

"When I go out with my pal in the evening, I have to be home and in bed by eleven," Conrad told Alison.

"And I'm expected to be tucked up by ten," Clara said with disgust.

"I'm usually asleep by half-past-eight," Emma confided to Alison. "But of course during term time I have to get up early for school."

Emma attended the local high school and, unlike most of the girls and boys with whom she had shared her primary education, would remain there until she was sixteen. Many of those with whom she had gone to primary school were now working in the cotton mills.

"Good old Hulme Grammar School!" Conrad said nostalgically. "Clara and I went there, too," he told Alison.

"I ended my schooldays last summer," Clara said loftily.

"What do you do all day, now you've left school?" Alison asked her.

"That's a good question!" Lottie snorted.

Clara changed the subject. "I never heard of a girl of your age staying up until midnight, Alison."

"Everything is different in the theater," Alison felt constrained to reply.

Her relatives had no doubt that indeed it was. Alison had brought, for a brief spell, the heady aura of her world into the Steins' home. When she was gone, it was this they would attach to her and remember, as an exotic perfume is remembered when its wearer is no longer there.

"I don't mind in the least going to bed early, while I'm here," Alison said with a smile. As she was sharing Emma's room, it would be no hardship.

"I'm glad to see you're not the kind to give me trouble about your bedtime," Lottie chuckled, with a sidelong glance at Clara. "When I said you don't have to do like we do, Alison, I was only referring to religious matters," she added dryly.

"And there's no reason why you shouldn't go to

church tomorrow morning, just because you're staying with us over Christmas. Conrad can walk you there, and call for you when the service is over."

"Sure I will," Conrad said. "And if I ever visit Alison during one of our festivals, I'll expect her to escort me to synagogue!" he joked.

Alison took him seriously. "So long as there is one in the town where we're playing, I certainly will, Conrad."

That's how it should be, Lionel thought while the young people chattered on. Mutual respect for each other's religion. It was a pity everyone didn't have it, but that couldn't be helped. In the case of his kids and Alison, it was essential.

Lionel glanced at Lottie, who had the wisdom to realize it. Religious differences couldn't be hidden away in a cupboard, between youngsters who were blood relatives, or there would be the kind of awkward incident there'd been about Alison wanting milk in her tea after a meat dinner.

Lottie was a clever woman, and had managed to make it seem to her children and her niece that Alison's not being Jewish was incidental to their relationship. Lionel noted the satisfied expression on his wife's face and went to kiss her cheek. He had lived with Lottie long enough to have learned that what she made seem so, eventually became so.

On Christmas morning, Conrad introduced Alison to his friend Albert Battersby, whom they encountered while walking to church.

"Albert and I went to school together," Conrad told Alison. "He works in his father's mill now, like I do in my dad's shop."

Alison gave Albert her white-gloved hand and her charming smile. "How nice to meet you."

"Same here." Albert shifted his mesmerized gaze from Alison's eyes to her tam-o'shanter and resorted to brusque humor to disguise his flustered feelings. "Where does this lass hail from, Conrad? Buckingham Palace?"

Alison's English was devoid of accent or dialect. Like the Steins, Albert had a Lancashire accent. But it wasn't just the way Alison spoke, Albert thought. It was her whole manner.

Alison, conscious that she hailed from nowhere, felt like making a sharp reply. But this sneery boy was her cousin's friend.

"She's from the theater, actually, Albert," Conrad said with a smile.

"What the heck does that mean?" Albert asked bluntly. "Which theater?"

Alison decided that, Conrad's friend or not, it was time to put him in his place. "My cousin used the word in its wider sense, which seems to have been beyond your understanding. He meant that my parents are theatricals," she said with a withering glance.

Albert looked her over. "That doesn't surprise me," he declared, then slipped on the frosty pavement and skidded flat on his back.

"It's those new boots I bought from your shop," he said accusingly to Conrad, after he had picked himself up and dusted himself down.

"I'd say it's more likely that you weren't looking where you were walking, or you'd have seen that patch of ice," Conrad answered with a grin.

Albert's gaze had been glued to Alison from the minute they were introduced.

"Have you hurt yourself?" she asked him.

"That's a silly question if ever I heard one!"

Conrad eyed his friend's stocky figure. "Of course he hasn't hurt himself. He's too well padded."

Albert glared at him. "I can do without being insulted on Christmas Day."

"Then perhaps you would apply that to others," Alison told him.

Conrad laughed. "I'm getting the feeling that you two haven't exactly taken to each other."

Albert had quite another feeling. Looking into Alison's eyes had set his heart thudding. Why was he behaving so badly toward her? He'd taken to her all right! But not to her superior attitude.

He managed to collect himself. "Where are you off to, at this time of morning, Conrad? It's not like you to be up and about early, when you've got a day off work."

"I'm taking my cousin to church."

"Don't be funny!"

"It seems to me that you are the one who keeps being what you call funny," Alison intervened crisply. "Though I don't find you in least amusing. And for your information, Conrad was being serious."

"Who writes your speeches for you?" Albert countered. "And what's this about you going to church?"

"Why shouldn't I? I happen to be a Christian, like you. Though I doubt that our Savior would consider your behavior very Christian," Alison, who was not in the least pious, declared. "Do you usually conduct yourself in this unfortunate manner?"

Albert was rendered momentarily speechless.

"He doesn't, as a matter of fact," Conrad said with a laugh. "It must be the effect you have on him, Alison."

They had reached St. Thomas's Church and paused beside the gate.

"My parents'll think I'm not coming," Albert said to Conrad. "I was still in bed, when they left the house. They always set off to church earlier than necessary."

"Like my parents, when the family goes to synagogue," Conrad answered with a smile. "I'll call back for you," he told Alison.

"If you like, Conrad, I'll walk her back to your house. Save you coming," Albert offered.

Alison gave him a glance that matched the frost on the church steeple. "No thank you, Albert Battersby. I am sure that calling back for me is no trouble to my cousin. And I certainly would not wish to trouble you."

She strode up the church path before Albert found his

tongue, a proud and striking figure in her dark-blue coat and flowing, emerald scarf that toned with her beret.

"She's a right one, isn't she?" Albert said with admiration, though Alison's parting shot had emphasized her hostility. "And how do you come to have a Christian cousin, Conrad?"

Conrad told him about the skeleton in the family cupboard.

"I thought it was only Catholics who made a fuss if their children married outside their faith," Albert said.

"No. It's Jews, as well. Or I'd have had my eye on your sister," Conrad grinned. "Like you've got yours on my cousin Alison," he added slyly.

"What makes you think that?"

"Come off it, Albert! You went goo-goo eyed the moment you set eyes on her. But you'll have to forget it. She's only fourteen."

"I thought she was about your Clara's age," Albert said with surprise. "But she'll be old enough for courting, one of these days—and I don't suppose this will be the last time she'll visit you," he added.

"You're really smitten by her, aren't you?" Conrad laughed.

"But she's not very smitten by me," Albert said ruefully, hurrying away to join the other latecomers heading into the church.

Alison had halted beside the porch, where the vicar was greeting his congregation as they entered. She knew he would welcome her, too, though she was a stranger. She had rarely been to any church twice, but in the past had always, at the Christmas morning service, had the company of her mother and her Plantaine grandparents.

Oliver never went with them. Nor did her father, and she had not known why until she learned he was a Jew. Why her uncle chose not to go was still a mystery to her. Was Uncle Oliver so ashamed of being a drunkard that he could not face God?

The vicar cut into Alison's thoughts. "Happy Christmas, my dear," he said shaking hands with her.

Alison gave him the reply she had heard Gregory Plantaine make on Christmas morning, year in, year out. "I am not one of your flock, but thank you for welcoming me."

"We are all Christ's flock," the minister answered kindly. "It is He who welcomes you, my child."

It's true, Alison thought as she entered the church. There were no strangers in His house. And today it was full to overflowing.

She stood halfway down the aisle, looking for a vacant seat. There was one near to Albert Battersby, who had entered behind her and was wedged between a very stout couple on a rear pew. They must be his parents, Alison surmised before dismissing her cousin's obnoxious friend from her mind. She wasn't going to share a pew with him!

"We can make room fer thee here, luv," an elderly man occupying an aisle seat said, tugging her sleeve.

He slid along the polished bench, squashing his wife, who was beside him, in the process.

The old lady fingered the feather in her hat, to make sure it was still intact. "Me husband can always make room for a pretty lass," she whispered to Alison. "That once included me, luv."

"Aye. In t'days when t'pretty lasses still had an eye fer me," her husband laughed with her.

Alison had often noticed that Lancashire folk didn't mind making jokes at their own expense, and thought again how warm-hearted they were. She was alone in their midst on this family day, but did not feel lonely. And it struck her that here, with wintry sunshine filtering through the stained glass onto the friendly congregation, was embodied the true meaning of Christianity.

There was a sprinkling of khaki among the worshippers, which did not allow one to forget that England was at war. But a sense of perfect peace was Alison's overriding emotion, as she knelt with her fellow Christians.

It was a feeling she had not previously experienced in church, or anywhere else, and perhaps never would again. Part of the maturing experience this trip north, alone, was for her. All her sensations were heightened. And, since she set forth on her journey, there had been times when she seemed to have stepped outside herself and was observing Alison Plantaine in this or that situation.

She had been momentarily affected that way last night, while feeding the sugared almond to her Uncle Lionel. It had happened, too, during the meal, when they were all seated together around the table.

It was not surprising that Alison was assailed by moments of unreality. This time last year, she had not known the Steins existed. Her brief meeting with Lottie had not, afterwards, seemed real. And her correspondence with Emma, charged with secrecy, had not dispelled the fairytale aura still surrounding the whole matter.

It would be some time before Alison's paternal relatives would entirely lose for her that quality, and slot firmly into the place they would hereafter occupy in her life.

But she was not thinking of them, as she stood in church that wartime morning, singing "Oh, Come All Ye Faithful," in an atmosphere of—incongruously—Man's goodwill toward his fellow men.

TWELVE

On arriving in London, Oliver had taken a taxi to the West End. Here, he thought, was where he would have been, if he had had the guts to break with family tradition.

Oliver was, and always had been, an outstanding actor and had not gone unnoticed by managers on the lookout for talent. How different his life might have been, if he had removed himself from his father's presence, which was a constant reminder that, in every way except acting, Oliver had let Gregory down.

He had paused in Piccadilly Circus to doff his hat, mockingly, to the statue of Eros; the god of love had not smiled upon Oliver Plantaine. And what is life, without love? Oliver thought. Was it not that, above all else, that was missing from his?

But why was he standing there, amid the Christmas bustle, taking stock of himself and his lot? Because today was, for him, a day of reckoning. The final disenchantment with his family had, this morning, been sealed by his sister's words. And the taste of total disillusionment remained bitter in his mouth.

He went for a stroll around theaterland and noted that, despite the war, business seemed to be booming. People were queuing at the box offices, and there was a fine selection of seasonal plays: *Alice in Wonderland* at the Savoy, *David Copperfield* at His Majesty's Theatre, *Peter Pan* at the Duke of York's Theatre, and *Charley's Aunt* at the Prince of Wales.

Oliver almost bought a ticket for the *Charley's Aunt* matinée—he could use a few laughs!—then decided against it and drifted toward Regent Street with the parcel-laden crowd. Where was he going to? Nowhere. But hadn't that been his destination all his life? His intention of seeking out some old acquaintances had suddenly lost its charm. And revenge its sweetness.

He needed a drink, but where was the nearest pub? Oliver knew the provinces like the palm of his hand, but had rarely spent time in the capital.

Someone caught his arm and halted him.

"Mr. Morton!" Oliver exclaimed.

"How nice to see you, Oliver."

"How are you? I thought you were in America."

"I managed to get there and back. War or no war."

Oliver did not ask how. Maxwell Morton was a wealthy impresario and had a reputation for being able to move mountains.

"You almost walked past me," Morton accused him.

Oliver eyed the greenery Morton was carrying. "One doesn't expect to encounter Maxwell Morton strolling amid the *hoi polloi,* clutching a bouquet of holly and mistletoe!" he said with a smile.

"Or Oliver Plantaine in London, on Christmas Eve, when the Plantaine Players are presenting *Twelfth Night* in Bournemouth," Morton countered.

Nothing went on in the English theater that Morton did not know about.

"Me with the holly and mistletoe is no mystery," he

said. "I'm giving a party tonight and was sufficiently imbued with the Christmas spirit to buy some. But what are
you doing here?"

"It's a long story," Oliver replied cryptically, "and I
don't propose to tell it."

The crowds were jostling around them and Morton
noted Oliver's wan expression. "Come and have lunch-
eon with me, Oliver. Everyone I know is busy today and
I dislike eating alone."

"I'll take you to the Ivy," Morton went on. "The food
is very good there."

And, Oliver thought with a dry smile, it was a place to
which theater people went to see and be seen.

"You don't have to join me if you have something better to do," Morton added as an afterthought.

"If I had, I should have declined," Oliver answered.

"But there are plenty who wouldn't!"

The sycophancy of the profession was well-known, as
was an impresario's power to make and break careers.
Men like Morton, and, to a lesser degree, Gregory Plantaine, were cultivated and courted by those seeking to
capitalize on their friendship, Oliver reflected.

But Oliver wanted nothing from Maxwell Morton and
Morton knew it. Unlike the hopeful young actresses with
whom he was known to surround himself, Oliver
thought. Morton was not entitled to be cynical about
those who sought to use him. He did his share of using.

They were ushered to a table by a deferential head-
waiter. Those who turned to look at Morton were acknowledged with a wave or a smile. In his own realm, the
impresario was a prince. Though not a handsome one,
Oliver thought, surveying his host while Morton perused
the menu. On the contrary.

Though he was not yet forty, Morton's was the kind of
face that had never looked young. His heavy-lidded gray
eyes lent it a somnolent appearance that belied the
shrewd brain in his leonine head. His physique was that
of a powerfully built man and it came as a surprise, to

those who saw him for the first time seated, when he stood up. His was not the kind of torso that went with short legs.

But his personality dwarfed everyone around him, Oliver had to admit, including Gregory Plantaine, and that was saying something.

"How is your dear father?" Morton inquired telepathically.

The adjective was not, in this case, an insincere superlative. Many people in the business harbored affection for Gregory, and a gruding admiration for his foolhardy idealism.

"The same as ever," Oliver answered enigmatically.

Morton smiled and sighed simultaneously. "One doesn't expect Gregory Plantaine to change. I don't believe I've seen him since that time I ran into you all at Euston station. I remember thinking what a delightful family the Plantaines are. And how remarkable it is that the company has remained intact for—how many generations is it, Oliver?"

"I'm afraid I've lost count," Oliver replied stiffly. He hadn't come to London to be reminded of Plantaine tradition!

"There was a child with your party," Morton recalled.

"My niece, Alison."

"Really? She didn't look like a Plantaine."

Hors d'oeuvres were set before them and Morton squeezed lemon juice on to his smoked salmon.

"How was Broadway?" Oliver asked him.

"Booming."

"It seems to be the same in the West End, I observed."

"The war doldrums are wearing off," Morton declared. "I've arranged to transfer one or two American plays to London," he revealed.

"Wasn't there an American play on recently at the Prince of Wales?"

"Broadway Jones," Morton supplied. "From the Cohan Theater in New York." He helped himself to a

slice of brown bread and butter. "I'm now thinking of staging a musical comedy, Oliver. In wartime, people want to be cheered up when they go to the theater."

"I have the feeling we're in for a period of theatrical escapism," Oliver said.

"But your father won't be part of it," Morton replied with a wry smile. He forked a slice of hardboiled egg into his mouth, chewed and swallowed it. "Hasn't Gregory given a thought to offering a contemporary repertoire?"

"Why would he do so now? When he never has before."

"If he doesn't, Oliver, I doubt that your company will survive the war. There'll always be a place for Shakespeare in the English theater—that goes without saying. The Old Vic has staged *The Shrew* this year, and the Savoy, *The Dream*—"

"That's on now at the Coronet Theatre," Oliver interrupted.

"But contemporary work is dominating the scene," Morton went on. "Shaw, and Galsworthy, and that doctor-fellow who's turned himself into a playwright, Somerset Maugham, are, I venture to predict, writing the classics of tomorrow. But your father is turning a blind eye to them, isn't he?"

Oliver could not deny it.

"He may live to regret it," Morton prophesied. "Others will grasp the opportunity to tour contemporary plays on a big scale, or try them out in the provinces. And that includes me."

"I have a distant recollection of your own father talking this way about melodrama," Oliver said while they were consuming Brown Windsor Soup.

Morton smiled. "Probably."

"But apart from Miss Ruby May's company's continued attempts to keep it alive, melodrama has had its day."

"I heard when I got back from America that Miss May's company has folded," Morton said. "It seems that even that tenacious lady has seen the wisdom of ceasing to flog the dead horse! Which bears out my late father's belief that in the theater, fashions and styles come and go and should be capitalized upon while the going is good."

"But the Bard's work is timeless and endures forever," Oliver replied.

"I have already said that," Morton declared impatiently. "But a sensible man of the theater, which regrettably Gregory Plantaine isn't, knows that audiences are fickle, and trends are not to be ignored."

He signaled to the waiter to refill Oliver's wine glass. "Do you share your father's ideas and ideals, Oliver?"

Was sharing, in that sense, the same as accepting? Oliver was forced to ask himself. The answer eluded him. All he was sure of was that he had accepted his father's ideas and ideals. Blindly.

"Presumably you do," Morton said when he received no reply to his question, "or you would not have resisted all attempts to lure you away from the Plantaine Players. My father couldn't have been the only one to offer you a part in a London production. And if you had taken it, you would by now, have been at the top of the tree."

"Possibly."

"There's no doubt about it, Oliver, or my father wouldn't have wanted you. His instinct about actors was never wrong. And he rarely made a mistake about a play. He had a feel for what's right for the times—and for what the public wants."

It had been said of the late Henry Morton that almost everything he touched turned to gold. He had arrived in London from Canada before the turn of the century, when the impresario function was monopolized by actor-managers like Gregory Plantaine.

Few businessmen would, in those days, have sunk their capital into the precarious enterprises of the theater world, or have thought themselves competent to judge and purvey its offerings. Initially, Henry Morton was considered an upstart and his success not expected to last.

But he had gone from strength to strength and had left his son a firm foundation upon which to build. Maxwell Morton was not yet thirty when he stepped into his father's shoes. They had proved a perfect fit.

Morton put down his soup spoon. "What would you say, Oliver, if I offered you a part now?"

Any desire Oliver had harbored to reach the heights of fame was long gone. And, despite everything, the need to redeem himself in his father's eyes was still there; a nagging ache inside him. He drank some wine to deaden it and put a bright smile on his face. Who can climb to the top of a tree with a bottle in their hand? he thought sardonically.

"No thanks, Mr. Morton," he said.

Morton changed the subject. "How long are you staying in town?"

"I'm not sure," Oliver replied. He would let the family stew, wondering where he was, until his cash ran out.

Morton watched him crumble the bread on his side plate. There was, today, something pathetic about Oliver Plantaine, he thought, while the waiter served them with large helpings of saddle-of-mutton.

But Morton did not know Oliver well enough to delve deeper than he already had—though he would like to help him. Oliver wasn't just any actor, but a member of one of England's distinguished theatrical families. Naive and improvident the Plantaines might be, but artistically, their work was renowned.

Compared to them, Morton was a Philistine and knew it. Descended from a long line of lumberjacks, he thought dryly. But like his father, who had turned wood into money, he respected what he himself could never be.

Morton helped himself to some red-currant jelly and dismissed the mystery of Oliver's forlorn presence in London from his mind. Oliver had probably fallen out with Gregory and, as the Americans would say, taken off.

Though family quarrels did not fit Morton's picture of the Plantaines.

"If you're not otherwise occupied, do come to my Christmas Eve shindig, Oliver," Morton said with a friendly smile.

Oliver took the card Morton handed him. "It's kind of you to ask me," he said noncommittally. "And to give me lunch." But Oliver had no intention of going to Morton's party.

By eleven o'clock that night he had changed his mind. He had spent the afternoon trying and failing to contact old acquaintances, and the evening pub-crawling, alone.

He was still alone—though on the streets of Soho, ladies of the town, and a sailor on leave, had invited him to go home with them—with the heightened loneliness a solitary soul feels in a crowd. Christmas revelers were milling around him and Oliver had discovered tonight, as many had before him, that a capital city, throbbing with life, can prove a lonely place to be.

Why aren't I drunk? he asked himself, pausing beside the statue of Eros for the second time that day. He had consumed a good deal of whisky, but it had not drowned his sorrows, or numbed his mind.

Instead of the addled jumble of thoughts that usually preceded his final, drunken oblivion, his brain had been sharpened to a greater clarity, and was telling him to take a cab to Morton's party.

For liquor to have the opposite effect upon him from that which he sought was a new experience for Oliver. Was he becoming immune to alcohol? Perhaps the time had come when it affected his liver more than his brain, he thought with grim humor on the way to Mayfair.

It was almost midnight but the party in Morton's flat was just beginning. Many of the guests had come direct from the theaters at which they were appearing.

A manservant let Oliver in and took his coat and hat. Morton was a bachelor—and not the kind who wanted to be mothered by a lady housekeeper, Oliver reflected.

Nor would Morton have found it easy to find one willing to lend herself to his way of life. The atmosphere in the spacious drawing room was thick with cigar and cigarette smoke. Plates of half-eaten food littered the occasional tables, and voluptuous young women in low-cut evening gowns were semi-reclining on sofas, or leaning against the walls, clutching goblets of champagne.

Oliver had heard about the theatrical parties in the capital, but had not been prepared for anything quite like this. His mother and sister would swoon with shock, Oliver thought as his eye fell upon an armchair in which a young girl was snuggled on a gentleman's lap.

"Oliver, darling! What are you doing here?" a lady in a chartreuse gown shrieked, detaching herself from a noisy group and pouncing upon him. She kissed his cheek rapturously. "I am in the new Galsworthy play," she went on without waiting for Oliver to answer her question. "We're in rehearsal now."

Oliver had not known there was a new Galsworthy play. Nor did he know who the lady was. He had begun to feel slightly befuddled; the liquor must be having a delayed effect upon him. Or was it the champagne he was drinking now?

The actress patted her hennaed hair and regarded Oliver fondly. "How is dearest Hermione?" she inquired, leading him to sit beside her on a gold, velvet couch.

Oliver registered with amusement that the blue sofa beside which they had been standing, would have clashed with her dress.

"The last time I saw you was when I played Bianca in your father's production of *The Shrew*," she reminisced.

And his sister had not been "dearest Hermione" to her then, Oliver recalled as she and that production returned to his memory. She had coveted the part of Katherina, which had gone to Hermione, and had lost no opportunity to make Hermione suffer for it.

"It's nice to see you again, Daphne," Oliver said, being as insincere as she was. "And you're looking as young

and lovely as ever," he lied, surveying her over-pow-
dered face, and the dyed hair which had not helped him
to place her.

"Thank you for saying so, darling. And where are the
dear old Plantaine Players now?"

Again, she did not wait for Oliver's reply and he remembered that she never had, but was the kind who
posed a question purely as a preface to talking about
themselves.

"When one is ensconced in the capital, as I am," she
was saying, "one hasn't time to remember one's early
struggles. Of course, the war has brought us all up short,
Oliver darling. But we are getting into our stride again. It
will take more than the Kaiser to close London's theaters."

"That goes for the provinces, too," Oliver informed
her.

"Does it, my darling?" she said vaguely, as though the
provinces had, for her, been removed from the map.
"Did you hear that Ruby May has retired?" she asked
irrelevantly.

"I heard her company had folded."

"Which doesn't mean Miss May has retired," said a
dapper gentleman seated beside them.

"She's been left pots of money by that old man she was
married to," Daphne put in. "She can take it easy for the
rest of her life. I heard that when he was alive, he kept a
tight hold on the purse strings."

"And I have it on good authority that she has bought
a house in London and is temporarily resting," the dapper man proclaimed. "Before resuming her career," he
added.

"From what I know of the melodrama queen, she
won't wear her widow's weed's for long," Daphne declared cattily.

"On the contrary, she's taken her husband's death
very badly. Her children told me so, this evening. They're
here—and talking to our host at present, I see."

Oliver, who was growing bored with the topic, grasped the excuse to escape, "It's time I had a word with our host, too," he said and went to where Morton was chatting with a young boy and girl.

"Come and have some supper, Oliver," Morton said gesturing toward the lavish buffet, beside which he and the two youngsters were standing. "And meet the terrible twins!" he joked.

"I'm Luke Appleby and this is my sister, Lucy," the boy said to Oliver. "And of course there is no need for us to be told who you are, sir."

Lucy gave Oliver a sweet smile. "Who wouldn't recognise Oliver Plantaine?" She looked at Morton and pouted appealingly. "Do you really think Luke and I are terrible, Mr. Morton?"

"Certainly," he teased her.

"We deserve it," Luke said contritely.

Morton laughed. "But as it's Christmas, I've forgiven you." He winked at Oliver. "They dared each other to gatecrash my party!"

Oliver was captivated by the impish smiles the twins gave him, and by their tawny-haired, green-eyed beauty. They looked like a couple of sea sprites. But there was an air of vulnerable innocence about them.

"Anyway," Morton declared, "I've decided not to send them packing, Oliver."

"That's lovely of you, Mr. Morton," Lucy said.

"Didn't you expect me to let you stay?"

"We thought you wouldn't notice us, among all your guests."

Oliver was still surveying them. Their appearance was so arresting, they would always be noticed.

"I'll leave you to keep your eye on them, Oliver," Morton chuckled, going to mingle with his other guests.

"It was worth gatecrashing the party, just to meet you, Mr. Plantaine," Lucy said. "Don't you agree, Luke?"

"I certainly do."

"Thank you for those kind words, children," Oliver

replied with a laugh. But he was moved by the respect they were according him.

"We'll excuse you for calling us children," Lucy said.

Oliver smiled. "I keep forgetting that young people are in a great hurry to grow up."

"Everyone thinks we're younger than we are," Luke complained.

"And how old are you?"

"Sixteen," they chorused.

"We're ready to begin our acting careers," Luke added.

"And how shall you go about getting started?"

"That depends upon our mother," Lucy said.

Oliver remained glued to them, oblivious to everyone else in the room. They were the most engaging pair he had ever met.

Pair was the right word, he thought, watching them fill themselves with sherry trifle and mince pies. They were like a double act. Lucy would begin describing something, or recalling an incident, then stop midway and allow Luke to finish it. Or the other way round. And often they would answer a question in unison, as though they were not just twins, but shared the same mind.

"It's time we went home, Lucy," Luke said reluctantly.

"And tucked ourselves up in bed."

"Before Mother sends the police to look for us."

Oliver glanced at the carriage clock on the elegant, Adam mantelpiece and saw that it was one-thirty. The twins were such fascinating company, he had not noticed the time slipping by.

"You must share my cab," he told them. He might as well leave now, too, though he had no idea where he would spend the night.

Luke and Lucy placed themselves one on either side of him, in the taxi. Oliver allowed himself briefly to fantasize that they were his children and the three of them were returning home together. He was not old enough to be their father, but did not allow arithmetic to impinge upon his imaginings, which did not include the presence of a wife.

By the time the cab pulled up outside the twins' Kensington home, Oliver's fantasy had crystallized into a yearning for the togetherness to go on forever. It must be the champagne! For whatever reason, he was drawn to Luke and Lucy in a way that made him loath to part from them.

"Mother is still up," Luke said, noting a light in the front window.

"Do come and meet her, Mr. Plantaine," Lucy begged.

"I'd be delighted to," Oliver said rashly. Were it not for her lovable children, he would have run a mile in the opposite direction to avoid meeting the notorious Ruby May.

He mounted the several steps to the front door, with the twins still flanking him. They had linked his arms—bless them!—as though they feared he might turn tail and leave them.

"You've always been mother's idol, Mr. Plantaine," Lucy revealed as they entered the house.

"But please don't tell her we've given away her secret," Luke added, shutting the door on the quiet square.

The hall was dimly lit and dominated by a somber oil painting. An aspidistra on a tall pedestal cast a grotesque shadow on the wall. Beside it stood a brass gong that looked big enough to sound the knell of doom.

For a moment, Oliver had an inexplicable feeling that he was trapped. Like the fly in the spider's parlor. He had definitely drunk too much champagne! Or was it his preconceived impression of Ruby May?

Then he saw her standing in the drawing-room doorway, wearing a black satin robe that enhanced the spider-and-fly notion.

"We've brought you a lovely Christmas present, Mother," the twins chorused. "Mr. Oliver Plantaine."

Oliver felt as though he were being served up on a plate.

Ruby came to greet her guest. "Welcome to my home, Mr. Plantaine," she said as though Oliver's appearance at this hour was not out of the ordinary. "My children are never happier than when they are able to give me a treat."

Oliver was briefly tongue-tied in the woman's powerful presence. She exuded an earth-mother quality he had not encountered in any other woman. Her eyes were green, like her children's, but the resemblance ended there. The twins were small and slight. Ruby was statuesque; taller than Oliver and with a bosom like a comforting pillow.

"Happy Christmas, Miss May," Oliver said, finding his voice. He could think of nothing else to say.

"Oh I'm sure it will be," she replied. "Take Mr. Plantaine's hat and coat," she said to the twins, "then you can go and make us all some cocoa."

She led Oliver into the drawing room, where the sinister overtones he had felt on entering the house were dispelled by seasonal good cheer. A bright fire was burning in the grate and two vases of chrysanthemums combined with the holly on the mantelpiece to lend a festive air.

"Your children are adorable," Oliver said.

Ruby smiled maternally. "I agree." She sat down by the fire. "Sit anywhere you wish, Mr. Plantaine. Make yourself at home. I'm not a formal person."

Oliver took the chair on the other side of the hearth. "Or you wouldn't be entertaining me at two a.m." he said with a polite smile. "I mustn't stay too long."

Ruby stretched her slippered feet to warm them by the blaze. "Why not? Is somebody waiting for you?"

"On the contrary."

"And what does that mean, Oliver? May I call you Oliver?"

"Why not?"

"And you must call me Ruby."

"Thank you. And the answer to your question is that I am in London alone."

"Poor you. Nobody should be alone at Christmas," she declared.

"Or at any other time," Oliver heard himself say.

"I know what you mean," Ruby agreed with a sigh.

Did she? Oliver wondered. He could sense her sympathy and felt a rapport with her. As though she somehow divined his predicament, though she knew no details. Ruby May was not at all as Oliver had expected her to be.

There was no sign of the hard, formidable creature everyone said she was. Nor of the tarty, calculating one that went with her melodrama-queen image. The strident red hair Oliver remembered from when he once glimpsed her from afar, had been toned down to auburn.

Oliver observed her placid face in the firelight. They had fallen silent, yet he was at ease with her. The black satin wrapper seemed incongruous on someone so motherly. She was a comfortable and comforting person to be with. A nice lady, he decided.

Oliver would not have thought so had he been able to read Ruby's thoughts.

If she had known the kids would bring home Oliver Plantaine, she would have put on her white lace robe and doused herself with lavender water, instead of exotic scent. Ruby eyed Oliver surreptitiously. Ought she to offer him a drink? She didn't want him to think her improper. If the twins had been escorted home by Maxwell Morton, she would have known exactly what to do. But Oliver Plantaine was a very different kettle of fish. Hadn't she once heard that he was gay?

If he was, there was nothing about him that gave it away. He was no caveman, Ruby thought, eyeing him again. But nor was he a fop. It was possible, she supposed, that Oliver was one of the kind who liked sex both ways.

"Where are you staying while you're in town?" she

asked him pleasantly. "I do hope you won't find yourself locked out."

Oliver impaled himself upon the carefully dangled hook. "I made no arrangements to stay anywhere, Ruby."

"Then you must stay here, with us."

"I came to London on the spur of the moment," Oliver divulged after he had thanked her for her kindness. "And cut the performance, I'm afraid," he added with bravado.

"You naughty boy! But I'm sure you had a good reason."

"Oh yes."

"You can tell me all about it, when we get to know each other better," Ruby said, implying that there was no doubt that they would.

The twins entered with the cocoa.

"Has Mother told you about her lifelong ambition, Mr. Plantaine?" Luke asked.

"That she's always wanted to be a classical actress?" Lucy added.

Ruby tried not to look surprised.

Lucy handed round the steaming cups and gave Oliver a winning smile. "Wouldn't Mother be marvelous as Lady Macbeth, Mr. Plantaine?"

"Or as Portia?" Luke suggested.

"I wouldn't mind playing one of the Merry Wives of Windsor," Ruby said modestly.

The twins giggled. "That would be perfect casting," they said in unison.

Oliver was impelled to join in the game—a game was what it felt like. As if they were playing Happy Families, grouped around the glowing embers in the grate, cozily drinking cocoa from homely, willow-patterned cups.

"And Luke would make a delightful Ariel," he declared, surveying the slender boy who was seated cross-legged at his mother's feet.

Lucy had curled herself on the rug beside Oliver. "What about me?" she pouted. "I feel left out."

Oliver fondled her silky hair, as though she were a kitten. "You, my dear, need never feel left out."

"I should like to play Juliet," she told him.

"And I Romeo," Luke declared.

"I don't doubt that it will come to pass, one day," Oliver said, thinking how ideally suited they were to play the star-crossed lovers.

"With the Plantaine Players?" they chorused.

"Why not?" said Oliver recklessly.

"You mustn't let my children badger you, Oliver," Ruby said with a smile. "Once they get an idea in their little heads, there's no stopping them."

"I find them very refreshing," Oliver assured her. He would happily submit to what Ruby called their badgering for the rest of his life.

The clock on the mantelpiece chimed five.

"Good gracious me!" Ruby exclaimed. "It will soon be time for breakfast. And none of us has been to bed."

Luke shrugged. "Who wants to sleep?"

"When they're having such a lovely time?" Lucy added.

Oliver smiled his agreement. "But perhaps your mother is tired?"

"Not in the least," Ruby said, though she was exhausted. "Let's have breakfast now, shall we? And rest later, while the turkey is cooking."

She rose from her chair and led the way to the kitchen. "Nobody lives by the clock in my household," she told Oliver. "I don't believe in rules and regulations, outside the theater."

If Oliver had been more worldly, he would have considered this a somewhat odd household; that a mother who allowed her children to go uninvited to parties, and bring home strangers in the early hours, could not be quite what she seemed. And that the children were perhaps not the innocents they appeared to be.

A sophisticated man's conclusion might have been that he was being set up. But Oliver was as naive as the rest of the Plantaines, his debonair manner no more than a veneer. Nothing in his experience had prepared him for what was now happening to him. His sporadic homosexual encounters had brought him no joy; the accompanying shame had prohibited it. And the lack of love in his life had rendered him vulnerable.

Ruby had tied an apron around her waist and the twins were laying the table.

"How do you like your eggs, Oliver? Fried or scrambled? she asked.

"Fried, please."

She gave him an intimate smile. "I'll remember that."

Luke cut some bread and sat down by the fire to make toast.

Lucy brewed a pot of tea and poured a cup for Oliver. "Sugar, Mr. Plantaine?"

"No thanks."

She smiled at Ruby. "We must remember that, Mother, too."

Oliver seated himself at the head of the table. He was still playing Happy Families.

"It's lovely to have a man in the house again," Ruby declared dishing up the breakfast and seating herself opposite Oliver.

"Mother's been very lonely since our father died," Luke said solemnly.

"And sad," Lucy sighed.

Ruby found her handkerchief and wiped away a manufactured tear—they did not call her the melodrama-queen for nothing.

"You must have been extremely young when you married," Oliver said to her. She did not look old enough to be the twins' mother.

Ruby put away the handkerchief and warmed him with a smile that sufficed for a reply. In fact, she had married at twenty and had not expected to have to wait until she was thirty-six before becoming a wealthy widow. Or that a frail husband, well into his sixties, would impregnate her.

"Father wouldn't want you to be lonely and upset," Lucy told her.

"That's what we keep telling her," Luke said to Oliver.

"I can't help it. I miss having someone who understands me." Ruby got out her handkerchief again and dabbed her eyes, delicately. "Do you know what I mean, Oliver?"

"Only too well," he replied.

That afternoon, Oliver went for a stroll in Kensington Gardens with the twins. Ruby stayed at home, to cook the festive dinner.

"This is like having a daddy again," Lucy said taking Oliver's arm.

The trusting look she gave him went straight to his heart.

"Did your father ever bring you here?" he asked as they passed a whiskered gentleman flanked by two little girls in knitted mufflers and hats.

"We came here with him once," Luke answered.

"When we accompanied him to London, to see a physician," Lucy supplied.

They had stayed at a small hotel near to the gardens, and had taken their father for an airing in his bathchair.

Oliver patted Lucy's hand, then put a comforting arm around Luke's shoulders. He was not to know that the only emotion their father's death had stirred in them was relief.

The gardens were almost deserted today, though the weather was crisp and clear. Most people remained by their firesides on Christmas afternoon, Oliver reflected. The twins had fallen silent. Were they thinking of their fatherless plight? Christmas was a family time.

"How sad it is that your father was not spared to see you begin your stage careers," he said to demonstrate his sympathy for them. "I'm sure he would have been very proud of you."

The twins remained discreetly silent. If William Appleby had lived, he would not have allowed them to be actors. He had not looked kindly on them being pictured with their mother in the newspapers and had done his best to isolate them from her world.

Appleby had hoped that Ruby would abandon her career when Luke and Lucy were born. But he had not broken his betrothal promise to her that he would never demand that she do so. Nor had he refused her money to finance her own company, which he had considered less demeaning than having her work for someone else.

Ruby's husband had been a man of his word, and a conscientious father. Ruby's wish to take the twins on tour with her had met with his firm refusal. When they were very young, he had employed a nanny to care for them. Later, he had sent Luke away to school, thereby separating them from each other, as well as from their mother. Appleby was a childless widower when he married Ruby, and had retained the home in Epping in which he had lived with his first wife. Lucy had been brought up there, under the watchful eye of a vinegary housekeeper, who had been with Appleby for years, and whom Ruby could not persuade him to replace with a kindlier soul.

Their father's death had put an end to the twins' bleak childhood and had reunited them with their famous mother. They had always accepted that Ruby's professional commitments must come first and had never resented her for putting them second. It was their father whom they blamed for their unhappiness.

Under the circumstances, they did not mourn him. He had never kissed and cuddled and fussed over them, as Ruby did. Nor had he allowed them the freedom they were now able to take for granted. They had toured with Ruby for a year before the disbandment of her company, and felt more at home in the theater than they ever had in their father's house.

Theater was in their blood, as it was in their mother's.
And they did not like the turn things had taken, when
Ruby decided to bring them to London and set up house.

As Maxwell Morton had surmised, she had accepted
that there was no future in melodrama, but had as yet
made no alternative plans. Offers had been made to her
to branch out into music hall, to which her larger-than-
life talents were eminently suited. But their mother's
veering in that direction would not have suited Luke and
Lucy. They saw their own future in the straight theater
and needed Ruby as a stepping stone to help them get
there.

They had urged her to take a long rest and Ruby had
found their concern for her touching. She had yet to learn
the extent of their cunning.

The twins knew that a woman as attractive as Ruby—
doubly so, as she was now wealthy in her own right—was
bound to remarry. They would have preferred not to
have a stepfather, but as that eventuality seemed inevitable, wanted to be sure of acquiring one who would not
cramp their style as William Appleby had. The second
proviso was that he should be a man of the theater, and,
too, one who could help get them where they wanted to
be.

They had trespassed on Morton's party with their
mother's easy-going permission and had told Ruby, jokingly, that they were going there to find her a new husband. She had not taken them seriously, but had amused
herself by imagining them being escorted home by Morton, and had put on her most glamorous wrapper just in
case. Ruby knew she could not succeed in capturing the
impresario; too many had tried and failed. But an affair
with him could prove useful and was not an unpleasant
prospect.

She could not believe her eyes when the twins returned with Oliver Plantaine.

Luke and Lucy had had to pinch each other to believe
their good fortune. Their captivating charm worked with

everyone, but Oliver was positively putty in their hands. The ideal candidate with a bonus.

They were strolling on the western shore of the Long Water and paused to admire the recently erected sculpture of Peter Pan.

"When I was last in Kensington Gardens the statue wasn't here," Oliver said.

"And Lucy and I have not seen the play yet," Luke said.

"Then I must take you to see it," Oliver answered. "It's on at the Duke of York's now, I think."

Lucy gave him a rapturous smile, then addressed her brother. "Imagine that, Luke! You and me going to the theater with Oliver Plantaine."

Oliver was watching some small boys playing on the frost-rimed grass with a shiny red ball, watched over by a gray-garbed nanny.

"I've always liked children," he remarked wistfully.

Lucy exchanged a glance with Luke. "What a pity you have none of your own, Mr. Plantaine."

"Someone who had you for their father would be very lucky," Luke declared.

Oliver linked their arms and continued along the path, unaware that the angels at his sides were devils in disguise.

"We shall miss you, when you are gone," Lucy sighed.

"Will you?"

They nodded.

"So will Mother," Luke thought it opportune to add.

Oliver glanced down with affection at the two tawny heads, upon which wintry sunlight was beaming through the trees.

"How long shall you stay with us?" Luke asked him.

"I can't bear to think of your leaving us," Lucy said with a catch in her voice. "It's as if we've always known you."

They were still working to win him. But Oliver was already won.

He laughed recklessly. "I shall probably stay until I am sent packing."

THIRTEEN

Alison remained with her Jewish relatives for a week. During that time, her antipathy to Clara had deepened. She could not bear to witness Clara's treatment of Emma, nor understand why Emma allowed it.

"If I had a sister like yours, I wouldn't let her get away with the things she does," Alison told Emma on the last night of her stay.

They were in Emma's room, preparing for bed, and Emma paused with her hairbrush in her hand. "With you it would never happen, Alison."

"I'm not sure what you mean."

"That nobody would think of behaving that way with you." Emma smiled and shrugged. "But I'm the sort of person—well, everyone knows they can get away with things, with me."

"If you're going to go through life thinking that about yourself, I'm sorry for you," Alison declared with feeling. "You'll be taken advantage of, Emma."

"I can't change the way I am, Alison."

"Have you tried to?"

"What's the use of trying? I know it can't be done. Can we talk about something else, please?"

"What for instance?" Alison asked, slipping her nightgown over her head and buttoning it.

"You," Emma answered. "You're a much more interesting subject than me." She picked up Alison's brush. "Sit down at the dressing table. I'll brush your hair for you."

Alison submitted to her cousin's ministrations. She had at first protested when Emma wanted to do things for her, but Emma was never happier than when she was doing things for people. For Alison especially.

"What shall you do when you leave school?" Alison asked her. "And don't tell me that isn't an interesting subject!"

"I still have two years left."

"But oughtn't you to be thinking about it, Emma? So you'll have made up your mind, when the time comes."

Emma shrugged and swept Alison's mane of hair to the top of her head.

"What are you doing that for?"

Emma studied Alison's reflection in the mirror. "To see what you'll look like, when you wear your hair up. And you're going to look even more beautiful, Alison," she said, letting the silky locks fall.

Alison was taken aback. She had never before been told she was beautiful. Nor did she see beauty when she looked in the mirror. Alison's conception of beauty was of her mother's fragile loveliness.

"I expect people pay you compliments all the time," Emma said.

"They don't, as a matter of fact."

"They will when you're an actress, Alison. People will flock to see you on the stage."

Alison laughed. "And shall you come to see me perform?"

"If you invite me."

"You may be sure that I will. You can come and help me dress, and brush my hair, if you like, Emma," Alison said, allowing her imagination to leap forward. "And then you can stand in the wings, to watch the play."

Emma was infected by Alison's sudden surge of excitement and allowed her own imagination to catapult her into the glamorous world Alison's words had conjured up. "Don't actresses have a maid to help them get ready for a performance?"

"Oh, yes, they're called dressers," Alison informed her. "But the Plantaine Players can't afford them."

"You won't have to pay me anything," Emma said.

Then they began giggling, as it struck them how they had let themselves be carried away.

"It reminds me of a Jewish joke," Emma spluttered.

"Another one?" Alison had heard so many in the past week, especially from her Uncle Lionel, she had not thought there were any left to tell. Nearly everything a person said reminded Lionel of a Jewish joke, she had discovered.

"This one's about the young wife, who isn't even expecting yet, who has a row with her husband about whether their grandsons will be doctors or lawyers," Emma said. "But it doesn't sound funny when I tell it. I don't have the knack."

"Your father does. Though I didn't understand the one about the old lady who spilled a pan of boiling chicken soup and only scalded the tip of her thumb. Why did the Christian friend she showed the blister to think she had a strange Jewish disease, when she told him she'd got off lucky?"

"The Yiddish accent Dad puts on when he's telling Jewish jokes isn't as good as he thinks it is," Emma said. "That's why you didn't get it, Alison. The Christian thought the old lady was saying, 'Look. I got a flucky'— and he'd certainly never heard of that disease before!"

Alison shrieked with laughter. "I must tell it to my papa, when he comes home from the war."

The thought of her father sobered her, as Emma could see from her expression.

"God will watch over him, Alison."

"Then why is He letting soldiers be killed and maimed?"

There was nothing Emma could say in reply. "Our Conrad wants to join up, but my parents have begged him not to," she confided. "It was the same with his pal, Albert Battersby, or both of them would be in the army now."

"I'm surprised to hear that dreadful Battersby boy was brave enough to want to volunteer," Alison said.

They got into bed and Emma turned out the light. "Albert's very nice, really, Alison. You don't know him."

"I have no wish to know him! He's utterly detestable."

"He and Conrad will be drafted, if the war goes on for a long time, Alison. If Albert gets killed, you'll be sorry you said that about him."

"We're back to the joke about the young wife rowing with her husband about what their grandsons will be!" Alison said. "Wasting our breath about what may never happen. That Battersby boy is still safe and well in his father's cotton mill and the war might end tomorrow. He may never go near a battlefield, Emma, let alone get killed on one—and you're telling me not to speak ill of the dead!"

Emma snuggled down under the covers. "A person ought to think of the future, Alison."

"I haven't noticed you thinking about yours. I asked what you plan to do when you leave school, but you were more interested in putting up my hair."

"What is there for me to do but stay at home and help my mother?" Emma laughed tolerantly. "Like Clara is supposed to be doing."

"Wouldn't you prefer to take some kind of job, Emma?"

"Not really, Alison. And my father wouldn't allow it. He doesn't think women should go to work unless they need the money."

Alison felt her cheeks redden with anger. "In other words, all women are fit for is waiting upon men and bearing their children! Well, I don't agree."

Alison had been raised in an ethos where women worked side by side with men, and had not previously considered the lot of those outside the theater.

"I wouldn't let anyone stop me from being an actress," she declared.

"Perhaps I should feel like that, if there were anything I wanted to be," Emma answered.

But Alison had come to realize that Emma would never be prepared to fight for anything, and was immensely sorry for her, though she was not sure why. Her cousin was not unhappy, but was not exactly bursting with joy, either.

Alison, on the other hand, could be beset by gloom one day and aglow with happiness the next; sometimes for no apparent reason. Emma seemed to exist placidly between the two, untouched by either.

Emma leaned over to kiss Alison's cheek, before settling herself for sleep. "It's been lovely having you here, Alison," she murmured. "The nicest school holiday I've ever had."

She had not said that she wished Alison could stay longer. But that doesn't mean she's had enough of me, Alison reflected after they had said goodnight. Emma made the most of the few simple pleasures that came her way and neither expected nor asked for more.

Contented was the word to describe Emma, Alison decided before slumber overtook her. She had never once seen her cousin upset or disappointed, though Clara gave her cause to be both, every day. Alison's last waking thought was that Emma was a lovely person and that it was not necessary to pity her.

But the compassion was still there when Alison awoke

next morning; and had crystallized into a feeling that Emma was missing out on something, though Alison knew not what.

It would be some years before Alison fully understood her cousin—or thought that she did. And several eventful decades were to pass by, before Emma would choose to reveal her innermost feelings to Alison.

Meanwhile, they were two fourteen-year-old girls, born into different worlds, brought together by family relationship. But the rapport between them owed nothing to the blood tie. A person cannot choose their relatives, nor does kinship insure compatibility, but each of these two knew, beyond doubt, that she had found a true friend.

Conrad and Emma accompanied Alison to Manchester, where she would board the London train.

"By the way, Alison," Conrad said when they reached the station. "Albert sent his regards to you."

"Hypocrite!" Alison exclaimed hotly. She could not now remember exactly what Albert had said to upset her. But the mere thought of him had an inflammatory effect.

"You've really got it in for Albert, haven't you?" Conrad said when he and Emma were standing on the platform and Alison was leaning out of the train window.

Alison did not reply.

Conrad took a paper bag from his overcoat pocket and handed it to her. "These are for you to suck on the journey."

"That's very thoughtful of you, Conrad."

"They're from Albert, not me. I'm not the thoughtful kind."

"Does he think he can buy my forgiveness with a bag of sweets?" She opened the bag and grimaced. "Wouldn't you know it! They're mint imperials. Someone must have told him I hate peppermint."

"You can give them to me, then. I like them," Conrad said.

Alison thrust the bag into his hand. Emma was looking

distressed and Conrad had a stiff expression on his face. Trust that Battersby boy to spoil her last few minutes with her cousins!

The guard blew his whistle.

"Best get yer 'ead stuck in, luv, or yer'll be losin' yer tammy in t'wind, when t'train moves off," a kindly porter advised Alison. "Folk've bin knowd ter lose their 'eads'n all, doin' what tha's doin'," he added ominously.

"Please spare me the gory details," Alison requested.

But he would not have had time to dwell upon them; the train was moving.

"I'll write every week!" Alison called to Emma.

"Me too!"

Alison remained at the window, holding on to her hat, her scarf flowing like a brilliant green flag in the breeze, until the train turned around a bend and disappeared from her cousins' view.

"If Alison were a bird, she'd be a peacock," Emma said.

"Don't you mean a peahen? But I know what you mean, our Emma. And if you were a bird, you'd be a sparrow, wouldn't you, love?" Conrad answered with a smile.

"Probably." Conrad could not have expressed more succinctly, for Emma, the difference between herself and Alison.

"But what's come over you?" Conrad teased her as they walked toward the ticket barrier. His little sister wasn't given to descriptive extravagances.

Emma laughed. "Alison has, I suppose!"

"Well, she's gone now, love, and we'll all have to come down to earth. Talking of which, we'd better get a move on," he said as they left the station. "Dad gave me the morning off work, not the whole day!"

"And I've got the silver and brass to polish," Emma reminded herself. "Clara's invited out."

Conrad snorted. "Trust her to wangle an invitation

somewhere on a Thursday, when Mam likes everything made nice for the weekend!''

"I told Clara it was all right for her to go, that I'd manage the polishing on my own.''

Conrad gave Emma's arm a big-brotherly squeeze. "You're a real gem, our Emma.''

Emma glanced up at him and smiled. "It's nice of you to say so, our Conrad.''

"I may as well say it as think it.'' A wry expression flitted across Conrad's homely face. "How do you like the way our cousin speaks? Proper posh, isn't she? You wouldn't catch Alison saying 'our Conrad' and 'our Emma'.'' Conrad chuckled. "And I'll never get used to her calling her parents Mama and Papa!''

They were walking down Market Street, jostled by shoppers. "You wouldn't think there was a war on, would you?'' Conrad remarked. "Except for the soldiers on leave helping their mothers to buy in for New Year's Eve,'' he added, dodging past an army private approaching with a laden basket. "They must be doing a roaring trade today at Smithfield Market—''

"I'm not interested in whether they are or not,'' Emma said with uncharacteristic sharpness. "I have something to say to you, Conrad, and I shall only say it once. If you must make fun of Alison, kindly don't do it in front of me!''

Conrad was taken aback. He had never before heard Emma express herself with such force. Years from now, his mind would return to the moment when the little sparrow had fleetingly sharpened her bill to defend the bird of a brighter hue. And he would see himself and Emma turning into Corporation Street on their way to Victoria Station, their comfortable relationship momentarily marred by Alison, though she was no longer with them.

At present, Conrad registered only that Alison had had a strange effect upon his sister.

"Promise me that you'll never do it again,'' Emma said

stiffly. "Alison can't help being—posh. It's the way she's been brought up. It's no different from us not dropping our aitches, because Mam was always very keen on us speaking nicely, wasn't she? She made sure we didn't talk broad Lancashire, like the kids we went to infant school with—or we'd be saying 'owt,' instead of 'anything', and 'nowt' instead of 'nothing', like most of our neighbors and friends do."

"That was quite a speech, our Em! But I wasn't making fun of Alison. I like her."

"Good. So do I."

That was an understatement if ever Conrad had heard one. Emma's feeling for Alison was more like worship. A cautionary bell rang in Conrad's mind.

"I hope you won't get upset, Emma, if Alison doesn't write to you every week, like she said."

Emma smiled. "I'm not expecting her to, Conrad. I know she means to, but sometimes she'll be too busy. Or forget."

They had arrived at the station in time to hurry through the barrier and leap on to a train, and said no more until they were seated in a compartment.

"That's all right, then," Conrad resumed their conversation. "It's best not to expect too much, then you won't be disappointed. Or feel let down."

"Alison would never let me down in any way that really matters," Emma said with conviction.

Conrad eyed her shining expression. "But her life is very different from ours, isn't it? Things that are important to people like us might not be to her."

"What sort of things, Conrad?"

But Conrad was unable to translate his misgivings into words. All he was able to say was, "Well, here're you and me on our way back to Oldham. Me to Dad's store and you to Mam's kitchen. And there's Alison, traveling in the opposite direction—in more ways than one! And you've only got to look at her to know she's something special. I've seen a lot of good-looking girls, in my time—

some of them prettier by a long chalk than Alison—but none of them had what she's got. I keep thinking how does a girl like that come to be our cousin."

"As she's the only one we've got, you'll have to make do with her," Emma said with a smile.

"But it's hard to believe we're related to her. I mean she's going on the stage, isn't she? And what do the Steins know from actresses?"

Emma fanned away the pipe smoke being puffed in their faces by a sergeant seated nearby. "I expect Alison is sitting on the train she's on, thinking it's hard to believe she's related to us."

Alison's thoughts on her journey south were not quite as Emma had surmised. The unreality of her relationship to the Steins and Shragers had by now receded, though Emma was the only one of them who had fitted immediately into a special place in her life.

The rest of the Steins were still, to Alison, a family entity; she had accepted them as a whole, complete with her antipathy to Clara. Though she felt she had begun to know them as individuals, there was still, in that respect, a long way to go.

Her grandparents had remained an enigma, though she had visited them several times.

One afternoon, when Emma had left her with them for an hour, while she went on an errand for her mother, Alison had hoped it would provide an opportunity to talk with her grandmother alone. But they had remained in her grandfather's sickroom and it had crossed Alison's mind that possibly her grandmother did not wish to be alone with her.

Minna had made her welcome, but Alison sensed a wariness, almost as though she were afraid of saying the wrong thing. Walter Shrager had by now recovered his strength sufficiently to spend his days seated in a chair. Was it his presence that was inhibiting her grandmother? Preventing Minna from being herself with Alison? Because, Alison reflected on the train, inhibiting her grandfather certainly was.

He had taken no part in the conversation, but had sat with an open book on his lap—though Alison was certain he had not been reading it. It had just been something for him to look at, so he need not look at her.

And her talks with her grandmother, even when Emma was present, had been almost entirely about Alison's father. As if, she had thought feeling hurt, Papa was Minna Shrager's only reason for talking to her.

Alison was left with the feeling that she had helped her grandmother to piece together a jigsaw; that Minna had been fitting all the bits and bobs of information she gleaned from Alison into place in her mind. As though, until now, the picture she had of her son's life had been incomplete and she was grasping the opportunity to fill in the empty spaces.

But the quizzing about Papa hadn't been entirely one-sided, Alison had to admit. She had asked a lot of questions about her father's childhood and youth, and had been shown some photographs of him as a lad.

In one of them, he had been wearing a little round cap, like the ones Uncle Lionel and Conrad had worn on Friday night, when Aunt Lottie lit candles.

For the Steins it was their Sabbath Eve and for Alison, Christmas Night. But there had not been an awkward atmosphere around the table. Uncle Lionel had blessed a silver goblet of wine and had passed it around for everyone to take a sip—including Alison, who though not of their religion was nevertheless part of the family.

Nor had her own religion been ignored that evening. Aunt Lottie had baked a special cake for dessert, because, she had said, it was "Alison's Christmas." And everyone had told Alison they hoped she had had a happy one.

Had she? she mused on the train. It had certainly been different from any previous one. Coming down to breakfast, in a house where there was no tree, had felt strange,

and the absence of holly and mistletoe had stripped the
festival of its traditional gaiety. Missing, too, was the customary festive meal. This was the first time that Alison
had not, on Christmas Day, eaten turkey, plum pudding,
and mince pies.

Alison would have been less than honest with herself,
had she not been prepared to admit she had been disappointed to find that Jews did not celebrate December
25th as Gentiles traditionally did. Briefly, she had felt
deprived.

But the feeling had been dispelled by the Steins' warm
hospitality. Of course she had had a happy Christmas!
she thought, gazing through the train window at the
northern industrial panorama she was leaving behind.
She had been surrounded by goodwill and that was what
Christmas was all about.

The compartment in which Alison Was seated was
crowded and noisy. Again, the military was well represented among the passengers. Uniforms were nowadays
a familiar, sobering sight.

Especially on trains and on station platforms, Alison
reflected, glancing at the soldier seated opposite her,
whom she had seen bidding farewell to his family, at
Manchester.

The lad had a set expression on his pale face and sat
gripping his cap. Was he thinking he may never come
back? Alison wondered. Would it seem forward to chat
to him, to cheer him up?

But he might then engage her attention for the rest of
the journey, and she wanted to sit and think, she decided
selfishly. While her impressions of her stay with her relatives were still fresh in her mind.

Her thoughts returned to the last afternoon, when she
had gone with Emma to say goodbye to her grandparents. In her mind's eye, Alison saw again her grandfather
seated by the window in his chair. Minna had given Alison and Emma tea beside the fire, and had asked Alison

to let her know when a letter arrived from her papa. The Shragers had not heard from him for some time.

Walter had appeared to be dozing, but Alison had had the feeling that he was drinking in and recording every word she said.

Before she left, he had—to her surprise—paid her a compliment. "You have a beautiful voice, Alison," he had said.

His expression had not changed, and his tone had been casual, but Alison had felt that he would have liked to take her hand, but could not bring himself to do so.

When her grandmother saw her to the door, she had given her a parting hug, and that too had come as a surprise. It did not fit into Alison's impression that she was, to Minna, nothing more than a link with her papa. As the final moment with Walter belied his apparent indifference to Alison.

There was no way Alison could have known, or understood, the mixed emotions her sudden entrance into their lives had stirred in her paternal grandparents. What she represented—the symbol of their only son's union with a Gentile woman—was, in theory, anathema to them.

Before meeting her, it had not been difficult for the Shragers to ignore her existence. Presented with the living proof, who bore the physical hallmarks of the Shrager family coupled with an irresistible charm all her own, it was another matter. And, unknown to Alison, an emotional conflict had awakened within both Minna and Walter.

Neither had admitted this to the other. Walter's nature prohibited it; to do so would be to him a sign of weakness, in his own and his wife's eyes. And Minna would not have dared to tell him how she felt.

Alison stopped brooding about her grandparents. Soon she would be back in the life to which she was accustomed. Theaters and lodgings, she thought with a wry smile, and wondered what Emma and Clara would say if they saw some of the seedy houses in which the Plantaines stayed, and the dank and drafty passages and dressing rooms, backstage.

Those whose lives were spent in comfort, like her cousins, would probably be horrified by what Alison took for granted, she reflected. And the things they took for granted were a novelty to her.

It had dawned on her gradually during her stay with the Steins, that there was a good deal she had missed. The company of other children had been denied her, because she had not gone to school. Nor had she known the pleasure of sharing an outing with friends and returning home to all that home meant.

It was the last thought most of all that summed up Alison's feelings on her journey south. And it struck her that though the Plantaines were a family who worked and lived together, they had no family life.

Alison was not too young to have assessed her northern relatives as being eminently ordinary people, the kind she had always considered less fortunate than herself, whose place was on the other side of the footlights. But she had found herself envying her cousins their stable existence, though she was not yet mature enough to see it in those terms. Her brief experience of a way of life hitherto unknown to her had given her a taste for the permanence theatricals could not have.

Would she like to change places with her cousins? she mused later, on the train to Bournemouth. The answer was no. It would be lovely, though, to combine the advantages of their life with the excitement of her own. Alison wanted the best of both worlds.

As the train neared the coast, the world to which she was returning claimed her thoughts. How would her mother greet her? The prospect of facing Hermione filled Alison with trepidation. Nor was she, now, devoid of contrition. Mama had probably had a miserable Christmas.

Night had fallen and some of the passengers on the

train had begun celebrating New Year's Eve. People were offering each other sweets and cigarettes, and one man was swigging whisky—which reminded Alison of her Uncle Oliver.

Someone was eating mint imperials, which reminded her, too, of Albert Battersby—would she never again smell peppermints without thinking of that horrid boy?"

" 'Ave one, love?" the plump gentleman said, offering her the bag.

Alison managed to smile. "No, thank you."

"If there's one thing I likes on a journey," he said, "it's a nice mint. I'm off to visit me auntie. The dear old thing is on 'er last. Lives down in Christchurch. Know it, do yer, love?"

Alison shook her head. She was then required to hear a detailed account of how Auntie came to be ending her days in Christchurch, though she had begun them in Stepney; including how the old lady had spent the years between.

By the time the saga ended, the train was grinding to a halt at Bournemouth station.

The gentleman got down her bag from the luggage rack and surveyed her over the top of his spectacles. "Anyone ever tell yer what a good listener you are, love?"

Alison wanted to reply that she had had no option. She had tried, several times, to divert him from his lengthy tale, but had not been allowed to get a word in edgeways.

The station clock told her that tonight's performance would just be ending. She might as well go directly to the theater.

"Nice to see you back, Miss Alison," the stagedoor keeper said, when she entered and left her suitcase with him.

"Thank you, Len. And I hope you had an enjoyable Christmas," Alison answered with a friendly smile.

Len watched her walk gracefully along the passage. She was a "real Plantaine," even though she didn't look like one. She's just like her mum and her granny, he reflected. They only had to smile at you to warm the cockles of your heart.

The smile had been for Alison an effort. She was about to face the music and doubted that it would be pleasant to her ears.

On the way to her mother's dressing room, she began rehearsing what she would say. But it would depend upon how Mama greeted her, she thought, abandoning the exercise. When she opened the door, would a blast of anger hit her? Or a wave of icy sarcasm? Stony silence was also a possibility.

Alison steeled herself for whichever it was to be, but was not prepared for total indifference.

"Oh, you're back are you?" Hermione said carelessly, pausing only briefly before continuing to remove her make-up. "But your partner in crime is still missing," she added in the same tone.

Alison found her voice. "I beg your pardon, Mama?"

"And so you should. But I am past caring. About you and the person who made what you did possible."

Alison sat down on the chaise-longue and tried to fathom what her mother meant. Who was this other person? She had momentarily forgotten that Oliver had provided the money for her train fare. Hermione's next words reminded her.

"You and your uncle are a fine pair. Did you plot the whole thing between you, to give me and your grandparents an unhappy Christmas?"

Hermione's tone was not in the least accusatory. As though, as she had said, she did not care, but was simply making some casual inquiries.

"Was it merely a coincidence that my brother absconded the morning after you did?" Hermione went on. "Not that I expect you to tell me."

She rose from the dressing table and went behind the screen to dress, leaving Alison to digest this startling information.

"I knew nothing of Uncle Oliver's intention, Mama," she declared.

Hermione did not reply and Alison sat feeling like a criminal in the dock, listening to the hiss of the gaslights and the rustle of her mother dressing.

Hermione emerged wearing a blue taffeta frock, with a white lace collar that matched the pallor of her complexion. The strength had drained from her, and the color from her face, as day after day had passed by and neither Alison, nor Oliver, had returned.

Alison, on the other hand, looked remarkably well, Hermione observed. And not in the least contrite. But Hermione could not summon the energy to lecture her on the error of her ways.

"Don't bother telling me that your uncle knew nothing of your intention, Alison," she said with a weary smile.

Alison's throat had dried. Her mother's lifelessness—there was no other way to describe Hermione's tone of voice and limp deportment—was frightening. Anger and sarcasm would be easier to deal with than this.

Alison got up and poured herself some water from the carafe on the dressing table. "As a matter of fact, Mama, Uncle Oliver didn't know what I planned to do with the money he gave me."

Hermione surveyed her for a moment. How could she look so innocent, yet be so underhand? "I'm afraid I don't believe you, Alison. You have proved yourself capable of duplicity in the past and have given me no reason to think you have rid yourself of that regrettable trait in your character. I now know from whom you have inherited it, that there are two people in my family whom I can never again trust."

Alison had to bite her lip to stop herself from crying out that her mother was not only being unfair, but also conveniently forgetting that she had struck Alison.

It had been that blow from Hermione's own hand that set in motion this whole train of events. Had it never been dealt, Alison would not have been impelled to flee north, nor Oliver from his sister's wrath. But Hermione had never been the kind to see the part she had played in bringing about a situation that caused her pain.

Alison watched her brush and put up her hair. There was now a long-suffering expression in Hermione's eyes. As though she were the tragedy figure in a play and her brother and daughter the villains! Alison thought. She had briefly felt sorry for her mother, but resentment had replaced the compassion.

"You may think what you wish about me, Mama," Alison said coldly. "But you are doing Uncle Oliver an injustice on my account, and I can't allow that. I'm sure if he had known what I wanted the money for, he wouldn't have given it to me."

Hermione went on securing her coiffure with hairpins. "If what you are saying is true, and I have lost interest in whether it is or not, it makes you none the less deceitful, Alison. And adds a distasteful irony to the entire matter. All it means is that you duped your uncle into paying your way, as he duped your grandfather into paying his."

Alison did not pause to work this out. "Did you hear from Papa while I was away?"

Hermione shook her head, adding to Alison's depression. Momentarily, Alison wished she was in her Aunt Lottie's kitchen, with the comforting aroma of simmering soup in her nostrils, instead of cold cream and grease paint and all that they presently implied.

She had prickled with excitement when she entered the theater and, despite her dread of facing her mother, had felt glad to be back. The theater was her place, though she had not yet made her debut upon a stage. But the memory of that cozy haven up north had not receded and would, though Alison did not yet know it, in her bleak moments continue to beckon her.

Alison switched her thoughts from Lottie to Oliver. Was her uncle lying drunk somewhere?

Her mother was still fixing her hair, taking her time

about it. She reminded Alison of a rag doll. Even her eyes had lost their sparkle. But Alison was unable to muster sympathy for her.

She could not have known the extent of Hermione's distress. Not for anything would she let Alison—or Oliver, when he returned—know how devastating was the effect upon her of their behavior. That, with one fell swoop, they had ripped apart her life.

It had been rent when her husband went to be a soldier; but between them, Alison and Oliver had put the finishing touches to it. Upon whom could a woman with no man at her side depend, if not her own daughter and her own brother? Hermione was thinking, though she allowed not a flicker of emotion to shadow her face.

Thank God she still had her parents to turn to. But she had never been able to unburden herself to them. Oliver had been her trusted confidant and she had thought herself his. But he had proved himself closer to Alison and had conspired with her, behind Hermione's back.

Despite her differences with Alison, Hermione had hoped, in Horace's absence, that their shared love and anxiety for him would draw them together. So much for my hopes! she thought, powdering her nose.

A surge of anger rose in her, but she did not let that show, either. She would waste no more affection or concern upon her daughter. Or her brother. They were unworthy of it and could both go hang!

Hermione got up to fetch her hat and seated herself before the mirror again to put it on, tilting the big-brimmed, blue velvet frippery to a fetching angle. Right now, she could not have cared less what she looked like. And indeed, she thought grimly, would be wearing black, were her feelings to dictate her dress. But an actress must, at all times, maintain her public image, it would not do for Hermione Plantaine to be seen leaving the theater looking other than the vision of loveliness she appeared onstage.

"Where do you suppose Uncle Oliver is, Mama?" Alison asked her.

Hermione added a touch of color to her cheeks.

"Who cares?" she replied.

FOURTEEN

On January 24th, 1915, the British public
learned over its toast and marmalade that
Miss Ruby May had become Mrs. Oliver
Plantaine.

Gregory opened his *News Of The World* and choked
on his tea. He handed the newspaper to his wife, while
Alison pounded him on the back.

A moment later she ran to fetch smelling salts for her
grandmother, whose color was now as ashen as her
grandfather's was puce.

When Alison returned from upstairs, it was her
mother who looked about to faint.

Hermione waved away the bottle of pungent crystals,
"Nothing can help me now, Alison. Or any of us, I fear."

Alison noted that her grandpa was now sitting with his
head in his hands. Her grandma was clutching her heart.
And tears had begun trickling, unheeded, down her
mother's cheeks.

It's like a scene from a melodrama, Alison thought,

managing not to giggle. All that was missing was the mustache-twirling villain! She had yet to learn why these three pillars of her life had suddenly crumbled before her eyes. But the word "villain" made her think of Oliver.

Alison no longer wanted to giggle. Had something terrible happened to her uncle?

She forced herself to pick up the newspaper, which had fluttered from Hermione's fingers to the floor, and found herself looking at a picture of Ruby May and Oliver, flanked by the twins.

Ruby was not one to overlook the publicity value of her marriage into the Plantaine family and had made sure that the press photographers would be waiting outside Caxton Hall when she emerged on Oliver's arm.

"How absolutely marvelous!" Alison exclaimed. "I've now got two more cousins and don't they look nice? But fancy Uncle Oliver having a whirlwind romance!" she added, quoting from the much embelished details included in the caption. "I'm so happy for him."

But nobody else seemed to be—on the contrary. "One would think you'd seen a picture of Uncle Oliver's funeral," she observed to her elders.

They did not tell her that, in their opinion, in effect they had.

"Not his wedding," Alison went on. She eyed her grandmother's gloomy countenance. "I've heard you say, lots of times, Grandma, that you wished he would get married."

But not to that common creature, Jessica thought. "I would have preferred him to choose someone more suitable," she said.

Exactly, Gregory thought. He had not dared to hope that his son would one day take a wife. Now, miraculously, Oliver had encountered a woman who aroused in him manly feelings. But why, Gregory asked God, did it have to be Ruby May?

Neither Gregory nor Jessica had met Ruby. But her

reputation and appearance were enough to cause them to recoil.

Hermione's feelings were more personal. Ruby had continued to be for her inexplicably a threat. The earthy, full-bosomed, magenta-clad figure, viewed from afar on a railway platform, had been grotesquely enhanced by Hermione's imagination. Now, she had entered Hermione's life.

Alison saw her mother shudder and her grandfather make an effort to pull himself together. Her grandmother was staring down at the congealing fried eggs on her plate.

"Is my new aunt really as dreadful as all that?" Alison was impelled to ask.

"We must hope not, Alison dear," Jessica said. "Ask Mrs. Harvey to kindly make us a fresh pot of tea, would you, dear?"

Alison did as she was bid, but she knew her grandmother's request was a ploy to get her out of the room.

"The woman is a monster!" Hermione declaimed the moment Alison was gone. "She married an old man for his money and now he's dead has got her claws into Oliver."

"There is nothing to be gained by allowing one's preconceived notions to run away with one," Gregory answered. "And I intend to give my daughter-in-law the benefit of the doubt."

"You're prepared to accept the marriage, are you, Papa?"

Gregory had recovered sufficiently to resume his customary bland facade. "I am not in the habit of trying to change situations I can do nothing about."

As always, Jessica followed her husband's lead. "We have no option but to accept it, Hermione dear. We must give Oliver a warm welcome, when he comes back to us with his wife and stepchildren."

Hermione buttered some toast, to busy her trembling hands. "As he no longer needs us, he might not come back. His wife is wealthy enough to support him," she added viciously.

Gregory gave her an icy glance. "Are you suggesting that is why he married her?"

"I wouldn't have thought him capable of it, once. But now, I wouldn't put anything past him," Hermione said with distaste.

Gregory put down his knife and fork. "I will thank you to remember that your brother is a Plantaine."

"And I am coming to think of him as a viper in the family bosom!" Hermione retorted.

"Then kindly keep such thoughts to yourself," her father instructed her. "It might help you to do so if you remembered that your own choice of marriage partner was not what your mother and I would have wished."

If Gregory had picked up the cup of cold, milky tea curdling beside him and flung it in her face, Hermione could not have been more stung. "There is no comparison between Horace and that woman!" she flashed.

"I agree," Gregory replied smoothly. "But he has never really fitted in, has he, my dear? Nevertheless, we have made the best of it, for his sake and all of ours. And we must do the same with regard to Oliver's wife."

"So you've been making the best of it, all these years, have you?" Hermione said, as the full import of her father's words sank in. "Well, I must say you had me fooled. Being the accomplished thespian you are, Papa, I had no idea you were acting. I believed that you had come to respect my husband's many fine qualities."

"And you believed correctly," Gregory assured her. "But I should never have discovered them, should I, Hermione dear, had I not given him a chance." Though his son-in-law's materialistic streak was abhorrent to Gregory, there was no denying that Horace had proved himself a man of integrity.

"That is what your father has been trying to tell you, Hermione dear," Jessica put in.

But Gregory had done himself no good in his daughter's eyes by the way he had gone about it. It struck Hermione that never again could she be sure that her father was as sincere as he seemed.

Her mother, either, she thought, watching Jessica spoon some honey on to her plate. Her parents were probably in league about everything, united in their resolve that nothing must affect the *status quo* of the Plantaine Players; not even their personal feelings about their children's spouses.

Until now, that had only meant putting on a show for herself and her husband, Hermione reflected bitterly. And what a good show it had been! So convincing, Hermione had thought Horace was by now accepted without reservations.

Her mother and father were now readying themselves for a repeat performance, this time for Oliver's benefit, Hermione thought, surveying the handsome couple with whom she had, all her life, felt safe and secure. Her brother would not be allowed to know their true feelings about his wife.

Hermione had always been aware that her parents were capable of prevarication when necessary, as she herself was, but had never suspected them of employing it with her. The discovery was as though her last remaining solid ground had turned out to be shifting sand. Her parents had become for her two more people whom she could not trust.

Alison entered with the teapot and set it down on the cork mat beside Jessica. "Mrs. Harvey asked me to make it and bring it in. She was up to her elbows in flour, baking an apple pie for our lunch. And she's terribly excited about Uncle Oliver. She doesn't take a Sunday paper, so I told her the news."

Hermione emptied the cold tea into the slop basin. "I am not interested in our landlady's reaction to your uncle's unfortunate alliance, Alison."

"Mrs. Harvey doesn't think it's unfortunate, Mama. She said having Ruby May in our productions will bring people flocking to see the Plantaine Players. That we'll never have poor audiences again," Alison conveyed.

Her elders had not yet paused to consider the professional aspect of the erstwhile melodrama queen's arrival in their midst.

Hermione voiced their thoughts. "Ruby May in a Shakespearean production?" she exclaimed derisively.

"It would perhaps be better if Oliver didn't return to the company with his wife," Jessica could not prevent herself from saying.

"And if he does?" Hermione asked her father.

Gregory summoned a reassuring smile and the well-worn words he employed to end conjecture. "I shall cross that bridge if and when I come to it."

*Here's much to do with hate,
but more with love.*

ROMEO AND JULIET

ONE

In 1916, Hermione began going to officers' mess parties after the nightly performance. She said it was the least she could do for the men parted from their wives and families and Alison accepted this, as did her grandparents. But Jessica and Gregory Plantaine's acceptance would not extend to what Alison now knew. She had discovered that her mother was not a faithful wife.

Alison had awakened with toothache at one a.m. and had gone to her mother's room for the tincture of cloves. Hermione was not there.

Even so, Alison would have given her the benefit of the doubt. But there was only one conclusion to draw from what she saw from her bedroom window an hour later. Bidding an amorous farewell to a soldier was a good deal more than the least her mother could do.

Alison had stood nursing her aching jaw and her disillusion. Her father was miles away and the last shred of her respect for her mother gone, compounding her feeling that the war had sent everything haywire including the moral values instilled in her from childhood.

The free-and-easy ways of some theatricals had always been frowned upon by the Plantaines and it had come as a shock to Alison when her Aunt Ruby began accepting supper invitations from the stage-door Johnnies who sent flowers to her dressing room. Ruby made no secret of her extramarital excursions and Alison was doubly shocked that her Uncle Oliver seemed not to mind.

Her father would mind, if he knew about her mother. But he would never know, which made Hermione's transgressions worse than Ruby's. Papa would return to a woman whom, in his ignorance, he believed was a loyal wife.

In his last letter he had said how thankful he was that the company's traveling days were over. They were now based in Hastings and Alison had hoped the family would set up house here. Instead, they had taken permanent lodgings.

Their landlady, Mrs. Fawcett, was an excellent cook and the accommodation spacious and pleasant. She had told the Plantaines to consider her house their home, but for Alison it remained just the place where she ate and slept.

The word "home," to Alison, was epitomized by Lottie Stein's cheerful kitchen and there were times, like now, when she longed to be there, with those whom she knew would never do anything to hurt her.

Alison had not visited her northern relatives since the first wartime Christmas when she had fled to them. In the interim, events had served to dull her into a state of inertia.

Even her fears for her father's safety had become part of the apathy within her. It was as though she were lying low, washed over by time, and by circumstances she could not change.

The companionship she had expected from her stepcousins had not materialized. Lucy and Luke had from the outset been patronizing toward her, and the closeness the twins shared had emphasized her solitary status.

Increasingly, she had come to feel she was existing on the perimeter of other people's lives, waiting for her own to begin.

These were boom years for the theater. Soldiers on leave, or convalescing from wounds, sought forgetfulness in the world of entertainment during their brief respite from the battlefields.

For civilians, too, the theater had become a means of escaping from everyday cares. You bought your ticket, entered its magic portals, and for a blessed interlude, were moved to laughter and tears that had nothing to do with the war.

But Alison had not yet taken her place behind the footlights. Traditionally, Plantaine females did so when they were sixteen. Alison had celebrated that important birthday in August. It was now the first week in September, but she would have to wait a while longer before making her début.

Her grandmother had made hers playing Ophelia, and her mother Juliet. Alison had assumed that she, too, would be presented to the public in one of those two coveted roles. But her grandfather had produced *Hamlet* last season, and *Romeo and Juliet,* which was to open the autumn season, was in preparation now. With Lucy playing Juliet! Alison thought with a pang.

On the sultry day she had discovered her mother's infidelity, Alison sat in the theater auditorium watching the rehearsal. Her toothache had gone; so, too had the resignation with which she had dulled the sharp edge of her disappointment.

What kind of grandfather would not take into consideration his granddaughter's début, when arranging his repertoire? As for her mother and grandma! They had let the oversight pass, as if it were of less importance than their personal preoccupations. And her Uncle Oliver had his own reasons for letting it pass.

But Alison had held her tongue about it and would continue to do so. Grandpa now had a step-granddaughter, too, and not for anything would Alison emulate the jealous actresses whose backbiting she had always despised.

Oliver had just come to sit beside her; he was playing Mercutio and not presently required onstage.

That should be me, up there, Alison felt like informing him. But he wouldn't agree. His attention was riveted to the twin apples of his eye, who were rehearsing the balcony scene. In Oliver's opinion, Luke and Lucy were God's gift to the English theater, Alison thought, noting his besotted expression. And her own chance to prove her worth, in the right part, had been snatched from her.

Gregory could feel Alison's gaze boring into him, but he had expected her natural resentment to boil over sooner or later. Would she, henceforth, join the ranks of those who ruffled the once smooth tenor of his days?

Contrary to Alison's supposition, Gregory's scheduling of *Hamlet* and *Romeo and Juliet* was a carefully calculated move. Casting of the latter play had been settled in June, long before Alison's sixteenth birthday, and before the opening date was set.

As Horace had had cause to conclude, Gregory Plantaine was a cunning old fox. Had he cast Alison as Ophelia or Juliet, Ruby May's fury would know no limits. The alternative would be Hermione's wrath, if Alison were eligible and Lucy favored. One way or the other, Gregory had reckoned, the fur would be bound to fly, on their own and their respective daughter's behalf.

Characteristically, Gregory had opted for the easy way out. It would be some considerable time before these two plays were included in the repertoire again, and he had never believed in facing today a dilemma that could be put off until tomorrow.

Nineteen difficult months had passed since the news of Oliver's unwelcome alliance shattered the family's complacency. But Gregory could not have foretold that Oliver's return with his wife and stepchildren would herald the end of an era for the company as it had once been.

They were now securely ensconced in a playhouse that Ruby's money had enabled them to lease. Touring, with all it implied, was for the Plantaines a thing of the past. Gregory's financial situation was stable, his life, without the need to travel, less burdensome, and his dream of a permanent theater for his company realized.

On the face of it he had every reason to be a contented man. But he felt like a lapsed missionary, seduced by Mammon and condemned to suffer for his sin.

The materialization of his dream had proved to be a living nightmare. Gregory Plantaine, the autocratic actor-manager, was no longer a free agent, nor his repertoire solely Shakespearean. The latter was the consequence of the former, Gregory frequently apologized to the Bard's revered memory; to his distinguished ancestors', too. If they knew that the Plantaine Players were currently presenting *The Second Mrs. Tanqueray*—and with a onetime melodrama queen topping the bill—their skeletons would rattle in the family grave.

How had this come to pass? Gregory would ponder when he lay sleepless. The honest answer was that he had let himself be duped. But it was beneath his dignity to admit it; he preferred to see himself as the victim of circumstances not of his making. In truth, he had fallen prey to his own ego; which included the kingly notion that nobody tried to pull the wool over Gregory Plantaine's eyes and had made him fair game for Ruby May.

Gregory had, with his customary light touch, avoided the pitfalls while crossing the bridge erected by Oliver's marriage. But he had failed to recognize the trap awaiting him at the other side.

Ruby's desire to provide the theater he had always wanted had seemed a fitting illustration of her wish to ingratiate herself with the Plantaines. Gregory had deigned to accept the offer, as though he were doing her a favor, not the other way round.

When she told him her solicitor would insist upon a formal business agreement, he had not wasted time perusing the lengthy document presented for his signature. Had he done so, he would not have taken its contents seriously. He had never encountered a woman over whom he could not get the upper hand.

Underestimating Ruby was Gregory's big mistake. Not until she exerted her legal rights did he learn what they were, or that he had more than met his match. There were times when he still found it difficult to believe that beneath her soft, feminine exterior was a granite will and a shrewd, masculine mind.

In return for her capital outlay, Ruby had acquired a half-share in the Players' profits. This was of less concern to Gregory than her equality with him in dictating company policy. There was nothing, be it casting, costumes, decor, or choice of play, in which Ruby did not have an equal say.

Box-office takings had risen in consequence, exacerbating Gregory's sense of grim irony about the entire affair. The advice he had refused to take from his son-in-law had been forced down his throat by his daughter-in-law. "Give the public what it wants" was the essence of it and how bitter, for altruistic Gregory, was the taste.

He imagined that Horace and Ruby would get on well together, when Horace returned from the war. Gregory did not allow himself to use the word "if" in that respect. He had, to his surprise, found that he missed his son-in-law's dependable presence; and that he harbored a reluctant affection for the young Jew whose personal integrity was unquestionable.

It would be a relief to have him back, and Gregory had decided—though he had not yet told Hermione—to appoint Horace his business manager and thereby remove himself from that distasteful arena to the artistic plane on which he belonged.

But nothing could relieve Gregory of the necessity to

direct and act in productions he did not wish to present. Plays by Shaw and Maugham, Pinero and Galsworthy, Barrie and Ibsen, were a painful diversion from his own life's work, but they were now included, along with Shakespeare, in the company repertoire.

Gregory vented his spleen upon the twins, though their rendering of the balcony scene was not at all bad. "How I shall transform you two into Romeo and Juliet—!"

"If you stopped trying to transform them, they'd be fine!" Ruby cut in sharply from the wings.

Oliver, too, defended the twins, from his seat in the front stalls. "They're doing their best, Father."

Gregory turned and froze him with a glance. "Then I'm afraid their best is not of a high enough standard for my company."

"Whose company?" Ruby said.

Gregory cleared his throat. If he had known Ruby was lurking in the wings, he would have watched his words in the first place, though he didn't take kindly to having to do so. But it was too late now. He was aware of an air of waiting in the hushed theater, and that the carpenters fixing something overhead had stopped work.

Then Ruby came onstage to confront him.

Luke and Lucy moved to her side and Alison was not sure if they felt in need of their mother's protection, or thought she required theirs. Ruby and Gregory were silently eyeing each other, like boxers in opposite corners of the ring—which in effect they were, it now occurred to Alison. And it was no secret that, so far, Ruby had won every round of their subtle contest.

But it was subtle no more. Ruby had finally abandoned discretion. She had never before publicly challenged Gregory's authority. Would he, too, now discard his diplomatic mask and pick up the gauntlet Ruby had just thrown down?

Alison was not left to conjecture for long. Ruby left him no option but to do so. "I hate to have to remind you,

Pa, but this is now my company, too," she said, smoothing the skirt of her cinnamon silk frock, which looked as if it had been molded to her ample curves.

Gregory controlled a shudder. He would never accustom himself to his daughter-in-law addressing him, in her own common vernacular, as "Pa." Beads of perspiration had broken out on his brow, but he would not add to his humiliation by fumbling for his handkerchief and mopping the telltale moisture.

Alison saw him swallow hard and, despite his thoughtless treatment of her, was sorry for him. Suddenly, the eternally youthful Gregory Plantaine looked like a weary old man.

But he had retained his dignity, as his next words and the manner of their delivery revealed. "I need no reminding of our—bargain," he said with an equal blend of cool politeness and distaste, "but it did not include something money can't buy."

"And what might that be?" Ruby asked warily.

Gregory treated her to a patronizing smile. "I am not surprised that you require telling. Regrettably, there is a good deal you have to learn, my dear Ruby. Much to which you aspire is of a quality you cannot hope to attain. As for the point at issue, I am referring to the Plantaine heritage, which is simply not purchasable. It cannot be converted into pounds, shillings and pence."

Gregory drew himself up to his full height and looked his protagonist squarely in the eye. "I am its present guardian, as my father and grandfather were, before me, and theirs before them," he declared in a voice that resounded electrically throughout the theater.

"In that respect, this company, and what it stands for, remains, in my lifetime, mine," Gregory said finally.

His tone brooked no argument and there was a moment of awed silence. Alison felt the gooseflesh rise on her arms. She wanted to applaud her grandfather's superb performance. But there was more to it than that. Gregory's words had evoked for her the family history;

the long line of Plantaines who had gone before her. She could feel their ghosts all about her. How proud they would be of her grandfather's routing of the interloper, as Alison was. The heritage Gregory was protecting was hers, too.

Ruby had put a humoring smile on her face, but her discomfiture was plain to see.

Alison wished, unkindly, that the rest of the company were there to witness it. Ruby May had taken to giving herself airs and graces, as though she had been reborn a lady when Oliver bestowed upon her his distinguished name. Evidently Ruby wanted to forget that she had once purveyed low-class entertainment and had deluded herself that she was an actress of the same high caliber as those with whom she now worked. But Alison would have had more respect for her, had Ruby not tried to pretend she was something she was not.

By the time Ruby had composed herself, Gregory had left the stage.

He was thankful that it was time for the dinner break; he would not have to resume the balcony-scene rehearsal in Ruby's presence. The unaccustomed confrontation had left him limp, but nobody watching his regal exit would have known it. And, he thought with satisfaction, there was no question about who was the victor and who the vanquished.

The triumph was sweet, but did little to raise Gregory's flagging spirits. The philosophy that had once sustained him was no longer possible. Only a fool would hope that tomorrow would be brighter than today, when the cloud in his sky was permanent and without a silver lining. Ruby and the havoc she had wrought were here to stay.

But she had, this morning, received her comeuppance, Gregory consoled himself as he entered the Green Room, where tea and sandwiches awaited him. He doubted that she would risk a second dose.

Oliver remained seated in the auditorium until the carpenters had clambered down their ladders and gone for their midday pint.

Some of the actors would be in the pub, too, and would be regaled with the details of the real-life scene just enacted onstage. By this evening, the entire company would know that Gregory had put Ruby in her place, and would be delighted to hear it. Ruby was not popular.

Alison had given Oliver a commiserating kiss before she left the auditorium, which, by and large, epitomized the family attitude toward him. His parents' unspoken sympathy had in it an element of injured reproach and his sister's was tinged with rebuke. But Oliver was left in no doubt that, collectively, they were sorry for him.

Why did they think sorrow on his behalf was called for? He had never been happier in his life. Complete fulfillment was beyond his reach—God, who had made him, had ordained that—but Oliver asked for no more than he now had.

"Are you going to sit there all day?" Ruby shrilled to him.

Oliver smiled tolerantly and made his way to the stage, where his wife and children were waiting for him. Even Ruby's sporadic nagging could not mar his new-found contentment.

"I'm afraid you asked for what you got," he told her mildly. "You must try to be diplomatic with my father."

Ruby's green eyes blazed with righteous anger. "Why should I let him think he's cock o' the walk, when it's my brass that bought him his own chicken-run?"

"I find the way you put it somewhat distasteful, dearest," Oliver replied.

"You would, darling!" Ruby countered. "You're a bloody Plantaine."

In times of stress, Ruby forgot her airs and graces and reverted to her natural earthiness, which included using language Oliver had not heard any other woman employ. She was now standing with her arms akimbo, glaring at him.

"How lovely you look, when fury takes you in her grip," he said lyrically. "Like a painting of a comely fishwife."

"Go away, Oliver!" she flashed.

The twins winked at him, a signal for him to leave things to them. Oliver blew some kisses and made his exit, Ruby's outbursts came and went, as rainstorms on a summer day, and her tolerance of his deficiencies was ample compensation.

He had failed to make love to her, but Ruby had not allowed it to matter. Instead, she had cradled him in her arms and had said there was more to love than sex.

Nor did it matter to Oliver that his wife sought and found elsewhere the physical pleasure he was unable to give her. She was the means of his acquiring the status of a family man and thereby, sameness in the eyes of his fellows. And the twins remained a constant joy to him; suffering Ruby's bouts of temperament would be worthwhile for that reason alone.

But Ruby, too, was a comfort to him. Incongruous companions though they were, their shared concern for Luke and Lucy, and the personal intimacy even a sexless marriage dictated, had forged a bond between them.

Its name was friendship. Oliver had not needed a drink since he met Ruby. It was as if, until then, he had been floundering. She was the anchor his life had lacked.

These were Oliver's thoughts when he left her to be calmed by the twins, and a whimsical smile played around his lips as he entered the Green Room, contemplating the tactics his precious young monkeys might employ to restore their mama's good humor. Would they cajole, or flatter her? Oliver wondered. He had long ago divined the guile beneath their angelic exteriors, but worshipped them none the less.

For Luke and Lucy, love had begotten love. The man whom they had, for their own purposes, ensnared into marrying their mother, had become their respected and adored Pappy.

"Why did you have to upset him?" Luke was presently demanding of Ruby.

"You didn't have to take it out on Pappy, just because the dragon was horrid to you, Mother," Lucy said, referring to Gregory by their private name for him.

Kids! Ruby thought with chagrin. A person would think I was the stepparent around here, not Oliver! Usually, she was amused when her children sided with him instead of with her. But it didn't strike her as funny now.

"Go and get something to eat," she snapped to them, "or you'll be late for afternoon rehearsal and the dragon will breathe fire at you again."

She watched them hasten away, without so much as an "Are you all right, Mum?" But she couldn't expect them to understand how she felt. Nor could she put her churning emotions into words.

Depression was uppermost. For two pins, she'd put her head in a bloody gas oven! Oh, no, she wouldn't. Ruby May Plantaine—what a mouthful it sounded—wasn't the giving-in kind, or she'd have gone under when she was still a snot-nosed brat.

May was the surname the orphanage had given her. It was in May 1877 that she was dumped, like a bundle of rags, on their doorstep. If the mealy-mouthed misers who ran the place had known she'd end up on the stage, they'd have left her lying there!

But Ruby had something to thank them for. Her Dickensian childhood had strengthened her to face the world. She had left the orphanage determined never to go hungry again.

Nor had she. The first man who bought her a meal had said she needed some flesh putting on her bones. Ruby walked to the wings and surveyed herself in the long cheval mirror that was kept there for the actors to check their make-up and costumes. Was that voluptuous woman really the scraggy fourteen-year-old whom remembrance had just conjured up? It was difficult to believe. But so, looking back, was her whole life.

The name Ruby had been printed on a bit of paper pinned to her shawl, when she was found on the doorstep—like a waif in a melodrama, she thought with irony. Had the girl who had abandoned her been ordered by her parents, in the same melodramatic style, never to darken their door again? Where was she now?

Ruby would never know. But her unknown mother had named her after a precious jewel. This had been no consolation to a deprived child, but meant something special to the woman that child had become.

Many men had wanted Ruby, but none had cherished her. The nearest she had come to a loving relationship was with Oliver, who wanted no woman. There was between them a warmth not present in the brief affairs with which Ruby satisfied her sexual needs.

As for her first husband, she reflected dispassionately, the less said about warmth the better. William Appleby—he was not the sort anyone would think of calling Bill—had been infatuated with her, in the autumn of his years. When the false flame flickered out, he had done his duty by her and their children. Love had not entered into it.

Ruby's mind returned to the night she met Appleby. She was playing a minor role in a melodrama, at a Leeds pub where entertainment was offered along with the ale. When the curtain fell, the manager had told her that the owner of the brewery had seen the show and would like Miss May to have supper with him.

With the leading lady's jealous catcalls ringing in her ears, and unable to believe her own good fortune, Ruby had found herself seated opposite a stringy little man, old enough to be her father.

Throughout the tête-à-tête meal, during which William had talked solely about his poor health and inability to recover from the loss of his dear wife, Ruby had been fascinated by his wobbling Adam's apple. And he by her bosom, she had noted.

He had made it clear that he was visiting the pub on

business, and was not the type who frequented the establishments from which he made his lucrative living.

Ruby recalled thinking him a hypocritical old devil. Then she had switched her gaze to his diamond tie pin. Her determination never to go hungry again had, by then, equated with the acquisition of money and she did not allow the wealthy brewer's hypocrisy to deter her from leading him, step by step, to the altar. As his double standards did not include expecting to bed a woman—even an actress—without marriage, the task was not difficult.

They were married three weeks later and, with Appleby's bank balance behind her, Ruby had never played a minor stage role again. It had not taken her long to equate money with power.

Ruby's journey down memory lane returned her, full circle, to the hurtful matter that had propelled her there. Her powerful position in the company had not bought her the esteem of the Plantaines.

They treated her as an equal—how could they not, when she had married into the family and was Gregory's business partner? But there was something about them that made Ruby feel inferior, though she could buy and sell them.

The only way she could hit back at them was by insisting on her legal rights in the company. If they had made her feel welcome, she would not have done so. She'd have considered it an honor to be one of them; to let her money boost the work for which they were renowned. With Ruby in the cast, the kind of play wasn't important. People would queue to see her stand on the stage and recite the alphabet, she thought. Gregory could have gone on producing nothing but Shakespeare, if he hadn't cooked his own goose.

But he had! His wife and daughter, too. They had got what they deserved—and Ruby would make Gregory pay for rubbing salt into her wounds today. She would make him stage a musical comedy, like the wartime ones in London. The bloody Plantaine heritage could go hang!

Gregory had by now brushed aside the morning's unpleasantness and was holding court in the Green Room. Had he known what Ruby was plotting, he would have choked on his cucumber sandwich.

Oliver and the twins were seated at his table. Several actors and actresses had gathered around to listen to their director's opinion of Ibsen.

It was rare for Gregory to discuss the playwrights upon whom he frowned, but Luke had mentioned the contoversial Norwegian admiringly and Gregory had felt constrained to reply.

Gregory's personal obsession with Shakespeare did not prohibit him from taking an academic interest in lesser works, nor from acknowledging merits he thought were due. The latter applied to Galsworthy and Barrie, and he would probably have enjoyed directing and acting in their plays, had he not viewed his present necessity to do so through Plantaine eyes.

"The most I can say for Ibsen is he knew how to construct a play," he now declaimed. "What I quarrel with are his themes. The man was seeking, through his work, to make a mockery of accepted standards of behavior, and of woman's place. I considered he had gone too far with *A Doll's House*. Then he topped that piece of outrageousness with his sordid *Ghosts*."

Luke would have liked to discuss *Ghosts*, but its theme was socially taboo. He would be in Gregory's bad books forever if he raised the subject of venereal disease! And Luke wanted to shine in the dragon's eyes.

As Lucy did. "We ought to be talking about *Romeo and Juliet*, and how my brother and I shall manage not to let you down, Grandfather," she said giving Gregory her impish smile.

Oliver patted her hand. "Have no fear, my pet. You won't."

"They had better not," Gregory declared. "As their name is now Plantaine, they must live up to it."

He had not been displeased when the twins decided to adopt their stepfather's name. They were talented and refined and Gregory had accepted them as ready-made grandchildren. Indeed, it was hard to relate them to their dreadful mother, he frequently thought.

For their part, Luke and Lucy both feared and respected Gregory. From him, they were learning the tricks of their trade—though Gregory would have been horrified to know that they viewed his teachings that way.

Above all, the twins knew on which side their bread was buttered. Fate and their late father's money had given them this privileged foothold on the ladder they were dedicated to climbing. Both were determined, with Gregory's help, to reach the top.

Luke's ambition was not limited to acting. "When I'm older, I'd like to try my hand at directing. Combine it with performing, like you do, Grandfather," he confided.

Gregory felt himself blanch and hoped it did not show. "Would you indeed?" he chuckled. "That's a high aspiration to have, when you're only eighteen!"

Those around the table joined in Gregory's amusement.

Luke took it in good part. "Everyone has their dreams."

And Luke's did not bode well for Gregory's future. He could see himself, a few years hence, sharing the directing with this lad. Ruby would enjoy making sure that he did.

Oliver had slipped away to fetch her and found her in the downstage wing chair she would occupy tonight when she played Mrs. Tanqueray. Rehearsals for the next production were held on the set of the current one and furnishings removed only as necessary.

"Come, come, my dear," Oliver said, scanning Ruby's expression. "This isn't like you."

"How do you know it isn't?"

"From living with you, of course. And I've never seen you sit sulking."

Ruby gazed at a vase of roses on the Tanquerays' heavily carved sideboard and it struck her that the artificial blooms—it was said to be unlucky to use real flowers onstage—were like herself. She had spent the past nineteen months pretending to be a lady, so the Plantaines wouldn't look down on her. Even her husband had seen only flashes of the real Ruby.

"You don't really know me, Oliver," she said wryly. "If you did, you wouldn't have made me your wife."

"Now you are being ridiculous."

"No. I'm being honest, for once."

Ruby studied Oliver's handsome face and, suddenly, he was very dear to her. But was she dear to him? "Why did you marry me?" she asked him. It had certainly not been for sex. And Ruby was sure the reason was not money.

Oliver went to kneel beside her and took her hand. "You're what I need, Ruby," he said simply. "And that is the truth, make of it what you may. Why did you marry me?"

"Because I was lonely, Oliver, and you are who you are. I'd reached a turning point in my life, personally and professionally. And I had the twins to think of, as well as myself. They'd always been mad on Shakespeare and idolized the Plantaine Players. Did I ever tell you that once, when my company and the Plantaines were playing the same town—I think it was Birmingham—Luke and Lucy visited me and stayed over Saturday night, but they went to see your show, not mine!"

They shared a laugh and Oliver was glad to see his wife her usual self again. "So you married me because of who I am, did you?" he said with a dry smile.

"Because of what it could do for me and my children," Ruby declared. It was a relief to know that with Oliver, if not with his family, she could revert to her habit of calling a spade a spade.

"It doesn't matter," Oliver told her. And added, avoiding her eye, "Who I am is no secret. But you could not have known what I am."

Ruby did not tell him that rumor had prepared her for it. "That doesn't matter, either, Oliver. I told you so, on our wedding night. And I meant it."

Oliver turned to look at her. They gazed for a long moment into each other's eyes and each knew that the other had spoken the truth. And the feeling now flowing between them, born of their mutual need and strengthened by honesty, was, in the purest sense, love.

Oliver was still kneeling beside Ruby and she gently stroked his hair. "I'll never do anything to hurt you, Oliver."

"Or I you."

"And I want you always to remember something," Ruby added.

Oliver prickled with foreboding.

"I married you, not your family." Ruby's voice hardened. "Your father is more beholden to me than I to him. He would never have got his own theater without me. But I want you to know, Oliver, that nothing I say or do, regarding the company, is intended to hurt you."

The midday break was almost over and most of the company had left the Green Room. Afternoon rehearsal was to begin with the Capulets' feast, a large-scale scene with which Gregory was not yet satisfied.

A mischievous quirk had impelled him to cast Hermione as Lady Capulet. Ruby had reluctantly had to make do with playing Romeo's mother, Lady Montague—a lesser part.

For Shakespearean productions, Gregory had the final word on casting, and Ruby for other plays. Ruby had suggested this as a workable arrangement and Gregory had been relieved that she had. It was a way of keeping her hands off his beloved Shakespeare, and of ensuring she did not make a travesty of his work, by casting herself in major roles.

Jessica had the plum part of the Nurse, which she had played many times.

"Come along, my dear!" Gregory said to her. "Duty calls."

"There's more than one kind of duty, Gregory dear," Jessica replied.

She was seated at a corner table with some middle-aged actresses and all of them were busily knitting. Masses of mufflers, balaclavas and gloves had been produced and sent by them to the Front.

Alison was sitting with them. "As they couldn't turn me into a knitter—I kept dropping stitches—they've made me a wool-winder, Grandpa!" she joked, displaying the ball of khaki wool she had just wound.

Jessica finished a row of knitting and started another. "We didn't succeed in making Lucy into either," she said, glancing at that young lady.

"I have weak wrists," Lucy sighed. "And such teeny hands," she added, gesturing gracefully to display them. "I'm not a big, strong girl, like Alison."

The remark made Alison feel like a raw-boned peasant, as it was intended to do. She shot Lucy an arrow of her own. "Can that be why you have such a small voice, Lucy? I couldn't hear you from the back at this morning's rehearsal."

Occasional inaudibility was one of Lucy's problems. She had not yet learned to project her voice and knew it. "My mother is not very pleased with the acoustics here," she lied.

"They are probably different from what she has been accustomed to," Alison replied sweetly.

It was not necessary to add that the acoustics in the drinking establishments in which Ruby had often performed were not to be compared with those of a real theater.

Luke exchanged a glance with his sister and gave Alison a baleful look. "We shall have to see how your voice fares, when the time comes, Alison."

Alison eyed him coldly. "I have no fears on that account. The time cannot come soon enough for me—except that I don't look forward to sharing a stage with you."

"Now, now, children!" Gregory intervened. He had not known his granddaughter had any claws to show, until she revealed them. "Let us not have any dramas offstage."

The older people present laughed, but the three youngsters had their tongues in their cheeks. In the Plantaine family, there were more dramas offstage than on, these days, and Gregory could not be so blind that he did not know it.

Gregory consulted his watch. "Where is your mama, Alison? I was about to inquire, before you dear children began practicing your histrionics upon us, if she is lunching out again? If so, I hope she won't return late."

It occurred to Alison, then, that her mother had taken to lunching out, recently. Alison had seen no significance in it. Until now. "I don't know where Mama is," she replied stiffly. Nor did she care! But the painful matter of Hermione's infidelity had returned to the forefront of her mind.

Jessica glanced up from her knitting, but her needles continued clicking. "She is probably in her dressing room, Gregory dear. Talking to that nice young officer."

"Which nice young officer?" Gregory asked.

Alison felt her cheeks flush with shame, on her mother's behalf. It had to be the man she had seen embracing Hermione. How dare Mama invite him backstage!

"I met him by the stage door, when he was asking for Hermione," Jessica said. "I believe he said his name was Brown? Or was it White?"

"It was probably Green!" Gregory said to everyone's amusement.

Jessica's vagueness had increased since the company was restructured. The mixed repertoire, after a lifetime of undiluted Shakespeare, and her husband's unprecedented failure to maintain their former *status quo,* had disoriented her.

"Whichever color it was, he was absolutely charming," she declared.

Grandma is easy to fool, Alison thought with affection for her. But she didn't know what Alison knew!

"He had come to return Hermione's gloves—or it may have been her scarf—which she had left at the officers' mess, last night," Jessica supplied.

"How very gallant of him," Alison could not stop herself from saying.

Only Lucy and Luke interpreted the comment for the sarcasm it was. Both looked as if they would like to snigger and there was no mistaking the knowing glance they exchanged, or the snide way they were eyeing Alison now. But their mother was no better than hers! Alison thought defensively. Or perhaps she was? Ruby's supper engagements with her officer admirers did not, so far as Alison knew, include kissing them goodnight.

Gregory rose from his chair, which was the signal for the others. Alison found herself alone in the Green Room with a mound of khaki knitting wool. The table was heaped with skeins of it and her grandmother had draped one on the back of a chair, for Alison to wind.

Alison averted her eyes. The color had combined with her feelings to conjure up a picture of her father risking his life on the battlefield, carrying away the dead and wounded, while her mother—!

But Alison wouldn't let herself think about it. Nor would she sit here winding wool, though she had nothing better to do. How was she to spend the afternoon? The evening, too, stretched endlessly ahead of her. Hours and hours of emptiness.

When she was younger, she had been content to sit and watch others rehearse. And to watch performances from her privileged place in the wings, mouthing the actors' words with them, anticipating their moves, with which she was as well versed as they were.

She had, too, spent time in the wardrobe room, watching Nellie and her assistants fashion splendid costumes from the lengths of velvet, brocade and muslin picked up at bargain sales and kept in a glorious tangle in a huge wicker skip. Alison could go there now and watch the *Romeo and Juliet* costumes taking shape. It would be a change from sitting in on rehearsals. But she had no taste for either.

She left the Green Room and came face to face with her mother. Was that a guilty look in Hermione's eyes? Alison could not be sure.

"All by yourself, Alison?" Hermione said for want of anything else to say. Her daughter's piercing gaze was making her feel uncomfortable.

"I've decided to go up north for a few days," Alison said, though she had not known she was going to say it. The words had sprung to her lips as suddenly as the need to escape had stirred within her.

"I don't recall you asking for my permission," Hermione answered coldly.

"What would be the point of my asking? I wouldn't get it."

Alison's blunt statement crystallized for Hermione that her daughter had, somehow, become mistress of her own life.

"You'll be late for rehearsal," Alison said.

"I think you may leave me to worry about that, dear."

The maternal rebuke made no mark upon Alison and Hermione felt that she herself was making a last stand. There was no longer any question of treating Alison as a child.

"When shall you go?" Hermione inquired.

"Tomorrow morning. This afternoon I shall wash my hair and pack my suitcase."

Hermione surveyed the assured young lady Alison undoubtedly was. Where was the little girl who had once clung to her skirts? It was a feeling all mothers experience when their children metamorphose, as if overnight, into adults, but for Hermione there was an added poignancy. Her husband was far away and her daughter had withdrawn from her.

She wanted to fling her arms around Alison and tell her that she loved her, but dignity forbade it. It would be tantamount to begging forgiveness for she knew not what.

Hermione had still not acknowledged her own contribution to the state of affairs between them. Nor had it occurred to her that Alison, too, was endowed with Plantaine pride.

To Hermione, it was still as though Shrager blood alone ran in her daughter's veins. And the rift had widened irrevocably when Alison fled to her Jewish relatives. Hermione blamed them for everything. Not quite everything—the war had played its part, too, she thought, leaning against the wall outside the Green Room, engulfed by self-pity.

Alison stood fiddling with a button on her blouse. Her mother's frock, she noted, looked crumpled. No doubt from Lieutenant Brown-White-Green's furtive embraces in her dressing room!

"I had better bid you goodbye now, Mama," she said and was surprised that her voice displayed no emotion. She had not yet learned that she was blessed with a self-possession that was to stand her in good stead all her professional life.

"You won't be returning to the lodgings before tonight's performance, will you, Mama?" she went on lightly.

"But aren't you coming back to the theater, after you've packed?"

Alison shook her head. "And I shall, no doubt, be fast asleep long before you return from your night out."

"I don't recall mentioning I had an engagement tonight," Hermione said, avoiding her eye.

"Haven't you?"

"Well yes, as a matter of fact."

"Well then, Mama."

"Well then what?" Hermione found herself asking defensively.

"Well then I'd better bid you goodbye now. As I said." Alison flicked a speck of fluff off her blue serge skirt. "As you don't rise in time for breakfast nowadays, Mama, I'm unlikely to see you before I leave."

On the surface, the remark was innocent enough. But an enigmatic smile was hovering around Alison's lips. Barely noticeable, unless you knew there could be a reason for it, Hermione thought.

Alison's aversion to confronting her mother with what she knew, need not, she had decided, prevent her from implying it. Or from savoring Hermione's reaction, which was that of a person with a guilty conscience. Mama's hand had fluttered to her throat.

Hermione pulled herself together and put a stage smile on her face. Her daughter was playing some sort of cat-and-mouse game with her and how dare she! If Hermione didn't throw her hat over the windmill, it would be no thanks to Alison. And it was small wonder if soldiers' wives did—as their husbands were probably doing, with the mademoiselles. Loneliness led people to behave in wartime as they would not in peacetime. And Alison was no comfort to Hermione. On the contrary!

They exchanged a duty kiss and went their separate ways, which in effect they had been doing for some time.

Hermione turned her thoughts to Lady Capulet and, with satisfaction, to Ruby's disappointment when she did not get that part. Hermione had, to her surprise, found it an interesting challenge to perform in the more contemporary plays. But the pleasure of stretching her talent was tempered by a sense of disloyalty to her father and the Bard; and of injustice, because Ruby always had the leading role. Only in Shakespearean productions was Hermione able to score over her.

Professional rivalry apart, Ruby was, to Hermione, the materialization of the menacing, larger than life figure who had haunted her from afar.

To a woman of Hermione's refinement, Ruby could not help but seem monstrously overripe. She exuded sexual promise from every pore.

As for her menacing quality, Hermione was unable to account for it. Since marrying into the Plantaine family, Ruby dressed less flamboyantly, as her position demanded. But her earthiness defied camouflage and the inexplicable threat she represented to Hermione was still there.

Hermione had initially pinned it down to a fear that Horace might find Ruby more attractive than herself. She now knew it was rooted in the effect Ruby had upon her personally.

For Hermione, as for most women, sex lived side by side with romance, and the latter was possible without the former. But not the other way round.

Her marriage had satisfactorily provided both, dispelling her conditioned belief that its physical aspect would be but an unpleasant wifely duty. She had learned she was a passionate woman and it had not been easy for her to sustain her refusal to let Horace make love to her.

After Horace went away to the war, her longing for him had increased and she had assuaged her aching nights with remembrance of the intimacies they had once shared in each other's arms.

That innocent comfort had, of late, been replaced by sexual fantasies of another kind, in which Hermione and her husband did not feature. They centered upon Ruby, stripping herself naked; slowly and languorously displaying her lush white body to a man whose face eluded Hermione. But she knew he was not her brother. Oliver was fair and slender. The man with whom the nude Ruby did things no decent woman would do was swarthy and built like a bull.

Night after night, Hermione was an unwilling voyeur of these scenes of depravity, born in her own mind, from which she drew a vicarious sensual pleasure that left her spent and filled with self-disgust.

In the daylight hours, she did not think about it and became again the perfect lady she knew she really was. Hermione was not prepared to admit that the shadowy threat Ruby represented to her was the darker side of herself. Ruby symbolized lust and Hermione was, in her own eyes, gentility personified.

It was this genteel person who made her way to afternoon rehearsal, ten minutes late, in her white-collared gray frock, her pale-gold hair drawn back into a demure bun.

Her visitor had told her she looked like a Quaker girl today. That did not stop him from kissing her lips, and holding her hand despite the wedding ring on it.

Captain Andrew Browne-Hogg was a still boyish twenty-six—ten years younger than Hermione—and unmarried. He had been posted to Hastings three months ago and had showered Hermione with attention from the moment he set eyes on her at a mess party.

Ruby's supper engagements—which Oliver called his wife's public appearances—had impelled Hermione to begin accepting invitations to army social functions. In the matter of public adulation, she would not be outdone by her sister-in-law if she could help it.

But it had not taken Hermione long to find herself enjoying her hosts' admiration on a personal level. Or to think, in her loneliness, "Why not?"—and take her pick of them. When wifely conscience pricked her, she told herself that what her husband didn't know couldn't hurt him; nor was there any harm in her pleasant flirtations.

Andrew was not the first, but had lasted longer than the others. He was a regular, reluctantly deskbound by a leg wound incurred in the first year of the war. Timely

postings to the Front had conveniently ended Hermione's previous encounters, but Andrew might conceivably remain in Hastings for the duration and she could
not bring herself to break his heart.

Hermione cast aside these personal thoughts when she
reached the wings. Switching off was second nature to
her; she had been doing it all her adult life.

Ruby switched her on again, as she was wont to do.
"Oh there you are, darling! Had a nice lunch?"

"Delightful, thank you, dear," said Hermione, who
had eaten nothing.

Ruby surveyed her. "I'm pleased to hear it, Hermione
love. I have always thought you need feeding up."

"I've always considered my slenderness an advantage,
Ruby dear. It allows me a professional versatility those
less fortunate do not have. With the benefit of padding, I
am able to play female characters of any girth. And you,
darling, have my deepest sympathy. It must be absolutely
dreadful to be limited by your size. My heart has always
gone out to actresses whose padding cannot be
removed."

Round one to my sister! Oliver thought dryly. Hermione's sympathetic tone could not be faulted, nor her
sweet smile, but she might just as well have said in plain
words that Ruby was fat. These sugary exchanges were
not uncommon and Oliver knew his wife would not let
Hermione get away with it.

Ruby did not let him down. "Forgive me for mentioning something so personal, but I can't contain my surprise. I always thought you were a natural blonde," she
said to Hermione.

"I am."

This Ruby knew and her prey was now wide open for
the kill. "Oh dear! I've put my foot in it," she said, feign-
ing contrition. "I didn't mean to draw attention to those
dark hairs on your collar."

But she had cunningly succeeded in doing so. The as-

sembled actors and actresses had fallen silent, to listen to
the sparring match.

Hermione felt a warmth in her cheeks and knew that
she had blushed. Andrew Browne-Hogg had dark hair.
Some of the company had probably seen him in the
dressing-room corridor before lunch. And those who
hadn't would have heard of his visit—the backstage
grapevine was all too efficient.

Ruby removed the telltale hairs from Hermione's collar, as a thoughtful sister-in-law would.

"Thank you, darling," Hermione said with a grateful
smile. What she would have liked to do was pull Ruby's
hair from her head.

Her father, who was seated onstage making notes on
his director's pad, had stopped scribbling to look at her.
But Papa would not interfere with her private life. As
always, he would close his mind to what he would rather
not know.

Gregory rose from his chair. "Conversational dal-
liance is all very well, but let us not forget the immortal
words—'The play's the thing'!" He smiled fondly at
Hermione and Ruby. "If you dear girls have concluded
your friendly chat, we'll start work."

One of them was not in the least dear to him, and knew
it; and the saccharine sweetness of their exchange coated
a bitter pill, as the pleasant demeanor Gregory was now
displaying toward his daughter-in-law belied his real
feelings.

Theatricals were well practiced in maintaining a facade of all-round amicability. Without it, the teamwork
theater demanded could not be achieved. Tantrums
were thrown and forgotten. Enmities lived on, veiled by
false *bonhomie*. Hence the prevailing atmosphere of everyone being everyone's best friend.

These were Gregory's dispassionate thoughts as the
actors playing Maskers and Servingmen positioned
themselves onstage for the Capulets' feast. He went into
the auditorium, to see how the grouping would look from

out front when Capulet had entered with the Guests and Gentlewomen.

The male members of the company were in the main elderly or middle-aged—some far too old for the parts they were playing. But Gregory had no option but to engage them. The war had denuded the profession of young men. Drafting had begun in May and Luke's imminent departure would add to Gregory's casting problems.

Ruby, and Jason Standish, a fruity-voiced actor engaged to play her husband, came to join Gregory in the stalls; Romeo's parents, the Montagues, did not feature in this scene.

"Do make yourself comfortable, my dear," Gregory said graciously to his hated daughter-in-law.

Jason tipped down a seat for her. "There you are, Ruby darling!"

"How kind!" Ruby gushed to both of them. Her punishment would be meted out to Gregory all in good time. As for Jason, his habit of upstaging her called for a kick in the arse!

Jason adjusted the yellow silk cravat he wore to hide his sagging neck, smoothed his mane of silver hair and sat down beside her. Had Ruby been able to read his mind, she would have learned that the feeling was mutual.

Gregory gave the signal for Capulet and his entourage to make their entrance, and the sense of theater that was the core of his being took him in its grip. There were times, of late, when he felt he might suffocate beneath the verbal syrup ladled out by himself and those around him. But it was a small price to pay for the pleasure of pursuing his art.

TWO

Journeying north, Alison put from her mind the troubles she was briefly leaving behind. In most respects—if not all, as her future would demonstrate—she was a sensible person, and had counseled herself on the futility of seeking a respite, if what she was escaping from went with her in her head.

Instead, she concentrated her thoughts on those to whom she was going. Emma's letters had kept her in touch though, typically, they made little mention of Emma herself.

Alison had learned that her Grandpa Shrager had grown pernickety, as time passed by and ill health continued to prohibit his return to the family business. Emma had confided that he was giving Grandma a difficult time, though Minna never uttered a word of complaint.

Emma had written, too, that Conrad had joined up and that her mother worried about him night and day, though he had not yet been sent to France.

It would be good to see Emma again, Alison thought with an anticipatory smile when she was changing trains in London. And to have a good laugh, when Uncle Lionel told his Jewish jokes. Clara was the only blot on Alison's immediate horizon. In retrospect, Alison's antipathy to her was no less.

Some months ago, Conrad had scribbled in a postscript to one of Emma's letters that Clara now had a steady boyfriend and was more impossible than ever. He had been home on leave at the time, and Alison had replied that with a sister like Clara she didn't blame him for joining up.

But she knew that patriotism had impelled him to do so. Only his father's pleas had stopped Conrad from volunteering immediately when war was declared. Lionel Stein had used Grandpa Shrager's illness as a lever, and Conrad's family loyalty was strong. But in the end he had not waited to be drafted. Allegiance to his country had won.

And he would not take Alison's joke the wrong way, she thought with an affection for him that was hard to relate to their brief acquaintanceship. With one exception, she was fond of all the Steins and sometimes wondered how it was possible for her to feel so close to people who had entered her life less than two years ago and with whom she had spent so little time.

Alison was not yet mature enough to realize it had happened because the Steins had allowed her to get close to them.

Lottie Stein had not hesitated to open her motherly arms and embrace within her family her brother's child, despite her initial reservations about Alison.

Little by little, the reservations had dispersed. The week Alison spent under her roof was sufficient to reveal to Lottie that her young niece's assured manner was not arrogance, as she had at first feared, but bespoke the shining confidence with which Alison was endowed. Lottie had come to know, too, that despite that confidence Alison was emotionally vulnerable.

Lottie had been aware that Alison was hurt by her Grandpa Shrager's apparent indifference to her. And that whatever had caused Alison to desert her mother at Christmastime, when she arrived unheralded on the Steins' doorstep, was a source of distress to her, not pique.

Alison's eagerness to fit in had both moved and puzzled Lottie. Why does this elegant, beautifully spoken girl want to be one of us? she had pondered; Alison was not of the Steins' humdrum world. Then Alison's marked resemblance to herself had brought Lottie up short and had dispelled her misgivings. And soon, there was no doubt in Lottie's mind that her Gentile niece felt herself as much a Shrager as a Plantaine.

But what had the Plantaines done to her? Lottie had wondered. Or was it something they had failed to do? Why had a girl raised among her mother's family fled to her father's, displaying what Lottie had come to realize was a pathetic need to belong?

Lottie would have been gratified to know that the Steins had fulfilled that need. As the train from Manchester to Oldham neared its destination, Alison's impatience increased. It was as though she was going home.

Day was fading to twilight when she reached the Steins' house. How lovely it looked at this time of year, she thought drinking in the sight of it. Though it was early September, and officially autumn, the tangle of rambler roses adorning the trellis arch above the garden gate were still in bloom.

A light shower had freshened the lawn and a grassy fragrance rose to Alison's nostrils as she walked up the neatly paved path, which had shimmered with frost when she was last here. So, too, had the bare branches of the laburnum, now abundant with foliage that provided the front parlor with shade on sunny days. Alison wished she could see it when its leaves turned to autumn gold, but by then, she would be long gone.

Briefly, she was assailed by the feeling she had had on the train the first time she came here, when she had thought of herself as a straw on the wind. But now she had the comforting haven her life had lacked. Somewhere to run to when things went wrong. How warming that thought was.

Alison set down her suitcase on the doorstep, savoring the moment. She had no doubt about the kind of welcome she would receive. She raised her hand and lifted the doorknocker.

"There's nobody in, luv!" a voice cried shrilly to her from across the street. "T'family's gone on their 'olidays."

Alison let the heavy brass knocker fall with a dull thud that matched her lowered spirits. How silly of her not to have remembered that the Steins took their summer holiday late. Last year, Emma had sent Alison a picture postcard from Blackpool; of a very fat lady in a bathing costume. Mama had picked it up with the rest of the mail and had pronounced it vulgar. Sometimes Alison thought her mother had no sense of humor—but she didn't want to think of Mama.

While she had been doing so, the Steins' nosey neighbor had come to have a word with her.

"Aren't you that relation o' theirs, who's one o' them there theatricals?" Mrs. Ramsden inquired. "What came to stop wi' 'em for Christmas, in 1914?"

Alison nodded and, despite her dejection, had to smile. The Steins didn't need to keep a diary of who visited them, and when—all they need do was ask Mrs. Ramsden, who had pigeonholed Alison as "one of them there theatricals!" Technically, Alison did not yet qualify for the appelation, but was amused to learn how the general public thought of those who did.

"It was kind of you to come and speak to me," she said summoning her charm. "I remember my aunt saying that you're a very good neighbor." Lottie had mentioned the nosiness, too.

" 'As there been some sort o' mix-up, luv? You look as if you came expectin' to stop wi' 'em," Mrs. Ramsden replied. Alison's suitcase had not escaped her eagle eye. "There must've been a mix-up," she decided.

"Not exactly," Alison answered. "I just wasn't expecting my relatives to be away." She mustered another smile. "Please don't let me keep you from whatever you were doing."

"Your relations'll be back tomorrow," Mrs. Ramsden said.

Alison's spirits lifted. She had already decided to go to her grandparents, but that wouldn't be like staying with the Steins. Now, she could look forward to sharing Emma's room tomorrow night.

She picked up her suitcase and Mrs. Ramsden walked with her to the gate.

"I'm surprised you didn't know this is Oldham Wakes Week, luv," Mrs. Ramsden said. "A lot o' folk'd like it to be in August, like it is in some other mill towns, but I don't mind when it is, so long as folk get their week off. If there weren't no Wakes Week, your uncle'd never take a break from 'is shop, nor me 'usband from 'is mill. I'm all-us tellin' me old man that 'e works 'arder than them what works for 'im!"

"My family never take a holiday," Alison told her. "While others are taking theirs, the theaters remain open."

"That's a shame, luv. There's nowt like a plateful o' cockles 'n' mussels for puttin' a sparkle in your eye. Me an' me 'usband went for t'day to Blackpool, it bein' Wakes Week," she said, returning to her subject. "We 'ad a plateful each, fresh from t'stall on't seafront. You should've seen t'lasses, walkin' arm-in-arm along t'prom, laughin' an' singin'. It'll take more'n Kaiser Bill to stop Oldham folk from makin' t'most o' their week off."

They had paused by the gate before parting, and Alison felt as if she had just been hearing a sermon, and a very stirring one. The homely woman—whom Alison had been surprised to learn was a millowner's wife—had made it plain that the spirit of this small Lancashire town was undiminished by the war. Alison felt proud to be British; she had no doubt that Mrs. Ramsden's sentiments were echoed throughout the realm.

"I 'ardly recognized you, luv," Mrs. Ramsden said. "Since t'last time I saw you, you've grown a lot bigger."

Alison did not require telling. It was not just her five-foot-ten height to which that word applied. Since donning the corset necessary as a foundation for grown-up clothes, she had become conscious of her shapely bust and hips. The wardrobe mistress had said that Alison had an hourglass figure which many females would envy. To Alison it was a source of embarrassment.

So, too, were the glances she received when she walked in the street. As Alison kept her gaze fixed firmly ahead, she had not registered the admiration with which men of all ages beheld her. Awareness of her own beauty was still a pleasure to come.

"I'd offer to put you up for t'night, if you didn't 'ave your gran around t'corner," Mrs. Ramsden said.

Alison gave her a warm smile. The woman's kindness made up for her nosiness, as Aunt Lottie had said.

"Best be off wi' you, then, lass, afore it gets proper dark. An' that's a luvly outfit you've got on. Specially your 'at."

"Thank you, Mrs. Ramsden. Our company wardrobe mistress made my hat," Alison said, touching the big-brimmed millinery Nellie had concocted from a remnant of coral silk, to add dash to Alison's beige linen jacket and skirt.

"It's like them 'ats Princess Mary wears," Mrs. Ramsden declared.

Alison laughed. "I know. And my Grandma Plantaine wears hats like the Queen's. Nellie is very clever—she cuts out the newspaper pictures of the royal ladies and copies their hats for us. Nellie used to be a milliner when she was a girl."

"Tell 'er she'd make a fortune if she opened a shop round 'ere," Mrs. Ramsden said before she and Alison parted.

Their conversation, from which Alison had at first impatiently longed to escape, had served as a welcome back to the friendly north of England, and she made her way to her grandparents' home cheered by the encounter.

When she arrived, it was Conrad who opened the door.

"You've done it on us again!" he exclaimed. "Arriving without notice seems to be your speciality, Alison." But his face was wreathed with smiles.

"What a marvelous surprise!" Alison said delightedly. She had thought him miles away, in an army camp. "How nice you look in your uniform, Conrad."

"I hope you've noticed the stripe on my sleeve," he answered bashfully. "Lance-bombardier!"

"I didn't, until you pointed it out. I was too busy looking at your funny face."

"And me at yours. But it didn't stop me from noticing how big you've grown."

Oh, that dreadful word! But I shall have to get used to it, Alison thought resignedly. She was doomed to bigness for the rest of her life.

Their light-hearted banter continued for a moment or two longer. Then Alison asked where her grandmother was. It was unusual for Minna not to appear from her kitchen when someone knocked at the front door.

"She's trying to persuade our grandfather to come out of the conservatory," Conrad replied. "He spends all his time messing about with the plants, nowadays."

"That sounds like a good sign," Alison said. "I'm sure it's good for him to have something to do," she added sensibly.

"Not to the extent he does it. It's become like a mania

with him. The doctor ordered him to rest in the afternoon, but Grandma can't get him to."

Alison was beginning to understand what Emma had meant when she wrote that Minna was having a difficult time. "I must go and tell Grandma I'm here," she said, thinking how nice it was to be able to take it for granted that she could stay the night. Though she did not know Walter and Minna very well, the fact that they were her grandparents assured her of her welcome.

"Stay and talk to me for a few minutes," Conrad said as Alison headed toward the breakfast room, which had French windows leading into the conservatory.

Alison paused and turned to look at him. His expression was pensive.

"I'm going to France when I return to camp," he said. "But don't tell Grandma. She's already worrying herself into the ground about your dad."

Alison sat down on the hall bench. "But you'll have to tell your parents, won't you?"

"I wish anyone luck to keep anything from Mam! But she'll go mad when she gets home and finds she's missed a day of her precious son's embarkation leave."

Conrad leaned against the oak paneling and whistled a few bars of *Mademoiselle from Armentières*.

Was he scared? Alison wondered. Who wouldn't be? The heavy casualty lists were enough to put the fear of God into anyone, but had not stopped boys from volunteering. It was as though the war had somehow endowed them with a special strength to steel themselves against whatever came. But even the bravest soldier was only human. How did those in the trenches make themselves obey the terrifying order to go "over the top?" Alison was sure that she could not do it.

Everyone thought that America was bound to enter the war eventually; that great country would not stand by indefinitely, but would lend its might to crushing the enemy. How did Germany become our enemy? Alison mused briefly. In company with most people, she was not clear what, exactly, the war was all about.

All that was clear were the consequences of war. This one was said to be the war that would end all wars and Alison hoped and prayed that this would be so. Meanwhile, people must live with their fear for loved ones at the Front, and, to a lesser extent, for their own safety.

Alison had never seen a zeppelin and could not believe it possible for bombs to rain from the sky, until it happened. Nor could she believe it when she learned that a zeppelin raid had damaged London's Lyceum Theatre. The dressing-room block had been hit and the theater was closed for repairs.

It had reopened last Boxing Day, with the pantomime *Robinson Crusoe*—and if that wasn't thumbing your nose at the Kaiser! Alison thought with pride.

Conrad emerged from his own rumination and interrupted Alison's. "By the way, Albert Battersby is on leave with me."

Alison froze. "Albert who?" But why was she pretending she had forgotten him, when she very definitely had not?

"My old school pal, who you took such a dislike to when you were last here."

"Oh, him," Alison said disparagingly.

"We joined up together," Conrad told her. "When the draft was announced we knew it meant that things were getting really desperate and did what we felt we had to do. We're in the same artillery unit. Albert's just got his stripe, too."

"Give him my congratulations," Alison replied curtly. She softened her tone. "I ought to have congratulated you."

"I was only joking when I asked if you'd noticed. They're two-a-penny in wartime." He did not add what was becoming increasingly clear; that promotion represented dead men's shoes.

Conrad brushed aside that grim thought and surveyed

Alison. He would not have called her exactly beautiful when he last saw her, though she had always been something special. Now, she was a real stunner. "Albert will be tickled pink when he finds out you're here, Alison."

"If you mean he'll look forward to getting my back up again, he won't be given the opportunity to," she flashed.

Conrad laughed. "You're not still holding against him whatever it was he said that upset you, are you?" Conrad had never been quite sure how Alison's antagonism toward Albert had come about. "You were only in his company for about ten minutes," he reminded her.

"Ten minutes too long," she replied.

Her own recollection of what had transpired during the short walk to church, that Christmas morning, was as hazy as Conrad's. But engraved on her mind was a memory of herself, in her emerald tammy and scarf, and podgy Albert Battersby, whose overcoat had looked about to burst its buttons, having a shouting match.

Or the equivalent of one, Alison thought now. She would not have lowered herself to shout. She was sure she had put off that Battersby boy—as she had come to think of him—in a dignified way. But she could not recall what had caused her to do so.

Conrad was studying her tight-lipped expression. "Albert certainly had a funny effect on you."

"He did indeed!"

"I mean, you don't strike me as the kind of person who bears grudges, Alison."

"I'm not."

"Then why are you being like this about Albert?" Conrad came to give Alison's cheek a cousinly kiss. "Will you try not to be, Alison? He sent you a peace offering, didn't he?"

An edible one! Alison thought derisively, recalling the peppermints. He probably ate sweets himself all the time, which accounted for him being so pimply and podgy, she unkindly surmised.

"I didn't tell him you refused to take it," Conrad went

on. "And I hope you won't. You didn't see him again last time you were here, because at Christmas Albert gets invited to a lot of parties—"

"I wouldn't have thought him so popular," Alison cut in.

"There you go again!"

"Even had he not got my back up, I doubt that he would have seemed likable to me."

Conrad gazed up at the blue-and-white china displayed on the hall plate-rack. His impatience was plain to see. "And heaven help anyone you take a dislike to, Alison, is all I can say! But Albert Battersby was the most popular lad in our class."

"It was obviously a boys' school," Alison said cuttingly.

"We'd hardly have been likely to attend a girls school!" Conrad retorted. "You seem to have forgotten that Hulme Grammar is for boys and girls. And Albert did a lot better with the lasses than I did," Conrad added with a reminiscent grin.

"Why are you telling me this, Conrad?"

"Because you keep attacking Albert, so I have to defend him. What I was going to say, when you interrupted me, was that you'll be seeing more of him this time. As we're home together, we'll be at each other's houses a lot."

"I timed my visit badly," Alison said with chagrin. "Not that I'm not absolutely delighted that you're here, Conrad."

"And you wouldn't want to spoil my embarkation leave, by being funny with my best pal, would you, love?" Conrad answered, employing a little blackmail.

"All right," Alison conceded grudgingly. "I'll try not to be what you call funny with him, Conrad. But I can't promise to be nice to him."

Conrad breathed a sigh of relief. What Alison had promised was, for the moment, enough.

"Was that what you wanted to talk to me about?" she asked.

Conrad nodded. "I thought I'd get it over, while I had you to myself. I hope you didn't object to me speaking my mind."

Alison rose from the bench and smoothed down her skirt, which she had discovered wearing grown-up clothes demanded whenever she got up or sat down. "I hope you will always speak your mind to me, Conrad. As I shall, to you."

"It's a promise, Alison."

"For me, too."

Their lives were destined to be interlinked in a way neither could then have imagined, and rancorous words would one day pass between them. But neither would ever doubt the other's honesty.

Meanwhile, on this September evening in 1916, they had taken the first steps toward the friendship their kinship did not guarantee and felt they knew each other a little better.

They were standing smiling at each other, when their grandmother came into the hall.

Minna stopped in her tracks and stared at Alison. "I don't believe it!"

"You had better, Grandma," Alison laughed. "Unless you prefer to think it's my ghost who's going to spend the night here!"

"God forbid!" Minna's Jewish conditioning prohibited tempting Fate. With her son a stretcher-bearer on the battlefield, and a grandson who, sooner or later, would also be dispatched there, Minna Stein had enough potential ghosts in her family.

She embraced Alison warmly, as she had when she bade her farewell. "So what brings you here, Alison? Don't bother to tell me. I'm happy you came. The others will have two happy surprises when they get back from their holiday, tomorrow. Not just Conrad, but also you.

Let's go into the kitchen. I have supper cooking, I must peep in the oven."

"Is that what I can smell burning?" Conrad joked as they followed her.

Minna quickened her step. "To see the baked mackerel turned into a burnt offering is all I need!"

A delicious, fishy aroma was pervading the kitchen. Alison caught the tang of lemon, too, and recalled that when Minna baked mackerel she served it with a lemon sauce.

"Conrad's teasing you, Grandma," Alison said with a smile. "There isn't a charred whiff in the air."

"Of course there isn't!" Conrad grinned. "And I'm ordering a double helping in advance. Though food burnt by Grandma would taste better than anything not burnt by the army cooks."

Minna was peering into the oven. "There's enough for you both to have double helpings."

"We don't doubt it," Conrad said, sharing a laugh with Alison.

Minna had not expected either of them, but it was a family joke that she had never learned to cook for two.

"I must go and say hello to Grandpa," Alison said.

"First, we'll have a cup of tea together," Minna replied. "Your grandpa is so busy with his plants, nowadays, a person has to shout down his ear before he knows they are there."

There was no resentment in Minna's voice. She had accepted her husband's new preoccupation as she had his former one. Once, his business had been his main concern and now it was his plants. He gave more care and attention to both, each in its turn, than he had ever devoted to people, and Minna had stopped asking herself why.

Conrad took the tea caddy from her hand. "Sit down, Grandma. Give yourself a rest." He put her into a chair, beside the hearth.

Alison fetched cups and saucers from the dresser,

while Conrad was making the tea. Her everyday life precluded such homely tasks; which was perhaps why she took such pleasure in performing them when she came north, she reflected, setting the willow-patterned crockery on her grandmother's spotless white cloth.

"I'm a lucky lady," Minna declared, watching the young people busy themselves. "The way you two are waiting on me."

Conrad smiled and brought the teapot to the table. "We want you to have something to remember us by."

"A fine thing for a soldier to say to his grandmother!" Minna cried.

Conrad had not realized the implications of his jocular words and gazed uncomfortably down at his gleaming army boots.

"You shouldn't let the things Conrad says upset you, Grandma. You know what a tease he is," Alison said lightly, though her feelings were far from light. A thoughtless idiot was what she felt like calling her cousin, right now! But Alison had already divined that tact was not Conrad's middle name.

Minna sighed. "How could I not know he's a tease, Alison? When he's been teasing me all his life. If he stopped doing it, I'd think there was something wrong with him. But in wartime, some things are not jokes."

Minna removed her apprehensive gaze from her grandson's uniform and noted her granddaughter's stylish outfit. "Take off your jacket, Alison. It's stuffy in here. And Conrad can open the window wider, to let some cool night air into the room. In daytime, I only have it opened a chink, I'd rather suffer the heat than the flies."

Minna's return to the commonplace was, for Alison and Conrad, a relief. She was now herself again. For Minna Shrager to express herself emotionally was comparable to a placid brook suddenly bursting its banks.

"That's a nice blouse you've got on," Minna remarked to Alison, who had draped her jacket over a chairback and was now pouring tea. "Since I last saw you, you've turned into a young lady."

"That must be why she's sitting in the kitchen with her hat on," Conrad said snidely.

Alison took it off. "I don't know how your sisters have put up with you all these years!" she flashed.

Minna chuckled. "A minute ago she was telling me not to let what he says upset me."

Conrad sat down to drink his tea and gave Alison a cheeky wink. "I think Grandma's reminding you that the kettle shouldn't call the pot black."

"Touché," Alison had to concede.

"What does that mean?" Conrad inquired suspiciously. "I'd rather be insulted in English, if you don't mind!"

"I wasn't insulting you, Conrad. Didn't you learn French at school?"

"Sure. *Et vous étes ma petite cousine,"* he said to prove it.

Alison's present sensitivity about her size was such that she was surprised he had not sacrificed his seniority in order to use the word *grande,* instead of *petite.* She told him what *touché* meant.

Conrad replied with mock chagrin. "To think that all my life I've been saying, 'All right, you win,' when I could've been saying—"

He was allowed to say no more. Alison shoved a biscuit into his mouth.

"My education in French was limited to useless things like verbs and grammar," he bantered when he had chewed the biscuit and swallowed it down. "Fancy expressions, they neglected to teach us!"

Alison's lessons from Jessica had also been limited— but the other way round.

Minna was enjoying herself immensely, thinking what a pleasure it was to have grandchildren. Clara and Emma often dropped in to see her, but Conrad had always been the one who made her laugh.

Alison, whom she was still getting to know, was revealing herself to be a girl with plenty of spirit—a quality Minna admired in others and had always known was absent in herself. As it was lacking in gentle, little Emma, Minna reflected while sipping her tea. Clara had spirit, but it showed itself as petulance. Alison's was proud and fiery, but she was a girl who knew how to stand up for herself with dignity, Minna thought now.

Before meeting Alison, Minna had expected to feel toward her exactly as she did toward her other grandchildren. Minna had certainly felt drawn to her—but grandmotherly her feelings were not.

On Alison's first visit, Minna had not been comfortable with her. She had never before encountered a girl like Alison and had found her, in some ways, formidable.

Alison could not have known that this was why her grandmother had talked to her only about Horace. Minna had felt that he was all they had in common. And that discussing him was safe ground.

The situation had been made more difficult for Minna by her chats with Alison taking place in Walter's sickroom. She had been aware not only of her own unease, but of her husband's.

It was Lottie who brought Minna to her senses—which was how Minna had come to think of her adjustment to Alison's place in her life. Would I ever have seen my mistake for myself? she mused while listening with half an ear to Conrad regaling Alison with tales of barrackroom life.

"You can't expect to have for Alison the identical feeling you have for my kids, Mother," Lottie had declared when Minna confessed her guilt on that account. "And you needn't feel conscience-stricken about it," Lottie had gone on. "What you felt in your heart for your other grandchildren when they were tiny babies, snuggling in your arms, can't be stirred in you by a fourteen-year-old. Once you accept that, Mother, and stop making comparisons, you might find Alison easy to love."

Minna glanced at the lively girl seated at her kitchen table and exchanged a smile with her. Lottie was right. Minna had applied her daughter's sound advice and, on Alison's last afternoon in Oldham, had looked at her with new eyes. She had, too, noticed Alison eyeing her wistfully, as though wanting something from Minna that was beyond her reach.

It had occurred to Minna, then, that perhaps Alison too had had expectations of their meeting which had not been fulfilled. When they parted, she had been impelled to hold her granddaughter close and was moved by Alison's response.

Today, though almost two years had gone by since that revealing farewell, neither had found it difficult to progress from where they had left off.

"I'm so happy to see you, Alison," Minna declared warmly.

"It's lovely to be with you, Grandma."

"Can anyone join the mutual admiration society?" Conrad quipped.

Alison laughed. "No. This one's between me and Grandma. You'll have to start one of your own."

For Alison, this was a precious moment. Her supposition that her grandmother had only accepted her because she was Papa's daughter had been proved wrong. Their parting embrace had cast doubt on it, but there was no mistaking the affection with which Minna was surveying her now.

But how her grandfather regarded her, she was far from sure she reflected, going with Conrad to let Walter know she was here. Alison had yet to learn that nobody really knew where they stood in Walter Shrager's affections; not even his wife.

The seizure from which he had not been expected to recover had condemned him to permanent invalidity. He had escaped death but, paralyzed on one side, would never walk again.

To make things easier for Minna, the breakfast room

had been converted to a bedroom for him. It had seldom
been used, any more than the dining room was. Except
on the Jewish High Holy Days they ate in the kitchen, as
the Steins did. In both homes, the parlor, too, was rarely
used and Alison had wondered why, in view of their simple way of life they lived in such fine houses.

She could not have divined the reason. Her own background, precarious though the Plantaines' fortunes had
been, had not encompassed the dogged uphill struggle
her father's family had known.

Though they had no pretensions to grandeur, residing
alongside Oldham's wealthy millowners and tradesmen
was, to Walter Shrager and Lionel Stein, recognition of
their achievement.

In their day, it was against the odds that a Jew would
succeed as they had. Most were still living in ghetto conditions. Who could blame Walter and Lionel—whose
wives would have been content with lesser homes—from
wanting to tell the world they had arrived?

"Grandpa hasn't far to go to get to his plants," Alison
observed. The French windows of the former breakfast
room were opened wide and they could see Walter in his
bathchair, amid the potted greenery at the far end of the
large conservatory.

"The old troublemaker couldn't have a more convenient arrangement," Conrad agreed with a rueful grin.

"Why do you call him a troublemaker?" Alison asked.

Her cousin replied with the honesty they had promised
each other. "Because he never considers anyone but
himself."

"And how does that cause trouble?"

Conrad gazed absently at the gleaming mahogany
wardrobe which now stood where the never-used breakfast buffet had formerly been. "It's hard to explain."

"I thought you were going to reel off a list of our
grandfather's misdemeanors," Alison said dryly. The
sight of Walter trying to surmount his disability by keeping busy had moved her to compassion for him. How

could she, on her last visit, have found that frail old gentleman forbidding? Nor could she believe him capable of causing trouble.

"It isn't a question of misdemeanors," Conrad replied, thinking, as he had from the day he met her, that Alison never used a simple word if a fancy one would do. Anyone else would have said "misdeeds"—but this was, for Conrad, part of Alison's charm.

"Then what is it a question of?" she persisted. "Hurry up and enlighten me, Conrad, before Grandpa turns around and sees us standing here."

"I can't explain, Alison. Not because I don't want to. Because it can't be put into words. It has something to do with the way people being the way they are affects their family as a whole. You have to live with it, Alison, to know what I mean."

Alison did live with it. But only among the Plantaines. And it struck her then that there were still great gaps in her knowledge of her Jewish relatives as a family.

She entered the conservatory and walked the several yards to where her grandfather had stationed his chair.

"If you've come to tell me supper is ready for me, I am not yet ready for supper," Walter said without turning around.

Alison's footsteps on the tiled floor had heralded her approach. When she halted behind the chair, Walter addressed his irritability to the chrysanthemums. "Whenever I am doing something, I get interrupted."

"I know just how you feel," Alison said sympathetically.

Walter paused with a watering can in mid air.

Alison moved to his side and kissed his cheek, which she had never before done. Nor could she have said why she had done so now.

Walter collected himself and surveyed her. "So it's you, is it?"

Alison forgave him his ill grace. "Didn't you recognize my voice?"

"What is so special about your voice?"

Had he forgotten that the only kind thing he'd ever said to her was that she had a nice voice? Alison wondered.

Walter was remembering how, on her last visit, he had enjoyed listening to her perfect diction and mellifluous tone. But his face was expressionless.

Alison stood her ground, aware that her grandfather was fending her off. Last time he had done it with silence, she recalled. "I could be forgiven if I didn't recognize your voice," she said with a smile, "as you hardly spoke a word to me when I was last here."

Listening, Conrad had to admire Alison's nerve— which their grandpa would undoubtedly call impertinence. There was a moment of silence and Conrad waited for a verbal explosion from Walter to break it.

Instead, came what Conrad had never expected to hear from Walter's lips. A cross between an apology and an excuse. Walter Shrager had never been known to offer either.

"I wasn't too well when you were last here, Alison," he said grudgingly.

"But you are obviously feeling much better now, Grandpa," she replied firmly. "This absolutely splendid display of flora and greenery is here to prove it," she added in admiration.

Walter gave her a sheepish smile. "I haven't done too badly, I suppose. For a person with only five green fingers, instead of ten."

Conrad stood gaping. This extraordinary cousin of his had bearded the lion in his den and now seemed to have him momentarily tamed. Conrad had not entered the conservatory. It had become, for the family, Walter's sacred ground. If you wished to speak to him when he was in there, you stood in the doorway—as Conrad was doing now—unless he invited you to join him, which he did only when a plant required moving to where he could reach it from his bathchair.

Occasionally, Minna went in, to try to coax her husband to come for a meal. But nobody else ever did and Conrad had forgotten to warn Alison. He doubted that she would have heeded the warning. There was something about Alison that told you she thought rules were for other people, not for her.

"As you thought, Grandpa, we came to tell you supper is ready," Conrad called.

"And I wanted to let you know I'm here," Alison added, wondering if Conrad suffered from hayfever and was therefore keeping his distance from the plants.

"All right. So you're here, Alison," Walter said with a shrug.

As though her visit was of no consequence to him, Alison thought.

Walter softened the blow. "Even if I could stand on my feet, I'm not the kind to turn somersaults about things, Alison," he said dryly.

"I had already guessed that."

"You had, had you?"

They eyed each other for a moment.

"So you're a good guesser," Walter said with another shrug.

"If you say so, Grandpa," Alison replied enigmatically.

Conrad felt like a spectator at a sparring match.

"I'd also guessed that you don't like people to fuss over you," Alison added with a smile.

"Then you're a very good guesser indeed. It saves me the trouble of telling you something the rest of my family all know. And I hope you'll remember it better than they do."

Walter said no more, but allowed Alison to wheel him from the conservatory to the kitchen.

Conrad watched speechlessly as they swept past him. He was unable to believe his eyes.

Alison did not know, until her cousin enlightened her later, that her grandfather had conferred upon her a spe-

cial favor. Usually, Walter refused to be wheeled. He had
asserted his independence, by learning to maneuver the
wheels with his good hand and got where he wanted to go
under his own steam.

The favor was Walter's grudging compensation to Alison for his aloofness on her first visit. Grudging, because
he was, against his will, drawn to her. Before he met Alison, he had hardened his heart against what she represented. His family would have been surprised to learn
that he had a heart.

In truth, he was a man of strong emotions, but one of
those for whom revealing their feelings would be a sign
of weakness.

Walter's father had been a lovable man, but weak and
improvident to a high degree. His wife and children had
suffered in consequence. The family had come to England from Austria in the mid-nineteenth century, when
Walter was five and his sister three. Poverty, and his
beautiful young mother, were Walter's prevailing childhood memories.

By the age of ten, Walter knew that it was up to him to
better the family's hand-to-mouth existence, for his father never would. It was then that he came to terms with
his father's character and equated gentleness in a man
with weakness. Carl Shrager did not have what it took for
an immigrant to make good in a new land and if Walter
was to do that seemingly impossible thing, he must be, in
every way, the opposite of his father.

Walter had there and then got himself a job helping
some stallholders on Oldham market, and from those
small beginnings progressed to being the family pro-
vider. He was not yet sixteen when he set up his own
market stall—at night he knocked on doors, buying for
coppers a motley selection of throwouts, which he sold
by day at a profit.

This early entry into the retail trade had led Walter,
step by step, to where he now was. His abiding regret was

that those whom he had set out to raise from penury had not lived to benefit from his present-day affluence.

The mother he had idolized, the sister he had cherished, and the father for whom he had harbored affection but could not respect, had died in a scarlet-fever epidemic, before Walter opened the little shop that was now a sizable store.

Though he was by then a married man, Walter had wanted to die with them. He could not envisage life without his mother. He still dreamed of her, and in his waking hours sometimes thought of the things he could now have given her, had she been alive.

She had come from a comfortably-off family, but her dowry was frittered away long before her husband brought her to England. She did not allow poverty to diminish her elegance. Even in a simple blouse and skirt, she managed to look like the chic Viennese she had once been.

Thinking back, Walter could not imagine how she had done it. He could not recall seeing her around the house wearing an apron, as other women did. And in his dreams she always had on the rust moiré frock and stylish black velvet hat she had worn in the synagogue, when Walter was *Bar Mitzvah.*

Walter had bought the dress-length from a stall on the market and a neighbor had made it up. He had wanted her to have something new to wear on the great day and had gone without the new boots for which he had been scrimping and saving. There was no sacrifice he would not have made for his mother.

His adoration had not allowed him to see her faults. They had been plain to Minna, but she had not made the mistake of pointing them out to him—or that their eldest granddaughter Clara had inherited them.

Clara's combination of vanity, laziness and guile was the late Frieda Shrager to a tee. But Walter, in one of his rare communicative moments, had once told his wife that he could not, for the life of him, think whence Clara's nature came.

He could not have failed to see that Lottie was the image of his mother, though something indefinable was missing. Not until he met Alison did Walter know what it was. Alison not only looked like Frieda Shrager, she had her presence.

As a perfume is remembered, and equally elusive, so it is with the aura of a personality. It defies description, but, in remembrance, lingers on. There was about Alison the *je ne sais quoi* that sets a woman apart, enters a room with her and is gone when she departs. Walter's mother had been endowed with it. But for Walter, it was more than just that, Alison was to him like Frieda reincarnated.

He had felt it the moment she walked into his sickroom and he had wanted to reach out and take her hand. Instead, he had withdrawn into his crusty shell.

Alison was right in thinking he was fending her off. He had not expected her to engage his emotions—and more so than any of his other grandchildren did, though he cared for them all.

He was, too, affected by the bitter irony of the situation. He had prepared himself to be polite to the granddaughter he would rather not have had but was not prepared for Alison in the flesh. Or for the tug-o'-war between pride and emotion that meeting her had evoked.

If Minna and Walter had been two different people, they would have talked the matter out. As it was, Alison's first visit to Oldham remained a time of secret anguish for both.

Confiding in Lottie had been for Minna an immense relief. For Walter, there was neither counsel nor comfort. He had always borne his burdens alone.

After Alison's departure he had put her from his mind. But she came to him alongside his mother, while he slept. When he dreamed of Frieda now, she was wearing black. It was Alison who had on the rust moiré frock.

Alison's unexpected appearance in the conservatory had had the quality of a dream. The fact that she was wearing a beige skirt and blouse in the current style and not the Victorian gown of a different hue in which she appeared in Walter's sleeping hours, did not dispel it.

It had taken Walter a moment or two to collect himself; from Alison's greeting him with a peck on the cheek, too. Clara and Emma habitually made that dutiful granddaughterly gesture of respect—Walter had no illusions that he inspired his kith and kin with undue affection—but he was touched when Alison kissed him.

Minna had opened her heart and let Alison in. Walter was still trying not to do so. Alison could not have divined the battle raging within him, during their verbal exchange.

But he wouldn't have to see her often, he reminded himself while she was wheeling him to the kitchen. She would never be part of his everyday life. Were she to become so, which was unlikely, he'd get used to her being around. As it was, when she came it would continue to seem like a dream. And what was the harm in enjoying it?—though he wouldn't let anyone, least of all Alison, know it was a pleasure to have her here. There was little enough pleasure left to him in his disabled old age. And Alison, if you forgot she wasn't Jewish, and what her father had done to you, was a granddaughter to be proud of.

Thus Walter came to terms with himself. To do so, he had applied logic, uncharacteristic self-indulgence, and illogic, in equal parts. It allowed him to accept Alison, and the time would come when he thought of her as his "dear butterfly," because her fleeting visits briefly colored the drabness of his days.

Alison would, too, one day be proudly claimed by her Lancashire relatives, in their own vernacular, as "our Alison the actress."

Even down-to-earth Lottie found it hard to think of Alison as merely one of the family, though it was as one of the family that Lottie welcomed her the following day.

Lottie hugged her with one arm and Conrad with the other, when she found them awaiting her in the Steins' house.

"Are you going to make a habit of not telling us you're coming, Alison?" Lionel chuckled, leading the way to the kitchen.

"It's a lovely habit, Dad," Emma declared. "It means there's a chance that Alison might arrive any time. That gives me something to look forward to, every day."

"It's a pity you can't find something better to look forward to," Clara said crisply.

"Are you baiting Emma?" Alison inquired. "Or insulting me?"

"Neither," Lottie intervened giving her elder daughter a sharp glance. "Her young man wasn't at the railway station to meet our train and Clara hoped he would be. She had to take it out on somebody, I suppose."

Clara picked up her handbag and headed for the door.

"Where are you going to?" Lottie demanded.

"Out."

"Out where?" Lionel asked. "You've only just come home. You haven't even taken off your hat and coat yet."

"That saves me the trouble of putting them back on again," Clara retorted.

"Kindly remember who you're talking to, my girl!"

Clara paused in the doorway and gave Lionel an agonized glance. "Why are you doing this to me, Dad?"

"What am I doing? All of a sudden I'm the Criminal!"

"Humiliating me, in front of Alison."

"I'll leave the room if you wish," Alison said uncomfortably. She had seen Clara provoke her parents before, but this had the makings of a full-blown row, and chipped some of the gloss off Alison's picture of the Steins as the ideal family.

"I'd rather you stayed and I left," Clara answered.

"I insist on knowing where you're going to, Clara,"

Lionel thundered. "You seem to forget that you're still only eighteen."

"It's our fault, for giving her too much rope," Lottie declared to her husband.

"It's a pity I can't hang myself with it," Clara said.

Lionel and Lottie exchanged an anxious glance.

"I feel like throwing myself in the river," Clara added for good measure.

"I beg your pardon?" Lottie said apprehensively.

"You know our Clara, Mam. One, two, three and she's already hysterical," Conrad put in.

"This time I've got reason to be." Clara transferred her gaze from Conrad to her parents. "You'll have to know sometime, so it may as well be now. I'm going to have a baby."

Lionel paled visibly. Lottie sat down on the nearest chair, which fortunately was right behind her.

Alison was wishing that she had left the room. Emma was beside her and clutched her hand.

Conrad, who had learned a thing or two in the army, broke the shocked silence. "You're not the first nice girl it's happened to, since the war," he said, going to put his arm around Clara, which he had not done since they were young children.

Clara's situation *vis-à-vis* her family was not a happy one. She had always been at odds with her parents and brother, but was not the kind to attribute this to her own failings; her vanity prohibited her from knowing that she had any.

Conrad's opinion of Clara was no secret to Alison. It mirrored her own and she thought it somewhat hypocritical of him to be comforting Clara. But Alison was capable of being harder than she herself knew. Nor had she yet learned that in times of trouble a Jewish family sets aside personal differences and closes ranks.

"What's the war got to do with it?" Lionel flashed to his son after another silence. His demeanor was that of a dog uncertain whether to bite its attacker, or lick its wounds. He decided upon the former. "I can't wait to get my hands on my future son-in-law!"

"What future son-in-law?" Clara said.

"Are you saying you don't think Percy will marry you?"

"If I'd thought that, I wouldn't have kept on seeing him, would I, Dad?"

"You wouldn't have let him get you in the family way, either. I hope!"

Lottie emerged from her daze. "How far gone are you, Clara?"

"Two months."

Hearing these intimate details openly discussed embarrassed Alison. But bluntness, she reminded herself, was a northern characteristic. Up here, people didn't believe in beating about the bush.

Lionel confirmed it. "So you'll get married right away, Clara."

"Before you start to show," Lottie said.

"People will think it's a premature baby," Lionel added hopefully.

Emma found her voice. "Will you let me wheel it in its carriage, Clara?"

"You can change its nappies as well!"

"I hope it's a boy, then I can teach it to play football," Conrad said.

"Bring Clara to sit by me," Lottie instructed. Her legs felt too weak to take her to Clara. "And get her the footstool. She should sit with her feet up." Lottie managed to smile. "I'll have to own up to my age, now I'm going to be a grandma. And buy some white wool to knit the baby a shawl."

"If it's a boy, it can come into the business," Lionel said.

"Its other grandpa might have the same idea," Conrad pointed out.

"Wouldn't you rather have a professional man in the family?" Lottie asked Lionel.

"An accountant would be useful to both his grandfathers," Lionel decided shrewdly.

Alison wanted to giggle as the ridiculous conversation continued. The baby was not yet born and they were arranging its adult life. Time would teach her that having an eye to the future was a built-in Jewish characteristic, and she would come to think it an incongruous one for a people whom history had led to believe they had no future.

But Alison, though she was half-Jewish, had no knowledge of the deprivation of human rights from which her father's people had, down the centuries, fled. Not until events stirred her own Jewish blood would she begin to see the full picture.

Right now, Alison felt she was seeing the enactment of one of Lionel's jokes. She had not spent sufficient time among the Shragers and Steins to realize that the best Jewish jokes sprang from the capacity to know and laugh at themselves.

"We'll buy the knitting wool on Monday," Lottie rounded off what she had been saying to Clara.

Lionel returned to a more pressing matter. "Oughtn't you to buy Clara a wedding dress, first?"

Clara switched her mind from a fetching vision of herself in a frilly bedjacket, the infant beside her, and came down to earth. "For a wedding dress, there has to be a wedding," she said.

"And there's damn well going to be one," her father informed her.

"But only the bride might be there."

"Why did we think our Clara had an understanding with Percy Zeligman?" Lionel asked Lottie. He sat down heavily in the fireside chair, then sprang to his feet again and paced the hearth rug.

Alison and Emma exchanged a glance and each knew what the other was thinking. How could Clara have got herself into this situation with a boy with whom she did not have a serious understanding? How, indeed, could she have let it happen to her at all?

Clara supplied the answer to that first question. "I took it for granted we were courting."

"Who wouldn't?" Lionel flashed. "He brought your mother a bouquet. If I'd known they were conscience flowers, I'd have rammed them up his nose!"

"What makes you think he won't marry you?" Lottie asked.

Clara hesitated and played with a fold of her pale gray skirt. "Well, he wasn't at the station to meet me, was he?"

It was the first time any of those present had ever seen her look vulnerable. The cocksure Clara they knew had momentarily gone.

"That seems a trivial thing to have made you so doubtful," Conrad said.

A tear trickled down Clara's cheek. "It doesn't take much to make a girl doubtful, in my position."

Percy chose that moment to arrive at the house. Conrad let him in. When he entered the kitchen, he seemed not to notice the tense atmosphere, or his beloved's tears.

Alison took an immediate dislike to him, as she had to Clara, and thought them well matched.

Conrad eyed the diamond ring on Percy's little finger. "The army won't let you wear that, when you're drafted."

"They haven't reached my age group yet and the war could be over before they do," Percy replied.

Conrad eyed him with thinly veiled contempt. They had gone to school together and had been the only Jewish boys in their glass—Oldham was not thickly populated with Jews—but had not been friends. Percy, too, was the son of a local businessman and Conrad had not liked his habit of bragging to the working-class boys about the things he had, which they plainly had not.

Conrad had thought it not only distasteful, but an unwise thing to do. He had already learned that there is more than one kind of Jew, but that it was Percy's kind whom Gentiles remembered.

Conrad could not think of a brother-in-law he would less like to have. And Percy's seduction of his sister had, he thought, put the tin lid on it!

The truth would not have occurred to Conrad. He did not know Clara quite as well as he supposed. She did not have a romantic notion in her head, but was calculation personified. She had set her cap at Percy Zeligman because he was a wealthy young man, and a big spender. When no proposal of marriage was forthcoming, she had decided to hook him in the timeworn way. Until he failed to appear at the railway station she had been sure he would marry her. The sudden doubt had not yet been removed.

"Get me my handbag, Emma," she said. "Since we got home, I haven't had time to powder my nose," she added, smiling at Percy.

Alison would have told her to get the handbag herself, pregnant or not. She had never heard Clara say please, or thank you, to Emma—as though she thought her younger sister was her slave!

"Good old Emma!" Percy said as she fetched the bag.

"That's what everyone calls me," Emma answered cheerfully. It was to be her lot in life, though she could not at the age of sixteen have foretold it. Had she been able to do so, she would have maintained the philosophical smile on her homely face.

"Our Emma's a good sort," Lionel declared unnecessarily. Then he fixed his gaze studiedly on the mantelpiece. "And she's going to make a very nice bridesmaid."

"Who's getting married?" Percy inquired.

"You are, my lad. And not before time."

Percy's sallow complexion turned a mottled red.

"I must go and unpack, if everyone will excuse me," Alison said politely.

"I'll come with you and do mine," Emma said. She too was impelled to escape.

They took with them the image of Percy Zeligman looking like an insect impaled on a pin.

The entire affair was, for both, a maturing experience. "Getting into trouble" was not something that happened to girls like them. Clara's plight had, for Alison and Emma, the effect of a strong wind ruffling the placid waters of their conditioned beliefs.

When they reached Emma's room, they fell silent. It was not an awkward silence; these two would never be uneasy with each other. An aspect of life they had not thought to encounter had touched them via Clara. Neither would be quite the same again.

"When you were last here, I still didn't know how girls got pregnant," Emma confessed to Alison.

"I already knew The Truth, by then." It was still a matter for capital letters, in Alison's mind.

"Who told you, Alison?"

Alison's eyes had been opened by Ivy Baines, when the Plantaines were staying there in the summer of 1913. It had taken Alison some time to recover from learning what Ivy thought it was time she knew.

"It was our Clara who told me," Emma said after Alison had revealed the source of her own enlightenment.

"It's a pity Clara didn't bear in mind what she told you!" Alison replied with asperity.

Emma's face shadowed with distress. "We mustn't be unkind about her, Alison."

"It isn't you who's being unkind. It's me. Just because Clara has been seduced, I don't have to pretend to like her."

Emma looked shocked. "Don't you?"

"Frankly, no."

They were lolling on the bed, unpacking far from their minds. Emma got up and opened the window. The air in the room was stifling after the house having been closed for a week. Alison lay with her hands folded beneath her head, enjoying the fresh scent of the flowers now drifting from the back garden on the evening breeze.

Emma remained by the window. A silence had followed Alison's declaration.

"You mustn't let what I said upset you, Emma," Alison said, breaking it.

Emma turned to look at her. "I've always known you don't approve of Clara. Nor do my parents—but they still love her. How can you dislike your own cousin, Alison?"

"Very easily, as she isn't in the least likable. I have two others I don't like. They're step-cousins, as it happens, but it would be all the same if they were my blood relatives. The trouble with you, Emma, is you're prepared to like anybody and everybody. That's why people take advantage of you."

Emma smiled and Alison thought she looked like a little girl, in her simple, cotton frock. One whose mama had allowed her to put up her hair, for a game of pretending to be grown up. Emma was no taller than the five-foot she was when Alison last saw her. Nor had she gained an ounce.

"Disliking people would make me miserable," Emma declared.

"How do you know, when you haven't tried it?"

"Only the pepole I care about can make me miserable, Emma," she went on, realizing that this was so. And her mother was a prime example! A girl didn't stop loving her mama just because she had lost respect for her.

There was distress, too, as well as happiness in Alison's relationship with her father. She fell asleep every night worrying about his being in the war. There was, too, now the terrible knowledge that Mama was deceiving him with another man.

Alison's brief pensive interlude brought home to her that love could be a combination of pleasure and pain. As she had yet to experience those twin emotions for a man, her assessment was in the broadest terms.

She looked at Emma, for whom she cared deeply. "I'd

be grief-stricken if *you* didn't want me to be your friend anymore," she said with feeling, "but I wouldn't lose any sleep if Clara said she never wanted to set eyes on me again."

Emma avoided her eye. "I didn't know you could be so heartless, Alison."

"Is that what you think I'm being?"

Emma nodded.

There was a good deal Emma had yet to learn about Alison, that Alison would never be aware of herself.

At present, Emma was thinking how beautiful Alison was. At this stage of their relationship, Emma's feeling for her was still near worship. Initially, it had been blind worship, but Emma was too practical a person not to have become aware during Alison's first visit that her idol was human.

Nobody could share a room with Alison and fail to note that she was careless and untidy. Last time, she had not brought much with her, but had managed, nevertheless, to scatter her belongings here, there and everywhere. And, though she was meticulously fastidious about her person, Alison did not bother cleaning her hairbrush after she had used it. Nor did she clean her shoes.

Emma, being Emma, had done those things, and a good deal more, for her and had enjoyed doing them.

She had not enjoyed her cousin's delight, when it suited her, in using words to cutting effect. Alison had never delivered a verbal sting to Emma, but even if she had, Emma would have continued to adore her. Alison remained for her a magical being. An idol whose flaws had not caused her to reveal feet of clay.

Alison was watching an evening sunbeam kiss the room goodbye, and thought how glorious the light oak furniture looked, briefly turned to gold.

Emma saw only the week-old dust.

Alison and Emma would never occupy the same

plane. But the attraction of opposites, what each saw in the other that was not in herself, had drawn them together.

Alison sat up on the bed and leaned her back against the headboard.

Emma noted her graceful movements with admiration in which there was not a trace of envy.

"All right, so I was being heartless about Clara," Alison conceded with a shrug.

"I forgive you, Alison."

Alison smiled. "You'd forgive me anything, wouldn't you, Emma?" She could not have failed to divine her cousin's esteem for her.

Emma returned the smile and nodded.

"There'd be nothing to forgive, if you just accepted that I'm me."

"I do," Emma said fervently.

"Good."

Emma hesitated. "It's just that—well I'm still not used to the kind of things you sometimes say, Alison. And the way you say them. What I mean is I'm just an ordinary girl. And you're not."

Alison did not attempt to dispute either statement. To do so would be like saying black was not black, and white was not white.

Though she had not yet made her stage début, the ego without which stardom is rarely achieved was in her blood and already burgeoning within her. And her honesty would not permit her to employ false modesty, or to pay lip service to denying Emma's assessment of herself.

"If I had to find a word to describe you, my very dear Emma, I'd call you a gem," she said sincerely.

"That's what Conrad calls me. But wouldn't a pebble be more fitting?" Emma replied with the dryness she occasionally displayed. "Gems shine, don't they?"

Alison surveyed her cousin's nondescript appearance.

But her hazel eyes, which were like Alison's father's, lit her face and their gentle expression was a testimony to her kindness. Alison got off the bed and gave her a hug. "There is more than one way of shining, Emma."

THREE

A telegram addressed to Hermione was delivered to the Plantaines' lodgings the day after Alison had gone north.

It arrived at 10 a.m. and Hermione had not yet risen. She had returned in the early hours from an outing with Captain Browne-Hogg, and one of her sexual fantasies had lengthily preceded sleep.

Jessica brought the envelope to her daughter's room. Before doing so, she concealed a bottle of smelling salts in her skirt pocket. Gregory, whose habit of looking on the bright side had not entirely deserted him, had said the wire was probably from Alison, to let Hermione know she had arrived safely in Oldham. But Jessica's vagueness had not prevented her from noticing that nowadays Alison was not in the least considerate toward her mother, and was filled with foreboding.

Hermione could not open it. "You'll have to do it, Mama," she said pitifully.

Jessica paused. "Would losing your husband seem to you as if your own life had ended, my dear?"

"What a terrible thing to say, Mama! And at such a moment!"

Jessica had not intended to say it. She and Hermione were no more communicative with each other now than they had ever been. But Jessica felt she must prepare her dear daughter for the worst. She had not, in her confused way, done so kindly and hastened to make amends.

"Come what may, you will still have a life—your family and your profession, Hermione dear. And whatever is inside this envelope, tonight the curtain will still rise."

Hermione was able to sigh with relief on one count, if not yet on another. She had at first thought her mother was implying the presence in Hermione's life of a replacement for Horace. But Jessica wouldn't have implied it, even had she known that Andrew was hovering in the wings. It was all in her own guilty mind.

Her mother was eyeing her with concern, and the telegram had still not been read. Hermione slipped her woolen bedjacket around her shoulders. She was shivering, though the day was warm.

"As I'm a Plantaine, Mama, I don't require telling that the curtain must rise. Now would you please open the envelope?"

Jessica did so with trembling fingers. She had not wanted Hermione to marry Horace, but had grown fond of him over the years. She forced herself to read the telegram.

"It's from the War Office, isn't it?" Hermione said, scanning her face.

"Yes, Hermione. Horace is missing."

Hermione buried her face in her hands. She could think of nothing worse than not knowing if she was a widow or a wife.

Jessica patted her shoulder. Her daughter was distressed, but stronger than Jessica had thought. The smelling salts were not required.

Hermione raised her face from her hands and met her mother's sympathetic gaze. "From my point of view, it's like having been tossed, for however long, into limbo, isn't it, Mama?" she said displaying the customary Plantaine stiff upper lip. But she was unable to disguise the haunted expression in her eyes.

Jessica gave her shoulder another inadequate pat.

"I don't know how I shall bring myself to tell Alison," Hermione added.

"You must both take comfort, Hermione dear, from the War Office not having said missing, presumed dead. And so must your father and I," she declared with feeling and to Hermione's surprise. "Would you like me to bring you a cup of tea, dear?"

Hermione shook her head.

"Well then, I must hurry downstairs and give Papa the news. He'll be relieved to know it isn't the worst. He is probably still sitting in the hall, convincing himself that the telegram was not from the War Office," Jessica said as she left the room.

Hermione had not thought her parents wished Horace ill, but nor had she known they harbored affection for him. Horace, too, would be surprised to know it. He had once said with amusement that his in-laws had learned to put up with him. Hermione knew there was more than a grain of truth in this, but he would be pleased to know they had also learned to regard him with warmth. And how sad it would be if he had died without knowing it.

Hermione thrust that thought aside. She would not let herself believe he was dead.

She rose from her bed and seated herself before the mirror. How could she have allowed herself to be consoled by another man? She picked up the photograph that stood in a silver frame on the dressing table. It was of herself and Horace on their wedding day—and oh how young and happy we looked, she thought poignantly.

Hermione had pressed, in her copy of *Troilus and Cressida,* one of the tea roses from her bridal bouquet. She fetched the book from its place on the spacious window ledge, and took the time-dried flower gently in her hands. If she were not careful, it would crumble to bits. As with the years a marriage could, and just as easily, she thought.

Hermione's had shown signs of doing so before Horace went away. But she would put love before pride and set matters right, if her husband was spared to come back to her.

FOUR

Alison was enjoying her stay in Oldham, in blissful ignorance of the ominous shadow a telegram had cast on her life.

On her second evening at the Steins', Percy's parents—who thought, correctly, that their son had been entrapped—arrived with an injured air to confer with Lottie and Lionel about the shotgun-wedding arrangements.

The conference took place in the parlor and Alison and Emma were not present, nor would they have wished to be.

"Mrs. Zeligman's what my mam calls a parlor-person," Emma told Alison, who was helping her prepare refreshments.

Alison had been introduced to the couple and was still wrinkling her nose from the odor of mothballs that had entered the house with them. Mr. Zeligman was a dried-up little man, with pale, anxious eyes behind his pince-nez. His wife was a forbidding-looking lady, who towered over him like a lamppost, in a fur coat whence the camphor smell came.

Anyone who wore fur on a stifling September evening had to be a parlor person, Alison thought and smiled at Emma. "I know what your mother means."

Halfway through the evening, Clara came into the kitchen.

"I'll take the lemonade and cake into the parlor for you," Emma said to her.

Clara sat down at the table. "I haven't come for the lemonade and cake!"

"Clara isn't a tray-carrying person," Alison said, giving Emma a wink.

"Nor do I ever intend to be," Clara snapped. "But I haven't come in here to be got at, Alison. I've come because I had to get out of the parlor, before I spat in Percy's mother's eye!"

"What's she done to you?" Emma asked anxiously.

But Clara could not reply. "Lend me your hankie, Emma," she sobbed. "I don't want to make a mess of mine."

"You won't believe what I'm going to tell you," she said when she had soiled Emma's and recovered her composure. "That dreadful woman who's going to be my mother-in-law would rather have her only child killed in France, than risk their family name being disgraced!"

This was double-Dutch to Alison and Emma. They waited for Clara to simmer down and elucidate.

When she did so, her voice was like chipped ice. "Percy's mother says he must join up—immediately—so people will think that's why we're getting married in a hurry. But when he wanted to volunteer, so he wouldn't be thought a coward by his pals who did, she didn't let him. It doesn't make sense, does it?"

Clara rose to examine her appearance in the mantelpiece mirror and licked her finger, to twist a tendril of her blonde hair into a kiss curl on her forehead.

"I'd better go back into the parlor now, and keep my

lip buttoned—for the moment," she said in the same cold tone. "But if Percy gets killed, I'll never let his mother forget she sent him to his death. If he doesn't come back, I shall never let her see the only grandchild she'll ever have."

Clara swept from the room, leaving Alison and Emma in no doubt that she meant what she had said.

The following day, Lottie took her to buy a wedding dress. Alison and Emma elected to stay at home. Neither could imagine a less pleasant way of spending a sultry afternoon than watching Clara parade in a dozen gowns before deciding which to choose.

The two girls were relaxing in the back garden, when Conrad came to tell them he had invited Albert Battersby to tea.

"I was looking forward to a lovely peaceful afternoon," Alison groaned.

"There's no reason why you shouldn't have one," Conrad said cheerfully. "Provided you're civil to Albert—which you promised to be."

"But what makes you think Albert will be civil to me? The fact that he sent me a minty peace offering doesn't change the unfortunate effect we have on each other." Thinking back, though the details continued to elude her, it had struck Alison that the antipathy had been mutual.

Conrad made no reply. It was not for him to reveal that Alison's being in Oldham was the highlight of his friend's embarkation leave. Since meeting her, Albert had not been able to interest himself in any other girl.

"You ought to have told me sooner that he was coming," Alison said. "Emma and I would have arranged to be out." She had learned to take it for granted that she was the leader and Emma the follower. Anything Alison wanted to do was all right with Emma.

"That's why I didn't tell you," Conrad grinned. "And unless you want to come face to face with Albert on your way out, it's too late now. He'll be here any minute—and you wouldn't want him to see you beating a hasty retreat, would you, Alison?"

She replied as Conrad had calculated she would. "Certainly not!"

"I'll go and put the kettle on and see what we've got left for tea," Emma said, getting up from her deck chair. "Our Clara's future in-laws ate a lot of cake, last night," she added, hastening indoors.

"Want me to come and help you?" Alison called from the hammock, though it went against the grain to have to prepare tea for that Battersby boy.

"No thanks."

Alison gazed mournfully up at the sky.

"Cheer up, love," Conrad said.

"How dare you tell me to cheer up? When you invited you-know-who because you want me to suffer."

"Why would I want you to suffer, Alison?"

"That's what I am wondering," she sighed.

"Being civil to Albert is a chance to prove you're a good actress," Conrad said glibly. "If you can put on a performance with him, like you're doing for me right now, everything'll be fine," he added with a dry smile.

Alison glared at him. "I shall honor my promise to you, Conrad. Have no fear. But I shall have to grit my teeth to do it."

"Just so long as you don't bare them, like you did the last time."

"I shall, as you said, look upon it as a performance," Alison answered loftily. "My thespian blood will stand me in good stead."

Conrad laughed. "It always does. But you can't help it, can you?"

"Any more than you, my dear Conrad, can help your Lancashire prosaicness!"

"*Touché!*"

Albert's arrival prevented Alison from telling Conrad she wished she had never introduced him to that word. She transferred herself from the hammock to a chair. If she must re-encounter that Battersby boy, it would not be from a reclining position!

She smoothed her skirt and tucked in her blouse, steeling herself to be coolly polite to him. More than that could not be expected of her. But who was that tall soldier, heading toward her across the lawn with Conrad? He didn't look like the Albert Battersby Alison remembered.

"Good afternoon, Miss Plantaine. It's nice to see you again."

Nor did he sound like him. Albert's pleasant manner took the wind from Alison's sails. "There is no need for such formality," she managed to say. "Unless you had forgotten my Christian name?"

"No. I hadn't." Nor did Albert usually address girls so formally. But there was something about Alison that demanded special treatment, he thought.

He had been aware of it the day they met. And a picture of her striding away from him toward the church porch had remained with him. She had been wearing an emerald-green hat and scarf and today had a scarlet bow at the neck of her white blouse, but it wasn't just the bright touches she gave to her appearance that made her memorable. It was everything about her, Albert thought, feasting his eyes upon her.

It had been an effort to say to her the few words he had. He stood fidgeting with his cap, unaware that Alison was similarly affected.

Conrad was an amused observer. A mischievous one, too. "I'll go and ask Emma when tea will be ready," he said.

Alison wanted to call him back. How dare he desert her! For once, she did not feel mistress of the situation.

Albert noted her confusion and found his voice. "Don't worry, I shan't bite you," he said with a smile. "Though I did the last time we met, didn't I? In a manner of speaking. Lord knows what got into me, that morning."

"Or me," Alison was surprised to hear herself say. "I am not given to altercations with strangers."

Albert, who would have asked any other girl if she had swallowed the dictionary, had she used a word like "altercation," to Alison said, "Nor am I, believe it or not. So why don't we just forget it happened and start from scratch? Then we might end up not being strangers."

He really was being incredibly nice, Alison reluctantly thought.

Albert was thinking he had wasted his time telling himself he couldn't possibly have fallen for a kid of fourteen he had met for ten minutes and had a flaming row with. Alison at sixteen was quite the most stunning girl Albert had ever seen. Also, they were no longer at each other's throats.

They exchanged a smile.

"You've certainly grown," Alison said.

"So have you. But I like tall girls."

Alison was not sure how to interpret that. But, at least, he hadn't said "big girls!" Maybe he hadn't yet noticed her increased girth.

Albert certainly had and thought it was all in the right places, but managed to restrain his eye from lingering admiringly upon her shape.

"I believe I was taller than you, when we first met," Alison recalled.

"But you're not anymore, so that's all right, isn't it?"

She did not know what to make of that remark, either. Nor why it had made her feel flustered. "I must thank you for the mint imperials you sent with Conrad, when he saw me off at the station," she said, steering the conversation to a less personal plane.

Albert brought a bulging paper bag from his pocket. "Conrad said they were your favorites, so I've brought you some more."

Alison accepted the sweets with good grace. Were there no lengths to which her cousin would not go to make peace? Wait until she got her hands on him!

Meanwhile, as Albert had been kind enough to buy them for her—and in wartime, sweets were hard to get—she felt obliged to eat one of the hated things. Albert had declined when she offered him one.

"They used to be my favorites, too. But I seem to have lost my sweet tooth," he said, while Alison was forcing herself to suck one.

That must be why he had lost his pimples and podge, Alison thought, and was now not a bad-looking young man. His too-wide mouth, and a slight bump on the bridge of his nose, stopped him from being handsome. But his gray eyes were fringed with thick black lashes that gave his face an arresting appearance its other features did not merit.

Alison averted her own from them. It was an effort for her to do so, as though she had been momentarily magnetized and could not drag her gaze from Albert's.

She was to find herself presented with that difficulty throughout the afternoon.

When Conrad and Emma returned to the garden with the tea tray, both were astonished to find Alison chatting amicably with Albert. Conrad had half expected to find them at opposite ends of the lawn.

Albert had always had a way with the lasses, but Conrad had privately waged that Alison would not number among his conquests and had been sorry for his friend on that account. Was Alison giving one of her performances? he now wondered, observing her rapt expression as she listened to Albert.

There was a similar expression on Albert's face, when Alison was talking to him, but that was no surprise to Conrad.

"I can't imagine what it would be like to spend one's days in a cotton mill," Alison was now saying.

"Nor me what it would be like to be on the stage," Albert answered.

They shared a smile, as though, Conrad thought, their unfamiliarity with each other's backgrounds was in itself common ground. And suddenly Conrad feared for his friend. If Albert succeeded in capturing Alison, what could he hope to build on a foundation that had no substance? There was no way that such a structure would not, in the end, come tumbling down.

Conrad was bred of a people who married within their own community, and he was not the kind to step out of line as Alison's father had. Conrad was, too, equipped with the common sense to know that, irrespective of religion, it was hazardous for like not to marry like.

Conrad's was the kind of mind that stripped a situation down to its essence and did so that afternoon, as he witnessed the birth of a love affair. Alison's flushed face left Conrad in no doubt that she was not acting a part.

Emma, too, was prey to her private thoughts. She was Alison's age, but young men still treated her as though she were a child. No, worse than that. Before Conrad went into the army, Albert and two other lads had come to the house every Tuesday night for a game of cards. Emma had usually been in the kitchen, ironing, while Conrad and his friends played their game at the table. Except when she served them with refreshments, they had behaved as though she were not there. That had not been the case with Clara if she happened to be in the room; Conrad's friends had paid more attention to her than they did to the cards.

Emma had long since settled for her plainness. It might have been better had she not, for cheerful resignation does not radiate the quality that captivates a man. An ugly girl—which Emma was not—is capable, by her personality, of rendering her appearance unimportant. But this requires an inner belief in oneself that Emma did not have.

That her sister was a beauty had not helped, though Emma had never been jealous of Clara. Nor did she experience a pang of jealousy that September afternoon when she saw, for the first time, Alison's effect upon the opposite sex. It was not Emma's way to wish for the moon.

By the end of that garden interlude, Conrad, as well as Emma, had been made to feel he was not there. It was as though an invisible window enclosed Alison and Albert, shutting out the other two.

"How long are you staying in Oldham?" Albert asked Alison when he rose to leave.

"I'm not sure," she replied. "When are you—and Conrad—" she added as if her cousin was an afterthought, "going back to your unit?"

Albert told her.

"Perhaps I shall stay until then," she said with a blush and a smile.

"Alison can't get enough of my company," Conrad chuckled, though he knew her decision had nothing to do with them.

"Nor you mine!"

"Touché! Alison's taught me to speak fancy-French, Albert," Conrad joked.

"And aren't I sorry I did."

"Perhaps you'll all come round to our house for tea tomorrow?" Albert invited.

"How kind of you to ask us," Alison said.

Albert would have liked to see Alison alone, but knew her aunt would not allow it. He mustn't let himself forget she was only sixteen, or that the Steins were a very proper family, as his was. If Albert or Conrad brought a girl home for tea, on her own, it would be as good as saying to their parents, "Meet your future daughter-in-law."

Albert did not let his imagination attach this to Alison. He had managed not to get her back up and she now seemed to like him. For the present, that was more than enough.

Alison had not examined her feelings. But she wanted to see Albert Battersby again.

Conrad and Emma were one step ahead of them both.

Emma, who was a romantic little soul with respect to others, thought that Cupid had today visited the Steins' back garden.

Conrad saw only the writing on the wall and wondered why he feared for Albert, rather than for Alison. For a very good reason, he answered his own question. Fond of Alison though he was, he did not doubt for a minute that she was capable of being a very hard nut.

Alison saw a good deal of Albert during the rest of her stay in Oldham; but by prearrangement on only one occasion, when she and her cousins went the next day to his home.

Mrs. Battersby plied them with homemade bread and jam and an assortment of cakes that Gregory Plantaine would have pronounced excellent. But Alison was aware that Albert's mother kept eyeing her warily, and could not think why.

The homely Lancashire woman would have had to be blind not to see that her son was smitten by Alison, and began immediately to fear for him as Conrad did. She presided at the tea table, her imposing bosom encased in her best white silk blouse, her cheerful face belying her feelings. What were our Albert wantin' wi' a lass like yon? she was thinking behind her motherly smile. Now there were summat else to worry on—as if Albert bein' sent to France weren't enough.

Her husband had popped home for tea, though it was a working day. His son's request that the Crown Derby china be brought out for the occasion had impelled him to do so.

The Battersby home was, compared with the Steins', a mansion. Mrs. Battersby had drawn the line at employing more than one servant, but her mill-girl days were far enough behind her for her to enjoy living as befitted the employer class.

Meals were eaten at a long table in the splendid dining room and evenings spent in the parlor—she would never learn to call it the drawing room—where tea was being taken now. Mrs. Battersby's cupboards and cabinets housed treasured china. Minton was used on a Sunday and Wedgwood for everyday, but it had to be an extra-special occasion for the Crown Derby to emerge from its shelf.

When Mr. Battersby met Alison, he was not surprised that his son had made the request. She struck him immediately as being "the Crown Derby kind." And genuinely so. Not like us folk, he thought wryly. He had begun his working life as a weaver and still felt incongruous with a china cup in his hand. 'Is missis'd taken to it like a duck to water, but 'e never would. Their daughter'd fancied goin' to boardin' school. She'd cum back a proper little lady, he thought. But put 'er side by side wi' Alison Plantaine, an' anyone'd know Liza Battersby were a fake.

Mr. Battersby's reaction to Alison was the opposite of his wife's. Within minutes, he was charmed by her. But Alison would always have that effect upon men.

"I liked Albert's father more than I did his mother," she said to Emma that night.

"You and your likes and dislikes!" Emma replied with a smile. "You didn't like Albert when you first met him."

They were preparing for bed and Alison paused with her hairbrush halfway to her head. "Albert is the exception that proves the rule. I've never before changed my mind."

"I wonder why you did about Albert," Emma said, though she was sure she knew.

Alison resumed brushing her hair. "There can only be one reason, can't there, Emma? I misjudged him."

That was the only time Emma was ever to hear Alison admit that she had made a mistake.

Albert contrived to see Alison almost every day. As Conrad's friend, it was not unnatural that he would drop in at the Steins'. Or so it seemed to Alison. Her aunt and uncle, and Clara, did not fail to divine the truth. One look at Alison and Albert together and anyone would know.

And Albert had not previously been their constant visitor.

Clara was too immersed in her own affairs to make any snide comments to Alison, and Conrad refrained from teasing her. Lottie and Lionel discussed it solely between themselves. But Alison talked to Emma, non-stop.

She did not ask herself why Albert Battersby had become her favorite topic—to the exclusion of all others—but gave herself up to the newfound pleasure of talking and thinking about him.

Lottie watched her like a hawk. There was no way she was going to allow what had happened to Clara to befall her young niece. Alison never went out without Emma, whom Lottie knew could be trusted implicitly. She did not distrust Alison, but she had learned to her cost that it was dangerous to apply the usual standards of behavior to a girl in love. It would not have entered Lottie's mind that Clara's plight owed more to cold calculation than to love.

When Albert came to the house, Lottie made sure he was not alone with Alison for a moment. Conrad found this comical and on the last night of their leave tried to give Albert a few minutes of privacy with his beloved. It was another sultry evening and the young people had preferred to be outdoors.

"Let's go and make a jug of lemonade, Emma," Conrad said.

"Since when did it take two of us to make a jug of lemonade?"

"Come on. I'll squeeze the lemons for you," Conrad insisted, taking Emma's arm and ushering her toward the house.

When Conrad returned to the garden, he found his mother, who was not an outdoor person, sitting stoically beside Alison and Albert.

"Oh, my back!" she groaned when she tried to rise from the low deck-chair.

It required all three of them to lever her to her feet.

Conrad hid his amusement and escorted Lottie to the house; she was still clutching her back and groaning. He was not allowed to enter with her.

"Are you mad?" she said, smoothing down her skirt.

"With respect, I think you must be, Mam!"

"I couldn't believe it, when I happened to glance through the dining-room window and you and Emma weren't in the garden. But thank God I did."

"So that's why you and Dad are sitting in the dining room tonight!" Conrad chuckled.

"We're deciding how best to rearrange the furniture, for Clara's wedding reception," Lottie defended herself.

"I thought perhaps you wanted to do your spying from a less obvious vantage point," Conrad teased her. "If you kept peeping through the kitchen window, we'd catch you at it."

"Kindly stop this nonsense, Conrad!" Lottie peered into the gathering darkness, to where Alison and Albert were seated together beneath a tree. "And get back to you-know-where."

"Don't you mean to you-know-who?"

"You know very well what I mean, you terrible boy! While Alison's in Oldham, she's my responsibility."

"I was only away from the garden for a few minutes, Mam. It would take longer than that for them to do you-know-what."

Lottie slapped his behind and watched him return to the twosome beneath the tree. Tomorrow, Albert would be gone. Possibly never to return. Her son, too. She cast that frightening thought aside and allowed herself to wonder how Conrad knew how long it took to do you-know-what.

Alison and Albert, oblivious to the comedy played out on their behalf, had just agreed to write to each other. An hour later, they parted in the sight of the entire Stein family and Percy, too, all of whom flocked into the hall to bid farewell to Albert and wish him luck.

After Albert had left, Lottie thought it safe to take

herself and her aching back to bed. Clara no longer required chaperoning! And, in her case, a lot of good it had done.

Percy and Clara had returned to the kitchen to resume planning their short honeymoon. Blackpool and Southport were the customary venues for local couples, but Clara—who liked to be different—was trying to persuade Percy to take her to London.

Conrad drew Alison and Emma into the parlor. "Us three'll be better off in here. Who wants to listen to our Clara trying to get her own way?"

The little-used room felt to Alison as empty as she suddenly did. "I shall miss seeing Albert," she said forlornly.

"It would be strange if you didn't," Emma answered.

Alison sat down on the maroon velvet sofa that looked as new as it had when it was purchased, many years ago. "I'm not sure what you mean, Emma."

"Come on now, Alison!" Conrad exclaimed.

"And now I don't know what *you* mean."

Conrad looked at Emma, who had perched on the piano stool, but she was no help to him. He cleared his throat and plunged in. "You must have been sweet on a lad before, Alison. Had a boyfriend, I mean."

"No, as a matter of fact," Alison replied stiffly. "And if you're suggesting that . . ." Her voice petered out. Then she gave her cousins a radiant smile. What an absolute idiot she was! Conrad had had to tell her she was in love.

FIVE

lison remained in Oldham to attend Clara's wedding. Though she cared not a fig for Clara, the wedding was a family event.

Emma was her sister's bridesmaid. Alison had declined Clara's invitation to share that honor. Her Uncle Lionel had offered to buy her a frock, but Alison had not, to Clara's secret relief, allowed herself to be persuaded.

Clara wanted Alison's striking figure detracting from her own bridal splendor no more than Alison was prepared to be her train bearer. The antipathy was mutual and Alison thought it hypocritical of Clara to have asked her, and did not follow suit by accepting. She was not yet sufficiently conversant with Jewish family life to know that what she had interpreted as hypocrisy was, to Clara, a statutory cousinly obligation.

The day was, for Alison, memorable on many counts and she afterwards thought of it as a day of "firsts."

The wedding party was Alison's first experience of the

unique atmosphere when a crowd of Jews get together. The Steins had only a few, distant relatives, but the Zeligmans had many and had invited them all. Alison thought her aunt's house would surely burst its bricks during the reception. And not just from the number of people crammed into it; the noise seemed loud enough to explode the roof.

The wedding was also Alison's first time in a synagogue and evoked in her poignant thoughts of her father's youth. He had never talked to her about his religion, but her Grandma Shrager had shown her a photograph of him at his *Bar Mitzvah* and had explained what that meant. Her Aunt Lottie had said Papa was confirmed in the synagogue in which Clara would be married, and during the marriage ceremony Alison imagined him as a boy, standing before the Holy Ark.

Though she could not understand the Hebrew words, she was moved by the hushed solemnity and fascinated by the ancient ritual taking place beneath a red velvet canopy. She almost jumped out of her skin when the bridegroom raised his foot and stamped on something, and the entire congregation shouted *"Mazeltov!"* Emma told Alison later that what Percy had stamped upon was a glass. Every Jewish bridegroom was called upon to break one, and it was always the high point of the ceremony; everyone held their breath lest the bridegroom fail to smash it.

When Alison returned south she took with her, too, the memory of herself wheeling her Grandpa Shrager in his bathchair along the synagogue aisle.

From then on, she was to be known in the family as Walter's favorite. The aisle was too narrow for him to negotiate it himself and it was necessary for him to reach the marriage canopy, to play a Jewish grandparent's traditional role in the ceremony.

Though many willing hands were offered, he bestowed the privilege upon Alison. Allowing her to wheel his chair at a family wedding was Walter's way of telling the

world that he was not ashamed of his Gentile granddaughter.

Her other grandfather welcomed her back with an ef-
fusiveness that was entirely genuine. Alison arrived in
Hastings on a Sunday evening and found her mother and
grandparents in the Plantaines' private parlor at their
lodgings.

"My dear Alison!" Gregory said, rising to kiss her.

For a moment, Alison was assailed by a strange feeling
as though she were teetering between her two different
worlds. Then she pulled herself together and stepped
back into this one.

"You have arrived in the nick of time," Gregory went
on. He smiled at his wife and daughter. "Good fortune
has not entirely deserted us."

"In the nick of time for what, Grandpa?" Alison
asked.

"To make your début, my dear girl. Poor Lucy has
been striken by laryngitis and is running a fever. She will
be incommunicado for at least a week. You are now sixteen, Alison, and I have the utmost confidence in your
ability to play Juliet, when we open tomorrow night."

Alison sat down with a thump.

"Lucy's misfortune is your good luck, Alison dear,"
Jessica said unnecessarily and with a fond smile. "As my
poor mother's sudden death allowed me to step in and
prove I was capable of playing Lady Macbeth, though I
had not yet the experience for it," she recalled. "Indeed,
there are those who say that luck plays the major role in
an actor's life."

"They are probably the ones who use the so-called absence of it as an excuse for their own lack of talent,"
Gregory remarked sweepingly.

Alison was listening with only half an ear. Her flesh
felt goosey with excitement. Was she really to make her
début tomorrow night? Throughout her return journey
she had gazed through the train window thinking of Albert. Love was like a newly-lit candle lighting up her life,

she had thought lyrically on the train. Now, another candle had been lit. From tomorrow night on, she would be Alison Plantaine, the actress! But it was hard to believe and small wonder she felt as though in a trance.

Her mother, who had not yet uttered a word, returned her to earth.

"Yes," Hermione said crisply. "Luck, in the theater, is often dependent upon being fortuitously in the right place at the right time. Indeed, I have heard it said that acting careers can be made, broken, and mended thus. But I have learned not to attribute more personal vicissitudes to luck. As Papa just remarked, it is too often used as an excuse. And not just for oneself, but as a cover-up for painful deficiencies in those one loves."

Hermione flicked a non-existent speck from her skirt—a technique everyone present knew she employed onstage to heighten a dramatic pause. "What is the point of my telling myself it's my bad luck that I have a thoughtless daughter? Which implies that she cannot help her ways. She has been away for more than two weeks and in all that time has sent me only one, brief note. I would do better to face the truth and admit that I have allowed her to grow up to be an inconsiderate girl."

Her mother's unprecedented admission was lost on Alison. The lengthy discourse had been addressed to Gregory and Jessica, as though Alison were not present. But there was no doubt for whom it was intended and Alison registered only the rebuke to herself.

Well, I'm back! she thought ruefully. And the contrast between the atmosphere she had just left and that to which she had returned was almost too much to bear. Oh, how lovely it would be to have the kind of mother to whom she could say blissfully: "Mama, I'm in love!" A warm and comforting mother, like Aunt Lottie.

Alison surveyed Hermione's profile, which looked as if carved from marble. She and her mother lived in close proximity, but it was as though they were on opposite banks of the cold river of Mama's disapproval.

Alison could feel an icy blast blowing toward her from it now. But she would not let it snuff out her two candles of happiness.

Hermione's next words succeeded in doing so. "I have some distressing news for you, Alison—which has not made your long absence easier for me. Your papa is reported missing. The telegram came the day after you went north."

The blood drained from Alison's face. "Why didn't you let me know?" she asked when she was able to speak.

Hermione gave her a weary smile. "Believe it or not, Alison, out of concern for you, though you have none for me. How would you have felt, receiving such news when you were far away from your family?"

"Mama, the people I was staying with *are* my family."

Hermione interpreted Alison's statement of fact as a rebuff. "I see."

Alison sat listening to the click-click of Jessica's knitting needles. Gregory, who had recently taken to playing Patience, was gazing carefully at his cards. Alison knew that her grandparents were sorry for her, but it would have been nice if they had showed it! Only once had she ever seen either of them display emotion offstage—when they learned that Oliver had married Ruby May.

If Alison had received this painful news while she was up north, she and the family could have comforted each other, she thought. Because Papa was theirs, too.

She rose from the sofa, where she was seated alone. "If everyone will excuse me, I think I'll go to my room." There was no comfort for her here; and she could not bring herself to console her mother, who was an unfaithful wife.

"I would have liked to say something encouraging to her about Horace," Jessica said with a sigh when Alison had gone, "but what is the point of building up her hopes?"

"That was my feeling, too," Gregory concurred. "But nor did I feel that commiseration was called for. I hope and pray it never will be. In the meantime, what can one say to the poor child?"

Hermione sprang up from her chair. "Neither of you appears to have noticed that the poor child, as Papa chooses to call her, did not shed a single tear!"

"We must put that down to shock, Hermione dear," Jessica said.

"I agree with your mama," Gregory echoed.

"Then neither of you knows Alison," Hermione answered. "I am not saying that she didn't receive a shock. Of course she did. But my daughter is made of iron. There are times when I think she has no feelings. Any other girl would have broken down and wept."

"Alison is not any other girl," Gregory declaimed. "You have momentarily forgotten, my dear Hermione, that your daughter is a Plantaine and we are inclined to lick our wounds in private."

An hour slipped by while Alison lay on her bed, breaking her heart lest her father did not return. When her tears were spent, she rose and wrote to her Aunt Lottie.

Once the letter was sealed in its envelope, Alison set aside her sorrow. It was not easy for her to do so, but the inner resources she did not yet know were in her came to her aid.

She took her copy of *Romeo and Juliet* from her bookshelf and began studying her part. Lucy's "too sweet to be wholesome" interpretation of Juliet was not how Alison would play the role. There were fiery depths to the tragic heroine, which tomorrow night would not be left unplumbed.

Alison fell asleep that night thinking of neither Horace nor Albert. Only her début occupied her mind. She was more of a Plantaine than anyone yet realized.

The next day was peppered with temperamental outbursts from her fellow members of the company.

The young actress who was to have understudied Lucy, had Alison not unexpectedly returned, led the way by cursing her own bad luck.

This was Alison's first personal experience of professional jealousy. She had many times seen it suffered by others, but that was not the same as its being directed against herself.

"Kindly control yourself, Polly my dear," Gregory soothed the disappointed actress. "If you work hard, you will one day be rewarded with your chance."

It was then that Alison realized to the full her own good fortune. Plantaines were not required to prove themselves before being given their chance. And if success were solely dependent upon talent, Alison doubted that Polly Drew would get very far.

The next outburst came from Luke. "Alison is much taller than me," he pointed out sulkily. "What sort of Romeo is she going to make me look like?"

"An actor is not judged by his physical attributes," Gregory replied. "I have known those, smaller than yourself, who by the power of their performance are able to make an audience forget their lack of height—"

"But how am I to embrace Alison?" Luke cut in. Only desperation would have caused him to interrupt Gregory. "My head reaches only to her shoulder. I shall look an absolute fool."

Alison was wondering—for different reasons—how she would manage to embrace Luke. She loathed and detested him but would doubtless, now her career was beginning, be called upon to be loving onstage to many whom she hated offstage.

"I'm sure we shall find a way, Luke," she said evenly; but could not resist adding, "if all else fails, you can stand on a footstool. Or I can sit down."

Elsie, the assistant wardrobe mistress, was hovering nearby and intervened before Luke had time to make a sharp retort. " 'As it occurred to anyone, yet, that Miss Lucy's costumes ain' goin' to fit Miss Alison? Not unless she's goin' to wear 'em for little undervests! 'N even then, they wouldn't fit 'er!"

Gregory, though he was not one to go to pieces in an emergency, gave her a demented look.

"Miss Lucy's understudy was 'er size," Elsie pointed out unnecessarily. "Wot am I to do?" she demanded of Gregory. "Jus' my bloomin' luck that Nellie 'ad to take sick with the laryngitis, too!"

"It's my bad luck I didn't take sick with it!" Luke said, eyeing Alison sourly.

Several of the company then began expressing concern lest Alison's total lack of experience affect the balance of the performance.

Gregory quelled the nervous clamor. "Alison will not fail us," he declaimed. "Would that I had as much confidence in all with whom I work. And I have lately heard altogether too much of the word 'luck!' I suggest that we begin running through the play and allow my granddaughter to accustom herself to the role."

"Wot abaht 'er costumes?" Elsie bleated.

"I am sure you can be as ingenious as Nellie is, Elsie dear, if you care to try. There must be something in the wardrobe room in Alison's size, to which you can, with your clever fingers, lend the required look."

Flattery sent the woman scurrying away—as Gregory had known it would.

Alison was left to hope she would not have to make her début wearing a Juliet-cap and her Aunt Ruby's *Second Mrs. Tanqueray* gowns. She and Ruby were the same height.

They ran through the play twice and Alison found that everyone—even Luke—was helpful to her. Onstage, professionalism took over from personal feelings. And it was reassuring to have her grandmother playing the Nurse.

"You'll do nicely, my dear," Gregory pronounced with satisfaction when rehearsal was over.

"Thank you, Grandpa." But he had not yet seen what Alison could do. She had saved her real performance for tonight.

"I would advise you now, Alison, to cut along and rest."

Alison went to lie down in the dressing room that had Lucy's name on the door. In the tea break, she had tried on the costumes Elsie had managed to contrive for her and they were not at all bad.

Later, her grandmother dropped in to see her. "Would you like some assistance with your makeup, Alison dear? I could attend to myself now and come back to lend you a hand," Jessica said, eyeing her fondly.

"How kind of you, Grandma. But I'm sure I can manage."

Jessica surveyed Alison's calm expression and recalled the long-ago evening of her own début. Alison must be extremely nervous, but she was a Plantaine and Jessica would not expect her to show it. "Anything you believe you can do, I am sure you will accomplish, Alison dear," she declared with conviction.

Alison noted that her grandmother was carrying a package. "Have you brought me some sandwiches, Grandma, to strengthen me for the kill?"

"No dear. And I shouldn't think you are feeling hungry."

Alison laughed. "I couldn't swallow a morsel!"

"But I have brought you something," Jessica said, handing Alison the package. "It's your début gift, from Grandpa and me. And we are delighted that you'll be able to make use of it sooner than we had expected."

Alison removed the wrapping. "Oh! My very own makeup box!" she exclaimed, gazing with pleasure at the neat leather case on which her initials were embossed in gold. "How absolutely marvelous, Grandma!"

"I'm glad you're pleased with it, Alison."

Alison gave her a rapturous kiss. "I shall treasure and use it all my life."

When Jessica had gone, Alison opened the box and saw that her grandparents had thoughtfully stocked it with greasepaint for her, and was filled with remorse.

It struck her now that her début was a significant event for them as well as for her; that she meant a good deal more to them than she had supposed. She would never again make the mistake of comparing her two families, but think herself fortunate to have them both.

A few minutes later, her mother came to see her. "It's sad that your papa is not here to share tonight with you, Alison," Hermione said quietly. Her expression reflected her words, as she stood pensively toying with the locket and chain she was wearing.

Alison allowed herself to briefly forget her mother's disloyalty to her father. "I'm glad that you are playing my stage mother," she said impulsively.

"Are you?"

Alison nodded. "Grandma played yours, when you made your début, and it's fitting that you should play mine. It will become part of Plantaine family history, won't it?"

Hermione was moved to kiss her daughter's cheek. "And I'm sure you will add a proud chapter to it. I wish you well, Alison."

"I know you do, Mama."

Hermione removed the locket and chain from her own neck and put it around Alison's. "I want you to have this, Alison. You've always admired it."

Alison was overwhelmed. "But Papa gave it to you—" she protested.

"And me giving it to you makes it a gift from both of us," Hermione said, securing the clasp, "on this momentous occasion in your life."

A moment later they were hugging each other, and wishing their brief closeness could last. But each was painfully aware that sentiment accounted for it. Tomorrow, they would again be a mother and daughter who could not see eye to eye.

Alison's final visitor was Oliver. "All right, my dear?" he inquired.

Alison nodded. "But please make sure it isn't real poison in the vial you give to me onstage tonight," she joked.

"If young Polly Drew had any say in the matter, I am sure it would be!" he laughed.

"Nevertheless, I'm sorry for her," Alison said.

"From your superior position as a Plantaine," Oliver commented dryly. "That's a splendid wrapper you have on, Alison," he remarked, surveying the embroidered, black silk garment into which Alison had changed.

"It was a sixteenth birthday gift from my Stein relatives. And my Grandma and Grandpa Shrager gave me the slippers I'm wearing."

Oliver inspected Alison's feet. "Red velvet! My, my! I must say, my dear, that your relatives up north have excellent taste. The wrapper and slippers together are most effective."

"I'll tell them you said so."

"By all means do."

Alison had been wearing the striking outfit when her mother came into the dressing room, but Hermione had not remarked upon it. She had probably guessed whence it came, Alison thought now. Hermione had never inquired what was in the parcel that had arrived from Oldham and Alison had not told her, but had kept the wrapper and slippers for dressing-room wear when she began her career.

But it would have been surprising if her mother had mentioned them. Nothing concerning the Steins and Shragers was ever mentioned if the Plantaines could help it, and Alison was amazed that Oliver had said what he just had.

It occurred to her, too, that her Jewish relatives avoided mentioning the Plantaines, as though each family was an embarrassment to the other. Each was steeped in its own tradition, Alison reflected. It was small wonder that Alison was still, at times, beset by the feeling that she was of two worlds.

But she had now stopped comparing the two sets of people who inhabited them, and felt better for that.

"Well, my dear niece," Oliver said, eyeing her with affection, "it seems to me but yesterday that you made me a thirteen-year-old uncle. Your début leaves me in no doubt that I am young no more! Here is something to mark the occasion."

He took from his pocket a tiny velvet box and handed it to Alison.

Alison opened it and gave him a thank-you kiss. "How did you know I wanted a ring?"

"Your Aunt Ruby said you must, as you hadn't one. She said, too, that you had once admired her topaz necklace, so I chose a topaz ring for you. Fortunately, the jewelers had several in stock."

"It's beautiful, Uncle Oliver," Alison slipped the ring on to her finger. "And how clever of you to have judged my size correctly."

Oliver smiled. "I can't claim credit for that. Lucy managed to croak to me from her bed, this morning—the poor dear girl has great difficulty in uttering at present—that if I measured her thumb it would be like measuring your finger."

And no doubt she enjoyed that! Alison thought. "My hands go with the rest of me," she said with chagrin.

"Well you'd look somewhat odd with tiny ones, wouldn't you, my dear?"

"If, you don't mind, Uncle, I would prefer to forget my size."

"You would do better to consider it an asset," Oliver advised her. "You are one actress who will never find it difficult to make an imposing entrance, Alison."

"But not all entrances are required to be imposing," Alison countered. "And Juliet's certainly isn't!"

Oliver hid his smile. He had just been delivering a similar lecture to Luke; on the same subject, but the other way round.

"My dear Alison," he said, "you are not in the least ungainly. And believe me, your height and build will pass unnoticed when the audience hears you speak and looks at your beautiful face."

"It's kind of you to console me, Uncle, and I have no qualms about my performance. But I don't consider myself beautiful."

"That is your mistake, Alison. Not mine."

He left her to begin making up and Alison set down her grandparents' gift amid the clutter on Lucy's dressing table. From now on, it would be hers, too: she and Lucy would be required to share. The mirror was large enough for them both, but Alison was not looking forward to the intimate company of her step-cousin.

She draped a towel around her shoulders and a band of linen around her hairline. Was the face reflected in the looking glass beautiful? Albert had not said so. But he wasn't the kind to, she thought with amusement. What was it his mother had said about him? *Our Albert's a no-nonsense lad.*

Alison had felt that the remark had in it some kind of cautionary note, but it summed up her own impression of her loved one. Albert was kind and trustworthy, but not in the least romantic.

The night they parted, when they had been for a few minutes alone together in the garden, Albert had glanced heavenward and said "It smells like rain." Alison had been thinking that the sprinkling of stars were like diamonds in the sky.

But she had sensed from the beginning that difference between them. Alison was a diamonds-in-the-sky kind of person, and Albert the sort whose feet were planted firmly down on earth.

He was in no way the young man with whom Alison had expected she would one day fall in love. Though she had never been given to daydreaming of a knight in shining armor, she had felt, as every young girl does, that somewhere her romantic fate awaited her. It had come as a surprise when Albert turned out to be him.

She set aside these tender observations and selected a

stick of greasepaint. It was Romeo whom she would love tonight! While applying her makeup, she imagined she was Juliet, seated before a looking glass in her home in Verona, unaware of what Destiny had decreed for her, her heart still ungiven, and yearning for she knew not whom or what.

Alison wanted to present a flesh-and-blood Juliet, whose life is interrupted by events. It would be many years before theater demanded this realism. But from the outset of her career, the characters Alison played were to her real people, and it would be so until the end.

She was brushing her hair when the familiar call "Beginners please!" resounded from the dressing-room corridor.

Only then did Alison begin to feel nervous. Was she really as talented as she supposed? Juliet did not make her first appearance until Scene Three—time enough to find out!

Alison put on her costume and pinned the little jeweled cap to her hair. All she needed was for it to fall off, and turn the tragedy into a comedy!

Then came a rap on the dressing-room door. "Ten minutes please, Miss Plantaine."

"Thank you, Derek."

Alison's legs felt like jelly. It was said that the best actors never got over their nervousness. Oh, what a prospect, to feel like this every evening of her life! She sipped some water, which did not serve to calm her.

"Five minutes please, Miss Plantaine."

It was Miss Plantaine who emerged from the dressing room, but the girl who appeared onstage was Capulet's daughter. When Alison stepped from the wings she stepped too, into the ancient city of Verona and into the heart, soul and being of Shakespeare's best-loved heroine.

Had she not been newly in love, she might not have brought to the role quite the same magic that enthralled her audience that night. But even had that extra dimension been absent, nobody could have doubted that she was a born actress.

During the balcony scene, there came a moment Alison would remember always. Silence lay thick as a blanket in the darkened auditorium as she spoke her lines, and she knew she had made the audience forget they were seated in a theater; she had transported them backwards in time, into Juliet's life.

It was then that Alison became aware of her own power. With a word, a glance, a pause or a gesture, she could hold an audience spellbound; make them hopeful or fearful, laugh or cry, do with them what she willed. And oh, what a glorious feeling it was!

Watching from the wings, Gregory felt his throat close up and his flesh tingle. Those present at his granddaughter's début would never forget it. Alison had yet to acquire the technique experience would lend to her art, but the day would surely come when hers was an illustrious name.

"To thine own self be true."

HAMLET

ONE

Alison spent her nineteenth birthday rehearsing for a revue.

The vengeance Ruby had promised herself had been delayed, but not forgotten. Gregory's pained expression, while directing the company's first light-entertainment offering, was evidence that vengeance had surely been wreaked.

Only Ruby's cunning suggestion that her father-in-law might prefer to engage another director for this production had constrained Gregory to undertake the task—as Ruby had known it would. Seeing Gregory suffer at her hands was the object of the exercise.

Fortuitously, it would also be a highly profitable exercise. And for Gregory the beginning of a long list of similar sufferings. The revue had played to packed houses in London and the current trend was for provincial theaters to cash in on recent West End successes. Touring companies were also trying out in the provinces productions destined for the West End.

Is this really me? Alison thought while she and Lucy trilled a witty ditty onstage, accompanied by a tinkling piano and her grandfather's tapping foot. What was she doing, lending herself to this absolute drivel? Her classical background had ensured that she could not easily adjust to the wide spectrum of post-war entertainment, and she doubted that she ever would.

But, as Hermione had, Alison found herself responding with pleasure to the artistic challenge of contemporary plays. It had caused her to rethink the meaning of drama and to view Shakespeare as a dramatist whose work, like Shaw's and Glasworthy's, held up a mirror to his day.

The revue apart, Alison enjoyed her professional life. Sharing a dressing room with Lucy was the only blot on her working horizon. On her personal horizon, there were two and both loomed large. She did not see Albert very often. And her father's safe return from the war was marred by his poor health.

Horace had eventually been traced to a military hospital in Bologne. He was still unable to remember how he had got there; his stretcher-bearing had been to and from a field hospital close to the Front. He had awakened to find himself on a ward crammed with casualties, with a burning sensation in his chest and his mind a blank.

The amnesia had lasted for several months. Then a soldier from his own unit had been brought into the ward and the familiar face had served to unlock Horace's memory. Until then, he had not even known his name. His identification tag had been lost, which accounted for his being reported missing.

How he had become a casualty had remained a blank and the medical officers had said this was not uncommon; sometimes the mind drew a curtain over something it wanted to shut out.

Horace had been surrounded on the ward by men now disabled for life and had thought himself fortunate not to have lost an arm or leg. He did not yet know that he, too, was disabled. He knew he had been gassed—hence the searing feeling in his chest—but had not been told he must live out his years with impaired lungs.

This, he learned from a doctor in Hastings when he returned to civilian life. It was a prognosis that would be, to anyone, a bitter blow. For an actor, it was tantamount to being told he was finished. There were days when Horace could breathe quite well and others on which he found himself gasping for breath. On his good days, he would be capable of sustaining onstage a not too onerous role. On his bad days, he could barely walk.

He had entered the doctor's surgery expecting to be told he required a period of convalescence and a bottle of tonic. He left with the knowledge that his acting days were over.

More than two years had passed since then. Horace's discharge from the army on medical grounds had been in April 1917, on the day America entered the war. But he still had about him the air of a man totally diminished. The process had begun psychologically, long before he enlisted; between them, his wife and his father-in-law had unwittingly destroyed his confidence and his self-image. He had gone into the army stripped of the comforting illusions common to all human beings, but had still been whole physically. Now, he was not even that.

Alison, whose heart ached for him, noted that he had not dropped in to the rehearsal, as he usually did. During the midday break, she went to see him in his office.

"You don't mind me sitting on your desk, do you Papa?" she smiled, perching on a corner of it.

"You may set fire to it, if you wish, Alison."

"Now, now, Papa!" she said with a laugh.

"I wasn't joking, love."

"Get me a box of matches, then, and I'll do it."

"Nor did I mean it literally."

"I know perfectly well what you meant, Papa."

They exchanged a glance that said more than words. Theirs was a perfect understanding.

"Shall I tell you what is a joke, my darling?" Horace said in a brittle tone.

"I'm always game for a laugh, Papa."

"Then prepare to split your sides. I left home when I was a lad to escape from monotony. And now I'm back where I started, aren't I? Except that it's a desk I spend my days at, not a shop counter. Ha, ha!"

Alison could not muster so much as a smile.

Horace avoided her eye and gazed through the window. A lone seagull had strayed from its own territory to perch on a rooftop across the busy street. It ought to have had more sense—and reminded him of himself.

"He who makes his own bed, Alison, must henceforth lie in it—and I am proof of the proverb," he said brusquely.

"Has it been such an uncomfortable bed, Papa?"

"Lumpy, to say the least. And there are times when I wonder what my life has been all about, Alison. I broke my parents' hearts, and for what?"

"I'm sure they've forgiven you."

"Are you?"

Horace transferred his gaze from the seagull to a list of advance bookings on his desk, but his mind was in Old-ham, whither the sight of the lone bird had catapulted it.

Since leaving the army, he had visited his family three times and had been made welcome. The barrier his defection had raised between himself and them had loomed less obviously—but it had still been there.

"There are degrees of forgiveness, Alison," he said quietly. "Dependent upon the crime and the nature of the person against whom it was perpetrated."

"Surely it depends, too, on their relationship to the perpetrator?" Alison replied.

"What you're saying is it should be easy to forgive one's own child."

"Don't you agree, Papa?"

"In theory. But not necessarily in practice. When you

have a child, Alison, you'll find out how vulnerable parents are."

Alison was distressed by her father's words. "Have I done something to hurt you, Papa?"

"Of course not, my dearest girl. But I would say categorically that I am capable of being more hurt by you, than by anyone else, because I care about you so much."

Alison went to wind her arms around his neck. "I shall never do anything to hurt you, Papa darling."

"I'm sure you won't, Alison. But we've digressed from the subject. We were talking about what I did to my parents. I think my mother has forgiven me more wholeheartedly than my father is capable of doing. That's what I meant when I said the degree of forgiveness was related to the nature of the sinned against."

"You don't think Grandpa Shrager has a heart, do you?" Alison said.

"Does anyone?" Horace countered.

"Yes, Papa. Me."

Horace smiled. "I suppose he must have, in view of your having won it. When we went up north together, I couldn't believe my eyes. I've never seen my father look at anyone the way he looks at you."

"He told me I remind him of his mother."

"Something has to account for it! She died before I was born, but I've heard say she was a vain and idle woman—and my father was the only person who didn't see her faults," Horace said with a twinkle in his eye.

"People shouldn't believe ill of their dead grandmother," Alison rebuked him. "Especially when their own daughter is said to be like her!"

"In character you're not."

"Thanks for telling me what I already know, Papa. But it doesn't matter to me who I'm said to take after. So long as it isn't my mother."

"I would rather you hadn't said that, Alison."

"I didn't mean to, Papa. But having done so, I'm not going to take it back."

A tense silence followed.

"I find it very sad that you feel this way about your mother," Horace said.

"If you want the truth, Papa, I have no feeling left for her at all."

Horace got up from his chair and went to stare through the window again. The foolish seagull was still there. "You, too, find it difficult to forgive, don't you, Alison?"

You wouldn't find it so easy yourself, if you knew your wife had consoled herself with another man in your absence, Alison thought.

"I know all about Captain Browne-Hogg," Horace said, as though he had divined her thoughts.

"Who told you?" Alison asked when she had recovered from her shock.

"Your mother did."

"How dare she!" Alison cried. What a welcome home for a wounded soldier, she thought.

Horace noted her clenched fists and waited for her to calm herself. "You are a grown woman, Alison, and I can talk to you now about things you could not have understood when you were a child. Your mother and I began our marriage with several handicaps—"

"And one of them is that my mother is a snob," Alison cut in, "and no doubt thinks of your background as lower class to her own as top drawer. Add to that her aversion to Jews and it's difficult to comprehend why she married you, Papa. It has occurred to me more than once that it could be because I look Jewish that she has an aversion to me!"

Horace sidestepped Alison's outburst. "Your mother married me, and I her, because we loved each other so much, we were sure the handicaps could be surmounted. We have both learned that it's a mistake to believe that love, however strong, is enough. In moments of crisis, those basic differences always crop up and there is an irresistible temptation to use them against each other."

Alison surveyed her father's frail figure. He was not yet forty, but had the stooped posture of an aging man. Her parents were the same age, but Mama looked much younger. Thinking back, Alison recalled that her father had stopped looking young before he enlisted. The war had completed the damage his wife had begun. There was no doubt in Alison's mind about who had come off best in her parents' marriage.

"Do you still love Mama?" she asked.

"That's a very personal question, Alison."

"This is a very personal conversation."

"Yes, it is, isn't it?" Horace answered wryly. "Not the kind I would imagine is usual between father and daughter."

"We are not just father and daughter. You're my best friend, Papa."

Horace was momentarily too moved to reply. "I thought Emma had been accorded that honor," he chuckled, hiding his emotion.

"Emma is a perfect dear. But nobody will ever be to me quite what you are, Papa."

"What about young Albert?" Horace teased her.

Alison blushed. "What about him?"

"I'd got the impression he occupied a very special place in your affections. And you in his."

Alison could not deny it.

"What will you do, Alison, if Albert asks you to marry him?" Horace asked quietly.

"I don't know, Papa. As Grandpa Plantaine would say, I shall have to cross that bridge if and when I come to it."

"You may not find it an easy bridge to cross."

Alison thrust away the shadow of that possible future dilemma. "I'm sure we shall find a way out. Which returns me to the question you didn't reply to, Papa."

"I don't see how—unless you're telling me that you

truly love Albert? Because the answer to your question is yes. I still love your mother. Why should you think I don't, Alison?"

Because she doesn't deserve that you should, Alison thought. "This and that," she said. "I began wondering when you didn't kiss each other goodbye at the railway station, when we saw you off to the war. You just stood there, with stiff expressions on your faces."

Horace recalled that painful farewell. He had wanted to take Hermione in his arms, but pride had stood between them. As it had in bed, for the preceding weeks. On the final night of his embarkation leave, he had almost taken her by force, thrown his pride to the winds, and the hell with hers!

He turned away to the window so Alison would not see his face, which had flushed with the memory. He was aware of a stirring in his loins, which thoughts of Hermione in bed invariably evoked. But thinking about taking her was, since his return, all he was capable of. And God, how he despised himself.

Hermione's loving understanding only made him feel worse. But somehow Horace's plight had drawn them close in a way they had not been before.

It was Hermione's plight, too, Horace thought now. And it crossed his mind that his wife had possibly cast herself in the role of a martyr. Or had she accepted sexual deprivation as penance for her wartime disloyalty to him?

"What is so interesting about the view from that window?" Alison dryly prodded him. "I would imagine you know every slate on the rooftops, after—how long is it, now?"

"Two years, love." But it felt like twenty. Since his return to civilian life, Horace's days dragged slowly by. But he ought not to complain about his lot. Fate had kindly arranged for the Plantaine Players to be housed in their own theater, with a ready-made job for Horace, as administrator. Had the company still been touring, a crock like him would have been a burden; a hanger-on, contributing nothing.

"I was using the view as a background to my thoughts," he replied.

She noted his bitter smile and kept her tone light. "And we shall never complete this conversation, Papa, if your thoughts keep intruding on it!"

"When one is discussing something highly personal, isn't that always the case? Now where were we?"

"At the railway station, seeing you off to the war."

"And suffice to say, Alison, that your mother and I were not on the most affectionate of terms when I went away. As it wasn't a state of affairs either of us wanted to resume when I returned, your mother told me about the young man. She didn't want to harbor a guilty secret that would always be hovering in her mind, between us."

"How very sensible of her," Alison said frostily.

Horace paused. Defending his wife to his daughter was hazardous ground. And vice versa. Their coolness toward each other was a source of distress to him; and he wanted to mend the rift, not widen it. "Your mother hasn't your strength of character, Alison," he said carefully.

"Indeed she hasn't!"

Horace noted his daughter's curled lips. "You'll discover there's nothing to be gained, and much to be lost, Alison, if you go through life being contemptuous of those who are weaker than yourself."

"Emma's not a strong character, but I don't despise her," Alison answered. "It isn't weakness I have contempt for, Papa: it's disloyalty."

Horace toyed with a pencil on his desk. "Let me say, first, that I think you're wrong about Emma. I haven't spent much time in her company but I'd say that girl has inner resources she hasn't yet been called upon to reveal."

"Dear, sweet Emma is a veritable mouse, Papa! As

Aunt Lottie once said, a person could forget she's in the room."

"Nobody could say that of you! But returning to Emma, there is such a thing as quiet strength."

"How about returning to Mama? You haven't finished making your plea on her behalf."

"I ought not to have to plead with you to be charitable toward your mother. And I hope you won't continue to hold against her the way she behaved after your début," Horace added, though he was not sure that it was wise to have done so.

The frostiness returned to Alison's voice. "I'm afraid that is asking too much of me, Papa."

She left him again gazing through the window and went to her dressing room, wondering who had seen fit to tell him what he would have preferred not to know.

Alison was thankful to find she had the dressing room to herself. The pleasant veneer she and Lucy now maintained with each other was increasingly a strain. But Alison had found it necessary to pretend amicability toward several actresses, as they did with her.

When she was still sitting on the sidelines, watching others behave that way, she had vowed she would not enter into the charade. Once her career began, experience had taught her she must set aside her principles in the cause of work.

"I'm sure you didn't mean to upstage me, darling," she would say sweetly to whoever had deliberately done so. Initially, the insincerity had cloyed in her mouth. By now, the "dears" and "darlings" tripped lightly from her tongue.

Occasionally she had a temperamental row with another actress, but when it had blown over they both pretended to be abject with apology and forgot it.

Alison and Lucy had never had a row. But it would not have cleared the air if they had. Alison was the better actress of the two and Lucy knew it. So did the critics, who had not hesitated to say so.

Alison's début had received adulatory reviews in the local press. Lucy's performance was described as "insipid" by comparison, when two weeks later she rose from her sickbed and took over the role.

Lucy could no longer be patronizing toward Alison. Nor could her brother. Before Alison's début, the twins had considered her unworthy of their attention. Now, she was for Lucy a threat. Luke had secretly found playing opposite Alison a stimulating experience; but his professional admiration for her was swamped by loyalty to his sister.

This partisan feeling was, between the twins, mutual. Anyone who harmed one of them was instinctively hated by the other.

Alison would not have rated their veiled animosity toward her as strongly as hate. She sensed that Lucy was jealous of her; but in the theater, jealousy is an occupational hazard, and Alison was learning to take it in her stride. She would have stopped in her tracks had she known that her début had made the twins her enemies for life.

She removed Lucy's baby-blue robe from the chaise longue and sat down. How long ago it seemed since she had sat here in her Juliet costume, savoring for the first time the taste of success. And later—but she didn't want to think about it. Why had her father had to bring it all back to her? she thought with a stab of pain.

The company, with one exception, had flocked to praise Alison's performance and she had known that, for once, everyone meant what they said. That it wasn't one of those obligatory and embarrassing "You were absolutely marvelous, darling!" sessions, of which she had witnessed all too many.

Even those who had congratulated her in the wings had come to the dressing room, as though carried there on the wave of excitement that had that night pervaded the theater. And her grandfather had publicly awarded her the accolade, in five memorable words: "Alison, you will go far."

Not until the excitement had died down and she was left alone did Alison pause to wonder why her mother had not come. Mama probably wants me to herself, she had thought happily, and had sat down to wait for her. When the minutes ticked by without Hermione putting in an appearance, Alison had had to accept that she was not coming.

She had dressed and returned to the lodgings with her grandparents. As they left the theater, the stagedoor keeper had mentioned that Hermione had left some time ago. Alison had felt almost as sorry for Gregory and Jessica as she was for herself. True to form, both had chattered to her about everything but her mother's odd behavior. Alison would have given more than a penny for their thoughts, but pride had prohibited her from mentioning her mother's name.

Alison would not forget the hurt Hermione had inflicted upon her that night. The triumph could never be taken from her, but her mother had ensured that the memory of it would, for all time, be bitter as well as sweet.

She had arrived at the lodgings to find a celebration supper awaiting her, arranged by the kindly landlady. And was told by Oliver that Hermione was sick and had gone to bed.

Sick with what? Alison had thought contemptuously. Envy of the acclaim given to her own daughter! Alison had taken so many curtain calls she had lost count of the number. But it was many more than she had ever known Hermione Plantaine take. Nor could she recall her mother ever receiving a standing ovation—and Alison's must have been for Hermione more than her ego could bear.

There was no other way Alison could construe her mother's unnatural behavior. If Hermione had tried to put things right the following morning, Alison might have found it in her heart to forgive her, though she now doubted it. But Hermione had not said a word about her daughter's success, which Alison found difficult to relate to her good wishes before the event.

A rap on the dressing-room door returned Alison to the present. It was the stagedoor keeper, bringing the red roses which Albert sent to her each weekend.

"I'd think it weren't Friday, if these weren't delivered!" the cheerful old man said.

Alison took the flowers and breathed in their heavy scent. "Me too, Jim."

" 'E don't never let us down, does 'e? Reglar as flippin' clockwork, them roses always comes."

"He isn't the letting-down sort, Jim." And sending me roses is his one concession toward the poetic, Alison reflected with a smile. Dear Albert's idea of an expression of love was still the bag-of-peppermints kind and he would never change. Alison didn't want him to. She loved him just the way he was—and hadn't yet told him that she loathed peppermints!

"It's a pity 'e can't see your face, when you gets 'is weekly bookay," Jim declared, surveying Alison's radiant expression. "When're we goin' to meet this young chappie o' yours, Miss Alison?"

"One of these fine days," she answered airily.

"That's wot you says every time I asks you! A right mystery-man, 'e is, if you asks me!" Jim said with a smile as he left her to put the flowers in water.

Jim was not the only person who thought thus. The entire company was curious about the sender of Alison's roses. Only her father had met Albert, and there were those outside the Plantaine family who privately wondered if she was having an affair with a married man, and being unjustifiably faithful to him.

As the other young actresses did, Alison received flowers from young men who admired her from the stalls. The offerings were invariably accompanied by invitations to supper. Alison always refused them.

She set the vase of roses on her end of the dressing table. Lucy had three vases at her end and was currently indulging in flirtations with each of the young men who had filled them for her.

At a glance, Lucy's face was as childish and innocent as it had been when Alison first met her. Lucy had then been sixteen. And was now twenty-one going on thirty! Alison thought cattily. Lines to which a young woman was not entitled told their tale beside her step-cousin's eyes.

Lucy liked what she called "a good time," as her brother did. But the all-night parties to which the twins went were not Alison's idea of a good time. Nor would she have liked to look and feel as they did, the morning after.

They had become the center of a wild young set. Some of the boys in it were titled, and all had motor cars and private incomes. The girls wore expensive clothes and too much rouge. The whole set seemed to have been raised with nothing but fun in mind, Alison had thought after briefly making their acquaintance.

Luke and Lucy had once invited them all for Sunday tea at the Plantaines' lodgings, and Alison had required no longer than that to assess the twins' friends as the empty sycophants they were.

Alison was not unaware that the glamorous aura of theatricals is magnetic even to the rich. She had no doubt that this accounted for her step-cousins' popularity, or that it was available to her, too. If she wished, she could be part of the twins' set, or gather around her a social set of her own.

Alison did not wish it and never would. That is not to say that she would never go to parties, or enjoy the social adulation that accrues to a well-known actress. But though her career was then only three years old, Alison already saw herself as quite another kind of queen bee, the kind who would dispense favor only where and when it suited her to do so. And there would, with a few exceptions, always be for those with whom she mixed a once-removed feeling. Alison was capable of being warm and friendly while at the same time remaining aloof.

Her thoughts had briefly strayed from Albert and now returned to him. How much longer could she put off inviting him to Hastings? Why was she so reluctant to have him here? It was as though she was afraid of breaking the spell each of them had cast over the other, that had made them fall in love.

Alison nibbled the cheese sandwich she had brought to eat in the dinner break—and told herself not to be ridiculous. But the feeling remained. Albert was part of her other world, the one to which she, from time to time, escaped and returned refreshed. But he wouldn't be comfortable in her everyday world. The Plantaines would of course be charming to him, as they were to everyone. But Albert would see through it and feel like a fish on dry land.

Alison poured herself some water from the carafe on the dressing table and sipped it pensively. Was it Albert whom she wanted to protect? Or herself?

As Alison was able to go north but rarely, and had discouraged Albert from coming south, theirs was something of a paper love affair, she reflected whimsically. And Albert wasn't the kind to express tenderness on paper! He found it hard enough to do so when he held her in his arms. But his red roses said it all and their regular delivery bespoke his constancy.

Nevertheless, there were times when Alison felt that he and she were held together by the most tenuous of threads. One wrong move and the fragile, precious thing their love was might snap, she thought with a shiver of apprehension.

But it was not this alone that deterred her from inviting Albert to visit her on her home ground. She had not invited Emma, either. Though she knew not why, Alison wanted to keep her two worlds apart.

TWO

"**I**'m concerned about Alison," Horace told his wife.

Hermione had returned from the theater and found him brooding in their bedroom. She surveyed his pale face and the dark shadows beneath his eyes. "You would do better to have more concern for yourself."

"Did Alison get away in time to catch her train?"

Their daughter had gone north, immediately after the evening performance. Albert's twenty-first birthday was to be celebrated tomorrow night.

"If she missed the train, she'll catch the next one," Hermione said shortly.

"I feel bad because I wasn't there to take her to the station, as I usually do," Horace replied.

Hermione had taken off her hat and was arranging her hair. She eyed her husband through the mirror. "For goodness' sake, Horace! When are you going to accept that your daughter is more than capable of taking care of herself? As you weren't well enough to leave the house today, and Alison knows it, there's nothing for you to feel bad about. As for your being concerned about her—!"

Horace rose from the sofa and opened the window.

"You'll get your death of cold!" Hermione exclaimed.

"It might be better if I did."

Hermione went to put her arms around him. "Oh, my darling, it would certainly not be better for me. So let's shut the window, shall we? It is November, not June."

"If you insist, my love." This was one of the times when, with or without fresh air, Horace found it difficult to breathe. "I hope my not being too well today won't prey upon Alison's mind and stop her from enjoying the party," he said.

Hermione moved away from him and sat down on the sofa. "Alison, Alison! Don't you ever think of anyone or anything else?"

Horace went to sit beside her and took her hand. "Yes, Hermione dear, I think of you. But you seem not to share my concern for our child."

Hermione removed her hand from his. "Our child—who, may I remind you, is now a woman—did not appreciate the way I once cared for her. And what, specifically, is causing you to be anxious about her now?"

"Her relationship with her young man."

Hermione laughed humorlessly. "Oh yes. The mysterious Albert."

"He isn't in the least mysterious," Horace said. "Far from it."

"Until Alison sees fit to introduce him to me, he will remain so to me."

Horace gazed into the fire their thoughtful landlady always lit for him on days when he was confined to his room. Defending Alison to Hermione was as delicate as the opposite way around. "Have you ever thought why Alison hasn't asked Albert here to meet you?" he said carefully.

"I have ceased to waste my time wondering why Alison doesn't do what might be expected of her."

"That's a pity," Horace answered. "If you were to think about it, you might come up with a useful answer."

"Oh?" Hermione said guardedly. "And what do you suppose it would be?"

Horace plunged in, though he would doubtless regret it. "Haven't there been times, Hermione, when you have not fulfilled Alison's expectations of you?"

Hermione got up and went to lean her elbow on the mantelpiece. "You know about her début night, don't you," she said after a silence.

"Yes. Though I wasn't referring to that."

Hermione gave him a forlorn glance.

How lovely she looks with the firelight gilding her hair, Horace thought. Not that it needed gilding; the years had barely touched her. Apart from a fine line or two beside her mouth, she still looked like the fragile girl he had married, and her beauty still brought an ache to his throat. She had hurt him in a multitude of ways, but he would forgive her anything.

Sadly, she and Alison could not forgive each other. Both were afflicted with something that had nothing to do with Plantaine family pride. It was not present in Jessica or Oliver, but Gregory and his daughter and grand-daughter were all three bedevilled by it.

Horace was not the kind to be blind to the faults of those he loved. Since his return from the war, he had become aware that Alison had in her more of her mother than she would be prepared to recognize. Horace had not failed to note that his dear daughter had matured into a woman who set her own value higher than that of others.

Ego was the word for it and Horace had learned it was a quality without which fame in the theater is unlikely to be achieved. But it went hand in hand with living for one-self, and it was on that account that Horace was con-cerned for his daughter. Egoists do not find it easy to give and take, to share their life with another.

This was one aspect of Horace's anxiety about Alison's love affair with Albert Battersby, and would have worried him no matter who the young man was. Horace feared, too, that Albert might whisk Alison away from her profession. And that, he thought now, would be the theater's loss.

He had been gazing into the fire and now looked up at Hermione, who was still eyeing him forlornly.

"I can't pretend to have been a perfect mother to Alison," she said quietly. "But I accepted, long ago, that I'm not the right mother for her. Nor is she the right daughter for me."

Horace remained silent.

Hermione steeled herself to say what must be said. "Alison is an actress of rare talent, Horace. Her début revealed to me that I am not."

Horace had always known that, gifted though his wife was, she lacked the special quality that makes an actor or actress unique. He wanted to say something to comfort her, but knew that nothing could.

"Learning the truth about myself was a terrible shock, Horace," she said. "And as I am being honest with you, I have to confess that I was jealous of Alison and couldn't face her that night—lest she see it in my eyes."

"My poor darling," Horace said. He had not required telling that his wife's bruised ego had taken precedence over her maternal pride in Alison. He went to put his arms around her.

"You won't tell Alison, will you?" she whispered.

Horace stroked her hair. "What I am hoping is that you will find the courage to tell her yourself."

Hermione stiffened. "Nothing would persuade me to. And I doubt that it would help." She smiled bitterly. "What is one justified grievance among the long list of imaginary ones my daughter holds against me?"

"How about those you hold against her?" Horace said gently.

Hermione broke away from him. "Mine are not imaginary."

"I expect that's what Alison believes about hers. Wouldn't it be better if you sat down with her and talked things out?"

"Possibly. If we could talk to each other. But we never could. And one day Alison will go out of my life, and that will be that," Hermione said with sadness.

"If she marries Albert, you mean?"

"No, I do not mean that." Hermione strayed from the subject. "I should like to know who told you that I avoided seeing Alison after her début?"

"Oliver."

"That doesn't surprise me," Hermione declared acidly. "I have come to think of my brother as a mischief maker. And it's hard to reconcile that with what he once meant to me. Since his marriage, of course, he has no longer needed me."

"He thought it would be helpful for me to know what had compounded the bitterness between my wife and daughter," Horace told her. "Believe it or not, Oliver finds it as distressing as I do."

"Oliver has never in his life been distressed except on his own account!"

Horace let that pass. The Plantaine family was a veritable web of grievances, most of them rooted in the inability to communicate with each other. To plain-speaking Horace, there was no misunderstanding that the will and the words could not clear up.

"My brother didn't consider my distress, when he gave Alison the fare to go north, the first Christmas of the war," Hermione went on.

Oliver had told Horace the whole story, but Horace remained silent. What was the point of reminding his wife that Oliver hadn't known why Alison wanted the money? It never did any good to jog Hermione's memory about what she found it convenient to forget.

"That episode is over and done with," was all he allowed himself to say on the subject. "And I'm sure it must be a relief to you that your brother is, at last, a happy man."

"Why should it be a relief to me?" Hermione flashed. "You seem to have forgotten at whose expense his happiness was bought. His marriage has changed his life for the better, but the same cannot be said about mine, or our parents'. Our ancestors would turn in their graves if they knew what has become of the Plantaine Players. And the kind of people upon whom Oliver has bestowed the family name."

Horace had been calling himself by that name for twenty years, but still felt no more fitted to it than Ruby and her children were. "What's in a name?" he quoted wryly.

"A good deal," Hermione informed him, "when the name is Plantaine. Would that my daughter shared that sentiment."

"Alison is proud of being a Plantaine."

"But whether she is a loyal one, only time will tell."

"Would you think it disloyal if she abandoned her career to marry Albert?"

"Alison will not abandon her career," Hermione declared. "No matter whom she marries. I'm sorry for her husband, whoever he turns out to be. He will always come a poor second to her profession."

A short silence followed.

"I know what you are thinking," Hermione said. "That it's been like that with us."

"Well, hasn't it?"

Hermione went to kiss his cheek. "No, Horace. And if I had had to choose between being an actress or your wife, I should have chosen you."

"Would you still?"

"Oh yes. Now, the choice would not be at all difficult for me. It has taken years, but at last I know what matters."

Horace was both moved and surprised by his wife's

revelation. How big a part did pity play in the last bit of what she had said? he wondered, but did not let his mind dwell on it.

His thoughts strayed north. "Each time Alison goes to Oldham, I expect her to come back and tell us that Albert has proposed to her," he said, "and what worries me is how Alison will cope with the dilemma it would present."

"Then take my advice and worry no more," Hermione replied brusquely. "It won't be a dilemma to Alison. If she accepts him, it will simply be an inconvenience to Albert. He will have to reconcile himself to seeing his wife only at the weekends. And to the traveling that will entail for him. As you know, Horace, not every actress marries within the profession.

"Our sister-in-law didn't, the first time," Hermione recalled with the distaste mentioning Ruby evoked in her. "But that didn't stop her marriage from being all too fruitful—would that it had, then we wouldn't have to put up with her odious twins!"

"All I want is for Alison to be happy," Horace said.

"Alison, Alison!" Hermione exclaimed, leaving the room to fetch their supper. When Horace was not well enough to join the family downstairs, Hermione ate her nightly meal with him in the bedroom.

She had slammed the door behind her and Horace was left feeling that their conversation had turned full circle. His wife exclaiming, "Alison, Alison!" was how it had begun.

Hermione was beset by the futility of most of what had been said. How could she make her husband understand the way she felt, when it was distressingly inexplicable to herself?

Her jealousy of Alison had not ceased to exist as a result of her admitting it. It was there now, conflicting with her maternal love. It was as though she were two different people; it would be painful for Hermione the mother if Alison were to go out of her life, but Hermione the actress would be happy if the young actress with whom she couldn't compete went far away. It was like insult piled upon injury, that this superior actress happened to be her own daughter.

Hermione could not confess this to Horace. No doubt he was already upset enough about the unmotherly feelings she had confessed. Nor could she confide in him her other jealousy, the one that had always been there: Why did he love Alison more than he loved her?

When Horace returned from the war a semi-invalid, Hermione had made up her mind to devote herself to him. Within the restrictions of her working life she had honored that vow. She went nowhere without him, though social invitations still came her way.

Night after night, Hermione returned to her ailing husband, but it was not a penance. Her love for Horace had assumed a new dimension. She had not really valued him until she learned he was missing in France. When he was spared to come back to her, she begged God never to take him from her again.

In the intervening months, when Hermione had not known if she was wife or widow, the sexual fantasies that had sated and disgusted her left her in peace, to think about the man she had married. And, too, about herself, which brought her to the shameful realization that her husband was a giver and she a taker.

It was then that Hermione comprehended the depth of her own selfishness; she had demanded and received from Horace more than any wife had the right to expect. Throughout their marriage—except for the matter of Alison having contact with Horace's family—it had been Hermione who called the tune. But her husband was not a weak man; just one who had subjugated his own hopes and wishes to hers, in the name of love.

She was now doing her best to recompense him, proving herself capable of the undemanding love he had always given her. His impotency distressed her on his account, not hers; she was not allowing that lack in her life to loom large.

Hermione would not have been human had she not harbored a sense of self-sacrifice; the role in which she had cast herself was not one for which she was fitted. But her sole concern was to make her husband happy, and it went against the grain that he now seemed more concerned with Alison's happiness than with hers.

These were Hermione's thoughts as she returned to the bedroom with the supper tray. The landlady had, as always, offered to bring it upstairs; but ministering angel was integral to Hermione's new role and she allowed no one else to play it when she was available to do so.

Horace eyed the tureen of steaming broth Hermione had set on a small table beside the fire. "I wonder if Alison remembered to take a flask of hot tea, for the journey."

Hermione had just picked up the soup ladle and managed not to plunk it back into the tureen with an angry splash. It was difficult, too, for her to refrain from exclaiming, "Alison, Alison!" yet again. "If she didn't remember, she will just have to go thirsty, won't she, dear?" she replied lightly. "We cannot think of everything for her, as we did when she was a child."

She ladled the soup into two flower-patterned bowls and sat down opposite her husband.

"Alison has always thought for herself about important matters," Horace said, "but when it comes to the small, everyday things of life, she will always need someone to think for her."

"Then let us hope she marries a man like her father." Hermione helped herself to a crisp bread roll. "I enjoy our cozy tête-à-tête suppers, darling, don't you?"

"I would, were it not for the reason for them."

These intimate meals by the fire were the nearest Horace and Hermione had ever come to what their life would have been like, had they had their own home. Horace had long since stopped dreaming that one day they would have. And, he reflected now, a man who required as much sick leave as he did, but was paid his wages nevertheless, should be thankful to have a roof over his head.

If Hermione had divined his thoughts it would have broken her heart. In truth, he was too hard on himself; on days when he was not fit to go out, the mail, and any administrative matters with which he must deal urgently, were brought from the theater to him.

"It was unfortunate that this had to be one of my bad days," he said to Hermione. "Alison will be anxious about me while she's away."

"But it didn't stop her from going, did it?"

Horace put down his spoon. "You lose no opportunity to denigrate her."

"Let's finish our soup, shall we? Before it gets cold."

But their cozy togetherness had fled, as it too often did; dispatched by their daughter, though she was not present.

Am I never to know peace in my marriage? Horace thought. The blessed amnesty his wife had, with her new loving kindness, declared, was little by little being eroded by her jealousy of Alison.

THREE

Unaware that she had become the fly in her parents' marital ointment, Alison was looking forward to her brief stay in Oldham. Her anxiety about her father's health was ever present, but she made up her mind not to let it cast a shadow on her beloved's coming-of-age weekend.

Alison's sojourns in the north were no longer the giggly, carefree times they had once been. For this, Clara was responsible. The war had made her a widow before she became a mother. She lived with her family, whose household now revolved entirely around her and her child.

Or so it seemed to Alison. Emma was the little boy's unofficial, unpaid nanny, while Clara sat around blaming her mother-in-law for her plight. This was not a situation Alison enjoyed witnessing, nor did it make her happy to see Lottie and Lionel subjected to the repercussions of Clara's vengeful vow.

Clara had kept her promise to punish her mother-in-law if Percy was killed in the war. She was what Emma called "an eye-for-an-eye person" and was relentlessly making Percy's mother pay for insisting that he join up. Clara had not allowed her in-laws to see the only grandchild they would ever have, who was named after their dead son.

Mr. and Mrs. Zeligman had, of course, viewed the child from afar. Clara could not stop them from lurking near the Steins' home, or in the park when little Percy was taken for an airing. Their attempts to get closer to him were a constant source of strife and distress to the entire Stein family.

Alison arrived around midday on Sunday, and walked right into a painful scene between the Zeligmans and her aunt and uncle, on the front doorstep.

"Where is your heart?" Mrs. Zeligman was tearfully demanding of Lottie.

"In the right place, where it's always been," Lionel replied for his wife. "Mine, too. And believe me, it's breaking for you. But we can't add to our daughter's sorrow by going against her wishes, that you must understand," Lionel added. He had repeated the words so often, he was beginning to sound to himself like a Gramophone record.

Mrs. Zeligman took a handkerchief from her coat pocket and dabbed her eyes, which were permanently swollen from two years of weeping. "Your daughter didn't look so sorrowful to me. To me she looked pleased when, a moment ago, she whisked our grandson in his carriage from under our noses."

Mr. Zeligman said nothing. He rarely did.

Alison, who liked the couple no more now than she did when she first met them, was nevertheless sorry for them. For her relatives, too. This couldn't be easy for Lottie and Lionel, whose own son had miraculously survived the war without a scratch, as Alison's sweetheart had.

But there's more than one kind of battle scar, Alison thought. There was about Conrad, now, a hard edge that had not been there when he went to France. And Albert had come back with a streak of white in his hair, as though the horror he had witnessed at the Front had aged him irrevocably, overnight.

The Zeligmans were gazing beseechingly at Lottie and Lionel.

"Anything your daughter wants, she can have," Mrs. Zeligman declared. "All we ask is to hold our grandchild for a minute in our arms."

"You can't give me back my husband and it was you who sent him to his death!" Clara screeched through the parlor window. She spent a good deal of her time there, watching out for her in-laws, and had this morning seen them creeping up the garden path. "All I want now is for you to stay away from me and my child!" she added vehemently.

Mrs. Zeligman looked as if she had just been condemned to the gallows. If Clara had had her way, she would be, Alison thought.

Alison was standing in the drive, wishing she had not chosen this moment to arrive.

"Pick up your case, Alison, and come in through the side door," Lionel called to her. "On Sundays we can never be sure that our front entrance won't be blocked," he said with a weary smile.

Mrs. Zeligman added indignation to her churning emotions. "A fine joke!"

"Joking I wasn't," Lionel said.

"So what was it? An insult, maybe? When else can my poor husband come here with me? Sunday is his day off and without him I wouldn't come to your doorstep. My darling daughter-in-law could maybe pick up a poker and clout me over the head!"

Lionel felt it necessary to defend Clara, though she was responsible for all the gray hairs on his own head. "Now who is being insulting? I don't agree with the way our Clara is punishing you. But you did do the thing she's punishing you for."

"And isn't it punishment enough that I have to live with it?"

"So does my daughter," Lionel said.

"Your daughter can get another husband. I'll never have another son."

Alison exchanged a glance with Lottie, who looked about to join Mrs. Zeligman in another bout of weeping.

"Like I said, Alison, it's always like this on Sundays. So pick up your case and come in," Lionel repeated with a helpless shrug.

Alison found Emma in the kitchen, spoon-feeding the innocent cause of the commotion.

"Isn't Percy beautiful?" Emma said when she and Alison had greeted each other with a kiss.

Alison was constrained to nod, though doing so was a lie. Emma was a proud aunt and would not like to be told that her toddler nephew was the plainest child Alison had ever seen. He was the image of his paternal grandmother and Mrs. Zeligman had no claims to beauty.

He was, too, a peevish child—but had probably inherited that trait from his mother, Alison thought, watching little Percy kick the spoon from Emma's hand.

Emma retrieved it from the rug and rinsed it at the sink. "He's always doing that," she told Alison.

"He probably knows he can get away with it, with you," Alison smiled. "You ought to be firm with him, Emma."

"And don't think I wouldn't be, if he was my child," Emma replied. "But our Clara won't let me be."

"That's absolutely typical of her!" Alison exploded. "She's letting you do everything for him, isn't she?"

"I don't mind, Alison. I enjoy it."

"And it suits Clara fine! But if she's going to let you take care of her child, then she ought to leave how you go about it to you."

Alison took off her hat and coat and surveyed her cousin's placid expression. "I don't know how you remain so equable and cheerful, Emma. I shouldn't enjoy living in the midst of a family feud. I think it's unfair of Clara to inflict it upon you all. Your dad's hair is a lot grayer than when I was last here, and your mother has lost weight."

Conrad had entered the room while Alison was speaking and went to give her a hug. "It seems ages since you last visited us, Alison. And I'm sure Albert thinks so," he added quietly.

Alison stretched her arms wearily and stifled a yawn. "Was that a rebuke, Conrad?"

"Yes, as a matter of fact. Albert misses you, Alison."

"And I him. I miss all of you, too. But I don't think any of you quite realize what it entails for me to come here. I have to rush to the railway station, exhausted from my performance, to catch the last train to London. I then have to change stations and spend the night traveling to Manchester. There, may I remind you, I cross town to another station, to get the Oldham train. And I shall have to leave at the crack of dawn on Monday, to be sure of getting back to Hastings in time for curtain-up that night."

"Poor Alison," Emma said.

"But it still wouldn't kill her to come a bit more often," Conrad declared.

Alison took an apple from the fruit bowl and hurled it at him.

"We once promised to be honest with each other," he reminded her.

"Brutally so, on your part, apparently."

"*Touché.*"

"I'm moved by your desire to see more of me," Alison said sarcastically. The sarcasm was a cover for she knew not what.

"It's Albert you should be thinking of, not me," Conrad replied, taking her seriously. "And while I'm doing some plain speaking, why haven't you asked him to visit you? There's no reason why the mountain can't go to

Mohammed, is there? As it's difficult for Mohammed to come to the mountain?"

"Are you calling my visits north pilgrimages?" Alison fenced with a smile, and it struck her that in a way they were. And that Albert was not a mountain that could be moved. This crystallized within her the thoughts she had already had about her reasons for not inviting Albert to Hastings.

Conrad, who had neatly caught the apple, tossed it back to her.

"It won't be fit to eat, when you two have finished playing ball with it," said Emma.

"Percy want to play," her nephew whined.

"Apples are not for playing with, Percy dear."

Percy dear picked up his dish of mashed potatoes and threw it at her.

Emma stood with the mush dripping from her face and hair.

"Smacking time has arrived," Alison advised her. "And be blowed to Clara for not wanting you to be firm with the brat."

Clara appeared in the doorway in time to hear this. "Did I hear you correctly, Alison?"

"You certainly did. And as you are now here, I suggest that you put what I said into practice, while Emma cleans herself up."

Clara lifted Percy from his high chair and clutched him to her breast. "All we need is your second-cousin Alison coming here and telling us what to do, isn't it, my pet?"

"What we really need, Clara, is for you to move out of this house," Conrad said, "and conduct your Vendetta from where it won't affect the rest of us."

Clara burst into tears and swept from the room with her child.

"You shouldn't have said that to her," Emma told Conrad. "Who else has she got, but her family?"

"She'll find someone," Conrad replied. "Let me give you a piece of advice, our Emma. Don't let yourself get too attached to Percy. One of these days, when she gets bored with her widow's weeds, our Clara will get herself a rich husband and live the kind of posh life she intended to have with Percy's dad. She'll have a maid to run her home and look after her kids. You won't be needed anymore."

"Do you think I don't know that?" Emma replied. "Now if you two will excuse me, I must go and wash."

"Our Emma's a born mug," Conrad said when he and Alison were alone. "But she enjoys being one. It's useless giving her advice."

"You were giving me some, when your nephew rudely interrupted you," Alison reminded him. "This seems to be your day for ladling out advice."

"And I was about to say that if I were Albert, I wouldn't wait to be invited to Hastings. I'd turn up there, to make sure you weren't two-timing me with another chap."

"Albert knows that I'm not. And did you make that suggestion to him, Conrad?" Alison inquired.

"No. But I did ask him why he hadn't insisted on visiting you. And it might interest you to know what his answer was, Alison."

"Indeed it would."

"Your boyfriend has got it in his head that the Plantaines won't think he's good enough for you, and that you're putting off introducing him to them because of that."

"But Albert has met my father, Conrad. They got on very well together," Alison countered defensively.

"Your father isn't a Plantaine."

"If I wanted to marry Albert—and he hasn't yet asked me to—nobody could dissuade me, Conrad," Alison said. "I am, and always shall be, my own keeper."

Emma had laid the table for lunch and Conrad sat fiddling with the salt cellar. "There's no need to tell me that, Alison. But I doubt if Albert knows it yet. He's a pretty strong character himself, and if you two do get wed, he'll consider himself your keeper."

"Then I shall have to disillusion him in advance, shan't I?"

Conrad chuckled: "I see stormy seas ahead!"

"I shouldn't marry him, unless I was sure they were navigable," Alison said. She gazed pensively at the fruit bowl. "So far, our love affair has been smooth sailing, Conrad. And I suppose I've known in my heart, all along, that Albert meeting my Plantaine relatives would, one way or another, cause waves."

Alison looked up at her cousin, whom she knew was a true friend. "What I would like, Conrad, is for my beautiful love affair to stay just as it is now. I don't want any horrid, everyday, outside influences to touch it. I want it never to change."

"You don't want much, do you! Only the impossible. No situation can stand still, my dear Alison. Least of all a love affair. Tomorrow always comes."

Alison changed the subject. "So does tonight! I must take my suitcase upstairs and unpack the dress I shall wear for Albert's party. It will probably require pressing. Emma will have to do it for me; I'd probably burn a hole in it."

Good old Emma! Conrad thought wryly. Alison was always telling her that Clara took advantage of her good nature, but didn't think twice about doing so herself. That evening, when he saw Alison wearing the white silk gown she had bought for the occasion, Conrad withdrew the unkind thought. Alison was not intended for the domestic chores that were a woman's lot. She was born to electrify ordinary mortals like himself with her special magic.

"You look stunning, Alison!" Conrad exclaimed as she descended the stairs, her raven hair piled high upon her head, a black velvet cloak draped over one arm.

"A compliment from you is worth a dozen from anyone else," Alison laughed. He was not given to them.

"But I thank you, sir. And don't you think Emma looks rather splendid this evening?" she said, appraising the diminutive, taffeta-clad figure beside her. "But I wish I could persuade her to wear a color other than brown."

Lionel, Lottie and Clara had gathered in the hall to inspect the party goers.

"My sister likes fading into the woodwork," Clara said.

Emma smiled. "Anyone would, next to Alison, no matter what color they wore."

"You look a treat, love," Lionel told her affectionately.

"That cameo brooch I made her pin to her collar sets her dress off, doesn't it" Lottie put in. "I wanted to lend Alison my pearl necklace, Lionel. But she was afraid of breaking it."

"Alison doesn't need jewelry," Conrad declared, helping her on with her cloak.

"Why is our Conrad suddenly behaving like a gentleman?" Clara said nastily. She was still smarting from his frank words to her that morning.

She watched her brother hold Emma's rabbit-fur coat for her to slip her arms into it, and experienced a pang because she was not going to the party. She had been invited, but had declined. Clara's period of mourning was long past, but she was still cutting off her nose to spite her face.

Lottie observed the lines around her elder daughter's mouth. Bitterness could age a woman faster than the years. "You should be all dressed up and going with them," she told Clara.

"I'm not in the mood for celebrating, Mam. And what would be the point of me going to Albert's party, anyway? It won't be a Jewish crowd."

Lottie and Lionel exchanged a hopeful glance. This was the first indication Clara had given that her thoughts were turning to the possibility of remarriage.

Conrad opened the front door and ushered Alison and

Emma out. "With a girl on each arm, I'll make quite an entrance tonight!"

In the event, Alison made her entrance on Albert's arm. He had deserted his guests to pace the drive impatiently.

"Why didn't you get a cab to fetch you here?" he asked Conrad, hastening to the gate to meet them.

"For a ten-minute walk? On a fine night?"

"I thought you were never going to arrive."

Conrad grinned. "I think that was meant for you, Alison," he said. But she was too busy looking into Albert's eyes to reply.

Conrad gave his sister a wink. "I think the lovebirds would like to be alone," he said, steering her toward the house.

As ever, Albert was a lovebird unable to sing his song. He wanted to tell Alison that he adored her. That the sight of her, with the moonlight enhancing her beauty, had caused his throat to close up. That he wanted to make her his and never be parted from her again. But the words refused to leave his tongue. "I couldn't wait to see you," was all he was able to say.

"Nor I you."

Albert took her in his arms and kissed her. "We haven't been alone very often, have we?" he said, holding her close. He could count those few precious occasions on the fingers of one hand.

Alison's visits north had not numbered many more than that, and Albert could not contemplate continuing to worship her from afar. When they were apart, he could not, in his imagination, breathe life into her, nor did the thought of her excite him to passion.

Only her physical presence had that effect upon him and was doing so now; telling him that the divine creature who remained for him on a pedestal when he wasn't with her was a flesh-and-blood woman. He had to restrain himself from crushing her mouth with his, instead of giving her the tender kisses that were all he had, so far, allowed himself.

The fear of taking a step that might damage their relationship was present in Albert, as it was in Alison. He was as aware of its fragility as she was. They were not of each other's worlds and both knew it. But Albert had made up his mind to make Alison part of his.

"While we're alone, I'd like to give you my gift for your coming of age," Alison said. "But you'll have to unhand me, so I can get it out of my evening bag," she added with a soft laugh.

She took from her bag a silver keyring and sang the traditional coming-of-age ditty:

> "I've got the key of the door
> Never been twenty-one before!"

She pressed the keyring to her lips and then into her lover's hand. "This will insure that you think of me often."

Albert gathered her close again. "What I want, Alison, is for you and me to have keys to the same door."

Alison laughed shakily. "Is that a proposal?"

Albert nodded. "I'd like to make tonight a double celebration, announce our engagement," he said against her cheek.

"What a splendid idea," Alison's heart was brimming with love and joy. But her mind was envisaging the difficulties her career would present when she and Albert were married, and her apprehension had deepened.

Albert took her hand and led her to the house. "You look a real picture, Alison," he declared proudly as they entered.

Drinks were being served in the hall and Alison's arresting appearance caused heads to turn in her direction. She was aware, too, that the buzz of conversation had petered out.

Her dramatic black-and-white attire was partially responsible for the moment of silence. Women and girls who had thought themselves elegantly gowned were made, when they saw Alison that evening, to feel as Emma did; that her presence rendered them unnoticeable.

But Alison's personality, too, accounted for it, and her natural grace. As though drawn by a magnet, the male guests, young and old, could not take their eyes from her—and some were elbowed into doing so by their female companions.

In time, Alison would grow accustomed to creating a stir, and at more sophisticated gatherings than Albert Battersby's twenty-first birthday party. But this was her first such experience and she felt as if she had just walked onstage. That any moment her audience would begin applauding her entrance—or possibly the reverse! What she could sense all around her was admiration laced with—what? Disapproval? Probably. The stage had scandalous connotations for these homely people, Alison reminded herself, and it was the stage that she represented for them.

It struck her, then, that none but her intimates would ever see her as a real person. It was as though invisible footlights were between Alison and those gathered here tonight, prohibiting them from getting to know each other.

This was a lonely thought and, though she was not yet famous, with it came a chilling foreknowledge that loneliness was the price of fame. She wanted to move closer to Albert and to glance at Emma and Conrad and warm herself with their cousinly smiles.

Instead, she slipped off her cloak and gave it to the girl who was waiting to take it. "Thank you so much, Elspeth."

The Battersbys' general domestic, dressed for the occasion in parlor-maid's uniform, flushed with pleasure. "Fancy you remembrin' me name, Miss! I 'adn't forgotten yourn, o' course," she added shyly.

"Nor I that you were kind enough to brush the mud off my coat, after I had plodded through a puddle in the drive, last winter," Alison answered with a smile.

Those listening were surprised that Alison had paused to chat with the maid; it did not tally with her image. But Alison would never be condescending with servants. A long and assorted line of theatrical landladies had taught her that those who serve are human beings.

Albert, to whom she was a never-ending surprise—that she loved him had not yet ceased to surprise him—put a proprietary arm around her. "If you and Elspeth have finished chatting, I'll introduce you to the local high society," he joked.

"And I'm delighted to tell you all that Alison and I are engaged to be married," he announced after he had done so.

Mrs. Battersby's glass slipped from her fingers and shattered on the parquet floor. "That's news to me, Albert!" she declared when she found her voice.

Alison greeted this with a charming smile. Oh, how useful it was to be an actress! "But I'm sure you were happy to hear it," she said, knowing that nothing was further from the truth. Albert's mother had been wary of her from the moment they met and dismay was now written on her face.

Mr. Battersby saved the situation. "So long as you'n our lad's 'appy, t'rest on us is 'appy for thee, lass," he pronounced kissing Alison's cheek.

Alison gave him a grateful glance. She knew that he liked her, as she did him, and she didn't envy him the task of reconciling his wife to being an actress's mother-in-law.

"Oh, well," that lady said, and gave her attention to gathering up the broken glass.

"Really, Mother!" Liza Battersby hissed. "Elspeth will clear up the mess."

The guests observed the moment of family drama with interest. Mrs. Battersby's reaction to her son's announcement would not be forgotten, and Albert's sister wanted to curl up with shame. Her mother would never learn to hide her feelings and be dignified. She wasn't a lady and never would be, Liza Battersby thought. Not in any respect.

Mrs. Battersby reluctantly left the glass. "Make sure thee picks up all t'tiny bits, luv," she instructed when Elspeth arrived with dustpan and brush. "Folks' feet tramplin' 'em into t' wood floor won't do it no good."

Mrs. Battersby had not wanted this big party in her house. Nor strangers in her kitchen, she was thinking with resentment. But Albert had requested a buffet meal beyond her homely ken. She had never sampled *vol-au-vents* and asparagus, let alone cooked them.

Ham 'n' egg pie, wi' tomatoes, an' cheese 'n' pickles, were wot Lancashire folk were used to! she said to herself with asperity, as her daughter steered her toward the dining room. Wi' custard 'n' jelly for puddin'. Folk in these parts were used ter no-nonsense party food! 'Er friends, who'd been invited along wi' their children'd wunder wot'd come over 'er when they saw t'supper table.

"Wot were t'names o' them fancy puddin's your brother's ordered for tonight, Liza?" she asked her daughter when they entered the dining room.

The lavish spread was being inspected by the guests and, as Mrs. Battersby had predicted, a cluster of well-corseted matrons were raising their eyebrows.

"I shall look a right lemon, if I don't know wot's bein' served in me own 'ouse, if anyone asks me," Mrs. Battersby whispered to Liza.

Liza eyed the *baba au rhum* and *meringue Chantilly*. "If I told you, you wouldn't be able to pronounce the words, Mother," she said with a superior sigh. "And please remember to pick up the asparagus with your fingers. It's bad manners to eat it with a knife and fork."

Mrs. Battersby also allowed herself a sigh. She no longer recognized her son and daughter. Boarding school had transformed Liza into a girl who looked down on her parents; sensible Albert had lost his head over an actress.

While the meal was being enjoyed by everyone except the hostess, who had made up her mind not to, Alison surveyed the guests. She reckoned that there were at least fifty people present, but the house was spacious enough to accommodate them.

What would it be like to be the mistress of a home like this? Alison wondered. She supposed that one day Albert would inherit it. But by then it would be too big for Albert and me, Alison thought. Our children will have grown up and left home.

What children? she checked herself. There it was again—that Jewish joke! She and Albert weren't even married yet and she was thinking ahead to their children leaving the nest! But even one child would be difficult enough to fit in with her career, and she would not bring it up as she had been raised, in lodging-house rooms with no place to call home. Alison's child would not have cause to think of itself as a straw on the wind. She'd find a little house in Hastings, that Albert could come to each weekend.

He was talking with a group of young people and she exchanged a happy smile with him. Emma and Conrad were beside her, eating mushroom *vol-au-vents* and asparagus; the Jewish dietary laws prohibited them from tasting the non-kosher cold cuts.

"What a shame you can't have any. This beef is absolutely delicious," Alison told them.

Conrad smiled. "Not being allowed to eat this, that, and the other is only one of the penalties of being Jewish."

"But there are plenty of compensations," Emma reminded him.

"Sure."

Alison did not need to be told what they were. All were rooted in the security of Jewish family life. They could fight like cats and dogs, she thought with a smile, but in a crisis they were as one.

Conrad had not yet finished airing his thoughts on the penalties. "This room is full of pretty girls," he said, allowing his eye to rove, "and most of 'em are still single." His gaze came to rest on a fresh-faced blonde. "That one I could really go for. She's intelligent, too."

"Who is she?" Alison inquired.

"Doreen Higginson. She works in the office at the Battersby mill. I'd like to take her out, but what's the point when nothing could come of it?" Conrad said, dismissing her from his scene. "So far, I haven't run into a Jewish girl I could get excited about," he added.

"Really, Conrad!" Emma exclaimed with embarrassment.

Conrad laughed. "I didn't mean it that way, Emma. I should have said enthusiastic." He eyed Doreen Higginson again. "Me, I go for blondes."

"So I'll run to Manchester, where there are lots of Jewish girls, and tell them all to bleach their hair!" Emma joked.

"I suppose that's where whoever's waiting for me is," Conrad said contemplatively. "If I'm ever going to find her, I'd better start going to dances in Manchester, instead of spending all my free time in Oldham with Albert, who'll soon be a married man."

He grinned at Alison. "I said that no situation stands still, didn't I? But yours has leapt ahead like a kangeroo!"

"You mustn't desert Albert after we're married," Alison requested. "As my work is in Hastings and his is here, we shall only be together at the weekends."

Conrad put down his fork and eyed her incredulously. "Are you out of your mind, Alison? What kind of marriage is that?"

"A theatrical one."

"Albert isn't a theatrical."

"But he's marrying one. Separation from those we

love is something theater people often have to accept, Conrad. The Plantaines are lucky in that respect, because the family happens to work together. As I'm marrying outside the profession, there's no question of my husband joining the company, as my father did when he married my mother. I shall be in the same position as some of our actors and actresses whose wives and husbands are on tour with other companies."

"Hm," Conrad muttered.

"A theatrical's life isn't the garden of roses the public thinks it is," Alison added. You don't know the half of it, she thought.

"Nor is Albert's going to be," Conrad replied. "I don't think I could put up with having a weekend wife."

"If you loved her, you'd put up with anything," Emma said with a smile. "I would, if I loved someone."

"Let's hope you don't have to," Conrad answered, observing his sister's earnest expression. Was Emma going to end up being made a mug of by some man? Probably. It was her nature, as it was Alison's to expect to call the tune.

"Have you and Albert discussed what we were just talking about?" Conrad asked Alison.

"There hasn't been time, as we only became engaged tonight."

They fell silent until they had been served with dessert.

"Albert would do anything to please you, Alison," Conrad declared, digging into his *rum baba*. "And a person could get drunk on this pudding! It's a good thing our Emma chose the other one, or I'd be carrying her home."

He surveyed the now depleted buffet. "All this was for you," he informed Alison. "Including the fancy tablecloth that's making me feel I'm at a Buckingham Palace banquet. Albert isn't a chap with high falutin' ideas—he leaves all that to his sister."

Conrad glanced at Liza Battersby, whose brittle-blonde appearance was tonight enhanced by a clinging crimson dress. "I used to like Liza, but not any more.

She's turned out to be our Clara's sort. What my mam calls a social climber. It wouldn't surprise me if our Clara sets her sights on a solicitor, or a doctor, when she gets around to finding her second husband. And Liza is probably hoping to marry into the landed gentry!"

"They're both pretty enough," Emma said.

"If all a man wants is an ornament for a wife," Conrad declared.

Alison returned him to the topic from which they had strayed. "What has all this to do with Albert and me?"

"As I said, it's because of you that Albert's twenty-first party is so elaborate. He didn't engage expensive caterers from Manchester to impress the locals. At my twenty-first, my health was drunk in milk stout," Conrad said, watching a waiter filling fifty odd goblets with champagne.

"Are you saying that Albert set out to impress me?" Alison demanded. "If that is what you mean, you're contradicting what you just said about him, which I already knew. Albert isn't that kind."

"Of course he isn't," Conrad answered. "And that's the whole point, Alison. He did it because he thinks only the best is good enough for you."

"And I love him dearly for it," Alison said with a happy smile.

"Enough to give up your career for him?" Conrad inquired, and watched the smile fade from her face.

"Why are you presenting me with a hypothetical dilemma, Conrad?"

"Because I think it could become a real one."

"Stuff and nonsense!" Alison laughed.

Then Albert came to lead her into the center of the room, where everyone had crowded to toast them.

"Next time our health is drunk, we'll be the bride and groom," Albert whispered to her. "And I want it to be very soon."

The words held an urgency Albert had not, until now, allowed himself to express to Alison. His lips against her ear, as he said them, held the same message, awakening in her the passionate womanhood she had not known was there.

When she looked up at Albert, his eyes told her that he desired her and a ripple of excitement coursed through her. She wanted to wind her arms around his neck and lay her body against his—and hoped that the blush that was warming her cheeks was not recognizable as shame.

"If you two lovebirds can spare the time, everyone is waiting to drink a toast to you!" Conrad chuckled.

Alison dragged her eyes from Albert's and lent herself to the convivial formality. Suddenly, she understood how good girls "got into trouble"—which she hadn't when it happened to Clara, she was thinking while Conrad made a jokey speech. Oh, how childish her notion of love had been until now. But red roses would no longer be enough.

After the party, Albert drove Alison and her cousins home in his father's car.

"Coming in for a cup of coffee?" Conrad invited him.

"I was waiting to be asked."

It was past midnight, but Lottie had not thought it necessary to wait up for the girls when Conrad was with them. In that respect, she ought to have known better than to trust her son.

"Let's take this rare opportunity to give these two a bit of time alone," he winked to Emma when the tea had been drunk.

Emma hesitated. "Mam would have a fit—"

Conrad took Emma's arm and steered her to the door.

"See you soon, Emma," Alison said.

"Very soon. I hope!"

"Poor Emma," Albert said wryly when he and Alison had the kitchen to themselves.

"Why do you say that?" Alison asked.

Albert got up to stir the dying embers in the grate. "Well she lives in hope, doesn't she? But people have to make things happen."

Alison giggled. "If I stay down here with you too long, Emma will probably make one of her hopes happen! She'll come to fetch me."

"I was speaking in general, Alison."

"I know you were, Albert. But what you said is one of the things about dear Emma that upsets me and I don't like to think about it. That girl will spend her life just waiting around hoping for the best, if nobody prods her out of it."

"I expect some man will," Albert said, coming to sit beside Alison on the couch. He took her hand and kissed her fingertips, one by one. "It's usually a man who changes a girl's life, isn't it?"

"Or the other way around. And what you're doing feels—well the only way I can describe it, my darling, is that I'm all of a tingle, tonight."

"Me, too."

"Why haven't you made me feel this way before?"

"Haven't I?"

"No."

"It doesn't matter, Alison. What matters is that we're going to be married and you feel that way now," Albert declared before he sought her lips.

His hand strayed to her breasts. She could feel the heat of it burning through her thin silk gown and uttered a low moan.

"I'd better go home, or I shall undress you," he said huskily against her mouth.

"I want you to," Alison murmured recklessly above the thudding of her heart.

Not until he raised her skirt to explore her thighs did Alison somehow find the strength to push him away. She didn't want to lose her virginity on Aunt Lottie's kitchen couch.

"Forgive me," Albert said contritely.

"My dearest darling, there is nothing to forgive. And I want us to be married without delay."

"I feel like rousing the vicar from his slumbers and asking him to marry us right now!"

"So do I, but we don't happen to have a license," Alison said with a smile.

They sat silent gazing at each other, but Albert did not allow himself to touch Alison. When she cast her spell over him she was only fourteen. He had waited five years for her and their wedding night would be all the sweeter for the waiting.

"I must come and meet your mother and the rest of the clan," he said. Now that he and Alison were engaged, he had no qualms about meeting the Plantaines.

"Come next weekend," she suggested. Nothing could cast a shadow over her love affair now. "Our landlady will be glad to put you up in her spare room, Albert. Since the Plantaines became her permanents, she hasn't bothered to take any other guests," Alison smiled. "It's a double room, as it happens. After we're married, it can be ours at the weekends—"

"Hold on a minute," Albert cut in. "I'm not sure what you mean."

Alison's stomach turned a somersault. Had Conrad been right? There was only one way to find out. "Well, you'll be spending your weekends in Hastings, when we're married, won't you?"

"My God!" Albert said.

A short silence followed and the clock ticking on the mantelpiece sounded painfully loud.

"I took it for granted that marrying you wouldn't affect my career," Alison said, when she could bear the tension no longer.

"Then you took too much for granted," Albert replied.

Alison stiffened. This reminded her of their first meeting, when animosity was all they had shared. But the strength of it had ensured they would not forget each other and, incongruously, from it had sprung love.

"Or maybe I took too much for granted," Albert con

rected himself. "To me, Alison, once a woman is married, her husband, home and kids are her career."

"Then you'll have to adjust to the situation, won't you?"

Albert got up from the couch and stood with his back to the hearth. "No, Alison. You will. Because I don't intend to fit my married life into the time you can spare from the theater. I want my wife where she belongs."

"Then you've chosen the wrong girl, Albert. Because I belong in the theater."

Alison had not even had to pause to think about it. Right now, where she belonged was the only thing of which she was sure. In every other respect it was as though the ground had slid from under her feet. A minute ago, she'd never felt more secure in her life; would not have thought it possible that anything could come between herself and Albert. Now they were like two people on opposite sides of a ravine.

Albert's expression reflected Alison's own misery. She wanted to hurl herself into his arms, let love mend the breach that words had created. But hovering at the back of her mind was her father's warning that love was not enough; that it hadn't enabled him and her mother to surmount the handicaps with which they had begun their marriage.

Alison glanced longingly at Albert, who was not prepared to try. He had never before struck her as masterful, but now she knew that he was. And oh, how she loved him! Briefly, she allowed herself to relive the moments of ecstasy they had just shared, then shut out the treacherous memory. In its place came a painful sense of loss for what might have been; for the simple domestic pleasures with which her working life would not, now, be interspersed; for the child she and Albert would never have.

Albert saw Alison blink away a tear. If he wasn't a man he'd be crying himself! For two pins, he'd grab her and kiss away her tears, agree to be a weekend husband. Take a chance on her coming to her senses and giving up the stage once she was married—and pregnant. But supposing she didn't? A chap couldn't stake his future—and his children's—on what, knowing Alison as he now did, was only a remote possibility.

The motley of emotions churning within Alison culminated in a great gust of anger. "How could you do this to me, Albert?" she cried. "I want you so much, but you've made it impossible for me to marry you."

"From where I'm standing," Albert replied quietly, "that's what you've done to me."

A heavy silence followed, then Alison pulled herself together.

"That seems to be that, Albert," she said flatly.

"Are you sure, Alison?"

"Absolutely certain." She was still aching for him but managed to muster a smile. "Ours must have been the shortest engagement in history."

Albert gave her an agonized glance and made his exit. It was for him like saying goodbye to an impossible dream. But better before than after, as his mother would surely say.

Alison sat gazing into the dying fire. In the space of a few short minutes she had learned that she was a passionate woman and that she could not always have what she wanted. That even Alison Plantaine could not have the best of both worlds. It would not be easy for her to forget Albert, or the feelings he had aroused in her. But she had also learned tonight that the theater was her one true love.

FOUR

Alison could not pinpoint the moment when she began to feel unfulfilled in her work. The Plantaine Players had continued to present a mixed repertoire. One month she would be performing in Shakespeare and the next in a revue, or a contemporary play. She and Lucy were, each in her own way, the darlings of local theater-goers. Nothing in Alison's working life had changed, but she was aware of a change in herself. Once, every performance had been to her a fresh challenge. Now there was a gray sameness in all she did and a restlessness in her blood.

She had at first attributed this to her personal life, which since her love affair ended was like an empty vessel. When, by the early Twenties, the feeling was still with her, she knew that personal loneliness was not solely responsible. She had long ago stopped pining for Albert and experienced no pain when Emma wrote that he was to be married.

The letter arrived on a day when there were no rehearsals. Alison had risen late and read it at the breakfast table, which she had to herself.

Albert's future wife was his father's typist, Doreen Higginson, Emma wrote. Alison recalled the fresh-faced blonde girl at the party, whom Conrad had said he fancied. Well, she thought wryly, Albert couldn't have chosen anyone more different from me.

Doreen would give him the apple-pie homelife his mother had raised him to expect, and would enjoy doing so. Had Alison chosen Albert instead of the theater, it would have been for her like acting a never-ending part for which she was ill cast.

As Albert had, the night they parted, Alison had eventually accepted that her beautiful love affair was not meant to culminate in marriage. The fairytale quality it had had for her was not reconcilable with that everyday institution, and it was with the aura of a fairytale that it was receding into the past.

Only their few moments of physical passion remained real to her, but she had not since encountered a man who her instinct told her could arouse her that way.

She was still reading Emma's news bulletin when her father entered.

"Having a lazy morning?" he smiled. It was not Alison's habit to lie abed late.

"I didn't sleep too well last night, Papa. And when we're not rehearsing, what is there for me to get up for?"

Horace did not like the sound of that. "It's a lovely day for a walk," he said, glancing through the window into the back garden, where daffodils and crocuses were heralding spring. "I'd join you for a stroll, Alison, if I could spare the breath," he added dryly.

"You look quite well this morning, Papa," Alison said, noting that there was a little color in his cheeks.

"Well, I'm something of a human barometer, aren't I, my dear? When the weather is cold and damp, my health runs down like the mercury in the glass."

"You mean a thermometer, don't you, Papa?"

"Whichever is applicable, love. You know what I mean. I am fit enough to be at my desk today."

"Why aren't you?"

"My office is being spring cleaned. Any tea left in that pot?"

Alison poured some for him. He and her mother always had an early breakfast, in their room.

"I see you've heard from Emma today," Horace said, observing the blue stationery his favorite niece used. "Any special news?"

Alison told him of Albert's forthcoming marriage. "I wish him well," she added.

"Why should you not?" Horace had been immensely relieved when the affair ended, though he had not told Alison so. "I'm sure he wishes you well, too, Alison. I'm not an authority on love affairs, as the only one I've experienced is my lifetime one with your mother, but I shouldn't think you will ever entirely forget Albert. He was your first love."

Alison smiled. "That isn't so, Papa. The theater is my first and abiding love."

Apprehension rippled through Horace. "But it is not to be confused with the love between a man and a woman, Alison. I shouldn't like to think that your single-mindedness about your art is to take precedence over your personal life."

"But it has already done so, hasn't it, Papa? Or I should now be married to Albert. Though I've since come to realize that he wasn't right for me, or I for him, I wasn't thinking that when I made my choice."

"When you meet the man who is, you'll put him first," Horace assured her and reassured himself.

"We shall have to wait and see. But I doubt it," Alison said. "I've learned to know myself, Papa. And it might be best if you really knew me, too, as you are the one I care most about in the world. The man I marry must be prepared to come second to my career. Which I suppose is the same as saying he would have to come second to me."

Horace had thought he did know his daughter, but the extent of Alison's egocentricity was a shock to him. Her mother's shrank into insignificance beside it.

Alison had risen to gaze through the window. When she turned to face him, Horace saw in her a formidable quality he had not before detected. He could not only see it in her expression, but feel its power coursing toward him.

She was standing quite still, her hands at her sides, her chin slightly tilted, with sunshine beaming through the window like limelight on to her hair. It was then that Horace knew his daughter had in her the makings of a great star. Her mammoth ego was part of what she would one day be.

Alison's next words were out of key with the moment. "But for some reason, Papa, I am suddenly disenchanted with my career." She returned to the table and confided to her father the restlessness with which she was beset.

"I should think that most actors feel that way from time to time," Horace said. "I certainly did and I know that your mama does, occasionally."

"But I've been troubled by it for almost a year, Papa. I seem to have lost the sense of—challenge. And once that has gone, where is the excitement in one's art?" Alison hesitated, then plunged in. "To tell the truth, I'm bored with Grandpa's productions, but I wouldn't, of course, want him to know it. Including the Shakespearean ones, Papa."

Alison got up to pace the room. "There are shades of meaning in the Bard's work that Grandpa has not divined," she declared. "Grandpa is obsessed by the pageantry and the words, as I was when I was a child. I would like to interpret my roles with much greater depth, but if I did so, it would affect the other actors' performances, and Grandpa would have a fit."

This and more Alison poured out to her father.

"What you're saying, Alison, is that you've outgrown the Plantaine Players," Horace said when she had finished speaking. And it was inevitable that she would, he thought in the light of his new assessment of her.

"You are not in the least disenchanted with your career," he told her. "What's getting you down is the lack of opportunity to stretch your talent."

That this was so became clear to Alison as her father pronounced it. "I wish Grandpa would allow Luke to direct another play," she said. Though she cared for her step-cousin no more than she ever had, she thought him a talented director.

Luke's chance to prove himself in that respect had come last winter. Gregory had succumbed to influenza, the day that rehearsals for Shaw's *Major Barbara* were to begin. A fortnight later, he had risen from his sickbed too weak to do more than protest about the innovations the young and eager opportunist had inflicted upon the production. Gregory had instructed Luke to "go by the book." Luke had taken one look at Gregory's notes and thrown the book away.

"I doubt if Luke will remain with the company," Alison said to Horace.

As Ruby's agreement with Gregory made no provision for an alternative director, she was unable to impose upon him that final ignominy. And Gregory's demeanor, when *Major Barbara* opened, was the opposite to that of its enthusiastic audience. It was plain that he would have to be on his deathbed before entrusting a production to Luke again.

"In my opinion, London is the place for Luke," Alison declared.

"And in mine, it is also the place for you," Horace said.

Alison, who had just picked up her teacup, put it down with a clatter. "That's ridiculous, Papa," she said confusedly.

"On the contrary, it was stating the obvious, Alison. You know as well as I do that you are wasted here."

"Possibly. But I am a Plantaine. And the Plantaine

Playhouse is here. It would be nice if we could pick it up and resite it in the West End," she added with a smile.

"I don't agree. What would be the point of taking with you a company you've outgrown? I agree, Alison, that Luke will sooner or later leave us. And Lucy will surely leave with him—they are twin peas as though they had never left the pod. And the time has come, Alison, for you to leave the company."

Alison gazed at her father incredulously. Her mother, if she were present, would accuse him of preaching treason. "Do you realize what you're suggesting? Luke and Lucy are not Plantaines, Papa, though they've adopted our name. They won't be expected to show family loyalty. The same would apply to you, as you weren't born into the family. But it is wrong of you to suggest that I break a theatrical tradition that has stood fast through generations of Plantaines."

Horace smiled. "Well, well, Alison!"

"It is I who should say that to you—and not with amusement!"

"I was thinking that you are not, after all, as single-minded as I thought you." Horace toyed with his teaspoon. "About your career, I mean. Because single-mindedness, Alison, entails allowing nothing—and I mean nothing—to stand in your way."

"I am finding this conversation distressing, Papa."

"That doesn't surprise me. But I don't doubt that you found breaking with Albert distressing. That didn't stop you from doing it. And I hope, Alison, that you will find the same strength to grasp opportunity—at whatever cost—whenever it comes your way."

Horace said no more, but he had made up his mind. The thought of being parted from Alison was not pleasant, but there was no future for her with the Plantaine Players. As a neglected plant withers and dies, so it would be with Alison's rare gift if loyalty kept her chained to the family company. She needed the artistic stimulation that was not available on her home ground.

The London theater was now an increasingly exciting scene and Horace recalled reading in *The Stage* about some young actresses who had metamorphosed into overnight stars. Several names had been mentioned, but he could remember only two: Edith Evans and Sybil Thorndike. Miss Thorndike had been acclaimed by the critics for her performance as Hecuba in *The Trojan Women,* at the Holborn Empire.

Alison, too, had played that classic role. But the impresarios who promoted talent did not spend their evenings sitting in the stalls in small seaside towns like Hastings. Unless they were invited to, Horace thought after Alison had gone to her room to reply to Emma's letter.

He then began considering which impresario he would invite. The company was currently staging *The Taming Of The Shrew* and Alison was playing Kate. The production had three more weeks to run. If Horace wrote to whoever it was to be, today, it could be hoped that that gentleman would have an evening to spare before the play closed.

Oliver helped him decide who the lucky impresario would be; Horace had no doubt that his daughter's potential would be immediately recognized and capitalized upon. Only a fool would fail to realize there was money to be made from promoting Alison Plantaine, and theatrical money men, though some were occasionally foolhardy, did not lack business sense.

"Guess who I ran into in town?" Oliver said when he returned that afternoon from a visit to London.

The family, as was their habit, were taking tea in their private parlor, before leaving for the theater to prepare for the evening performance. On this occasion the twins were present. More often than not they spent their free days with their friends and arrived at the Playhouse with little time to spare before curtain-up.

It was to them Oliver addressed the question, and with a mischievous twinkle in his eye.

"Never mind who you ran into," Ruby intervened. "What did the doctor have to say to you?"

Oliver reluctantly made regular trips to Harley Street to see a heart specialist. If his wife had allowed it, he would have put from his mind the defect that had kept him out of the army. So far it had not troubled him but the fact that one day it might troubled Ruby.

"Your anxiety about me is quite unnecessary, dearest," he told her. "My ticker is still ticking as it was when I last saw the doctor. So is Mr. Maxwell Morton's," he added to the twins.

"I had no idea that Morton had a heart condition," Gregory said. "Though I have had no contact with him for years."

"Nor had I," Oliver answered. "He emerged from the consulting room when I was waiting to enter it. I hadn't seen him since the twins know when!"

He and his stepchildren shared a laugh and Ruby gave them all a smile.

"You must forgive us our little private joke," Oliver apologized to the others, none of whom knew that Morton was indirectly responsible for Oliver's now being a family man. He had kept the details to himself.

"But Morton is no more sick than I am," Oliver said with a smile, "though it seems we are prone to the same fraudulent complaint."

"It would take more than a heart murmur to cut Morton's capers," Horace declared. "He has several shows on the road at present, hasn't he? Not to mention his activities in the West End."

"He said he would quite like to see the twins perform," Oliver remarked.

"Oh?" Horace said guardedly. The twins, eh? But it would be Alison with whom Morton was enthralled. Her portrayal of The Shrew was magnificent. And it seemed fated that Morton would be the lucky impresario.

"Who is this man you are all talking about?" Alison inquired from behind her magazine.

"If you read *The Stage* each week, instead of *Punch,* you wouldn't need telling, dear," Lucy replied. "He's an old friend of mine and Luke's, as it happens."

"And something you probably wouldn't believe happened to us at one of his parties," Luke added, winking at his stepfather.

Nothing that happened to Lucy and Luke at parties would be beyond Alison's belief. Morton's being a friend of theirs was sufficient to prejudice her against him, sight unseen. Nor could she summon the energy to reply to Lucy's sugary jibe about her reading matter. Alison read theater reviews in *The Stage* and the daily newspapers, but had no interest in those who promoted the plays. Impresarios' names did not register with her.

"Do let's invite Mr. Morton to see us perform, Pappy," Lucy said to Oliver.

"I don't see how we cannot," Luke declared, smiling at his mother. "In view of the kindness he unwittingly did us."

"Then allow me to send him some tickets on behalf of the company," Horace put in smartly. How very fortuitous this was, he thought.

"That's very obliging of you, Horace," Oliver said. "If it were left to me, I should probably forget."

"I'll suggest the final night of *The Shrew,*" Horace answered. "Then we can entertain him in the Green Room."

The usual final-night party would provide a chance for Morton to meet Alison socially, Horace thought. He cast a guilty glance at his wife, who was seated by the window reading, unaware that Horace was plotting their daughter's escape.

FIVE

Morton accepted the invitation. It would, he said in his reply to Horace, afford him the pleasure of seeing Shakespeare produced by the man his father had called "the maestro," in addition to reacquainting himself with old friends.

The compliment was a shot in the arm for Gregory Plantaine and aroused in him nostalgia for what he thought of as "the good old days," when Morton's father was alive. It served, too, to emphasize how far behind him that shining era of English theater now was.

The adjective he would apply to the post-war era was "glittering," for a good deal of it was to him worthless entertainment lent a false sparkle by lavish costumes and settings. But Gregory was a purist through and through, prohibited by his nature and conditioning from moving with the times. He was, too, among the last of a dying breed. The impresarios were taking over and the old institution of the actor manager was on the way out.

Revues in particular were anathema to Gregory, though he was occasionally constrained to put his tongue in his cheek and produce one. Professional curiosity had impelled him to see several in London's West End. He had drawn the line at performing in those of his own productions he considered artistically beyond the pale, and consequently was often free nowadays in the evenings.

In 1921, he and Horace had gone together to the opening night of *A to Z* at the Prince of Wales theater. Horace had enjoyed it. Gregory had thought it a waste of time, but had been riveted by the performance of a young actress called Gertrude Lawrence, making her West End début. Gregory had recognized in her the potential greatness that was in Alison.

Alison was one of the few members of the company unaffected by the prospect of Morton seeing them perform. The news that he was coming threw all but the born Plantaines into a frenzy of excitement. But, for them, Morton's presence in the audience lacked the hopeful element it presented to their fellow players.

Alison hid her amusement as the last Saturday in April drew near. She had long since assessed the company as mediocre, yet all of its members seemed to think that Morton would see in them star material, though many had, in this production, non-speaking parts.

What he would think of her own performance, Alison did not care. Her place was with the Plantaines; the family tradition and her career were inseparable.

When the curtain rose on the final performance of *The Taming Of The Shrew,* it was for Alison just another Saturday night at the Playhouse. The auditorium was full, as always at the weekends, and Alison played to the whole house, not to one influential man seated alone in a box.

She forgot that Morton was there until Lucy, who was playing Bianca, began deliberately upstaging her. When it happened for a third time, Alison registered that the first occasion was during Bianca's line: "Sir, to your pleasure humbly I subscribe." Lucy had been sending a coy

message to Morton, at the expense of Alison's performance, and was moving heaven and earth to ensure that
her own face, not Alison's, was turned toward his box
when she and Alison were onstage together.

It was then that Alison felt her fighting blood rise,
which accounted for there never having been a more
tempestuous Shrew; nor one who reduced her sister
Bianca to an object of derision the Bard had not intended.

The twins' friends, who were in the audience and had
been invited to the closing-night play, afterwards told
Gregory that they had never before seen a performance
like Alison's. Gregory agreed, though it had unbalanced
the performances of her fellow players and he was not
pleased in that respect.

It had left Alison drained and she would have preferred to return to the lodgings, but her grandfather had
made it a rule that the family be present at the company's
monthly social occasion.

Present, too, were local patrons of the arts, with whom
Horace was playing his administrator's role when Alison
entered the crowded Green Room. As always, her
mother and grandparents were dispensing charm to all
and sundry.

Oliver and Ruby were chatting to a group of theater
goers whose long-standing enthusiasm for the company
had won them the privilege of socializing with the actors.

Alison got herself a cup of coffee and went to stand by
the ornate fireplace that was the room's sole distinguish-
ing feature. The theater was not as old as the provincial
playhouses of the Plantaines' touring days, and its backstage accommodation was consequently less warrenlike.
In truth, it was a good deal more comfortable and convenient than the theaters to which the company had been
accustomed, but for Alison it had always lacked the special ambience she associated with her childhood.

Alison's idea of a Green Room was those in which she
had spent lonely hours awaiting her parents, epitomized

by peeling walls, gilt-framed mirrors and velvet ban-
quettes. A far cry from this modern decor and furniture,
she thought with nostalgia. Ruby had recently had the
room refurbished, thereby removing the modicum of
character it had previously had.

But why am I standing here sizing up the Green
Room? Alison asked herself. She was behaving like a
wallflower at a dance, instead of the sensation of tonight's performance. Because she wanted to remain
apart from the sycophancy going on around her. Those of
the company who were unable to get near to Morton had
extra-bright smiles plastered on their faces lest he glance
in their direction, and kept eyeing him hopefully over the
top of their coffee cups and beer glasses.

Suddenly, this was no longer amusing to Alison. None
of them had what it took to reach the top, but hope was
eternal within them. Different from Emma's kind and all
the more pathetic because of it, Alison reflected.
Doomed to futility though it was, theirs was the kind of
hope that impelled them to try to *make* what they
wanted, happen.

Morton was penned into a corner by Lucy and Luke
and their smart set, and some determined actors who
were endeavoring to engage his attention. Alison
thought him repulsive looking. She had heard on the
company grapevine that he was known to have women
falling at his feet, and did not doubt that this was so.
There were actresses of Alison's acquaintance whom she
knew would sell themselves for a leading role.

Not until Morton's glance briefly met hers across the
room, did Alison become aware of the man's personal
magnetism. There was about him an animal masculinity
that weaker women than herself might find compelling.

Her parents appeared at her elbow. "Why are you
being so unsociable?" her father asked.

"I've given my performance for tonight, Papa," she
replied dryly.

"On the contrary," her mother corrected her, "there

are still members of your public here, Alison." Hermione eyed her daughter's attire. "Though you seem to have forgotten that there would be, when you selected your dress for tonight."

"There's nothing wrong with my dress, Mama." Alison had on a simple black suit, with a long coral scarf lending it a splash of color. She had not yet succumbed to the shapeless, leg-revealing outfits Lucy and her flapper girlfriends now wore, and prayed that this hideous fashion would not last. Nor had Alison learned to dance the Charleston, which she considered beneath her dignity. And nothing would persuade her to cut her hair, she thought glancing at the shingled heads of Lucy and her friends.

Her mother was still surveying her. "A jacket and skirt is not my idea of evening wear," Hermione declared with a rustle of her full-length, blue taffeta gown. "But you and I have never shared the same ideas, have we, Alison," she added superfluously. "Mine include making a special effort when the company is entertaining an important guest."

"Come and be introduced to Mr. Morton, Alison," Horace intervened before the exchange had time to sharpen.

"No thank you, Papa."

"Why not?" Horace demanded.

"I wouldn't want him to think I was kissing his feet, like those who have dressed themselves to the nines for the company's monthly get-together, when they don't usually do so."

Hermione knew this was not directed at her. She and her mother always wore full evening dress for the occasion, as befitted their superior position as Plantaines. In that respect, Alison seemed to enjoy letting the side down, she thought with a sigh.

"Mr. Morton is not important to me," Alison declared vehemently.

Isn't he just! Horace thought. "Calm down, Alison," he said. "You are not still onstage playing the Shrew."

"And that is another thing!" Hermione exclaimed. "I expect your grandfather will have a word or two to say to you about what you did this evening, Alison. I have never before seen an actress toss her fellow players to the dogs, as though she cared only for her own performance."

"What came over you, Alison?" Horace asked quietly.

"Lucy came over me! She didn't care a fig about anything but impressing *that man*. As it was largely at my expense I didn't let her get away with it."

Although Alison was by now ashamed of having allowed her personal feelings to override her professionalism, she was not prepared to admit it. "Everyone is allowed one mistake," was the most her pride allowed her to say. And she would take care that it never happened again.

Hermione, who could no longer pass as a Kate, or a Bianca, had had to settle for the role of the Widow. The inevitable transition to playing older characters, which every actress must eventually face, came no more easily to Hermione than to her peers. Nevertheless she paid her daughter an unexpected compliment, "You are much better cast for Kate than I was, Alison."

Alison was not sure if it was a compliment.

"Indeed, your portrayal would require some beating," Hermione declared. "You are capable of a fieriness that isn't present in me and it will stand you in good stead."

"It's nice of you to say so, Mama," Alison replied coolly. But a little late in the day for you to praise me, she would have liked to add.

There was no need. Hermione read it in her eyes and felt the specter of Alison's début night rise between them.

Horace, too, felt its cold breath and put a comforting arm around his wife. Hermione would be hurt by the manner of Alison's going from her, but relieved that she need no longer look her daughter in the eye.

The thought impelled him to glance at Morton, whom Lucy had just drawn aside. What was that little madam up to? Like her flamboyant mother, Lucy had no sense of propriety. Morton was old enough to be her father and there she was, ogling him fetchingly! It wouldn't be Lucy's fault if she didn't go far.

Alison, too, was watching them. But who wasn't? she thought with contempt. Not that Lucy cared. It struck Alison then that she had underestimated Lucy, that beneath the flighty facade was a will to succeed as strong as Alison's and, too, a wily brain.

Something else crystallized for Alison at that moment. As a Plantaine, the heights to which she could rise were limited to within the company. It would not be so for Lucy. And suddenly Alison resented the shackles that bound her. She could feel them chafing now, and wanted to break free.

Oh God, she thought, what am I to do? There was nothing she could do. She was the only Plantaine of her generation. When her elders were gone, it would be Alison and her descendants who ensured that the curtain continued to rise on the company that bore the family name.

"Are you feeling unwell, Alison?" Horace asked, eyeing her anxiously.

Alison was not surprised that he had. She had felt the blood drain from her face as her treacherous thoughts whirled in her mind. "I'm feeling tired, Papa, and if you don't mind I'd like to leave now."

Her mother had gone to join Gregory and Jessica who were deep in conversation with the group of Playhouse regulars, and it seemed a suitable moment for Alison to make her escape.

"You haven't had a word with our guest yet," her father reminded her.

Alison stiffened. "Why should I bother to? He didn't

have the courtesy to come and say he enjoyed my performance."

Horace sipped some lemonade. The atmosphere was airless and smokey and his sick lungs were telling him so. He would suffer for it tomorrow, but would suffer anything for his daughter's sake.

The evening had somehow gone terribly wrong. Morton wasn't the kind who paid congratulatory lip-service and his failure to speak to Alison did not bode well. Nor would he take kindly to a young actress giving him the cold shoulder.

Horace eyed his daughter's stubborn expression and mentally threw up his hands. Alison could charm a poker into bending if she so wished, but was equally capable of maintaining an iron rigidity herself.

Lucy blew them a kiss from the doorway, where she and Morton were now hovering. "See you soon, Alison darling!" she called fondly, as though Alison were her best friend. "Dear Mr. Morton is taking me to his hotel for a bite to eat. Isn't it sweet of him?"

Alison gave them an actressy smile. "Enjoy your supper," she said, hoping they would both choke on it.

Morton waved benignly to the gathering and ushered Lucy out.

"Well, that's that!" Luke pronounced with a laugh. "Maxwell Morton has been and gone and now we can all relax."

"That's that," summarized Horace's feelings as he escorted Alison and Hermione to their lodgings. It had been Lucy's night, not Alison's. And Lucy would probably put the rest of the night to good use, to ensure herself a part in Morton's next production.

Horace would not be surprised if Ruby was amused by her daughter's machinations. Oliver, of course, would read no evil into them; he seemed to think that butter wouldn't melt in his stepchildren's mouths!

Horace glanced down at his own daughter's proud profile, lit by the moon to a marble purity. Alison would never be like Lucy. She would get where she was going on her merits.

The Players' next production was *The Importance Of Being Earnest.* Gregory would have preferred not to present Oscar Wilde's work—the author's scandalous reputation reminded him that he had once feared that Oliver was headed for a similar fate. But Ruby, who wanted to play Lady Bracknell, had exercized her right to select the company's non-Shakespearean productions.

Lucy arrived late for the final run-through. She had spent the whole of Sunday sleeping and Alison had not seen her since she left the Green Room with Morton on Saturday night.

It was now Monday morning. Dress rehearsal was scheduled for this afternoon and the play would open tonight.

"Thank you for coming, Lucy, dear," Gregory said, giving her a frosty smile. "Now you are here, we can begin." He had not liked her coquettishness with Morton and now wished she had not changed her name to Plantaine.

"Did Mr. M. offer you a part?" Polly Drew, who was again her understudy, asked her.

Lucy giggled. "I didn't audition for him. But I shouldn't be surprised if he does."

"Then she can talk him into letting me direct some of his touring productions," Luke said.

And the sooner the better, Gregory thought. His initial illusion that Oliver had brought him two ready-made grandchildren, who would lend themselves to the Plantaine tradition, had not lasted long. Thank God for Alison, he thought, giving her an affectionate glance. Then he gave his attention to the run-through. The company could survive without the twins! And the play, even when by an author of whom Gregory didn't approve, remained the thing.

Later, when Alison and Lucy were in their dressing

room making up for the dress rehearsal, Alison inquired what Morton's next production was to be. They had to talk about something when they were closeted together, and it was a more interesting subject than Lucy's gossip about the people she called her friends.

"It's a drama by a new playwright," Lucy said while coloring her cheeks.

"That's very adventurous of Mr. Morton," Alison declared.

Lucy smiled. "Mr. Morton is a very adventurous man."

Alison did not encourage her to continue along that track. "What are the characters in the play, Lucy?"

"It's only a small cast, and I was only interested in the part that sounded right for me. He said it's set in a cottage hospital and there's a nursing sister in it."

"Well there would be, wouldn't there?" Alison said, blocking out the image of herself in a nurse's uniform. She had better stamp on her treachery here and now, before the rot set in!

They said no more about it, but Alison noted that Lucy was rising early each day to await the postman's arrival. On Friday, an envelope bearing the Morton Theatrical Enterprises crest landed on the mat. It was Lucy who handed it to Alison.

Alison had just come downstairs and they were alone in the hall. She was riveted to the spot when she saw whence the envelope came and that it was addressed to her.

"If he's offered the part to you, I'll never forgive you for it!" Lucy exclaimed venomously. "And why else would he be writing to you?"

She ran wildly upstairs and Alison heard her bedroom door slam shut. Then Horace appeared on the landing.

"What on earth is going on, Alison?" he said, coming to join her in the hall.

Alison handed him the envelope and watched his face light up when he saw Morton's business crest.

"I shan't bother to open it," she said.

"Then allow me to do so for you." Horace read the letter and smiled. "So much for Morton's not congratulating you on your splendid Kate! He is obviously a man who conducts his affairs in his own style—and knows a good thing when he sees it. He wants you in his new production Alison."

"I didn't imagine, Papa, that he was writing to invite me to tea—it was Lucy with whom he got on those terms, not me. Who is going to reply to him that I'm not available and never shall be? That I'm under contract for life to my family company. Would you like to do it, Papa? Or shall I?"

Horace pocketed the letter. "Your opportunity to be what you were born to be is not to be tossed aside so lightly, Alison."

Alison was too good an actress for her father to divine that her feelings on the subject were far from light.

"With your permission, I shall discuss the matter with your grandfather," Horace said.

"You don't have my permission."

"Then I shall have to talk to him without it."

They eyed each other silently for a moment.

"I am obviously not the only person who thinks you are worthy of better things," Horace said. "Maxwell Morton is an excellent judge."

Alison stared up at the colored glass in the fanlight so her father would not see that tears had sprung to her eyes. But they were selfish tears, and she would have to live with her personal disappointment. Try, somehow or other, to raise the company's mediocrity to the heights she knew she could achieve.

"It can't be done, Alison," Horace declared when Alison conveyed this to him.

"Why not?"

"Because your grandfather has given up the fight. The company's artistry is, in the final analysis, dependent upon him. And though his idealism has not wavered, and never will, events have sapped his strength. He's like a man swimming against the tide, Alison. He is a director with no sense of direction, since the agreement with Ruby diverted him from his path. That isn't to say that I approved of his path—I didn't. For me it was always too narrow. But plodding along with his feet firmly planted on it and his eye fixed to the rainbow he continued to see in the distance, kept your grandfather artistically alive. You said yourself, Alison, that you're bored with his lack of innovation. And you must surely know that his heart is no longer in it."

"Poor Grandpa," Alison said softly. The rainbow had gone from his sky. "You're not only suggesting that I desert a sinking ship," she said coldly to her father, "you're telling me to hit a man when he's down."

"I'm telling you to do what's necessary to pursue your own art, Alison. To thine own self be true."

"A fine time to quote Shakespeare to me!" she said with a bitter smile.

Horace did not delay saying what he must to his father-in-law, which did not include telling him that he had lost heart.

"Alison didn't want me to mention the matter to you, Gregory," he concluded. "But I don't think the decision should be left entirely to her."

The conversation took place that evening, in the Plantaines' parlor. Gregory was not appearing in the Wilde play and had settled down for a quiet read when Horace joined him.

"No Plantaine has ever left the company to go their own way, Horace," Gregory said, though it did not require saying. "And Alison's being offered a part in London is not unprecedented in the family. In my youth, I received many offers. Oliver, too. We had no hesitation in refusing them."

"Nor had Alison."

"Then what is all this fuss about?"

"Your granddaughter's future. And if you're honest with yourself, you'll admit there is none for her here."

Gregory smiled wearily. "You haven't changed, have you, Horace?"

"Possibly not. But the company has."

"I am well aware of that."

"I'm sure you are, Gregory. And, in my opinion, it's criminal to let Alison sacrifice herself to a tradition that no longer exists."

Gregory stiffened. "I beg your pardon?"

"The tradition your ancestors began and that you hold so dear hasn't existed since you entered into partnership with Ruby," Horace went on undeterred. "What you've been doing since then, Gregory, is making the best of a bad job."

"So that's your opinion, is it?"

"And I was about to add that I doubt if you're proud of what you're doing."

A short silence followed. Then Gregory sagged in his chair.

Horace wished it had not been necessary to confront him with the painful truth. Gregory had never been prepared to look the truth in the face, but Horace knew he was doing so now and was moved to pity. He had not thought the time would come when Gregory Plantaine looked a beaten man.

Gregory gazed into the fire and a long sigh escaped him. "You are right, Horace. What the company once stood for is no more and there's nothing to be gained by holding aloft a flag that is at half-mast."

Horace put a kind hand on his shoulder and thought emotionally that, though their lives had been entwined for twenty-odd years, this was the first warm, human contact they had shared.

"Alison must go her way," Gregory said.

"I think you should be the one to tell her."

SIX

On a May morning in 1923, Alison stood on the platform at Hastings railway station, surrounded by Plantaines. Only Lucy had not come to see her off to London and she was surprised that Luke had.

"You're looking very fetching, darling," he said, admiring her lime-green outfit and matching cloche hat. "All ready to knock 'em dead in the big city! Remember you have a cousin who's a budding director, when you get there," he added jokingly.

So that's it! Alison thought dryly. He's keeping in with me. She gave him a sweet smile. "How could I possibly forget, Luke? When you are sure to remind me?"

"You will take good care of yourself, won't you, Alison dear?" Jessica urged her for the umpteenth time.

"London is rather different from Hastings, Alison," Oliver warned.

"And you must watch out for the traffic, love, when you're crossing the street," her father cautioned her.

Ruby gave her a wink. "And for gentlemen waiting to take advantage of you."

Alison laughed. "Anyone would think I had never been anywhere alone before!"

"But you have never had to fend for yourself," her mother said. "Nor have you lived alone."

Suddenly, Alison's excitement was tinged with trepidation. What her mother had said was true. Alison would not know a soul in the lodgings Mr. Morton's secretary had found for her, and London was vast and impersonal.

"We shall miss you dreadfully," her grandfather said when she had boarded the train and was standing by the window.

"And I you."

"Alison isn't going to another country," Luke said, observing his elders' expressions.

But Alison knew that in effect she was. The moment of parting was nigh and she was putting behind her the familiar figures who had peopled the landscape of her childhood and youth.

"Fare thee well, proud maid!" Oliver said when the guard blew his whistle and the train began to move. He doffed his hat and smiled. "I doubt not that thou shalt."

Gregory entered into the mock-Elizabethan spirit. "I wager that yon maid shalt bring forth glory upon our fair name!"

"It won't be her fault if she doesn't. And she couldn't have had a more fitting send-off, could she?" Luke grinned.

Though emotion had dried his throat and he had to unclamp his tongue to speak, Horace had the last word. "God bless you, my dearest daughter! And keep you safe," he called as the train gathered speed.

Alison leaned out of the window and watched the family group recede, and it was as though they were receding into her past. Leaving her beloved father was her one regret. The Plantaine Players would always be part of her and she of their long heritage. But Alison Plantaine was on her way to her future.

A former journalist, Maisie Mosco began writing fiction in the sixties and is the author of fourteen radio plays and twelve novels. Originally from Manchester, she now lives in London.

HarperPaperbacks *By Mail*

BREATHTAKING SAGAS
BY MAISIE MOSCO

ALMONDS AND RAISINS

The families are as different as night and day. The outgoing Sandbergs are from Russia. The bookish Moritzes are from Austria. They meet in England before the First World War and form a strong, fiery friendship that would shape the destinies of three generations.

SCATTERED SEED

It is the matriarch Sarah's children who decide the future. Children like David, the eldest son, whose obsession is a business that threatens to steal his faith...and Nathan who falls in love and breaks all the rules...and Marianne, the granddaughter, who asks the unthinkable questions—and seeks the answers on her own.

CHILDREN'S CHILDREN

The next generation are successful men and women, social and sexual rebels, who think they can break the laws of God and family and survive without roots. Only Sarah, the proud matriarch, has the wisdom and compassion to heal the wounds of a dynasty.

OUT OF THE ASHES

When her husband dies, all Marianne has left is her career. But soon she finds herself stepping into her grandmother Sarah's shoes as matriarch of the proud but troubled Jewish family. Somehow Marianne must maintain her career as well as nurture the age-old family traditions that have almost slipped away.

———•———

FOR LOVE AND DUTY

When young Bella Minsky's mother dies in a tragic accident, Bella must take over the family clothing store. She builds the store into a high-fashion international business. But happiness does not come as easily as success for Bella. It is only when Bella begins to recognize her own strengths that she finds the love she deserves.

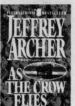

OUTER BANKS
Anne Rivers Siddons

Four sorority sisters bound by friendship spent two idyllic spring breaks at Nag's Head, North Carolina. Now, thirty years later, they are coming back to recapture the magic of those early years and confront the betrayal that shaped four young girls into women and set them all adrift on the Outer Banks.

"A wonderful saga." — *Cosmopolitan*

MAGIC HOUR
Susan Isaacs

A witty mixture of murder, satire, and romance set in the fashionable Hamptons, Long Island's beach resort of choice. Movie producer Sy Spencer has been shot dead beside his pool. Topping the list of suspects is Sy's ex-wife, Bonnie. But it isn't before long that Detective Steve Brady is ignoring all the rules and evidence to save her.

"Vintage Susan Isaacs."
— *The New York Times Book Review*

ANY WOMAN'S BLUES
Erica Jong

Leila Sand's life has left her feeling betrayed and empty. Her efforts to change result in a sensual and spiritual odyssey that takes her from Alcoholics Anonymous meetings to glittering parties to a liaison with a millionaire antiques merchant. Along the way, she learns the rules of love and the secret of happiness.

"A very timely and important book...Jong's greatest heroine." — *Elle*